My Foolish Heart

**Center Point
Large Print**

Also by Susan May Warren and available
from Center Point Large Print:

> *Nothing But Trouble*
> *Double Trouble*
> *Licensed for Trouble*

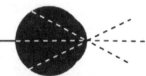

**This Large Print Book carries the
Seal of Approval of N.A.V.H.**

My
Foolish
Heart

Susan May
WARREN

CENTER POINT LARGE PRINT
THORNDIKE, MAINE

This Center Point Large Print edition is published in the the year 2012 by arrangement with Tyndale House Publishers, Inc.

Copyright © 2011 by Susan May Warren.

All rights reserved.

Most Scripture quotations are taken from the *Holy Bible*, New Living Translation, copyright © 1996, 2004, 2007 by Tyndale House Foundation. Used by permission of Tyndale House Publishers, Inc., Carol Stream, Illinois 60188. All rights reserved.

Philippians 4:23 taken from *The Message* by Eugene H. Peterson, copyright © 1993, 1994, 1995, 1996, 2000, 2001, 2002. Used by permission of NavPress Publishing Group. All rights reserved.

This novel is a work of fiction. Names, characters, places, and incidents either are the product of the author's imagination or are used fictitiously. Any resemblance to actual events, locales, organizations, or persons living or dead is entirely coincidental and beyond the intent of either the author or the publisher.

The text of this Large Print edition is unabridged.
In other aspects, this book may
vary from the original edition.
Printed in the United States of America
on permanent paper.
Set in 16-point Times New Roman type.

ISBN: 978-1-61173-434-8

Library of Congress Cataloging-in-Publication Data

Warren, Susan May, 1966–
My foolish heart / Susan May Warren.
pages ; cm
ISBN 978-1-61173-434-8 (library binding : alk. paper)
1. Women radio talk show hosts—Fiction.
   2. Disabled veterans—Fiction. 3. Minnesota—Fiction.
   4. Large type books. I. Title.
PS3623.A865M9 2012
813′.6—dc23

2012001921

To the Cook County Vikings football team—
coaches, staff, and players.
You make us proud.

Acknowledgments

Like any great football team, a book needs a team of great players to help score a goal. I'm deeply grateful to the following people for their specific contributions to this story:

Coach Mitch Dorr—Head coach of the CCHS Vikings, who constantly impresses me with his vision of sports as a way to build character and football as a way to build boys into men. My sons are becoming "men built for others" because of the excellent coaching staff. I am deeply grateful for all your help on the specifics of football in this story and especially for writing the Quarterback Chaos play. (What a fun play! May it win a state championship someday!) All mistakes in calling the game are mine alone.

Peter Warren—My amazing fullback/middle linebacker, who helped me break down practices and drills, and for answering the question "What would you do if you were the coach?"

Noah Warren—My amazing defensive end and the inspiration for Caleb.

David Warren—Oh, how I miss you and your plotting abilities! Thank you for helping me sort out those story kinks during your summer break.

Andrew Warren—The football player of legend in our family.

Thank you for helping me understand football and for being my cohort as we trek to every football game, rain, sleet, or shine.

Sarah Warren—My daughter with the advice for the lovelorn. Thank you for helping me create the callers on the show and for the "top-ten" list.

World's Best Donuts—The best place on the planet to get donuts (including the skizzle!).

Rachel Hauck—My writing partner. I'll write your book; you write mine, okay? Thank you for helping me break free of the Paralyzing Premise!

Ellen Tarver—Who knows how to ask the tough questions and make all the story threads tie together. You are my secret weapon.

Sarah Mason—Wow. Again, wow. My amazing line editor, who makes me sound pretty good.

Karen Watson—My Editor Extraordinaire. Thank you for believing in me.

Steve Laube—You rock, O Amazing Agent.

For I can do everything through Christ,
who gives me strength.
PHILIPPIANS 4:13

For Your glory, Lord.

I

For two hours a night, Monday through Saturday, Isadora Presley became the girl she'd lost.

"Welcome to *My Foolish Heart*, where we believe your perfect love might be right next door. We want to send special greetings out to KDRT in Seattle, brand-new to the Late Night Lovelorn Network. BrokenheartedInBuffalo, you're on the line. Welcome to the program."

Outside the second-story window of her home studio, the night crackled open with a white flash of light and revealed the scrawny arms of her Japanese plum, cowering under a summer gale. Issy checked the clock. Hopefully the storm would hold off for the rest of her show, another thirty minutes.

And the weather had better clear by tomorrow's annual Deep Haven Fisherman's Picnic. She couldn't wait to sit on her front porch, watch the midnight fireworks over the harbor as the Elks launched them from the campground, and pretend that life hadn't forgotten her.

Tomorrow, she'd watch the parade from her corner of the block, wave to her classmates on their annual float as they made their way toward Main Street, then linger on the porch listening to the live music drift up from the park. Maybe she'd even be able to hear the cheers from the annual log-rolling competition. She could nearly taste the tangy sweetness of a fish burger—fresh walleye and homemade tartar sauce. Kathy would be pouring coffee in the Java Cup outpost. And just a block away, the crispy, fried-oil tang of donuts nearly had the power to lure her to Lucy's place, World's Best Donuts. She'd stand in the line that invariably twined out the door, around the corner, and past the realty office waiting for a glazed raised.

She'd never, not once in her first twenty-five years, missed Fish Pic. Until two years ago.

She'd missed everything since then. She swallowed down the tightening in her chest.

"Thank you for taking my call, Miss Foolish Heart. I just wanted to say that I listen to your show every night and that it's helped me wait for the perfect man."

BrokenheartedInBuffalo had a high, sweet voice, the kind that might belong to a college coed with straight blonde hair, blue eyes. But the radio could mask age, race, even gender. Truly, when Issy listened to her podcasts, sometimes she didn't recognize her own voice, the way it softened with compassion, turning low and husky as she counseled listeners.

She could almost trick herself into believing she knew what she was doing. Trick herself into believing that she lived a different life, one beyond the four walls and garden of her home.

"I'm so glad, Brokenhearted. He's out there. What can I do for you tonight?"

"Well, I think I found him. We met a few weeks ago in a karate class, and we've already had three dates—"

"Three? Brokenhearted, I know that you're probably smitten, but three dates isn't enough to know a man is perfect for you. A great relationship takes—"

"Time, trials, and trust. I know."

So Brokenhearted listened regularly. Good, then maybe Issy could slow her down, help her to part the heady rush of the "love fog"—another of her coined terms.

"Then you also know you don't develop that in three dates, although Miss Foolish Heart does advise calling it quits after three if there is no visible ten potential."

"But it feels like it. He's everything I want."

"How do you know that?"

"I have my top-ten list, just like you said. And of course, the big three."

"Big three essentials. Sounds like you know what you're looking for."

"That's just it—he has *most* of them, and I'm wondering if it's essential for him to have all of them. Isn't . . . let's say, seven out of ten enough?"

"You tell me, Brokenhearted—would you settle

for a seven romance? Or do you want a ten?"

"What if I don't know what a ten feels like?"

What a ten feels like. Yes, Issy would like to know that too.

"Good question, Brokenhearted. I think it must be different for everyone. Stay on the line and let's take some calls and see if anyone has a good answer. Or you can hop over to the forum at the *My Foolish Heart* website—I see that Cupid27 has posted a reply. 'Love feels as if nothing can touch you.' Nice, Cupid27. Any other callers?"

She muted Brokenhearted and clicked on another caller. "TruLuv, you're on the air. What does a ten feel like?"

A gravelly, low voice, the two-pack-a-day kind: "It's knowing you have someone to hold on to."

"Great response, TruLuv. Here's hoping you have someone to hold on to." She muted TruLuv. "Go ahead, WindyCity."

"It's knowing you're loved . . . anyway."

Loved, anyway. Oh, she wanted to believe that was possible. "Love that, WindyCity. Anyone else?"

The forum had come to life, replies piling up. On the phone lines, PrideAndPassion723 appeared. Pride called at least once a month, often with a new dilemma, and kept the forum boards lit up with conversations. Issy should probably give the girl a 1-800 number.

She clicked back to Brokenhearted. "Do any of those replies feel like what you feel?"

"Maybe. I don't know."

"Miss Foolish Heart suggests you hold out for the ten, Brokenhearted. The perfect one is out there, maybe right next door."

She went to a commercial break, an advertisement for a chocolate bouquet delivery, and pulled off her headphones, massaging her ears.

Outside, the rain hummed against the house, a steady battering with the occasional ping upon the sill, although now and again it roared, the wind rousing in anger. Hopefully she'd remembered to close the front windows before she went on the air. Lightning strobed again, and this time silver leaves stripped from the tree, splattered on the window. Oh, her bleeding heart just might be lying flat on the ground, after all the work she'd done to nurture it to life.

The commercial ended.

"I see we have PrideAndPassion on the line, hopefully with an update to her latest romance. Thanks for coming back, Pride. How are you tonight?"

She'd expected tears—or at the very least a mournful cry of how Pride had stalked her boyfriend into some restaurant, found him sharing a low-lit moment with some bimbo. Pride's escapades had become the backbone of the show, ratings spiking every time she called in.

"I'm engaged!"

Issy nearly didn't recognize her, not with the lift in her voice, the squeal at the end.

"Kyle popped the question! I did it, Miss Foolish Heart—I held out for true love, and last night he showed up on my doorstep with a ring!"

"Oh, that's . . . great, Pride." Issy battled the shock from her voice. No, not just shock. Even . . . okay, envy.

Once upon a time, she'd dreamed of finding the perfect man, dreamed of standing on the sidewalk at the Fisherman's Picnic with Lucy, hoping they might be asked to dance under the milky starlight of the August sky. But who had the courage to dance with the football coach's daughter? And as for Lucy, she simply couldn't put her courage together to say yes. Sweet, shy Lucy, she'd used up her courage on one boy.

It only took Lucy's broken heart their senior year to cement the truth: a girl had to have standards. She had to wait for the perfect love.

Issy had come up with the list then, refined it in college. A good, solid top-ten list, and most important, the big three must-have attributes in a man besides his Christian faith—*compassionate, responsible,* and *self-sacrificing*—the super evaluator that told her if she should say yes to a first date.

If any came around. Because she certainly couldn't go out looking for dates, could she?

"Oh, Pride, are you sure?" Silence on the other end. She hadn't exactly meant it to come out with that edge, almost disapproving. "I . . . just mean, is he a ten?"

"I'm tired of waiting for a ten, Miss Foolish Heart. I'm twenty-six years old and I want to get married. I don't want to be an old maid."

Twenty-six. Issy remembered twenty-six, a whole year ago. She'd celebrated her birthday with a jelly-filled bismark that Lucy brought over, and they'd sung ABBA at the top of their lungs.

And as a finale, Issy ventured out to her front steps. Waved to Cindy Myers next door, who happened to be out getting her mail.

Yes, a red-letter day, for sure.

"You're so young, Pride. Twenty-six isn't old."

"It feels old when everyone around you is getting married. I'm ready, and he asked, so I said yes."

Issy drew in a breath. "That's wonderful. We're all happy for you, right, forum?"

The forum, however, lit up with a vivid conversation about settling for anything less than a ten. See? Not a foolish heart among them.

"Good, because . . . I want you to come to the wedding, Miss Foolish Heart. It's because of you that I found Kyle, and I want you to be there to celebrate with us."

Issy gave a slight chuckle over the air. High and short, it was a ripple of sound that resembled fear. Perfect. "I . . . Thank you for the kind offer, Pride, but—"

"You don't understand. This is going to be a huge wedding. I know we're not supposed to reveal our names on the air, but I am so grateful for your help that you need to know—my father is Gerard O'Grady."

"The governor of California?" Former actor–turned–billionaire–turned–politician?

"Yes." A giggle followed her voice. "We're already planning the wedding—it'll be at our estate in Napa Valley. I want you there, in the front row, with my parents. You've just helped me so much."

"Oh, uh, Pride—"

"Lauren. I'm Lauren O'Grady."

"Okay, Lauren. I'm so sorry, but I can't come."

"Why not?"

Why not? Because every time Issy ventured a block from her house, the world closed in and cut off her breathing? Because she couldn't erase from her brain the smell of her mother's burning flesh, her screams, the feel of hot blood on her hands? Because every time she even thought about getting into a car, she saw dots, broke out in a sweat?

Most of all, because she was still years away from breaking free of the panic attacks that held her hostage.

"Our station's policy is—"

18

"I'm sure my father could get your station to agree. Please, please don't say no. Just think about it. I'll send you an invitation."

And then she clicked off.

Seconds of dead air passed before Issy found the right voice. "Remember to visit the forum at the *My Foolish Heart* website. This is Miss Foolish Heart saying, your perfect love might be right next door." She disconnected just as Karen Carpenter's "Close to You" signaled the close of her show.

Yeah, sure. Once upon a time, she'd actually believed her tagline.

Once upon a time, she'd actually believed in Happily Ever After.

The next show came on—*The Bean*, a late-night sports show out of Chicago that scooped up the scores from the games around the nation. She had no control over what shows surrounded hers and was just glad that she had the right to control some of the ad content.

Stopping by the bathroom, she closed the window, grabbed a towel, and threw it on the subway tile floor, stepping on it with her bare foot. She paused by her parents' bedroom—it hadn't seen fresh air for two years, but she still opened the door, let her eyes graze the four-poster double bed, the Queen Anne bureau and dresser, the window that overlooked the garden.

For once, she left the door cracked, then

descended the stairs. Front door locked, yes; the parlor windows shut.

Light sparked again across the night, brachials of white that spliced the blackness. It flickered long enough to illuminate the tiny library across the street and the recycle bin on its side, rolling as the wind kicked it down the sidewalk. A half block away, and down the hill toward town, the hanging stoplight suspended above the highway swayed. The storm had turned the intersection into a four-way stop, the red light blinking, bloody upon the glassy pavement.

She pulled a knit afghan off the sofa and wrapped it around herself, letting the fraying edges drag down the wooden floor to the kitchen. Here, she switched on the light. It bathed the kitchen—the spray of white hydrangeas in a milk glass vase on the round white-and-black table, the black marble countertops, the black-and-white checked floor. Part retro, part contemporary—her mother's eclectic taste.

Thunder shook the house again, lifting the fine hairs on the back of her neck. How she hated storms.

She snaked a hand out from the blanket, turned on the burner under the teakettle. She'd left the last donut from her daily Lucy delivery upstairs in her office. Her gaze flicked to the index card pasted to the cupboard. *"If God is for us, who can ever be against us?"* Indeed. But what if

God wasn't exactly for you? Still, she wasn't going to ignore help where she might get it.

Another gust of wind, and something tumbled across her back porch—oh no, not her geraniums. Then, banging on her back door. The glass shuddered.

Why her mother had elected to change out the perfectly good solid oak doors for one solid pane of glass never made sense to her.

The kettle whistled. She turned the flame off, reached for a mug—

A howl, and no, that wasn't the wind. It sounded . . . wounded. Even afraid.

She swallowed her heart back into her chest. She knew that kind of howl. Especially on a night like this.

Tucking her hand into her blanket, Issy moved to the door, then locked it. She turned off the kitchen light and peered out into the darkness.

No glowing eyes peering back at her, no snaggletoothed monster groping at her window. She flipped on the outside light. It bathed the cedar porch, the cushions of her faded teak furniture blowing in the wind, held only by their flimsy ties. Her potted geraniums lay toppled, black earth muddy and smeared across the porch, and at the bottom of the steps, the storm had flattened her bleeding heart bush.

At the very least, she should cover her mother's prized Pilgrim roses.

Issy dumped the afghan in a chair, rolled up her pant legs, grabbed a Windbreaker hanging in the closet near the door, and pulled the hood over her head.

Unbolting the door, she eased out into the rain. The air had a cool, slick breath, and it raised gooseflesh on her arms. The deluge had stirred to life the Scotch of her white pine, a grizzled sentry in the far corner, its shaggy arms gesturing danger.

But who would hurt her here, in her backyard? Not only that, but her father had built the Titanic of all fences, with sturdy pine boards that hemmed her in, kept the world out, with the exception of Lucy, who used it as a shortcut on her way to town.

It wasn't like Issy actually locked the gate. Okay, sometimes. Okay, always. But Lucy had a key to the gate as well as the house, so it didn't really matter.

Splashing down the stairs, she dashed across the wet flagstones, past her dripping variegated hosta, the verbena, the hydrangea bush, too many of the buds stripped. The rugosa, too, lay in waste.

She wouldn't look. Not until tomorrow. Sometimes it worked better that way, to focus on what she could save. On what she still had.

Reaching the shed, she dialed the combination and opened it. She grabbed the plastic neatly folded on the rack by the door, scooped up two bricks, and dashed back to the porch. Rain couldn't quite smatter the roses here, under the overhang. Still, just in case . . . she weighted one end of the plastic with the bricks on the porch, then unfolded it over the flowers. Grabbing stones from the edging of her bed, she secured the tarp, then ran back to the shed for another pair of weights.

The howl tore through the rain again, reverberating through her.

She froze, her heart in her mouth.

Something moved. Over by the end of the porch.

The sky chose then to crack open and pour out its rage in a growl that lifted her feet from the earth.

And not only hers.

Whatever it was—she got only a glimpse—it came straight at her, like she might be prey. She screamed, dropped the bricks, and sprinted for the porch. Her foot slipped on the slick wood and she fell, hard. Her chin cracked against the wood, and then the animal pounced.

"No! Get away!" But it didn't maul her, didn't even stop. Just scrambled toward the door.

The pane of glass waterfalled onto the floor as the beast careened into her kitchen. Issy froze as the animal—huge and hairy—skidded across the linoleum.

It came to a stop, then lay there, whining.

A dog. A huge dog, with a face only a mother

could love, eyes filled with terror, wet and muddy from its jowls down.

"Nice doggy . . . nice . . ."

Lightning must have illuminated her, and the animal simply panicked. It turned and shot off through her house. Toenails scratching her polished wood floors.

"Come back!"

In the front parlor, a crash—not the spider plant!

The dog emerged back out into the hall and shot up the stairs.

"No! C'mere, boy!" Issy's bare feet stopped her at the threshold. The glass glistened like ice on the floor. Perfect. "Don't break anything!"

She darted off the porch, around the path of the garden, opened the gate, and ran through the slippery grass to the front of the house.

Thumper the rabbit still hid the key, and now she retrieved it and inserted it into the door.

The squeal of rubber against wet pavement came from her memory—or perhaps she only hoped it did. Then a crash, the splintering of metal, the shattering of glass.

She turned. *No.*

Under the bloody glow of the blinking stoplight, a sedan had T-boned a minivan. Already, gas burned the air.

Her hand went to her face, to the raised memory on her forehead, and she shook her head as if to clear away the images.

She should call 911. But she could only back into her house.

She shut the door and palmed her hands against it, the cool wood comforting. *Just . . . breathe. Just . . .*

Her breath tumbled over her, and she felt the whimper before it bubbled out.

God, please . . . What was her verse? *"If God is for us" . . .* No . . . no, the one Rachelle had given her. *"God has not given us a spirit of fear and timidity, but of power—"*

She heard shouts and closed her eyes, pressed her hand to her chest, heat pouring through her.

Just breathe.

Issy slid to the floor.

You're safe. Don't panic. Just breathe.

Caleb Knight had been in Deep Haven less than three hours and God had given him his first opportunity to be a hero.

"How many people in there?" The petroleum odor of the asphalt poured through him as he laid his cheek against the ground, peering into the overturned Caravan. The driver hung upside down, his belt securing him. A laceration separated his eyebrow, dripping blood into his scalp, his skin white and pasty. He opened his mouth, but nothing emerged.

Already the rain plastered Caleb's T-shirt to his body, his jeans turning to paste, stiffening his movements. Good thing he'd finished moving in the last of his boxes and fallen asleep fully clothed in a heap on the sofa or he'd never have reached the accident so fast.

But that crash, practically right outside his front door, could have woken the dead.

"Sir, look at me. Who else is with you?" Getting the victim talking and focused aided in preventing shock.

"My wife . . . my . . ."

Good, the man could speak. Shining his flashlight, Caleb located a woman, unconscious—at least he hoped just unconscious—hanging upside down and bleeding from a wound in her scalp. In the seat behind her hung a toddler still strapped in her car seat. He guessed the child was about three years old and when he flicked his light over her, she jerked, then screamed.

The driver—probably the father—came to life. He clawed at his belt. "Jamie!"

Caleb grabbed his hand. "I'll get her! Let's get you free." Glass glittered in the frame of the door like teeth, so Caleb shucked off his shirt, wrapped it around his hand, and broke the shards free before he reached in past the man, searching for his belt buckle. "Put your arms around me—I'll try to catch you, but brace yourself." He unlatched the buckle. The man slumped against him. Caleb hooked his hands around his shoulders and backed out, pulling the man with him.

Thank You, God—he didn't fall.

The toddler's screams tore at Caleb as he hobbled away, the man's arm latched over his shoulder.

"My daughter—my wife!"

"I'll get them. Stay here."

He set the man on the curb, then glanced down the darkened road, dead and eerie this time of night. Where were the police? Across the street, the other car had begun to flame. He ran over to it, found the driver—a young man the size of a has-been linebacker who reeked like he'd taken the pub home with him—slumped at the wheel. Caleb pressed two fingers to his carotid artery but found no pulse.

The flames flickered under the hood, stabbing out like blades around the edges. He tried the door once. It wouldn't move, so he left it.

Where was the fire department?

The rain slickened the pavement, more so for him, but he scrambled back to the passenger side of the Caravan. He'd done a few vehicle extractions while in Iraq, but then he'd had tools, of course. He leaned in but the woman's girth wouldn't allow him access. He slid his hand across her belly, trying to find the buckle and—

Pregnant. The woman was pregnant. *Oh, God, please . . .*

Behind them, the toddler's frantic howls ate at him. "C'mon!" He stifled a word, even as he tried

27

once more to reach the woman's belt. When he yanked his arm back, his hand came away wet, sticky.

Blood.

Caleb pressed his fingers to the woman's carotid artery. Yes, a pulse. For now. "Ma'am, wake up."

"It's on fire—the van's on fire!" The voice of the panicked father raked him out of the passenger window. The gasoline from the other car bled a lethal trail to the Caravan, and eye-biting smoke blew into the window on the driver's side.

Caleb tried the back passenger door, fought with it. Nothing. He put his weight into it. They'd need Jaws . . .

The child's cries turned hysterical and galvanized him. He turned his back to the van, then, with everything inside him, put his elbow through the window.

Pain spiked up his arm, but he whirled around, sliding over the shattered glass. Flames had already begun to devour the seats, the ceiling fabric, churning acrid smoke into the cab. The toddler thrashed in her seat. He unlatched the first thing he saw—the buckle holding the seat. Catching the car seat, he dragged it out behind him, the toddler still strapped inside.

The father struggled to his feet, and Caleb practically shoved the child into his arms. "Get back!"

"My wife—she's pregnant—"

Now—*finally*—sirens. Only the man's wife didn't have time, not with the flames moving swiftly across the ceiling.

God, please don't let her burn! Caleb dove inside again, this time shoving himself against the woman, fighting for a handhold on the buckle. He touched it. It sizzled on his skin, but he depressed it.

The woman fell hard against him. He backed out of the window, grabbed her shoulders. He needed more leverage. He would have braced his foot against the vehicle, but of course, he couldn't do that—not and keep his balance.

You have to get used to the fact that you can't do the things you could before.

Collin's voice in his brain only strengthened Caleb's grip on the woman. He pulled her through the window, but her belly scraped against the frame, imprisoning her.

She roused fast, hard, her eyes on his. "I'm burning—I'm burning!"

Burning.

No, he wouldn't go there.

He found his medic's tone, the one he'd honed in Iraq. "I'll get you out." Preserve life in the living. Yes, *that* voice he'd listen to.

A fire engine pulled up, firefighters swarming onto the scene.

She gripped his upper arms, her eyes wide. "Don't leave me—pull me out! Pull me out!"

He forced her body through the window even as she screamed.

Then water. He heard it more than felt it, the rush killing the fire, spitting into the Caravan, drenching him as he slipped, hit the ground.

He nearly cried out as his knee twisted. He struggled to push the woman away, wrenching his leg even more out of whack.

"We have survivors over here!"

He pushed up, lifting himself onto his good knee. Turned to the woman.

An EMT knelt beside her, her blonde hair pulled back in a ponytail. "We need a stretcher over here!" She glanced at Caleb, at the way he held himself, probably at the angry rumpled skin up his rib cage, his arm and shoulder. "Where are you injured, sir?"

He didn't even know where to begin to answer, but that wasn't really her question. "I wasn't in the accident. I'm fine."

Confusion swept across her face; then she turned away, gesturing at two firemen who appeared with a litter to carry the woman to the curb.

Caleb made it to his feet and followed them, limping.

The EMT gave him another stray glance. "You sure you're okay, sir?"

"What took you guys so long?" Behind him, water had killed the fire, the generator for the

Jaws of Life growling into the night as it gnawed open the door of the dead driver.

She frowned at him. "We're volunteers. Seven minutes isn't a terrible response time, considering that most of us were in our pajamas. You got a complaint, talk to the chief."

She gestured to a firefighter, the one with the white hat, and Caleb took a breath, hobbled over to the man. One look told him that *volunteer* was the operative word. Paunchy, with a day's beard growth and tired eyes, the man looked like someone had dragged him out of his feather bed, where he'd been hibernating.

He glanced at Caleb. "You okay, sir?"

"No, I'm not—I want to know why it took you guys seven minutes to get here."

The man pursed his lips and turned away to supervise the removal of the other victim. "Joe, what do you see?"

The firefighter turned, appearing undone by the accident. "It's Zach Miller." He shook his head.

What looked like real pain flashed across the chief's face. He faced Caleb again. "Are you new in town?"

His question swiped the anger from Caleb. "Uh . . . yeah. I'm the new football coach. Just got here tonight."

The chief stared at him, his eyes narrowing for a second. "Then you should probably know that kid in the car was one of the best defensive tackles

31

in the state a couple years back. And now all his parents and the town are going to remember about him is that he died nearly killing three people."

Caleb had no words for that.

An officer wearing a rain slicker sidled up to them. "Pastor, you want me to talk to the parents?"

The chief shook his head. "I know Marci and Greg. I'll tell them."

Pastor? Caleb gave the man a long look. He could appreciate a preacher who ministered with action as well as words.

Caleb turned, watching the EMTs trundle the woman, now sedated, into the ambulance, the lights splashing red and yellow across the nightmare. "I'm sorry about the kid." He didn't look at the pastor.

"I hate this intersection. In the winter, or whenever it rains, that hill is like a sheet of ice. It's killed more people than I want to think about." The chief blew out a breath. "Listen—you probably saved that whole family tonight. But if you have a complaint, feel free to get involved. Come down to the station, join the crew." He took off a glove and held out his hand. "Dan Matthews."

Caleb met his grip, nonplussed by the chief's offer. Maybe the darkness hid him more than he suspected. "Caleb Knight."

"Nice to meet you, Coach."

Coach. Yes, that had a ring to it Caleb craved. "I would love to, but . . ." That part of his life was over, despite his desire to save lives, to invest in people. "I don't think so."

"Shame. We could use someone with your instincts."

Caleb backed away to the curb.

The blonde EMT shut the back of the rig. "You should get that leg looked at."

Yeah, he should do that.

But frankly, he spent way too much time looking at his leg. Or perhaps trying not to. That was the battle, wasn't it?

The rain began to slack as he limped home. He hadn't realized how smack in the center of town he lived—on the corner a half block up the hill from the highway intersection, with a view of the lake, and within walking distance to the library, grocery store, gas station, and coffee shop. And on the other side of the highway, a quaint downtown that overlooked Lake Superior.

Maybe here he could find a new life. A fresh start. A place where people saw Caleb Knight, not his scars.

The porch light sprayed over the backyard of the house next door, although the lights upstairs had switched off since he'd moved the last box in.

Maybe the neighbor, too, had voices in his head that kept him thrashing away the night hours.

Your life is different now, but you'll get used to it.

There's no shame.

You're a hero for your country.

Your disability can be a good thing, if you let it.

Yeah, sure it could. Although it had opened his eyes to God's grace, to second chances, and set his focus on being the man he should have been. The man he would be.

But it didn't make it any easier to sleep. Not when the sounds and smells of the desert, the taste of fear and his own tinny blood, could crawl back to haunt him. Hence his addiction to late-night talk shows. They filled his brain with sounds that couldn't hurt.

Hopefully he could get an Internet connection, pick up *The Bean.*

Caleb steadied himself on the porch rail as he climbed the steps. He stopped to rest, to breathe deep. He had to get inside before someone saw him.

Then again, it had to be close to midnight. Who would see the new football coach limping to his house?

He opened his door and went inside.

Closing it, he braced himself on the side table. Ten more steps. He could do ten more steps.

No . . . he couldn't, not with the heat in his leg nearly making him howl. He turned around, leaned his back against the door, and collapsed to the floor. Fighting with his cuff, he tried to pull up his pant leg. Shoot, he couldn't get at it . . .

So he unbuckled his belt and peeled down his

jeans. Then, with hands that shook, he reached down and rolled off the elastic sock that connected his transtibial amputation to his artificial leg.

2

How Lucy Maguire hated 3 a.m. The world at 3 a.m. bore a hush that could turn her bones brittle. Not with fear, of course—because who could really be afraid in Deep Haven? A hamlet trapped in time, without a Starbucks, without a mall, without even a movie theater. No, the brittle, almost-breakable sense came from the loneliness of the hour, the fact that only her voice kept her awake as she kneaded dough, processed it through the donut cutter, plopped it into the hot oil.

Most of all, her solo humming reminded her that upon her size-two shoulders alone hung the confectionary legacy of three generations.

And she was going to let them all down.

Lucy slapped her hand on the alarm and buried her head in her pillow. Even if she tried, after all this time, her body simply refused to sleep past three fifteen.

It made for a stellar social life.

She rolled over, stared at her ceiling. Pulled out

her earplugs and set them on the white wicker nightstand, the one her mother picked up at a garage sale in the Cities when Lucy was twelve. In fact, the entire room overdosed on white wicker, all garnished with pink—a pink bedspread, pink carpet, pink plush pillows.

She padded across the hallway into the bathroom, dug her toes into the royal blue bath rug, and fished her toothbrush out of the cup. It must have rained in the night because the rug squished between her toes, a victim of her open window. She turned off the water. Sure enough, the random plinks from the poplars looming over the bungalow told her to put on rain gear for her walk to the donut shop.

A gal had to get her exercise somehow. Especially when she hung around donuts all day. The grease embedded her pores, and indeed, as she peered into the mirror, she resembled a teenager the week before the prom, little bumps of acne across her forehead, where she wore her baseball cap. Then again, she always looked like a teenager, or worse, a ten-year-old. It simply wasn't fair that Issy landed all the curves while Lucy could still shop in the juniors section at Dillard's.

But at least she *could* shop at Dillard's, at the mall some two hundred miles away. At least she wasn't trapped in her house. At least Lucy's mother was alive, albeit on a beach in Florida, having done her tenure at the donut shop.

Issy had good reason for her panic attacks, and Lucy, her best friend since first grade, wasn't judging.

She scrubbed her face, ran her fingers through her pixie cut, grabbed a red baseball cap, didn't bother with makeup, and returned to her room. Yesterday's jeans were good enough, paired with a clean T-shirt and a Deep Haven Huskies sweatshirt.

Wait—today was the Fisherman's Picnic parade. They'd expect her on the class float. Well, she'd just have to come home and change.

Or not. After all, she didn't have anyone to impress. There wasn't a soul in town who didn't know Lucy the donut girl, hadn't known her since she was three. And wearing pink. Sweet Lucy.

She hadn't been sweet since . . . No. Why did every Fisherman's Picnic have to rouse all the dark memories?

All her failures.

She grabbed her raincoat and slipped into her rubber boots. Not bothering to lock the back door, she cut through her yard to Issy's backyard paradise. Oh, to have one ounce of Issy's talent. Everything she did, she did well, from gardening to her crazy radio show. Trapped in her home, she was still someone. Miss Foolish Heart.

But Lucy—oh yes, *she* could make donuts.

She closed Issy's gate and turned onto the flagstone path. Stopped.

Someone had broken into Issy's house.

She ran up the back steps to the shattered door.

"Issy?" She didn't care if she woke the whole neighborhood. "Issy?" No light in the kitchen or the front room, or from the upstairs office. But Issy *had* to be here. What if she was hurt?

Her boots picked up the glass, which sliced into the ridges and crunched as she ran down the hallway. "Issy!"

"Here. I'm here." The voice emerged small, and even as Lucy searched, she couldn't find her.

"Where are you?"

"By the piano."

Oh, Issy. Wrapped in her father's coaching jacket, the one that still smelled of grass stains, Issy had crammed herself under the baby grand in the front parlor. Bare feet stuck out of her jeans, rolled up at the cuffs.

Lucy flicked on the lamp over the piano. "What happened? Are you okay? Your back door— there's glass everywhere." She crouched before Issy. Her long hair hung tangled and crunchy around her face, which was puffy as if she'd been crying.

"I think there was an accident."

"I know; I saw the door. Are you okay?"

"No, I mean . . . you know. At the light."

"At the . . . There was a *car* accident?"

"A couple hours ago. You probably had your earplugs in, didn't you?"

Lucy nodded, but what did that have to do with Issy's back door being demolished? "I don't understand."

"I heard the sirens. And I think there was a fire."

"Was anyone hurt?"

"I don't know. I just—" She drew in a breath, and Lucy had to give her credit for not burrowing back into her father's coat.

"Shh. You're okay. But what about your door?"

"Oh. There was a dog. I think he must have been afraid of the storm. He broke in."

Lucy took Issy's hands. They radiated heat, clasped as they'd been inside the arms of the jacket.

"Are you hurt?"

Issy swallowed, sadness on her face. "No."

"Good. You're okay. See, you're okay, right?"

Issy nodded. "I'm okay."

"Where's the dog?"

Issy looked past her. "I think he's upstairs."

"C'mon. We'll get him." Lucy held on to Issy's hand and led the way up the stairs.

Sure enough, the dog had invaded the second floor, helping himself first to the greasy white donut bags, now saliva sloppy and littered across the floor toward—

"Oh no." Issy pushed open her parents' bedroom door.

Lucy followed her in. The dog, his feet chunky with globules of earth, his sides slicked with grime, slept in the middle of Issy's parents' handmade wedding ring quilt. Mud layered into the creases of the squares. The animal had even settled his head on the matching pillow, dripping saliva into the cotton. The quilt itself was tangled in a circle around him, as if he'd tried to make a nest.

"Wow. That's . . ."

Issy made a strange sound. A burble at first, then a hiccup of something breaking free.

Lucy turned. *Please, don't let her be unraveling, not again.*

Issy put her hands over her mouth, looked at Lucy, and laughed.

Out loud. Louder, half-crying, half-laughing. "I guess he likes me." Her words emerged on more high-pitched giggling.

"Are you okay? Do you need to sit down, maybe put your head between your knees? Is this the beginning of a panic attack? I don't know what to do."

Issy pressed her fingers under her eyes. "The poor dog sort of looks like me, crazy with fear, trying to find a safe place. If I were him, I'd have done the same thing—gone for the donuts, then curled up in my parents' bed." She sat down, ran her hands over the animal. He opened one eye but didn't move.

"Issy?"

Issy's smile faded. "I'm so tired of this, Lucy.

Tired of feeling broken. Tired of letting fear beat me. Tired of hiding in the dark. I just want to be free."

Lucy sat next to her. "You will be. One day at a time."

"I hope so. One of my callers tonight asked me to go to her wedding. In Napa."

"Napa? California? That's wonderful."

Issy gave her a look. "Not so much."

"You should go."

"How, exactly, might I do that? I can't even stir up the courage to cross the highway and attend the celebration in town. Bree's called me three times to get me to ride on this year's float. Like that's happening."

"You don't need to ride on the float. I'll walk down to the corner with you. We can wave together."

Issy picked up the animal's floppy ear. Leaned into it. "Whoever you belong to is going to die a slow, painful death."

The dog yawned, groaned, then settled back into sleep.

Issy glanced at Lucy. "It wouldn't hurt *you* to ride the float, you know. A little free World's Best Donuts advertising?"

"And it wouldn't hurt you to go to Napa, a little free advertising for *My Foolish Heart*."

"Touché."

Lucy grinned. "I need to go to work."

"Go. I'm fine. I think I'll just join Duncan here."

"Duncan?"

"Doesn't he look like a Duncan?"

Lucy kissed her friend's forehead and let herself out. Sure enough, at the intersection, a couple tow trucks hoisted two dented cars onto their beds. She blinked away the too-raw image captured in the *Deep Haven Herald* of the fire department pulling the body of Issy's beautiful mother from the wreckage of their sedan.

As for Issy's father . . . well, the town had yet to find a replacement for their most winning football coach, the wound of his injuries still fresh. Thankfully, Coach Presley hadn't died—although it seemed like it sometimes with him trapped in his bed at the care center. That night had dismantled the football program with one swift, ugly blow. The assistant coach had barely managed to finish out the season and moved out of town. And the volunteers since then hadn't known the first thing about coaching, let alone how to fill the shoes of a man who'd helped build men of honor.

Or at least tried to.

Lucy detoured the other way, crossing a block down from the wreckage, intending on cutting back across the lakeshore toward the donut shop. After fifty years of renting, her family had finally purchased the tiny building on the edge of Main and First. It needed updating, however, the land beneath it worth more than the building. Unfortunately she owed too much money to the bank to consider updating the property.

She'd sold six hundred fewer donuts yesterday than she had last year at this time. Which meant she'd have trouble making her monthly loan payment yet again. With heating bills and the dip in tourism, clearly her decision to stay open last winter hadn't been a wise one.

Maybe she wasn't exactly cut out for business ownership.

What if she just called it quits, closed the shop? Then what?

She caught her reflection in the dark window of the Java Cup. Hood up, she looked like a waif or perhaps a vagabond.

Nearly tripping over something on the ground, she stopped. She'd stepped on a piece of cardboard—no, poster board, probably ripped from the door of the coffee shop by the storm. She read it in the dim light.

Freshly made donuts, sixty cents each. While they last.

Freshly. Made. Donuts. *Sixty* cents? She'd been charging eighty for the past two years. A person couldn't make a living for less than eighty cents a donut.

While they last? How many had the coffee shop made? Six hundred, perhaps? Almost five hundred dollars of her donut revenue?

She picked up the sign, her hands shaking, and debated putting it up against the door but then, suddenly, couldn't.

She was the donut girl. She ran World's *Best* Donuts.

Marching over to the Dumpster, she held it up to toss it in; then—yes!—she tore it in half. Again. And again.

She tossed the scraps into the Dumpster. Picked up a rock, threw that inside, too.

Oh, she wanted to scream, to awaken the town, or . . . something.

Issy wasn't the only one tired of being trapped, of being overwhelmed. Tired of the past haunting her, telling her how to live.

But Lucy was the donut girl. It was all she had. She wasn't going down without a fight.

"I doubt she was serious, Elliot." Issy cradled the phone against her ear as she piled the quilt and the sheets into a ball and carried them down to the basement laundry room. At the top of the stairs, she pulled the dangling cord, and light bathed the cobwebs, the cracked, ancient cement floor that had seen too many days as a hockey rink.

"I guarantee you that Lauren O'Grady was serious. So serious that I got a call this morning on my *home phone* from the governor himself asking for your number."

"Hence why you dragged me out of bed at 6 a.m.?" Although Issy had never visited Elliot in New York, she imagined him as an older fellow, well dressed, his hair slicked back, with sharp, dark eyes. He had approached her on behalf of Late Night Lovelorn after listening to her podcasts online.

Podcasts that Oscar, the producer from Deep Haven's local radio station, had posted after she'd hosted a few book club call-in shows from her remote location at home. Elliot had heard them online and cajoled her into starting a talk show. *My Foolish Heart* had been his creation, and in those early days, it kept her from the black hole of grief that wanted to suck her in, seal her off completely from life.

"Who are you kidding, Issy? You never sleep. You're always online."

What did he expect? *My Foolish Heart* had become her entire life. It had grown to a national show, with a forum and a chat room and a life to it that made her feel too much like the television host she'd once upon a time aspired to be.

Someday, she might even reveal her identity to the world. To Deep Haven. But not quite yet. She couldn't bear the comments that might follow.

Such a shame what happened to her parents.
Three days in the hospital after the funeral.
She didn't leave her house for almost a year.

And all this time that she was hiding out, she was pretending to be a romance therapist!

Talk about driving her back into her home, never to be seen again. "You didn't give my number out, did you?" She piled the laundry onto the dryer and opened the washer lid.

"I can't be bought, yet, but have you given any thought to your ratings, Issy? This could be a real boost. Imagine, broadcasting live from Lauren O'Grady's wedding."

She pushed the laundry into the washer, added soap, turned on the water. "I don't think she'd like that."

"Of course we'd wait until after the wedding, but we'd have some taped interviews from guests, talk about how *My Foolish Heart* helped her commit to marriage."

"All I did was offer some commonsense romance advice my mother gave me. 'Don't call boys; wait until they ask you out. Dress like a woman you want them to respect. Expect the best from your date. Don't give away the goods.' I never expected the show to go viral. I thought I was hosting a radio show for aficionados of classic romances." She climbed the stairs and turned off the light. Now to attack the back door. She'd already swept up the glass, but she needed to put a piece of plywood or cardboard over the frame to keep the mosquitoes—and apparently, wildlife—out.

She'd already fed Duncan the last of Lucy's donuts before the dog took off, tail wagging after his bed-and-breakfast stay.

She sort of hoped he came back. After a bath, of course. He made a nice companion. A man of few words. Kind eyes. Afraid of storms. Someone she could relate to.

"And that's what's made you so popular. Common sense. Principles. And the fact you are so well-read. You're the only talk show that reads passages from *Jane Eyre* and *Romeo and Juliet* and *Sense and Sensibility* aloud."

"We can always learn from the classics."

"But looking ahead to the future wouldn't hurt. Late Night Lovelorn Network is willing to pay for your trip, set you up in a hotel, provide you with transportation and a staff to make this happen."

She stepped through the door, surveyed the damage, and sighed. "No."

"I don't understand your phobia. What, do you think you're going to get hurt? I'd fly out, be right there with you."

Most people didn't understand panic attacks, really. It wasn't a fear of leaving the house. It was a fear of being out of control, of something happening that she didn't expect and then reacting poorly. Poorly, aka running away, hiding, dropping into the fetal position, weeping. Making a scene for the entire world to watch.

It was a fear of being in a place that reminded her of that moment when life careened so far out of control that she simply unraveled. She couldn't let that happen again. Ever.

"Unless you have had fear rule your life, you can't understand. But I'm trying, Elliot. Really. And you knew this about me when you contracted my show."

Elliot sighed. "I'm on your side, Issy. Really. But management wants you to do this. Your numbers are down recently, and we're losing advertisers. They think if you broadcast in Napa, you could pick up some new markets, add some new life to your show. You need to do something to boost ratings. Your contract is up for renewal at the end of September, and I'm afraid if you don't agree to cover this, Late Night Lovelorn just might drop you."

Drop her? So she could disappear back into the darkness? The show connected her with real people, safely. She couldn't lose the show. But—

"Issy?"

She sat down on one of the stools at her kitchen island. "I can't go to Napa, Elliot. I'm sorry. The fact is, I want to. I don't want to lose my show. If there was a way to boost my ratings, believe me, I'd be doing it."

He had no idea how she'd love to visit Napa. Or . . . anywhere. She'd even settle for downtown Deep Haven, just to make it to World's Best

Donuts and have a hot skizzle instead of waiting for leftovers. She'd long tired of the view of the pine boards of the backyard fence, the vacant, paint-peeling A-frame rental next door.

"Are you still seeing your counselor?"

"Of course."

"Then you're making progress."

"If you call being able to finally run around the block and visit the library across the street during quiet hours *progress,* yes."

"I do. There's no way you could talk yourself onto a plane?"

She considered it a moment. "I think that would take a miracle of epic proportions."

Elliot was silent as the words hung between them. Finally he said, "Hang in there."

"Where else am I going to go?" She meant it as a joke, but it fell flat.

He gave her a courtesy laugh anyway. "Do me a favor and get those recordings done." He hung up without a Minnesota good-bye.

A miracle of epic proportions. She glanced outside at the blue sky, cloudless after last night's storm.

"Please, Lord, send me a miracle. Set me free, if that's even possible."

She let her words hang there, just in case God still cared. She'd long ago figured that after everything she'd done to embarrass Him, He'd probably washed His hands of her. And why not? Christians were supposed to overcome fear. She'd embarrassed everyone, especially God.

Pocketing the phone, she slipped on her flip-flops and ventured out to the garage.

The storm had littered sticks into her yard, flattened more than her bleeding heart. She had hours of gardening before her today.

Sunlight poured through the grimy garage windows, over her father's boat and the shiny Chevy the insurance company had purchased to replace her car. Actually, Lucy had purchased it for her, driven it home from Duluth before the insurance check expired. Now, it radiated a barely-been-driven sheen.

She ran her fingers over the hood, then flipped on the overhead light and spotted the refrigerator box in the corner. Her mother had had the new appliance installed just two weeks before her death.

The perfect size to cover the back door.

She pressed the door opener and retrieved the box, pulling it into the driveway.

It was then she noticed the shiny white truck. Like a behemoth, its girth sprawled over the neighbor's driveway. Its giant wheels had ground up the pansies she'd grown from seed and planted, one by one, along the border between the houses.

She stalked over to it, glanced at the A-frame rental. Which, until yesterday, had been empty for nearly two years.

She had a new neighbor. And on his porch lay the furry culprit of last night's attack.

Seb Brewster just wanted to sneak back into town before anyone noticed.

He needed time to paste on his game face.

The sun had just begun to peek over the lake, denting the sky with gold as he coaxed his Dodge Neon over the last hill and into the hamlet of Deep Haven. Opening the window, he tapped the brakes, cruised to thirty, and drank in the piney tang of the air after a storm, the sound of gulls crying over lost opportunity.

Cars lined the streets, and as he veered away from the Main Street cutoff, he noted a band shell set up in the harbor park. Today's lineup was sure to feature JayJ and his band of blues musicians, probably still plunking out the same tunes they had when they'd slapped together sounds in his garage over a decade ago. Seb lasted about two practices at the trap set before football overtook his life.

A few early morning power walkers pushed athletic strollers or followed obedient city dogs on leashes, and a couple teenagers in shorts and Lake Superior sweatshirts skipped stones into the hungry water. One, two, three, four . . . He'd made it to fifteen once.

Back in his glory days.

The sweet breath of coming home stirred inside him and nearly slid his compact into an empty parking space in front of the Footstep of Heaven bookstore, daring him to dash down the street to World's Best Donuts, grab a fresh donut.

What if Lucy still worked there?

Maybe she had finally forgiven him.

He sighed and kept going, through the one stoplight, past the grocery store, the auto parts lot—aka junkyard—the forest service building, and finally, at the town limits, turned left at Dugan's Trailer Park.

His buoyant spirit deflated as he passed the rows of trailers lined up like railroad cars. A few displayed the efforts of beautification—a potted clump of geraniums, a bed of lilies. A freestanding swing and a turtle-shaped sandbox with a collection of Tonka trucks, their yellow tin glinting in the hazy morning sun, suggested small children still lived in the neighborhood.

As he drove farther up the hill, the nostalgia died in the clutter of weeds and a rusty white pine that loomed over a single-wide green trailer with dented screens in the two-by-two windows. A blackened plastic Christmas wreath hung on the door. A sorry reminder of his mother's last Christmas before she left.

Seb parked next to a dented Impala. A splotch of oil darkened the gravel under it, and he had to arc his leg out to avoid stepping in the grease. By the end of the week, he'd probably be lying in the puddle, replacing the oil pan.

The birds chirruped as if remembering him, and the old porch creaked appropriately, but no sounds of life drifted from the trailer's screened door—no bacon sizzling on the stove, no canned laughter from the television. He peered inside for a moment, gathering his breath against the cigarette odor that would saturate his clothes. Once upon a time, the smell would cause him to fling open the door and search the rooms for his father, home from the road.

Later, the smell told him whether he should stick around or take off for Coach Presley's place. Seb had awakened most Saturday mornings on the coach's front room sofa, his stomach aching at the smell of pancakes.

He eased open the door. It caught and he had to wrestle it the rest of the way, as if forcing himself back into his old life.

Perhaps, indeed, that's exactly what he was doing.

Dishes marinated in the sink, a swarm of flies lifting in greeting. Spaghetti hardened in a bowl on the built-in dining nook table. No television at all—maybe it had broken, although he hadn't seen it on the porch. Instead dust layered the television stand, the deer lamp on the side table. The brown carpet hadn't been vacuumed this side of the last election.

He eased down the skinny hallway, past the bathroom, then his old bedroom-turned-closet for his father's hunting equipment. The Marlin 336 lay on the bed—*great storage, Dad*—and against the wall leaned the Ruger rifle, with what looked like a new scope.

Seb sucked a breath, then pushed open the master bedroom door, half-hoping he wouldn't find him, a skin-and-bones man, his teeth yellow, his skin bled of color, his hair long and tangled over his face, life shucked from him one drink at a time.

But there he lay, fully clothed in a pair of greasy jeans and a T-shirt, his mouth open as if surprised that he might find himself in his own bed.

Seb walked up to him. Nudged his knee. "Dad. Hey."

Nothing.

"Dad, c'mon. Wake up." He shook him again, harder, his heart just a little in his throat.

The man roused. Groaned.

"Dad, it's me, Seb. I'm home."

An eye flickered open. Then the other. For a long, suffocating moment, he stared at Seb, those green eyes unfocused or simply climbing out of someplace Seb didn't want to know about. Seb fought the urge to drop and bury his head on his father's bony knees and weep. *It's me, Dad. Seb. And . . .*

I'm sorry. I'm so sorry. I meant to be more.

But he pushed his hands into his jean pockets, fisted them.

Finally his father broke through the fog and blinked at Seb. He wiped his mouth, then reached out his hand, gripping Seb's wrist. "It's about time you got here, kid."

About time. Yes, maybe.

"Do you need anything?"

A smirk tweaked his father's face. He followed it with a harrumph. "How about some breakfast?"

His father's grip fell away and he rolled back into slumber. At least the old man had made it home. Hopefully without hurting anyone.

Seb nodded, slipping into a rhythm, seventeen again, arriving home from practice to find his father passed out on the sofa, the bathroom floor, the bed. He'd fix himself a sandwich and watch the NFL channel until midnight, plotting his future. Back then, he'd planned on playing for the University of Minnesota. If he got lucky, if he did well at the Combine, he'd get picked up by the Packers or even the Bears. He wanted to stay close, in case his mother came home, in case she saw him in the papers.

Maybe she'd even want season tickets. He'd get her a box seat, of course.

Seb missed that, perhaps, the most—looking up out of a huddle when he was fifteen, already varsity quarterback, and seeing her, bundled for winter in the stands. Sometimes the only one.

But even his touchdowns hadn't kept her home.

As he reached the door, he heard his father rouse again. Seb stopped and swallowed hard before turning back to face what remained of his family.

"Welcome home, Son."

"Yeah. Thanks, Dad. I'll get those eggs for you."

3

Caleb could fall in love with a town that served fish burgers. Especially by a playful indigo lake that flirted with the laughing children running along the stone-tossed beach.

The intoxicating smells of grilled hot dogs, fresh kettle corn, and crispy french fries dripping with peanut oil had all conspired to draw Caleb to the annual Fisherman's Picnic. He'd put on a long-sleeved shirt, then walked down the street, crossed at the light—where glass and other debris still marked last night's tragedy—and sauntered over to the festivities along the harbor.

He'd beelined to the Elks Club's fish stand, where the "Have You Had Your Walleye Today?" sign made him fork over three bucks.

Walleye, deep-fried, slathered in tartar sauce, on a long hot dog bun. Only in northern Minnesota. Or perhaps, only in Deep Haven.

Yes, Caleb wanted to fit into this town. Wanted to look like the locals, in their cargo pants, their

Gore-Tex jackets, their hiking boots. Wanted to know the kids skateboarding down the center of the blocked-off Main Street—all three blocks of it—and know who to recruit for his offensive line. Wanted the blonde at the coffee stand to know his regular brew, like she did with every other person in line. He pictured his own mug on the shelf at the donut shop, where this morning he'd purchased a raspberry-filled bismark from the petite, doe-eyed brunette. He'd stopped for a long moment and just read the fifty or so cups on the rack, their first initial and last name demarking the owner's place in the community.

Coach K. That's what his label would read. He'd rise early every day, slide into an orange molded booth with a fresh donut, a hot cup of black coffee, and raise a greeting to the mayor or the hotel owner from across the street or the booth of local contractors. "Hello, Coach," they'd say without a trace of pity.

After Caleb grabbed a napkin from the stand, he ventured through the crowd with his fish burger until he found a place in the middle of Moose Park, below the stage. A long-haired guitarist picked out some bluesy tune, as behind him what looked like locals in their T-shirts, jeans, and Birkenstocks jammed to his beat. A few courageous souls danced on the cobblestones of the park. Caleb moved out of their way.

The rain seemed to have cleansed the clouds

from the sky—only the clear blue remained. The town rose on a hill behind the harbor with unpretentious houses amid the lush backfill of white pine and cedar trees. He raised his face to the heat of the sun.

"Hey—if it isn't the new coach."

He turned. "Chief . . . uh . . ."

"Dan Matthews. Enjoying the fish burger?"

"I've never had a fish burger before. They're . . ."

"Fabulous. We only get them twice a year—Fish Pic and Labor Day." Dan patted his belly. "I've had three already. But don't tell my wife—she'll have me eating low carb for a month."

Caleb grinned. "Your secret's safe with me. So how's the family from the accident?"

"I checked in with them this morning—the wife delivered a healthy baby girl by C-section but had to be airlifted to Minneapolis Medical Center's burn unit. The father and his other daughter were released. I'll check again, but I think everyone will survive, thanks to you."

"Right time, right place."

"And quick thinking. I really can't talk you into volunteering for the fire department? You'd get to take a place in our annual dunking contest." Dan gestured behind him. Caleb turned just in time to watch a victim splash into the drink at the hands of a little girl, her blonde hair pulled through the back of her blue and white baseball cap.

"Way to go, Wendy!" Dan yelled, and she turned, waved. "She's my oldest. Has the fastball of a Yankee pitcher."

A woman, her light brown hair in a matching ponytail, high-fived the girl. "And that's my wife, Ellie. She's the manager of our EMS department, and I promise, you don't want me to sic her on you. An able-bodied man fresh to our community? Turn yourself in under your own volition is my advice."

Able-bodied. And so far, even in daylight, the pastor hadn't given a second glance to Caleb's shaven head under his baseball cap or the puckered skin on his hand, the one holding the fish burger. "I think I'll be pretty busy with football practice, but we'll see."

Ellie waved her husband over and Dan made a face. "Busted. I think it's my turn in the tank." He clamped Caleb on the shoulder. Thankfully, Caleb no longer had to wince. "Swing by anytime or even come up to the church. We'd be glad to see you."

Caleb took the proffered hand and returned an I'll-do-that smile.

His first friend in Deep Haven, a pastor. Yes, this place felt right.

Finishing off the fish burger, Caleb made the rounds through the assembly of artisans who had set up shop in front of the local pizza parlor. Watercolorists, weavers, wood-carvers. He stopped in front of a pottery booth.

A foot-pedaled potter's wheel bulked the middle of the booth. Sacks of clay sat on a shelf behind it alongside unfired pots, some painted, some pale gray. The potter stood over a worktable, wearing an apron over her broom skirt and white T-shirt, her long black hair in a loose braid.

Caleb picked up a bowl painted in the earthy greens, ambers, and cedars of the north woods. A seagull flying above a shoreline etched the bottom.

"Let me know if you have any questions," the woman said. She took a bag filled with what looked like clay and water and began to knead it from the outside.

Okay, sure. "What is that?"

"A broken pot. It fell off the shelf before I could fire it. Thankfully, it wasn't completely hardened, or I would have had to grind it to powder and start all over. This one, I just took the pieces, let them soak in water for a few days to regain the moisture. I think it's just about ready to be remolded."

She opened the bag, worked her hand through the clay, finally fishing it out. She dumped it onto a wooden board and began rolling it into a ball.

"Do you have a store in town?" Caleb asked.

"Right up the road. I share commercial space with the bookstore."

"How long have you lived here?"

"About ten years. *Someday* I hope to be considered a local." She looked up at him, pushing back wisps of her black hair with her wrist. "Are you visiting?"

"No, I—"

"He's our new social studies teacher, Liza." This voice he knew, and Caleb turned into the handshake of Mitch O'Conner, head of the school board. A fishing cap, bedazzled with tied lures, protected his blond crew cut, but already the sun had turned his burly arms red. He shifted his coffee cup into his right hand. "You settling in?"

Caleb nodded. "Got here last night. Met the local fire department."

"So you were the one on the scene. I was talking to one of the firefighters this morning and he mentioned a Good Samaritan. You should volunteer—we could use more men on the squad. And a few of them are on the school board. You might recognize them from your interview."

Yes, Caleb remembered that interview, six weeks ago. Especially the question *Is there anything that might prevent you from doing this job?* They'd probably had their eye on his scars, those they could see. He'd answered as truthfully as he could.

Not in my estimation.

He'd just have to prove his words right.

"By the way, you should know that a couple of the guys from the board told me we have another candidate for the coaching position."

"But I thought I would be coaching." He knew he'd technically been hired to teach psychology and social studies, but he hadn't exactly hidden his true agenda.

"The candidate is Seb Brewster, an alum of Deep Haven High. He's filling a math aide position." Mitch took a sip of coffee. "Played quarterback, led our team to our last state championship. And . . . he wants the coaching job." He gestured with his cup. "He's over there in the green shirt, listening to JayJ and the guys."

The green shirt . . . oh, the guy who looked about six-four, built lean and fast, as if he still spent time on the field, throwing long and scrambling out of the pocket? The man finished his own fish burger and now rose to shake a hand and buddy-hug a couple linebacker-size locals.

"He's already got a fan club in this town, so . . . well . . . I had to swing a deal with the board."

Something about the look on Mitch's pale-skinned face made Caleb's chest tighten.

"We're going to have a competition." Mitch made an I'm-sorry face as he spoke, but it didn't lessen the pinch. A competition with the state champ over there? For the job?

Perfect.

Three years ago, Caleb might have outcoached the man blindfolded, his own impressive high school record as running back fodder for serious competition. Today, his leg already ached after an hour of tromping around town, and even with his degrees in teaching and coaching, he hadn't coached seriously since the year he'd graduated from college and worked for the summer youth football camps.

Then, of course, came his two-year National Guard stint in Iraq.

The fish burger soured in his stomach.

Mitch was still talking. "We're going to divide the team in half, and each of you will get a full line. You'll have a couple weeks to whip them into shape, learn a few plays, and then we'll have a scrimmage. We have one every year anyway to give our players a chance to stir up some excitement for the season, and this time, we'll get to evaluate coaches as well as the players. We're not guaranteeing the winner the job, but it won't hurt."

He took a sip of coffee. "We mostly want to see how you work with your players. This is a long-term gig and we have to make the right investment. We may be a small town, but we're a town that loves our sports teams. Especially football."

Mitch stared into his coffee as if it held some answers or words. "Frankly, we're still hurting over Coach Presley's accident. Just can't seem to find our footing. Our football program was more than a sport—it was a way to build character into our young men."

No pressure there. "I knew the old coach was in an accident, but what happened?"

Mitch looked at the kids running along the beach. "Coach got hit by a semi two years ago during homecoming weekend. The accident killed his wife, and he ended up a quadriplegic at the care center. He can't breathe on his own. Great guy. He used to coach me." Mitch sighed, his gaze bouncing off Caleb, back to the band and Seb Brewster. "It hurts to see him like that. Not to mention what happened to their daughter."

"Their daughter?"

"She was in the car. Her mother died in her arms. Tragic. She's got some sort of PTSD, had a breakdown."

PTSD. Yes, he understood that. Knew, too, how a person had to have a firm grip on the love of God to fight the panic attacks that came with it.

Mitch looked at him. "For what it's worth, I'm rooting for you, Caleb. Good luck."

Yeah, well, he didn't believe in luck. Divine providence, yes. Hard work, you betcha. Caleb smiled back and met Mitch's grip again.

Mitch walked away, but Caleb stood there for a long while, listening to the cry of the gulls, the harmonica solo from the local band, watching the high school boys doing tricks on their boards.

Turning back to the potter, Caleb found her still working the clay, kneading it with the heels of her hands, putting her weight into it as she pushed it into the board.

64

She looked at him and smiled. "It's nearly ready. The key is to make sure there aren't any air bubbles or hard spots because it'll make it impossible to work with on the wheel." She rolled the dark clay into a ball, then dropped it back into the bag, twisting it closed. Then she picked up a rag to wipe her hands. "Come by later—I'm going to throw it onto the wheel."

"What's it going to be?"

"Dunno yet. I guess it'll depend on the clay. How it will work with me." She put the bag on the shelf, picked out a dollar from her tip jar, and stepped out of the booth into the sun, smoothing the cash between her fingers. "When it's done, you won't even know it was once a broken pot."

She gave him a wink before crossing to the ice cream stand.

Across the park, Dan dumped into the water to the shrieks of the locals.

And a small crowd had formed around Seb, the local football hero, back for glory.

Back to fill the shoes of a man the town still clearly loved.

Back to steal Caleb's job.

"If it ain't the Seb-a-na-TOR!"

Seb heard the voice and cringed, fighting hard to wipe the dismay from his face. How he hated that nickname—it sounded so crude. But

Big Mike had never denied his redneck roots, football just taming them for a season.

Still, it didn't hurt to have so many of his old teammates happy to see him.

"Hey, Mikey," Seb said, his voice trying for enough enthusiasm to acknowledge their past camaraderie, not enough to inadvertently invite Mike over to the trailer at midnight with a six-pack of Bud Light.

He might savor the old glory, but Seb wanted a different kind of life this time around.

Mike slapped him on the back. "Just in time! You're gonna run that other guy right outta town."

"What other guy?"

"There's another guy who wants your job. Got a de-*gree* in coaching, don't ya know it." Mike gripped his shoulder, gestured past him with his drink.

Of course he did. If Seb had learned anything in football, it was to look out for the guy coming from the blindside, faster, stronger, tougher, ready to take you out. He'd forgotten it once, and it derailed his entire life. Now, he turned, sized up the . . .

Yep, competition.

The guy didn't seem any taller than himself, but he had wide shoulders—probably had a pull-up bar in his bathroom, a weight set in his kitchen. He knew the kind—living, breathing foot-ball, every second running plays in his head. Lean, with a shaved head under a red cap, a summer-vacation grizzle on his chin, he wore a stoic expression as if shaking down every kid in town, running him through his mental conditioning course.

"A coaching degree, huh?" Seb had barely passed his last online class. He'd landed the aide job by pulling hard on a few strings. He was hoping the board didn't look too deeply at his grades, the fact that he managed to stretch out his college experience into eight halfhearted, part-time years or that he hadn't exactly landed his teaching certificate. Yet. Thankfully, the school didn't require one for their aides.

It helped that they'd just had a slew of cuts at the school. Desperation, perhaps, made them ask few questions. Hire outside the unions.

Of course, Seb *might* have suggested that the teaching certificate was in the mail. He fully planned on passing during the next round of testing dates.

"Yep," Mike said. "Supposed to be some sort of superstar, led his team to state as a running back for three years. Set all sorts of records. Played in college, too." He turned to Seb. "But you played college ball for the Cyclones, so he's got nothin' on you. And you've got Coach's playbook."

Yeah, Seb had played college ball. For about 7.2 seconds. But as for Coach's magic playbook? "No, I don't."

"You don't? But weren't you his favorite?"

"No. I just needed a place to crash sometimes. He didn't give me the book."

"Maybe you can remember the plays."

He was counting on it. "I hope so. Do you?"

Mike lifted his glass. "I barely remembered them the next day. But go ask Issy for the book. She probably has it at her house."

"Issy is still in town? Last I heard she was headed out for some big anchor job in the cities."

"Not after the accident. She can't leave her own house now."

Seb stared at him, not comprehending. "What?"

"Yeah, she's . . . uh, what do you call it? Agraphobic—"

"Agoraphobic?"

"That's it. Although I saw her in her yard a few days ago, so maybe she's not." He took a drink. Burped. "Weren't you and she friends?"

Seb lifted a shoulder. Friends. Yes. And then after Lucy, no. But agoraphobic? Oh, Issy, what happened? "She was the coach's daughter, so of course we hung out."

"Weren't she and Lucy pretty tight?"

Lucy's name stirred up an image in Seb that clenched his teeth. His voice, pitiful to his own ears, emerged without permission. "I think so. Does she still work at the donut shop?"

"Owns it, I think. Hey, the parade's about to start. Aren't you gonna be on the float?"

Seb shook his head as Mike jogged away,

probably to inform what remained of their senior class that the Sebanator had returned.

He didn't even want to imagine the look on Lucy's face. *What was I to you, Seb? A fling? A mistake?* Her words could still turn his throat to fire. Of course, no. Never.

But in the end, yes.

And what had happened to Issy? He should stop by and see her.

The crowd began to push toward the sidewalk along Main. He found a place next to the kettle corn stand and stared up First Street to watch.

The Deep Haven parade lasted an entire twenty minutes. But crowds packed the sidewalks, anxious for everything from the old-fashioned cars carrying the Huskies Booster Club Fan of the Year, to the Humane Society float with children holding abandoned puppies and kittens, to the mayor giving a thumbs-up from the back of a convertible, to finally the North Shore Queen and her subjects, waving from a float decked out in green. He read the name on the side—Sarah Mulligan. Lucky Sarah, she'd have her face immortalized in a block of butter at this summer's state fair dairy pavilion.

Issy had been the North Shore Butter Girl the summer after their senior year. He'd made a point of avoiding the dairy pavilion.

He'd always believed the Butter Girl should have been Lucy. But Lucy had never been the kind to stand out, to vamp up onstage for a crown.

And by the time the pageant came along, Lucy had disappeared into her donut shop.

The "Class of" floats started in the sixties, sporadic as they worked forward by year until they reached his decade.

He had to admit that he was curious.

Curious about P-Train, his running back, and Bam, and DJ Teague, his wide receiver who could catch any of his passes, even when he threw them wide or long.

But most of all, yes, he wanted to see Lucy. Wanted to see that she'd made something of herself, that she'd healed. Even gotten over him.

He wouldn't dare to hope that she'd forgiven him.

The float came into view—a flatbed pulled by a Ford truck, and of course, Big Mike rode in the bed, waving for his fans. Seb waved to Bam, barely recognizing him with his beard and fifty extra pounds. Behind him—was that P-Train? What had happened to his running back's hair?

He searched then along the people sitting on the flatbed, their legs dangling off the edge. Monica Rice, Abby Feldstone, Bree Sanders.

No Lucy.

Except . . . there, behind the float, a slight girl—er, woman—wearing skinny jeans and a black T-shirt with white type that read *Got Donuts?*

She handed out flyers to the crowd, one by one, behind the float. A smile on her face, and although she'd cut her beautiful, silky long hair, she looked . . .

Breathtaking.

And was coming his direction.

For a moment, he panicked. He should slink into the crowd before she saw him. But maybe, maybe she'd smile at him. Remind him of their happy moments.

Tell him that she'd forgiven him for betraying her.

He blew out a breath, tried to keep his body from freezing, tried to keep his stomach from roiling.

Lucy handed a flyer to the man next to him.

Seb reached for one. Met her eyes. "Hi, Lucy."

Time stopped, or perhaps just his heart, as Lucy's gaze found him.

Her beautiful smiled dimmed. "What are you doing here?"

So much for his welcome home.

"I have a new neighbor. And I'm hungry."

"I just saw Seb Brewster."

Issy let a beat pass. "You win. Go."

"I don't have time. I've got a donut rush after passing out flyers at the parade. But . . . well, he looks good. Too good."

Issy switched the phone to her other ear. "Seb was at the parade?"

"Yep. Listen, if you need food, I'll be by after work with leftovers."

"So we're not going to talk about Seb's return? Okay, then I need something more than donuts. Vegetables, fruit. Diet Coke." She opened the cupboard. "What kind of lunch could I make with a stale half package of Ramen noodles, two packets of ketchup, a mail-sample bag of some new brand of healthy cereal, and a box of hardened raisins?"

Lucy laughed, then greeted the mayor. "You know, you could go to the grocery store." The ring of a cash register. "You're ready. This is the next step. You can do this, Issy. I believe in you."

Strange, once upon a time, it had been Issy comforting Lucy. A different lifetime.

Issy stared at herself in the microwave door. "Yes. Yes, I can do this," she said. Yes. She refused to let fear trap her in her house. First this, and then . . . maybe she'd tell her neighbor to get off her grass.

Then, someday, Napa.

"Go to the grocery store. I'll see you tonight." Lucy hung up.

How hungry, really, was she?

She grabbed the sample bag of cereal, worked it open, and peered inside. Granola of sorts.

Nudging open her back door, now covered in refrigerator-box cardboard, she walked out to her porch, sat on the steps, and surveyed her tiny piece of heaven.

Yes, sitting here in the backyard might be enough

to nourish her, with the August breeze reaping the fragrance of the Pilgrim roses next to the porch, the dainty tea roses along the path.

Issy could live right here, in her mother's backyard, forever.

To think, there'd been a time when she couldn't wait to escape it.

Thank You, God, for leaving me my mother's garden. But the thought twined around her like nettles.

She emptied the last of the cereal into her mouth and blinked back the moisture in her eyes.

Her stomach still growled.

Really, how hard was it to walk two blocks to the grocery store, fill her canvas bag with essentials, and walk home? She didn't have to talk to anyone. She could paste on a smile and not meet any gaze straight on. She visualized herself walking through the automatic doors of the tiny store. Saw herself picking up a red plastic basket. Plotted her route through the aisles. She'd start at the bakery for bread, then head to the frozen foods and finally the dairy section, grab some eggs, yogurt, milk. She'd end at the vegetable aisle for lettuce. Maybe pick up some dressing. All that could fit into her tote bag, the one just big enough to keep her from buying too much to carry.

She'd pay with her bank card, then walk home. Still smiling.

She could do this.

Take your time. There's no rush. You're in control.

Rachelle's voice pulsed in her head, and it pushed Issy off the back porch, to the front door. She found her flip-flops, her canvas grocery bag, her purse, her sunglasses. Glanced in the mirror by the door. When was the last time she wore makeup?

Probably the day of her mother's funeral.

The thought caught her up, filled her throat.

Use your tools.

"For God has not given us a spirit of fear."

"If God is for us, who can ever be against us?"

"I can do everything through Christ, who gives me strength."

She had no problem walking to the end of her block or the next. See? She was making progress. In fact, she'd pushed the boundaries of her world out that far just recently with her daily run. Only a light sweat beaded her skin as she crossed First Avenue diagonally into the parking lot of the Red Rooster Grocery Store.

Which, she noticed, overflowed with cars. What was wrong with these people? Didn't they see the celebration going on downtown? *Please don't let the place be packed with familiar faces.*

Including hers. Just her luck, someone would notice her. *Hello, Issy. How's your father?*

Of course, people had stopped offering condolences for her mother more than a year ago.

74

Issy pulled in a breath, something stalwart and deep, before she stepped onto the mat that opened the automatic door.

Cool, canned air, the beep of the scanners, voices and conversations, and the smell of produce sucked her into the store. She kept her sunglasses on under the fluorescence and went to grab a basket.

The bin was empty.

No problem. *No problem.* She took a breath in, out, then unhooked a cart from the stack and dumped her bag into the seat in the front.

She gripped the handle with two hands.

Bakery section. She kept her eyes on her goal even as she noticed a familiar face in the cereal aisle—Mark someone, from the Elks Club. And there, by the deli, Diann, who used to work in the school library.

Issy grabbed a loaf of wheat bread, dropped it into her cart, then cut toward the frozen foods.

She kept one hand on her cart while she opened the door, the air raising gooseflesh as she grabbed for a frozen entrée; she didn't care what flavor.

Across from her, Nancy from the café glanced at Issy as she grabbed a carton of ice cream. Her toddler daughter kicked her feet against the cart. Was that baby one or two?

Issy didn't stop to ask, kept her smile affixed as she nodded, despite the swelling of her throat. *Just keep moving.*

She picked up a carton of yogurt, a package of cheese, then beelined for the refrigerated dairy case.

A man dressed in a blue oxford, a red baseball cap on his head, stood contemplating the sour cream. He didn't seem familiar, but she didn't expect to know everyone in Deep Haven. Especially after all this time. She turned away, stepping back from her cart to grab a half gallon of milk.

The heat fogged the glass on her door even as she heard his section slam, heard his cart rattle.

She grabbed her milk, closed the door, turned.

No cart.

She looked up to see the stranger hauling her food away, dragging the cart behind him like an afterthought.

Wait. "Hey!"

The word came out more strident than she intended, panic laced in her tone.

He didn't stop.

She clutched the milk to her chest. "Hey! You!" She ran up and grabbed the cart, jerking him to a stop. "That's my cart." Had she shouted it? A woman looked at her from the cleanser aisle.

The thief turned to face her, his back to her momentarily, and that's when she saw it. On the opposite side of his body, emerging from the neck of his shirt and crawling up his head to underneath his cap, a wave of reddened skin, rumpled and shiny, as if it had been peeled back from his body. It touched his jaw and wrinkled his ear and she had no doubt that his cap hid something brutal.

"This is your cart?"

He was speaking, and she barely managed to rip her gaze from his scars to his eyes—blue, so blue that they sucked her breath from her with their intensity. "Uh."

"Oh, it is. I'm so sorry. I thought that was mine." He leaned down to take out his sour cream.

Her gaze followed his movements and affixed on his scars. The skin on the top of his hand snarled into a tight ball, and where his pinkie finger had been, there remained only a nub.

He'd been burned.

She froze, all other thoughts stripped.

Burned.

Her breaths came fast. She opened her mouth again, but only a mangled whimper emerged.

"Are you okay?"

Please, don't make a scene. But what was the man going to do with a woman hyperventilating before him?

"Can I help you with something?"

From the meat section, Diann looked up.

No. Don't look. Please, don't—

The cruel hand of the past reached up for her. She smelled the smoke, heard her mother's screams. Her own screams.

"Ma'am?"

A keening filled her brain and she prayed it wasn't audible as she pushed away from him, leaving the cart, her groceries, her bag right there. She quick-walked past the cereal aisle, the bakery, and heard her own breaths rip out of her as she picked up her pace, nearly crashing into the automatic doors.

As if in a tunnel, she heard the slapping of her feet against the pavement as she fled across the parking lot.

She lost a flip-flop, came down hard on the ball of her foot, scraping skin against pavement. But she didn't care, just ran, eyes on her house.

She climbed the stairs, threw open the door, and slammed it hard, breathing out. Her hands palmed the cool wooden floor as she dropped to her knees.

Then, losing her other flip-flop, she crawled over to the piano in the front parlor and slipped underneath, pulling her legs to herself.

So much for miracles.

4

After three years, Caleb thought he'd be used to the reaction of a pretty girl to his scars. Thought it wouldn't hurt so much for someone to freeze, polite words ripped from her mouth, leaving only a mumble in reply. Sure, culture had conditioned most people into a cool, *hey, I don't see that you're hurt* sort of facade, but Caleb could still read it in their eyes.

He was damaged. Scarred. Frightening.

And sometimes, when he looked at his body in the mirror, he might agree with them. When he stared at the pucker of scars along his arm, his back, down his leg, and remembered the body he'd had, it could cripple him into seeing only what he wasn't.

But he'd long ago refused to focus on his wounds.

And today, at the celebration, he'd actually forgotten them.

However, he'd never driven a woman away in a state of horror before. Caleb had watched her go, torn between wanting to run after her and apologize—for what, really?—or quickly walk away, pretend it never happened.

Pretend he'd never served his country? Pretend

that he hadn't survived when others didn't? No, that didn't seem right.

Which left only frustration.

And of course, a fresh wound where he thought he'd healed. Thankfully, the checkout girl smiled sweetly at him as he paid. He loaded his two bags of groceries into the back of his truck and drove the less than two blocks home. Probably he could have walked, but the jaunt around town had fatigued him and he needed to save his energy for practice.

The last thing he needed was an injury before he met the team. A football coach had to be tougher and smarter than his players.

Especially if he hoped to wrench the job away from Seb the champion. He couldn't believe that Mitch had roped him into this competition.

He would prove that he could be the best football coach Deep Haven had seen since . . . well, since they'd lost Coach Presley. Caleb knew what it felt like to lie on the sidelines, broken and defeated, and planned to do everything he could to restore the Huskies' winning streak and get the Deep Haven football program back on its feet.

Coach Presley cast a long shadow, but Caleb didn't plan to linger in it long. God hadn't given him a second chance for him to quit.

Caleb climbed out of the truck, touching down on the groomed lawn of his neighbor. They built these lots small in little towns, and his two-wheel paved driveway couldn't contain his truck, his tires flattening the edges of her grass. He glanced at the house—a two-story Victorian with dormer windows. Pretty, with light blue paint, a white railing, a couple potted geraniums on the steps, roses in the bed flanking the stairs. Still, it was only a hint of what lay behind the fence in the backyard.

The garden belonged in a designer magazine, not trapped inside this frozen wasteland just south of the Canadian tundra. Lilacs and roses— must be ten kinds of roses—and pots of over-flowing pink and red and white geraniums on the back deck, and a stone pathway winding through it all. In the center sat a royal blue birdbath and a wooden bench. It called to him to plop himself in the middle until the whir of his brain stilled to a soft flutter.

Yes, he liked his neighbor's garden. And when he'd stopped home after the parade, he'd seen the owner working in it, her long brown curly hair like a waterfall down her back, her skin baked by the sun.

He'd like to meet her.

Except, maybe not at this moment. Perhaps he'd let his ego heal first. Just in case she reacted the same way as the woman in the store. But if there was a way to meet a nice woman in this town, he wouldn't resist.

Caleb stood now, groceries in each arm, looking at her house, remembering her sitting back on her heels as she soaked in the sun, the way she lifted her face to the sky, wiping her brow with her forearm, and . . .

The woman in the grocery store. She'd worn sunglasses, but something about her . . . That long brown hair, the tanned arms. A pretty girl.

Oh *no*.

And to think he'd come to this town to start a new life. Perhaps he was dreaming too big for a guy with his scars. Maybe he should come to accept the horror in the eyes of women. After all, what woman would stick around long enough to get to know him, to see past his wounds?

He crossed around the back of the pickup into the forest of his front yard. He needed to mow, but he hadn't seen a mower in the shed. He heard his foot scuff on the cement pathway, shuffled up it, found his front steps.

He should put one of the bags down, hold on to the railing, but four steps wouldn't topple him, right?

Caleb managed the first, was on the second when he heard the barking. A deep, throaty bark that issued from the belly of something large. He turned and spied the dog rushing up the stairs beside him. It knocked him on his bad leg, and he was a goner.

The groceries flew as Caleb grabbed for the

railing, but it didn't stop him from twisting, going down, slamming hard into the steps. Pain spiked up his leg, all the way into his brain. He ground his teeth against the burn as he reached out to swat the dog.

"Dog! Get!"

The animal trundled down the stairs, then turned, his tail slicing the air. He barked as if saying, *Don't just sit there! Play with me!*

"You're the one who's been digging for gold in my backyard, aren't you? You're going to kill me, animal. Go decimate someone else's yard."

He'd describe the beast as a cross between a mastiff and a Saint Bernard, brown and black with saggy eyes and a tail that should be registered as a lethal weapon. Mud caked its coat, and balls of matted fur hung from its tail.

"Please don't tell me you're homeless." He reached for the dog, and it came to him, slurped him in the face as Caleb ran his hand down its neck. Frayed and caked with mud, the collar revealed nothing in the way of identification.

"Awesome. Are you hungry? What was this, an ambush?"

Sure enough, the dog scooped up the bacon and ran for the hills.

"I hope you get trichinosis!" Caleb yelled.

Groceries. All over his front yard. He looked to see if the neighbor might be peering out her window. Or if the folks across the street, next door to the library, might be on their front porch, staring.

Thankfully, no one saw his dinner scattered on the lawn. No questions to answer, no help to refuse.

Caleb moved to get up, and that's when the pain screamed through him. He had wrenched his knee harder than he realized yesterday. But he fought his way down to the yard, forced himself to pick up the crushed sour cream, milk, the sodden carton of eggs, the flattened bread, and the can of beans.

He blew out too many breaths as he worked his way back up the stairs with his loot, returned for the second bag, full of bruised apples, canned corn, and a package of crushed Oreos.

He piled it all in the entryway and closed the door behind him, refusing to listen to the small, dark voice inside that told him to quit and drive as fast as he could away from Deep Haven.

"I can't believe Seb Brewster is back."

Lucy sat on the back porch swing of Issy's house, nursing a cup of tea. Above Issy's head, the porch light had flicked on, drawing moths flirting with death. Cicadas chirruped, backdropped by the sound of "Twist and Shout," a local band playing the standards for the street dance. Tonight, after Issy's show, they'd sit on her front porch and watch the fireworks. She could stay up for that.

Lucy refused to imagine Seb at the dance. "He looks really good. I'm going to have to hate him for that." She watched the moonlight glisten on the freshly replanted hosta, the row of ostrich fern, Virginia bluebells, and . . . "What are those big red flowers called?"

"The ones against the fence? Hibiscus. They're perennials." Issy sat on the steps, leaning back against the post, one foot on the lower step, the other drawn underneath her. She picked at the take-out container of grilled corn, the now-cold fish burger Lucy had brought over. "Thanks for dinner."

"You really ran out of the grocery store?"

"I feel sick. Just ill. I cannot believe I treated him like that."

"You were in shock."

"I was rude. And hurtful." Issy drove her hands into her long hair, and Lucy didn't know how to comfort her. "I am just praying for a chance to apologize, but how's that going to happen? I swear I'm never walking out of this house again."

"Stop. I'm sure he understands."

"Oh, you don't know how bad it was. But it had nothing to do with his scars, which, frankly, aren't that bad. He has a handsome face—or at least amazingly blue eyes. I do remember that much. But, oh, Lucy." She shook her head as if to dispel the memory. "Let's talk about Seb. Did he say anything? What do you mean he looks good?"

"That black curly hair, those mysterious green eyes. He's filled out—big shoulders, thick arms. Definitely looks like he played football for some college team. . . ."

Lucy played with her tea bag, remembering Seb standing on the sidewalk, next to the kettle corn stand, as she'd passed out her scribbled *Buy one, get one free* flyers. For a second, seeing him had knocked the wind right out of her, rushed at her that feeling she'd had the first time he looked at her or, better, seeing him waiting for her after school astride his motorcycle.

Talk about rude—*What are you doing here?* But it was a good question.

"Didn't Seb play for Iowa State?" Issy said, reaching for dessert—a cold raised glazed donut.

"Two years, I think." Actually, exactly seven games and three quarters before a late, blindside hit blew out his knee, but telling Issy that would only ignite more questions. "Funny, he stood there, his hands shoved into his pockets, looking embarrassed."

"He should be."

"Not anymore. I mean, c'mon, that was eight years ago. I think I can forgive him for breaking my heart."

Issy looked up and for a second held Lucy's gaze, then shook her head. "You cried for six months."

"I was a hormonal teenager."

"You dated for a year. And he cheated on you."

Yes, that's what Issy knew. Lucy couldn't bear to tell her the whole truth.

Better to let Issy think that Seb had simply broken her heart.

Not stolen her virtue or turned her into a woman who betrayed herself.

Seb had left such deep wounds that sometimes she still bled. Like today.

"Seb Brewster has been out of my life for nearly a decade. Trust me, that's long enough to get him out of my system."

Issy smiled. "If you say so. And by the way, let's go back to the flyers you were handing out at the parade. Really? You were in the parade?"

"Yes, and Bree said to tell you hi and that if you need your hair done, she'd be glad to stop by."

"You always were so nice, Lucy. Even to Bree."

Lucy pulled out the tea bag, dropped it onto the saucer, pushing away the image of Bree in Seb's arms. Shoot, she'd thought she had deleted that from her memory. "That's me. The nice girl." She took a sip of tea and managed not to choke. "I declare a moratorium on nice. Did you know the coffee shop is serving donuts?"

She could have hugged Issy for her appropriate look of shock.

"Yep. They had a sign on their door—they're selling them for sixty cents. Sixty!"

"That's simply not right."

"Which is why I was out handing out flyers. Did you know that I made 2,486 donuts today?"

"That's a lot of donuts."

"Not enough. I'm down by six hundred from last year at this time."

"Six hundred donuts?"

"That's about five hundred dollars." She took another sip of tea. "Tell me I love my job."

"You love your job."

"Tell me that buying my parents' business wasn't a huge mistake."

"You made a stellar investment. It's the only donut shop in a hundred miles."

"Tell me I love donuts."

"You love donuts."

Lucy looked at her. "I hate donuts."

Issy took another bite. "You don't hate donuts."

"Oh, but I do. I've been making donuts every single solitary day since I was twelve. I hate donuts with everything inside me. I loathe donuts. I wish nothing but terrible things for donuts. I despise the dough and the glaze and the chocolate—"

"Please stop talking. You're hurting me." Issy took another bite. "And the donut. It's in pain. Shh . . . wait until I've eaten it."

Lucy bit back a smirk. "Fine, okay, I don't hate donuts. I'm just saying, I never thought, when Mrs. Childers assigned us to write, 'Where will you be in ten years' for our senior essay, that my answer would turn out to be 'Serving up coffee and donuts down at the harbor.' "

"Being a donut girl is a noble profession."

"Now you're just lying to make me feel better."

"Isn't that what best friends do?" Issy finished the donut. "And no, I'm not. Think of how lonely and donutless I'd be without you."

"My mission in life—to fill the earth with donuts."

"Donuts are joy in a little sugary package."

"No, donuts have a hole in them. Which says that something is *missing*. Probably a good metaphor for my life."

Oops, she hadn't meant to get quite that transparent. *Please, Issy, don't ask.*

"Oh, Lucy. You're the most beloved girl in town. You know everyone, and everyone knows you. What could you be missing?"

See? She had everyone fooled. She lifted a shoulder. "I might be missing my donut shop by this time next year if I can't make my payments. Which means I have to fight for donut control of Deep Haven."

"Maybe we could rally the community."

"Like when we tried to get Pierre's Pizza to start delivery? Yeah, that worked."

Issy made a face. "I miss their gourmet spaghetti, with the pepperoni and olives? Yum." She licked glaze off her fingers. "Talk to the mayor. Jerry loves the donut shop. Doesn't this town have some sort of no-compete clause? Or why don't you talk to Kathy? Find out why she's serving donuts."

"Kathy's wanted to serve donuts since my mother started making lattes and cappuccino."

"Then I think your mother started it."

"And left me to finish it. I have to get creative. Figure out a way to beat them at their game."

"What about delivery? I'd have a standing order."

"I don't have the money—or the manpower—to begin a delivery service."

"How about adding a drive-through?"

"A drive-through?" Lucy made a face. "It's so . . . big city."

"Listen, tourists love to drive. The Java Cup has a drive-through. The Dairy Queen has a drive-through. Why can't you? And it might cut down on some of those mile-long lines."

"What can I say? The tourists love their donuts. By the way, have you met your neighbor?"

"No. But when I do, I'm going to make the Neanderthal buy me more pansies."

"Neanderthal, huh? What is that, number two on the 'Issy's perfect man' list—no Neanderthals? What does that mean, really?"

"Number four. And specifically? No flannel, must be able to read above a third-grade level, and most importantly, *don't park on my pansies!*"

"You and your list."

"It's practical and keeps me safe."

"Your list will keep you safe because it's unattainable."

The sound of laughter lifted from the street. A group of locals walking home, perhaps.

"So, really, you aren't even going to talk to him?"

"Who?"

Issy raised an eyebrow. "Seb, of course."

"No. Why would I? It's in the past, and I'm over Seb. Completely."

"Mmm-hmm." Issy got up, carried her plate into the kitchen, leaving Lucy to contemplate the moths darting at the hot porch light.

Something about Lucy didn't seem right. Something in her tone, the way she described Seb.

Hello, but had Issy been the only one in the room when Lucy refused to attend school for three days after she broke up with him? And stayed in her bed, crying? Then for at least two months after, she walked around in a sort of daze as if a part of her had died when Seb broke her heart.

It had taken eight years for Lucy to come back to herself. Little by little, and especially after the Presleys' accident, she'd finally become the girl that Issy knew. Maybe, indeed, she was over him, but Issy had expected Seb Brewster's reappearance to rate more than a "He looks good."

Perhaps if Lucy had added, "The creep," Issy might feel like she wasn't hiding something.

Issy stored her leftover fish burger in the fridge for tomorrow. Maybe she'd attempt the grocery store again.

Or not. Oh, she'd never shake the expression of that poor man from her brain. How could she be so cruel? *I'm sorry, God. Please help him to forget me, forget what happened.*

Hopefully he was a tourist and right now was dancing to—

"Issy!" The panic in Lucy's tone brought Issy back to the porch, where Lucy stood—perhaps trapped, perhaps simply horrified by the monster unseating Issy's variegated hosta.

They might have been on reasonable terms this morning, but that was before he broke into her yard, started tearing up her garden. "Duncan! Stop!"

He looked at her, dirt hanging from his muzzle.

"Maybe he'll go away," Lucy said.

"You're a huge help. How'd he even get in here?"

The dog dug his snout back into the earth. The hosta tore and she cried out in actual pain when it flew into the air, green and white shrapnel. "No!" She turned and grabbed the broom still on the porch from this morning's cleanup. Then, shoving it into Lucy's hand, she said, "Back me up."

"What? Wait—you're not going in! What if he attacks?"

Issy didn't turn around. "Then I want you to bean him. As hard as you can."

"Isn't that dog endangerment?"

"I'm more concerned about the hosta endangerment." Issy took a breath, then grabbed the animal's grimy collar. Bracing her feet, she fought to wrench his face from the ground. "Oh, I am so going to kill him."

"Kill who? The dog?"

Her precious garden dirt, with the lava ball fertilizer and imported vermiculite, hung from the animal's mouth. With all her strength, she wrestled him away from the hole. Then, to Lucy, "No, my new neighbor, the redneck who can't keep his mule in his own yard." She cast a look at the hosta debris. "And while I'm at it, I'm going to tell him to get his tires off my pansies."

Lucy edged off the porch. "Why stop at a tongue-lashing? I'll get a rope."

"Stop grinning, Lucy, and just hold the broom."

When Issy reached the gate and unlatched it, Duncan catapulted through, tearing toward freedom. "Ow—don't take my arm off."

She braced her feet as the animal half dragged her toward the front of the house. "I don't know why you didn't just exit the way you came." A car rolled down the street and again she nearly lost

93

her arm at the socket as Duncan lunged for it. "No! Bad dog!"

"You tell him, Issy!" Lucy followed, a good ten feet behind.

The dog shagged a look back at Lucy, a sloppy grin on his face.

Issy hip-checked him toward his owner's travesty of a yard. She practically had to get her jungle waders on, take a machete to his grass to fight her way to the walk. Duncan got the general drift and bounded for the front steps.

Her bare foot stepped in something soft, gooey. Ew—what was that? Egg?

Disgusting.

Music—she should have guessed, some twangy country singer—rumbled through the open window. She rang, then knocked on the door. Then rang again.

"I'm coming, just a second!"

But the music didn't stop and the dog stepped on her foot.

"Get out here and get your dog!"

"Uh . . . my dog?"

"Yeah, your dog." Duncan slurped her on the face. Oh, for crying out loud. "Listen, you have to keep him tied up or something."

"I can't tie him up."

Of course not. It was probably against his redneck code. The music cut low and she heard banging. How long did it take him to get to the door?

"You should know that my hosta took me years to grow and your *buffalo* here chomped it out in one bite. Have you any idea how hard it is to get things to grow up here? This is a zone three, and *nothing* grows here, especially my variegated hosta. I'm just thankful he didn't get into the Pilgrims, and I'm telling you, if he had even sniffed at my tea roses, I'd be digging a hole for his grave."

"Listen—"

She heard a warning tone, and it sparked something inside her she couldn't place. "No, *you* listen. I live next door, and I'm tired of staring at this wreck of a yard. Show some respect for the neighborhood—for that matter, your new town. If you really want to win friends, paint your house. It looks like an old shoe left in the rain."

"I just moved in!" His voice sounded far away, deep inside the house.

She lifted her voice in case he couldn't hear her. "And could you please attempt not to drive on my lawn when you pull up? Here's a hint, if you *mowed* your lawn, you might actually find your driveway, and you could park on *that*. You took out six months' growth of pansies."

The door opened.

And then her world stopped. He wore a red bandanna—instead of his red hat—and a black National Guard T-shirt cut off at the arms, a pair of faded jeans, and a growth of scraggly whiskers.

She hadn't noticed that before.

Nor had she noticed the football girth of his arms, now dressed in shadow, or the way he filled out his shirt, his wide shoulders, lean hips. He leaned into the door, bracing himself even as he opened the screen.

This time she knew enough to keep her gaze off the scar running down one arm.

"Can I help you?"

Her stomach began to cramp. *God, this isn't fair.* She'd asked for a second chance, but . . .

"I'm sorry." The words trickled out small, without power. She let go of the dog. "I . . . Your dog was in my garden."

He looked at the animal like he couldn't care in the least. "He's not—"

The swirl inside roused, tightened. *Get off the porch; get back home. . . .*

"Just take him." Issy let go and the dog jumped on her. She grabbed its paws. "No, please, c'mon, Dun—dog."

She expected her breaths to pile up in her chest, expected sweat across her palms. Instead she just wanted to cry. "Keep him away from my yard and my hosta, and if you could keep him from committing any more felonies—"

Stop talking. She heard the voice as if it might be speaking to her outside her head. "Uh . . . welcome to Deep Haven."

She fairly pushed the dog into the house, past

the neighbor. He startled, gripping the door as the beast mowed over him, but she didn't stick around. Hopping off the porch, she all but sprinted back to her property, past Lucy standing sentry with the broom—what a huge help she turned out to be—up her own porch steps, and into her house.

Issy sank down on the stairs. Shook her head.

Lucy came in, set the broom upside down in the umbrella stand, and closed the door. "What was that all about?"

"He's the one."

"The one? As in, the perfect ten?"

"What?" Issy looked at her. "No. The guy from the grocery store."

"The guy with the scars?"

Oh yeah, his scars. Mostly she remembered his blue eyes. And the look of confusion in them. "Yeah. But . . . well, he actually is kind of cute." Had she said that? She winced, then buried her head in her hands. "And I made a fool of myself, yet again. What is it about this guy that brings out the worst in me?"

Lucy sat on the stairs. Put her arm around her. "And remember, Lovelorn, your perfect love might be right next door."

It's not my dog. Caleb had tried to push the words out, but every time he tried, she cleanly bit them off. He just might be bleeding.

He'd closed the door when she reached her

97

porch and now turned to the reason for his bruises. "Way to go, pal. Exactly the way I'd hoped to meet the pretty neighbor."

And, oh, his heart went out to her. The look on her face when he'd opened the door, the texture of shame in her voice. He wanted to go after her, but perhaps he'd wait until they'd both recovered.

His leg wasn't quite secured, either. He'd struggled to get it on as she stood outside, yelling at him, and had nearly given up and grabbed his crutches, but he didn't want a repeat of the grocery store.

The dog stared at him, a sofa pillow in his grimy jaws. Then he dropped low on his front legs like he wanted to play. Yes, she'd been right calling him a buffalo. "What are you? Horse? Part bison—hey! Don't!" But the dog took off as Caleb eased toward him, knocking over a glass of water he'd set on his stained mission table. As long as the animal didn't topple the flat screen—

Caleb dove for the television, righted it just as the dog skidded to a stop on the oval rug. He dropped the pillow as if Caleb would take the bait and lunge for it. His tail wagged with the power to destroy a couple small countries.

"I don't know who you are, dog, but frankly, I'm in her camp. You and I can't be friends if you're going to eat my groceries and decimate my yard. I need this town to *like* me." He approached the animal, but it bounced away—with the effect of a tractor trailer rumbling through his A-frame. "How 'bout if we scrounge around the fridge, find you something to eat, huh?"

Limping back to the kitchen, he opened the fridge, found a package of hot dogs he planned to cook this week on the grill, and wrestled one out. The dog slurped it up in one breath, his massive tongue licking his jowls.

He had a good mind to simply toss the package outside as far as he could, let the dog romp after it. "But that would be irresponsible, wouldn't it? She has a point. You are a bit ragged around the edges. Don't you have a home?"

The dog sat in the middle of Caleb's linoleum, depositing a slick of mud on the white floor, and swished his tail through it.

Nice.

"Okay, if you're going to sleep here, you have to at least be clean. C'mon . . . Roger. I think you're a Roger. Let's go." Caleb snagged a flannel shirt hanging over a kitchen chair and tucked the package of hot dogs in the pocket, then grabbed the liquid hand soap next to the sink.

Roger trotted out the back door, down to the yard.

Caleb flicked on the porch light and uncoiled the faded hose nestled behind the house. Then, holding out another hot dog, he caught Roger's collar. "Sorry, dude."

He turned on the hose and began to wet the

animal's coat. Mud sloughed off, puddling at his feet, and Roger's coat began to shine a lovely raven black. He pumped the hand soap, and as Roger finished off the last of the hot dogs, Caleb ran his hands over his coat, working up a brown lather on his body, his legs, under his neck. Then he sprayed the dog again.

Roger shook, drenching him with grimy suds.

"Nice, Rog. But you're kind of handsome without the mud." He'd hop over to the library tomorrow, pin up a Found ad on the community bulletin board. Until then, maybe he could teach Roger some manners.

At the very least, he'd keep the mutt away from the neighbor's hosta.

Caleb watched the dog dance through the jungle of his backyard. When he turned toward the house and took a step, his bad foot dropped into one of Roger's holes.

He pitched forward and went down hard. He tried to roll onto his back but bit back a cry as the leg caught in the hole.

Then his gaze went—of course—to the Victorian window overlooking his yard. Thankfully, no one stood in the outline, pulling back the curtains. Scrambling to his feet, he hopped toward the house, his leg hanging, useless. "Roger!"

The dog bounded up the stairs, danced on the porch, his tail taking out the dead spider plant in the plastic planter near the door. Caleb steadied himself on the porch rail as he turned, then scooted up the steps backward.

When he reached the top, he slid back and stretched for the light, disappearing into the darkness.

Breathing hard, he worked off his prosthesis. He might have damaged the hinge at the ankle. He'd have to make it work. At least until after the competition. He couldn't win the job out of pity.

A thousand stars winked above him. He listened to the wind brush the trees, smelled the pine, heard the faintest twang of the band downtown.

Lord, this might be harder than I thought. Are You sure I heard You right? Am I really the one for this job?

Roger sat down next to him. Put his soggy head on his lap. Sighed.

Caleb ran his hand over the dog's head. "Me too, buddy. Me too."

5

"Caleb, I hope you like butternut squash." Ellie, Dan's pretty wife, set the casserole dish on the table. "It's growing like a weed in my garden."

"Love it. My mother used to slather it in butter and bake it in the oven."

"Your mother and I would get along."

Wendy, their daughter, carried in a plate of meat loaf. "Daddy's favorite," she said and glanced at her father, pouring iced tea into glasses.

Dan winked at her. "Go call your brothers in for lunch, please."

Caleb watched her open the sliding door, call out over the deck to where twins Ethan and Joseph swung on their jungle gym. Caleb had learned their names this morning when they'd nearly knocked him over running down the center aisle after church. Thankfully, Ellie blocked for him. She had the moves of a right guard.

"Great sermon today, Pastor. I love Philippians and especially the 4:19 passage."

" 'This same God who takes care of me will supply all your needs from his glorious riches.' " Ellie added a Jell-O salad to the table. "Including lunch. We're so glad you could join us. Sorry the place is such a mess. I had to cover an extra shift at the firehouse last night because of the picnic."

A mess? The house—more of a log cabin—had the look of a firehouse. Everything in order, gleaming stainless steel appliances, a picnic table in the kitchen, a couple of comfy suede sofas in the open living room. A loft above the kitchen looked over the giant picture windows facing town. Caleb had stood way too long drinking in the view of the little hamlet perched on the curvature of the harbor.

"This is a beautiful place."

"Thanks. Ellie and I built it together." Dan pulled out his wife's chair.

Caleb took the one next to Wendy. "Built it? As in, hammer and nails?"

"Yep," Ellie said. She held out her hand for Dan, who took it.

Wendy nudged Caleb, her hand lying on the table. Oh. He caught it up, took Dan's on the other side. Bowed his head as Dan prayed.

In those brief seconds, he was home, sitting at the table, his father at the head, with the traditional words, the smell of a pot roast, carrots, onions, potatoes, and rosemary nudging open his eyes. Collin sat across from him, kicking him under the table—

Wait. He peeked open his eye. Sure enough, Ethan suppressed a grin.

"Amen," Dan said. He reached for the meat loaf. "I have to admit, I was surprised to see you today in church." He handed the plate to Caleb.

"Why? You invited me."

Dan loaded up some squash. "That I did. It's just . . . well, it's good to see the football coach sitting in the pews again. It's not an easy job, coaching all those boys into manhood. It's great to see that you're willing to accept some help."

He wouldn't exactly call it that. More like following through on his word to the Almighty.

After all, a guy could only expect so much help. "I grew up in the church."

"Where was that, Caleb?" Ellie scooped squash onto Joseph's plate, despite his grimace.

"Little town on the border of Minnesota and Wisconsin called Preston. It's a farming community. My father ran a hardware store."

"So were you a Packers or Vikings fan?" Dan asked.

" 'It's not whether you get knocked down; it's whether you get up,' " Caleb said, quoting Vince Lombardi, the Green Bay Packers' legendary coach.

Dan shook his head. "Well, we're going to have to keep it friendly when the Packers play the Vikings."

"Not too friendly," Ellie said, handing Caleb the salad. "So why did you choose Deep Haven?"

"I love small towns. I like the simple life, the slower pace."

"You won't think it's so slow when the school year starts." Ellie moved a napkin to Joseph's lap. Gestured for Dan to do the same for Ethan. "We can barely keep up with the sports, the carpools, ministry, and our shifts down at the firehouse."

"Actually Ellie is the only full-time firefighter."

"I was the chief a few years back. But now I just run the EMS department and do fire investigation."

No wonder Dan had obeyed his wife and

helped his son sit up straight, use his manners.

"Is this your first coaching gig?" Dan asked.

"I coached in the pro summer camps through college, but I got called up for the National Guard and went to Iraq right after I graduated. This is my first real job after . . ." He glanced at the kids. "After my injury."

A beat passed, and he took a breath.

Ellie smiled at him. "You're going to do a great job."

"How did you get hurt?" Ethan asked.

"Ethan!" Dan said.

"No, it's okay." Caleb smiled at the boy. "I was transporting some wounded back to base and we got hit with a roadside bomb. It blew up the truck and . . . hurt me."

Editing out his missing limb seemed the right move at the moment. They didn't need to know the darkness of those hours he'd lain in the ditch, the fear that he'd be captured so deep that it could scour out his breath, the pain so overwhelming that he just wanted to sink into it and die.

Until he'd cried out to God and discovered that God's grace was deeper than his lowest moment.

"We're glad you survived, Caleb. I'm so sorry." Ellie touched his hand. His wounded hand.

He didn't move it away, but neither did he clasp her grip. "Thanks." He drew a breath, then looked at Dan. "So what can you tell me about Seb Brewster?"

"He was the starting quarterback of the Huskies as a freshman. I remember him as young and cocky. But a nice kid. His mother used to attend church occasionally. His father drove OTR, would be gone for a week or so at a time. I do remember seeing him in the stands, though. They separated when Seb was in high school. Kid took it pretty hard. So did his father—he starting drinking. I remember Coach Presley praying for them in men's Bible study. I think Seb spent a lot of time on Coach's sofa."

Dan took a drink of his tea. Set it down. "Coach is a real prayer warrior. He might have been benched, but he's still very much a part of the game. You should stop by the care center and meet him. He's been praying for someone to fill his shoes—hasn't found a coach he could endorse yet."

"I'll do that, but I can't imagine that he'd endorse me over Seb."

Dan said nothing.

"Some apple pie, Caleb?" Ellie said. "Wendy made it." She glanced at her daughter, smiling.

"I won't be able to run tomorrow," Caleb said, now able to quip like that without a flinch. "But I wouldn't be a Minnesotan if I turned down a piece of apple pie."

Wendy grinned.

"What's your coaching plan?" Dan asked as he handed Ellie his empty plate.

"My plan is to focus on fundamentals. Teach them how to block and get off the line fast, how to get their head across the defender's body and drive, not to be soft on the block." Caleb smiled as Wendy brought him the piece of pie. "Yum."

"You'll have to run a few extra laps with your boys tomorrow. Thanks, honey." Dan leaned back as Wendy put a piece in front of him. Caleb noticed Dan's piece was considerably smaller than his.

"I called an early practice—6 a.m. It'll be a conditioning practice. At least for the first few days. Later we'll start to break out into positions. We'll work on tackling, how to handle the ball, stance for the linemen. Only after we have the fundamentals down will we start running plays."

"You have a lot of work to do before the scrimmage." Dan sipped his coffee. "Word's gotten around. I think you're going to have a pretty big turnout."

Caleb drew in a breath. Sometimes it did feel overwhelming.

Not unlike learning to walk again.

"They'll be in pain, for sure. But I want to teach them to fight through it, control their bodies instead of their bodies controlling them. I want them to learn what it means to get back up and even see a part of themselves that they never knew existed. Be men, not boys, or at least on their way."

Ellie wore a strange look. She smiled and glanced at Dan.

"Yes," Dan said, "you need to meet Coach Presley. You just might be the guy to fill his shoes."

The words lingered as Caleb drove home, as he greeted Roger, who had clearly decided that he belonged on Caleb's front porch, and let him into the house. Meet Coach Presley. Yes, he'd do that, maybe tomorrow after practice.

He couldn't deny the swirl in his gut at the thought of practice.

Caleb stared in his bathroom mirror, trying out his coaching face. "The man with the most heart wins!" He said it loud, full, and his voice thundered through the house.

From the sofa, Roger raised his head.

Okay, so he didn't exactly want the neighbors rushing in to check out the crazy new guy on the block, screaming at himself in the mirror.

They had to learn to play with their hearts, with every fiber of their bodies. Sure, it sounded cliché, but Vince Lombardi said it first, and when was he ever wrong? Unless a man believed in himself and made a total commitment to his career and put everything he had into it—his mind, his body, his heart—what was life worth to him?

Caleb ran water down his face, then shut off the light.

Maybe he should focus more on God's quotes.

"This same God who takes care of me will supply all your needs from his glorious riches." He had; oh, He had. Caleb hated to ask for more.

He knew in his gut that God had saved him that dark night, healed him, and sent him to Deep Haven for a reason.

Caleb wasn't going to let Him down.

He sat on the sofa and positioned his legs so they lay the length of it. Roger lifted his head from his paws, got up, set it on Caleb's knees. He toggled the dog behind the ears. "So now we're friends?"

Pulling his laptop from the floor, he connected to the Internet, found *The Bean*'s channel.

"Welcome to *My Foolish Heart*, where we believe your perfect love might be right next door."

He'd caught the week's recap of the show before it. He clicked on the link. *My Foolish Heart*, a talk show for hopeless romantics. He listened to the sultry-voiced hostess who called herself, appropriately, Miss Foolish Heart. Oh, brother. But *The Bean* would be on any minute.

He rolled his eyes at the responses to what it felt like to fall in love.

"It's knowing you have someone to hold on to."

"Great response, TruLuv. Here's hoping you have someone to hold on to. Go ahead, WindyCity."

"It's knowing you're loved . . . anyway."

Loved, anyway. If that were even possible. Ashley hadn't loved him, not really. And after the dust cleared, he hadn't loved her, either. They'd simply clung to each other through college because they both liked the glory. Sure, she said she'd stay with him after his injury, but he saw the pity in her eyes.

He couldn't be loved because of pity.

No, he didn't know what it felt like to fall in love. But he did know what he wanted.

Someone who wouldn't give up on him. Someone who didn't love him *despite* his handicap but didn't see it at all. Someone who believed in him.

He let the show play as he went to the kitchen and poured himself a glass of milk. The hostess had moved on to a new caller, someone announcing her engagement.

He stood in the doorway, listening, as the hostess gave a sort of high-pitched, tremulous laugh when the caller asked her to the wedding. Something about the hue of fear in the voice nudged something inside him.

He sat down and turned up the volume.

A commercial break, and she returned with an excerpt of yet another show. She solved the problems of a workplace romance and a long-distance relationship and headed off a would-be affair.

And by the end, he'd become uncomfortably

entwined by that soft, compassionate voice. Like she might really care about the saps calling in. Thankfully, *The Bean* came on and knocked him back to his senses.

What was a foolish heart, anyway?

Roger whined in his sleep, his legs twitching. Yes, that happened to him sometimes. He dreamed of running, or worse, his leg itched.

He turned off *The Bean*.

"Rog, try and stay home tonight, huh?" Walking past his bedroom, he saw the neighbor's light flick out. The summer wind, cool through his screen, drew him out onto the porch. He eased down on his front steps, stared at stars against the dark pane of night. The sky seemed so close, he wanted to reach up to heaven.

You just might be the guy to fill his shoes. Yes, he'd like to someday have the reputation that Coach Presley had. But fill his shoes? No. He wanted his own pair.

If Issy could, she'd skip over Sundays and go right to Mondays. Not that life inside her house felt much different on Mondays, but Sundays seemed to bring to life all her limitations.

She'd listened to Pastor Dan Matthews's sermon on the radio and couldn't push from her thoughts the image of watching him from the third pew, right side, the sunlight streaming in through the tall windows. Sometimes she could even see her father sitting beside her, his arm stretched out over the pew. Hear his rich tenor singing "Amazing Grace," the occasional "Amen!" muttered under his breath.

Yes, Sundays she missed him the most.

She tried to assuage the pain by sitting in his recliner under the puddle of lamplight, his marked Bible on her lap. Sometimes she read his playbook, the notes he scribbled in the margins.

Today, she simply tried to figure out just what Dan meant by his verse of choice. *"This same God who takes care of me will supply all your needs from his glorious riches."*

What was she supposed to do with that?

The teakettle whistled. She got up, went to the kitchen, took out a bag of chamomile, and dropped it into her mother's favorite cup, a souvenir she'd picked up in Germany during their twentieth wedding anniversary trip. Issy poured the water in, dunking the bag, the rusty brown bleeding into the water. Then she dropped the bag into the sink.

Bless Lucy for the bag of groceries she'd left this morning, probably reaped from her own pantry, or Issy would be relegated to the half-eaten fish burger and the cold corn.

"This same God . . . will supply all your needs . . ."

Okay, He'd supplied food, but that wasn't her real need, was it? She could barely look at

Lucy's kindness without weeping. What was she supposed to do with verses like *"For I can do everything through Christ, who gives me strength,"* or even, *"Don't worry about anything; instead, pray about everything. Tell God what you need, and thank him for all he has done. Then you will experience God's peace, which exceeds anything we can understand. His peace will guard your hearts and minds as you live in Christ Jesus"*?

She didn't know whom to blame for her failure, because she'd certainly spent hours begging God for peace. For strength.

So that left her where?

She picked up the cup, blew over the surface. From the living room, she could hear the replay of her show. Elliot always chose the best calls to replay on Sunday nights. She would take notes, sometimes checked into the forum, but not many discussions happened on Sunday.

Now, she heard her voice as Pride invited her to her wedding.

"Okay, Lauren. I'm so sorry, but I can't come."

"Why not?"

The *why not* hung in Issy's mind even as the conversation continued. She winced at the tremble in her voice.

She was tired of the *why not*s. Tired of sitting here every Sunday, listening to her church family worship from afar, knowing her father was probably listening too.

She reached up to touch his picture on the fridge, the one with him and his championship team her senior year. He was being carried off the field, dripping wet from the water bucket, on the shoulders of his team. And beside him, also carried, Seb Brewster. They were looking at each other, their hands locked above their heads. In a way, Seb had been the son Coach Presley never had.

"Daddy, I miss you," Issy whispered.

The worst part was, he lived only a mile away.

Past the highway, over the hill, in a room facing the lake. But the care center where he lived on a breathing machine might as well be across the Pacific in Bangkok.

Or in Napa Valley.

At least they had the telephone. Their daily phone call kept their prisons from strangling them.

She pushed open her cardboarded door, padded out to the porch. Night bathed the yard, the air cool, scented with pine and the heady fragrances of her hydrangea, her daylilies, the Pilgrim and tea roses.

"Come . . . see me, Isadora. I miss . . . you."

His voice in her head, the memory of their conversation this afternoon, could turn her inside out. It wasn't enough that he could only talk when his ventilator expired the air from his lungs, but the short bursts of speech, dying at the end,

114

always sounded like the end of his life. Every sentence, every phone call, every day could be his last.

"I want to, Daddy. I'm getting better. I am running around the block now and even to the coffee shop." Okay, she'd only run there once and hadn't gone in, but technically, she'd touched down in the parking lot.

"Don't let it rule . . . you . . ."

It had taken all of thirty-seven seconds for Coach Presley to kick in, for her father's go-get-'em tone to color his speech. She could almost see him pacing the sideline, yelling encouragement, his body more muscle than fat even at fifty, his dark hair containing just a touch of silver at the temples.

"Try to understand, Daddy. It's like, when I think about leaving the house, going into town, I can see what could happen. Every possibility. And then I start to feel this unraveling deep inside. After that, it's not about what could happen, but rather me making a fool out of myself. Sweating and crying and losing my mind in front of the entire town. I did it once—"

"Funeral. Everyone understood."

"I locked myself in the bathroom of the funeral parlor and they had to call the police to get me out." Her voice pitched low, even as she sat on the sofa in the privacy of her parlor. "They had to sedate me. And hospitalize me for three days."

He knew this, of course, but he'd been fighting for his life in Duluth's trauma ward at the time. Besides, how could he possibly know how it felt to hold her mother's hand as she bled out, trapped in a burning car? How it felt to watch the EMTs haul her father away, gray and unmoving? How her world had dismantled right before her eyes?

Her hand went to the scar on her forehead, raised but hidden by her hair. Just a scalp laceration. She'd been back home, walking into her empty house, by six the next morning.

"I am praying for you. . . ."

She flinched at that. "Please don't talk to me about God. I know, I know—just 'cast my cares on God.' Believe me, I have—"

"Honey . . ."

"The thing is, I can't figure out if I abandoned God, or if . . . well, if He abandoned me. But I'm broken, ashamed, and it feels like God is doing nothing to fix me. So, please, can we not talk about God?"

Part of her wanted to yank her diatribe back, even now. But sometimes she just had to say it aloud, to acknowledge the truth. She simply didn't matter to God. She'd embarrassed Him enough.

"It kills me . . . see you trapped," her father said softly, and she imagined him sitting on the side of her bed, brushing hair from her face with his big, wide-receiver hands like he had when she was seven.

She wiped her cheeks, held her breath in.

"I want to see you free, married . . ."

"I know, Daddy. But that's never going to happen." After all, who would want her, a girl who could barely leave her yard? Talk about a ball and chain.

"You win or lose in your head."

"Oh, Coach, love isn't a football game, you know." But she grinned, and she could almost see his smile on the other end. Or wanted to. She gritted her teeth and gave up on wiping her cheeks. "Yes . . . every night, you coach . . ."

"I give advice, Daddy."

"You're a coach at heart."

Just like her old man.

Now she sipped her tea, letting his words seep into her heart. Oh, she wanted to be like him. Storming out onto the field with the right plays, not letting defeat—or the fear of it—keep her on the sidelines. Believing in her players, seeing their potential, coaching them into strength.

She should start with herself. Because if she couldn't coach herself out of this dark place, how was she supposed to help others get over their fears, reach out with their hearts for love?

She got up, turned off the back porch light, returned to the family room. Her show was just ending and even as she heard her voice calling out hope, in her mind she heard Elliot's doom. *You need to do something to boost ratings. . . .*

Please, God. Don't let me lose the show, too. She stood there, staring out at the indigo darkness, the droplets of stars peeking through the canopy over the lake. *Help me figure out a way to save the show.*

She closed her eyes, longing to hear something, feel something. To know the peace that Jesus promised.

Instead, *The Bean*'s opening music played.

Through the window, she saw the neighbor's light flicker on; then he came out to the front porch and sat on the steps. Duncan—she should find out his real name—settled down beside him. Something moved inside her as she watched him run his hand over the animal's head. Despite his wounds that gave him every excuse to be jaded, even angry, he seemed kind. At peace, in a way.

If only she hadn't blown that so badly, if she wasn't so horrified by her own actions that she would make a point of never talking to him again, she might pray for another chance to meet him. In him she might have found someone who understood exactly what it felt like to be trapped inside something bigger than yourself.

He might have even figured out how to be set free.

6

No man will respect you unless you respect yourself!
Coach Presley's voice had chased Seb across three states, all the way to Deep Haven, and now, even into his sleep. *You can't blame others for your mistakes!*

Seb lay there, blinking into the early dawn, his narrow bed soggy with sweat, and everything hurt. His shoulder. His head—probably from too much sun on Saturday, because he'd turned down Big Mike's offer to hang out. Definitely his chest, where Lucy's razored gaze had left a bruise. *What are you doing here?*

Why did he think that coming back to Deep Haven would help him find the man he'd wanted to be? Because no, he didn't respect himself, and it had all started right here.

Seb pushed himself out of bed, wandered to the bathroom, hearing his father's snores motor down the narrow hall. He'd scrubbed away the mold layering the tiny shower and now could almost make out his warped image in the mirror over the sink. He'd also tamed the kitchen, moved the weaponry out of his bedroom, and opened the window to encourage fresh air to scour the trailer.

After Seb threw water onto his face, he pulled on a shirt, some shorts, then grabbed his running shoes. He took them out to the deck and put them on as the sun heated his shoulders.

Mostly out of a latent habit, he took the town route, the one that passed in front of the grocery store, the gas station, and along the lake. Today, the breeze from the lake slicked off the sweat as he settled into his pace.

As if he'd traveled back in time, the memory of Lucy rose from the quietness of the morning and latched on to his thoughts.

You want to study with me?

He'd sat on his motorcycle outside the school, too much hope in his voice.

She'd stood there, hands on her tiny hips, a messenger bag over her shoulder, wearing a pair of jeans and a pink blouse, looking so clean and smart. Then she'd smiled, and his words had vanished.

Even now, the memory of that spring, the summer months with Lucy, could fill him with a new breath, a sort of happiness that could deceive him. In those moments, he wanted to rewrite their ending.

Perhaps he could blame that hope of a new ending for driving him back to Deep Haven.

He ran past the fish house, where Arnie and Bubs were pulling out on their fishing boat for their early morning trip. Across the street, the bookstore remained dark. He ran up the hill, pushing hard.

He'd lucked out by partnering with Lucy, out of all the girls in their junior English class, for their spring semester project on Jane Eyre and her Rochester, a man throttled and deformed by his early mistakes. Sometimes, after they worked on their presentation together, after Seb had spent two hours watching Lucy twirl her beautiful caramel hair between two petite fingers, after she'd laughed so easily at his stupid jokes, after she'd made him feel smart and heroic, he imagined himself as Rochester, calling to her across the moor.

He could still hear that voice, sometimes, calling in his thoughts.

Seb cut his run past the care center, toward the school, picking up his pace.

Indeed, he'd become Rochester, a man unable to forget the one woman he ever loved, despite his mistakes.

I'm waiting, Seb, until I find the man I'll spend forever with.

The dawn slid across the tennis courts in front of the school, and Seb angled toward the football stadium. He always ended with a couple quick forties, then jogged the last half mile home in low gear.

I'm right here, Lucy. Right here.

As he rounded the school, he heard voices.

Or rather, a voice.

"Push through the pain, boys! Don't let your body control you—control your body!"

The words had the power to whisk him back through time to hell week under Coach Presley, when he'd lost ten pounds in two days, mostly in sweat and vomit. Sure enough, there they were, eighteen football hopefuls in workout gear, running bleachers.

The other coach stood on the track, watching. Taking notes.

"Push it, and you'll find out your new bounds."

Seb recognized the words, had heard them a thousand times in his own practices. Hearing them from his competition, however, raked a chill through him.

He'd returned to Deep Haven believing he could finally return to the man he'd wanted to be. The man of honor that Coach Presley had wanted of him. And that meant taking up the Presley coaching mantle. No, Seb didn't have a degree or even years volunteering, but he had Coach Presley's old plays in his head and the desire to reach into the past and find the old glory.

He hung on the fence, stretching, watching, reluctant to take the track. Instead he'd just stay and watch and chew himself out for not assembling his team at 6 a.m., in the cool of the day. In fact, he had nothing but a vague idea of what he might do this afternoon during their first practice, intending to lean on his instincts.

Back in the glory days, they'd never failed him.

When he'd lost his last job just weeks ago, instincts—and possibly desperation—had sent Seb home. Desperation also landed him on Mitch's doorstep begging for the coaching gig, a chance to coach their old team back to victory.

As he watched, the players descended the bleachers, and the coach wound them in, ordering them on a water break. The teens hunched over, grabbing for breath, some of them holding their sides, others falling to the turf, breathing hard. Coach Knight walked up to a few—he had a funny walk, as if he might be nursing a football injury too—bent down, and talked to them. He stepped away fast, awkwardly, as one spewed his breakfast onto the turf.

Knight even looked like a coach—thick, sculpted arms, wide shoulders, a red baseball hat. Probably an Ohio State logo on the grid.

Seb would have to order a Cyclones hat. Or perhaps he could find an old Huskies cap in the closet. That, at least, should inspire his team.

As Knight seated the team on the turf, began to talk to them, giving them a break before more con-ditioning, Seb turned away and jogged for home.

In fact, if he had any sense, he would just keep going, right out of town.

Lucy's earliest memory had to be of sitting on the front porch of World's Best Donuts in her cutoff jeans and flip-flops or swinging from the railing of the narrow blue steps, then pushing her face into the hole of the giant donut sign and grinning for the lineup of customers.

They sometimes took her picture. She always posed.

Her mother, clearly recognizing her strengths, moved her behind the counter at the age of eight. She'd been peddling donuts ever since.

And most of the time, she knew her customers by name. Even the ones from Missouri, Iowa, Nebraska, and California.

"Two chocolate cake donuts and a skizzle." She handed the white wax bag to the Geertsens, from Wisconsin. "Nice to see you again. And Annie is getting so big!" She leaned over the counter and blew a kiss at the eight-year-old. Annie grinned, a gap the size of a truck between her two eyeteeth.

"Hello, Margie!" Lucy yanked out a wax sheet, grinning at a red-haired, middle-aged woman in a jean shirt and sandals, who, as soon as she opened her mouth, would deliver the most charming Texas drawl. "Are we going with the chocolate raised or the six-pack of donut holes today?"

Margie leaned over the counter, kept her voice low. "I have the grandkids with me this time. So let's try a dozen powdered sugar cake donuts."

"You won't be sorry." Lucy grabbed a box, then pulled out the tray.

In the back, the two girls she'd hired for summer

124

help loaded up trays with freshly fried donuts. They came in around 6 a.m. to keep the supplies replenished, but by then, Lucy already had the dough for the day mixed together. Part of the World's Best secrets . . . the secret dough recipe.

"How are your parents, sweetie?" Margie said, handing over her cash.

Lucy pulled off one of her cellophane gloves to work the cash register. She could go through an entire five-hundred-pack on a good day. "Loving their house in Florida." She returned the change. "And of course, if you ever get to Fort Myers, they'd love to see you."

"Did they open a shop in Florida?"

"Oh no. This is the only World's Best Donuts." Lucy winked and grabbed another glove.

"But I noticed another donut shop in town." Margie opened her box, then glanced at Lucy with a grin, clearly seeing the extra donut she'd thrown in.

Lucy's day soured immediately, her stomach twisting. "It's not a shop. Just a . . . menu item. Next!"

She let the words tunnel through her, however, and drain the energy from her smile. Another donut shop in town. So the word already made it to the tourists.

She always stopped making fresh donuts around noon, and usually by two she'd run out. Today, the shop's doors lingered open until three fifteen.

Finally she bagged up the remains—two long johns, three cinnamon cake donuts, a soggy skizzle, and a glazed danish—and dropped them off at the local newspaper office. "Jerry here?"

Lois, the first woman to ever work for the *Deep Haven Herald*, white-haired now, looked up from where she read ad copy. "He's over at the Blue Moose Café."

Of course. The three-o'clock coffee break with the locals.

Inside the café, the cadre of regulars sat in the far booth, the one facing the street so they could survey interlopers. She knew them all—Dan, the town pastor, and Joe, the bestselling author that the town did a good job of hiding. And of course, Jerry. Editor and newly elected mayor.

"Howdy, boys," Lucy said. "What's the news of the day?"

"Dan's looking for more volunteers down at the fire department," Jerry said, smiling at her. *Jerry Mulligan, a deep-fried skizzle.*

Lucy flexed a muscle.

"It's like Minnie Mouse—"

"Mighty Mouse, Pastor. Get it right." But she smiled at him. *Pastor Dan, cream-filled long john.*

"Don't listen to them, Lucy. We'd love to have you." *Joe Michaels, a sugared cake.*

"I'd like to help you out, but actually, I need to talk to the mayor here. Official donut business."

Jerry moved to slide out of the booth, perhaps to

126

follow her outside, but Dan caught his arm. "You stay. I gotta run. But I'm heading up to take a gander at Seb's football practice. I want to watch the coach competition. I'm going to check out the new coach tomorrow morning."

"I'm on that." Joe pulled out a couple dollars, dropping them on the table. "See you tomorrow, Lucy."

She slid in opposite Jerry just as Nancy came up and plunked down a coffee cup. *Nancy Ryan, a six-pack of donut holes.* "Thanks."

Nancy winked at her.

Lucy poured herself a cup of coffee, just to have something to hold on to. Stared into it. "The Java Cup is serving donuts." When she looked up, she found Jerry pursing his lips and nodding like he already knew. "Jerry, it's just not right. I mean, when that other pizza joint tried to come in here, the council turned it down—"

"As I recall, they didn't have the right zoning. The coffee shop already has a license to serve food."

"But this is the home of the World's Best Donuts. It's—"

"It's competition, Lucy. That's what makes our society strong."

Or crumbled it. She blew out a breath.

"Listen—" he touched her hand, and she let him—"I know how much the donut shop means to you, to your parents, and frankly this town. But the fact is, your popularity is actually your demise. Your lines are out the door and halfway down the street. People don't want to wait that long for a donut. You want to keep people from drifting over to the Java Cup, figure out a way to move them through faster."

"How?"

"I don't know. Make an outside window."

"A drive-through? In this town? It's so impersonal. People come to World's Best for the donuts and . . . well . . ."

"To see you. You can say it. Your family has owned the shop for three generations. But you want to stay in business? Then you're going to have to sacrifice that hometown nostalgia." He rose and picked up the check. "I'm on your side, Lucy. But even the newspaper had to change. We lost our routes, and we had to move online, create a different business model. It's just business."

It wasn't the donut business. "But I can't afford to cut a hole in the shop. I'd have to hire a crew to move the electrical, the plumbing—I don't have that kind of cash." Not to mention the cash to pay this month's mortgage . . . again.

"Talk to Mark Bammer at the credit union. He's doing business loans now, and he'll get you fixed up."

Bam. Of course. He'd love for her to come slinking into his office. She pushed the coffee away. "Thanks, Jerry."

He gave her a smile before moving to the counter.

"You want anything, Lucy?" Nancy stood over her with a pad and paper.

Yes, but she didn't see freedom, courage, or even a money tree listed on the menu. "No thanks, Nancy."

Issy's perfect romance might not be next door, but she could find it across the street.

In the library bookshelves, of course.

In fact, other than in her garden, Issy never felt safer than when she was sitting in the library, on the gray-carpeted floor between the shelves, authors like Jane Austen and Charlotte Brontë peering over her, not to mention the slew of contemporaries. She had a spread of three new romances in front of her, reading the first chapters.

Sometimes she opened her show with a reading from one of her favorite scenes. It was what she loved best about *My Foolish Heart*—the freedom to sculpt the show to what suited the moment. Sometimes she began with a monologue about a celebrity romance. Sometimes a reader letter.

Today, it would be a passage from a classic, one prompted by Pride's . . . well, foolish heart. She hated to be the one to suggest it, but a reminder of ill-fated love might shake Lauren O'Grady free of her fog-induced agreement to marry a less-than-ten.

Three words, dear Romeo, and good night
    indeed.
If that thy bent of love be honourable,
Thy purpose marriage, send me word
    to-morrow,
By one that I'll procure to come to thee,
Where and what time thou wilt perform the
    rite;
And all my fortunes at thy foot I'll lay
And follow thee my lord throughout the world.

The last line still made her shake her head. And what if he led her into pain, heartache . . . death?

See, Juliet might have benefited from a list, no matter what Lucy said.

Out of the corner of her eye, she saw a pair of feet walk by. Black-and-white Adidas under faded jeans. Whoever it was, he had a limp. She leaned out between the rows.

What was *he* doing here? But now that she was prepared for the scars, they didn't look so shocking in daylight. In fact, she had to look for them, because, oh, my, he looked good. The kind of good that should be outlawed, especially for neighbors—how was she supposed to keep her eyes off him as he mowed the lawn?

If he mowed the lawn. But she could cling to hope, right?

He had slipped into the row marked "Local Reference."

A guy who spent his afternoon in the library couldn't be a Neanderthal, right?

Oh, she just wanted to hide inside her book.

He walked past her again, a case of tapes under his arm, a book in the other. And yes, he limped. Interesting.

She waited until he approached the front desk, then darted into the aisle across from the desk.

He'd asked to fill out a library card. What if he *was* a reader? What if he had hurt his leg, maybe broken it, and during his convalescence he'd taken to reading? Maybe the classics—Hemingway, *Les Misérables*, F. Scott Fitzgerald. She'd even tolerate a Jack London fan.

The girl at the desk—Mindy Scott—giggled. She must be a sophomore by now; Issy remembered babysitting her.

He picked up his stack—wait, was that a wink?—and lifted his hand to Mindy as he thumped out the glass doors.

"Who was that?" Issy hustled over to Mindy, not missing the blush pressing her face. "What's his name?"

Mindy's eyes widened. Okay, maybe Issy had been a bit forward. And maybe she shouldn't have picked up his freshly minted library card application sitting on the desk. "Caleb Knight."

"He's new in town." Mindy yanked the application from her grip. "And that's confidential."

"If he's new, then everyone will know about it by noon."

"Sooner than that. He had his first practice today. Had his team out running bleachers at 6 a.m."

His team? Bleachers? Oh. *No.*

"And he wore the cutest shirt—it said 'Sack 'em' on the front."

"Sack 'em."

"You know, like in football?"

"Yes, I know what it means." She pushed her books toward Mindy, faked a smile. Slapped her card on top.

"I just never thought the new football coach would be so cute." Mindy zipped Issy's card through the scanner. "Usually, they're old men." She looked up, her face suddenly white. "Oh, I'm sorry. I didn't mean anything by that."

"It's okay, Mindy. My father would have said the same thing. But take it from someone who knows. A football player is the last person you want to give your foolish heart to."

Issy didn't look back as she passed through the glass door.

"Are you doing your exercises? Keeping your stump clean? Making sure you're changing your socks?"

The way his brother acted, Caleb might be six years old again, with the chicken pox. "Collin, I'm good. Really."

132

Caleb leaned on his crutches, washing out today's sweaty socks and the nylon sheath that covered his residual stump. He would also have to clean his prosthesis with rubbing alcohol.

"You're doing your exercises? It's the little things that make a difference."

"Let's pretend that you're not my big brother, physical therapist extraordinaire, and that I've managed to live without your help for at least the last three years."

"I just want this to work for you."

"Me too. And it will. I promise."

"But you know, if you need it, the sofa is all yours."

"And listen to you and Maricel fight over who gets to take the dog out? Thanks, but everything here is great. I'm not sponging for an empty sofa quite yet."

"Call me if you need anything."

"I will. Stop worrying, Bro."

Caleb pressed the Off button. As if he'd *really* forget clean socks, a clean prosthesis, and to do the exercises that allowed him to be mobile.

Sort of like he might forget to breathe.

Caleb wrung out the socks, let them hang over the bathroom rack. It just wouldn't do to have to hobble around town on his crutches looking for a Laundromat.

Which he'd have to find, and soon, anyway.

He maneuvered out to the main room, where

he grabbed his exercise mat. Unrolling it, he let himself fall back on the pads of his hands, then lay down flat.

As the pressure on his leg released, he just breathed. The heat on his stump from being upright all day could grind his back teeth to powder. He stared at the ceiling. Began his quad sets.

Pushing the back of his knee down, he tightened his thigh muscle. Held for five seconds, then released.

Again. And again. While he ran over the practice in his mind.

He'd made the team run bleachers, then lines, then a couple laps around the track, followed by push-ups, pull-ups, and dips. He sprinted them against each other and finally put them in position drills.

While Caleb did a few gluteal sets, he considered his players.

The sophomore McCormick had running back written all over him, the way he cut and with his quick reaction off the line. He might be unstoppable if he had a few extra pounds on his bones.

The junior Merritt, Caleb would put on the line, at center. The guy had a good head on his shoulders. Caleb would teach him when to call the blitz, and the kid would learn fast.

He pulled his leg up to his chest as tight as he could, flexing his knee, held it, then straightened it. Repeated.

That sophomore Bryant would make a great wide receiver, with those sticky fingers. He and the senior quarterback, Ryan, could have great chemistry someday. And Ryan, he could be a star. The kid not only knew how to scramble, but he had a deep ball.

If only Ryan would ditch the cocky, solo act attitude. Caleb had watched one of the games from last year he'd found in the library today, and every time the option came, Ryan held the ball, refused to pass it off, and got tackled for a loss.

The kid had a college scholarship in his future, but only if he learned to play as part of a team.

Caleb bent his good leg, put his foot flat on the floor, and raised his residual leg straight to the ceiling. Lowered it. Again.

He'd spotted the other coach, too, during the early hours of practice. The guy came right up to the fence, stretching out on his run. Or at least pretending to. Caleb had watched him run off as he called his players in for a pep talk.

"If you want to be good, you'll have to give it your all, no matter how much it hurts." He'd stared at the red faces, most of them drenched in sweat and displaying tired eyes. "I want you to go home, ice your legs, go to sleep early, and don't eat a big breakfast tomorrow because you'll lose it if you do."

He'd wanted to tell them to stay the course, that there was nothing sweeter than testing your limits and going beyond. That they could become heroes in their own eyes.

And that was worth any pain he would dish out.

More than that, standing at the end of a season, knowing they'd left it all on the field, would enable them to look back without regrets.

Caleb put a rolled towel under the knee of his amputated leg, practiced lowering and straightening his leg.

Tomorrow he'd run them again, then put them in more position drills. He'd make the backs carry the ball over the bags. Then he'd like to have them practice hits and spins, but he really needed another coach, because he had to spend time with his receivers, helping them run routes.

And, well, he couldn't really do that, either.

Caleb blew out a breath.

He'd hoped for a staff, not this crazy competition. Not being pitted against the legacy of the Huskies.

The guy had even worn his jersey onto the field for his first practice today. He ran in to the high fives of his players.

Yes, Caleb had been watching from his truck. When he couldn't take it any longer, he drove away, down to the library, and checked out every tape he could find on the Huskies.

He even lucked out and found the state championship eight years ago. He'd downloaded it onto his iPod.

Now he rolled over to his stomach, lay prone, clicked Play, and listened to the game against the Lakeville Ravens—just the last quarter with the Huskies down by five, their best wide receiver on the sideline nursing a broken thumb, and the quarterback Seb Brewster marching the ball down the field with less than a minute to play.

Not unlike Caleb's own senior championship.

"It's first down on the twenty-five, and the Huskies are at the line. Brewster takes the snap, pitches it out to Teague, who takes it for a quick two-yard gain. Huskies forgo the huddle and Brewster drops back, is looking, looking, and here comes the blitz from the left side! Brewster scrambles out of the pocket, tucks the ball, and scoots over the line of scrimmage, a gain of one."

Caleb found himself holding his breath as he listened to Seb execute one more perfect play for the first down.

"On the sideline, Coach Presley is remarkably calm as he sends out fresh receivers on the field. Brewster takes the snap, drops back—and he connects with Kline at the fourteen-yard line for a first down! The Huskies are in field goal range, but with thirty-seven seconds on the clock, they're running out of time and a field goal won't win the game."

Caleb sat up, grabbed a towel, began to rub his leg, desensitize it.

Outside, he heard a roll of thunder. He listened

as Brewster was sacked for a loss on the next play and heard the cheers of the hometown fans as he completed a pass on the next play.

Finally, with twelve seconds left on the clock, Presley called a time-out.

Caleb got up and opened the door, peering into the night. "Roger?" Rain plinked on the roof of his truck, contributing to the jungle of his front lawn. He would mow. Tomorrow. Or soon.

"Don't forget, people, this game is brought to you today by Duke's Hardware, your one-stop shop for all your household needs."

Caleb smiled. How he loved a town that stopped their high-action play-by-play to deliver a commercial about the local wrench shop.

"The Deep Haven Huskies come back to the line. Brewster's in shotgun position. He calls the first hike and—wait, there seems to be some confusion on the field. Brewster is headed to the sideline, yelling something at the coach. The defense seems confused, is there a time—no, there's the snap to the fullback! Brewster is in motion down the sideline. The wide receivers are going deep and the fullback drops back to pass. He pumps once, looking for a receiver, and finds—no way, Brewster's in the end zone! And there's not a defender this side of Canada! Touchdown Huskies!"

Caleb listened to the cheers erupting, could imagine the town rushing the field, boosting

Brewster onto their shoulders, carrying him off.

How Caleb had loved being carried off the field.

But even more, what was that play? Some sort of sneak—he'd heard of a similar play called "wrong ball"—the offense acting as if they had the wrong ball on the field. But this—Brewster was clearly yelling something that threw off the defense. Wrong play, wrong ball . . . it didn't matter. Presley had tricked them all.

He clicked off the iPod.

If Seb Brewster remembered half the plays Presley taught him, if he turned out to be half the coach Presley had been, Caleb hadn't a chance of netting the coaching position.

He worked his way to his foot, grabbed his crutches, then leaned down to wind up his mat.

Next door, light glowed from his neighbor's upstairs window.

Interesting. He'd seen her today, at the library, hunkered down in the fiction section, that long brown hair curly upon her face, her tanned nose buried in a book.

She looked up as he passed, and he'd tried, just for a second, to hide his limp. He wasn't ready for her—or anyone—to know all his secrets. Although the loneliness of keeping them had begun to creep up on him. Wouldn't it be nice to talk to someone, tell them the truth?

Hobbling to the sofa, Caleb plopped himself down, put his leg up. On his side table lay a stack of tapes and DVDs, the recordings of the Huskies over the years. He'd also checked out a copy of the Deep Haven High School yearbook for Brewster's graduating year. It might help him understand his competition.

He opened to the table of contents, found the football pages, and spotted Seb, surrounded by thirty players in blue. And behind them, Coach Presley and his coaching staff. Yes, Coach looked like a man who could train boys into men. He flipped to the senior section, found Brewster as a fresh-faced jock, then paged through the other faces. He would like to see these faces today, if they found what they looked toward as they faced the camera.

He stopped on a face that looked familiar. Brown hair blowing in the wind, sitting on a rock in the harbor, smiling into the sunshine.

He knew that look.

The caption identified the girl as Isadora Presley.

Presley. As in Coach Presley's daughter?

No, it couldn't be.

Coach Presley's daughter was his *neighbor?*

Coach Presley, whose accident raked deep wounds into the community, who still held their hearts in his winning grip?

Coach Presley, whose daughter had run from him not once, but twice?

Coach Presley's daughter, the one with PTSD?

He glanced at her house. No wonder the woman had freaked out when she'd seen him. What had Dan said—her mother died in her arms?

So, yes, he'd forgive her. Again.

He knew what it felt like have wounds that no one could see. That no one except God could heal.

What if God had sent him here, not just for the Huskies . . . but for Isadora Presley? What if she needed a friend?

He closed the book. So many dreams, so many ambitions.

Leaning against the sofa, he reached for his laptop to pull up *The Bean*'s online station.

The page listed the show before it, still in progress.

My Foolish Heart.

He didn't exactly need help with romance, thank you, but he would like to figure out how to talk to his neighbor.

Perhaps a little coaching wouldn't hurt.

And perhaps she might have some insights on how to beat Seb at his own game.

Men rarely possessed the courage to call the hotline, so immediately Issy lowered her voice, kept it warm and patient, hoping not to spook him.

"Go ahead, BoyNextDoor." What a cute user-name. Creative. She ran her bare foot over Duncan's fur as he lay at her feet, or rather, sprawled under her table, a boulder that occasionally shook with the rumble of thunder. Still, his huge body radiated warmth and he almost seemed like another adult in the house, one who simply couldn't speak.

When the animal appeared on her doorstep this afternoon, looking forgotten, with the neighbor's truck absent from the driveway and the sky overcast, she'd found some luncheon ham in her fridge, then invited him in for a nap. Better than having him destroy her parents' quilt again. She'd closed the door to their room, despite his heartbroken look.

"I, uh . . . I'm not sure what to say."

BoyNextDoor had a low, resonant voice, a little on the roughened side, as if overused. Or perhaps not used enough. She pictured him in his midthirties, maybe slightly overweight with thinning hair, sitting alone in his two-bedroom apartment in Chicago, overlooking some parking lot.

"Is there something I can help you with tonight?"

"I hope so. I made someone angry."

"What did you do?"

"I'm not sure. I think she just doesn't like me."

"You're not sure? She didn't give you a reason?" She'd learned, with men, not to settle for the confused *I don't know what I did.* Most men knew when their words stung; they just didn't understand why.

"She did. A sort of list of reasons, I guess. But even if I fix all those things, I'm not sure if that will make her like me. We got off to a rough start."

"You don't know this girl?"

"No, but I think I'd like to. She's . . . intriguing. And I think she needs a friend."

"So you feel sorry for her?"

"No! I . . . I just think we could be friends if I had another chance."

Oh. He'd done something to blow it with her, and now he wanted another shot. How men hated to fail.

"Besides, I have this . . . *project* I'm working on, and I was hoping she could . . ."

"You want her help."

"Well, not help . . ."

Of course not help. Men didn't need *help*.

"Input?"

"Endorsement."

Huh. "You want her to like you."

"Exactly." His voice rose, and she could see him rising from his chair, maybe running a hand over his hair, striding to the window to peer out on the darkened, rain-slicked street.

Or not. But the rain pattering on her window only fed her imagination.

"So start with the basics."

"Do I send her flowers? Or maybe chocolate?"

Issy smiled. This one needed a lot of work. "Have you ever had a girlfriend, BoyNextDoor?"

"Yes. In college. We dated. But she pursued me, not . . . Well, let's just say that I didn't have to work too hard."

Hmm. On the forum, someone had opened up a discussion. *What about the BoyNextDoor?* The Lovelorn had already plugged in their assessment of him.

DorothyP: All he has to do is apologize.

GotMyHeart07: What for? I get so tired of men having to say they're sorry when they don't know what they did.

Proverbs31: It doesn't matter. Saying you're sorry breaks the ice. Remember, a soft word turns away anger.

Cupid87: He sounds like a jock. Didn't have to work too hard? Arrogant, too.

Issy found a smile even as Boy added, "That didn't come out right. It's just that we were both in college, and we weren't serious, and admittedly, I didn't put too much into the relationship. Then life sort of blew up for me, and she didn't stick around."

Issy wanted to ask about life blowing up, but something about the way his voice grew cold felt like a giant Keep Out sign.

And with the way the discussion board had lit

144

up, selfish her wanted him to call again. What if she did help him with his—how did he put it?—*project?* Could that boost her ratings enough to save *My Foolish Heart?*

Just like that, it hit her, and the words came out of her mouth almost instinctively. "Tell you what, BoyNextDoor. I'll help you woo this girl. You do everything I say, and within a month, she'll be in love with you." She said it without pride, more sweetness and encouragement in her voice than confidence. But, well, she did know what women hoped for in a man.

Or knew what *she* hoped for in a man.

After all, she had the list.

He made a little sound on the other end of the line, something like surprise. Or perhaps fear. Uh-oh, she didn't want to scare him off. "Oh, BoyNextDoor, don't you want to fall in love?"

Silence. Then, "I don't know."

He didn't know? But in his tone, she heard the slightest tremble. It vanished with "What do I need to do?"

Deflection. Yes, BoyNextDoor could be a very interesting, very lucrative caller.

"Start with listening. Whatever her list of complaints is, fix them. Show her that her concerns matter to you. Then call me back." *Please, call me back.*

"Am I supposed to say something? Like 'Thank you, Miss Foolish Heart'?"

She heard the mocking in his voice but somehow didn't mind it. As if he might be mocking himself, too.

"That'll do. Good luck, BoyNextDoor." She muted him, then ran a commercial, watching the forum board.

Cupid87: Do you think he'll do it?

MissFoolishHeart: If he wants to win her, he will. A woman likes to know her words matter. Look at Mr. Darcy. He listened to Elizabeth's fears and then, without telling her, went and found her sister, making sure she married Wickham. He made Elizabeth feel safe.

It always came back to that, didn't it? Safety. Duncan raised his head. His tail flopped once. *Don't you want to fall in love?*

Her question niggled at her for the rest of the show. Something about his pause—she understood that pause.

No.

Well, maybe.

Only if it didn't hurt.

She ended the show with her tagline and was just signing off when a chat request came in. From Elliot.

Elliot: Did you see the activity after BoyNextDoor's call? I think you have something there.

MissFoolishHeart: I know. Why do you think I told him to call me back?

Elliot: You're brilliant, MFH.

MissFoolishHeart: Now you figure out a way to turn it into advertisers.

She logged off. No doubt he'd spend all night working on proposals for new sponsors.

But perhaps, along with a ratings boost, she could make one woman's life a little easier.

She doused the light to her office, noticing that the neighbor's still glowed, bluish white across his jungle.

What about *his* to-do list? Just because she'd made a fool of herself didn't negate the fact that he lived in the Amazon or killed her pansies. Was it so hard to cut the grass? Maybe move his truck onto the street?

Duncan got up, thundering down the stairs behind her as she went into the kitchen and turned on the tea. And next door, the neighbor's light flicked off and settled the house into darkness.

7

"How are they looking, Coach?"

Caleb looked up from where he sat on the bench, taking notes on the players. "Hey, Dan." Great. Now Pastor Dan could report to the coffee slingers how he coached from the bench. He'd seen them sitting in the stands yesterday morning.

The fact remained, however, that his players simply didn't run as hard, as fast, without him standing over them. But he'd had to sit down, his eyes nearly crossed from hours of standing, running, hiding his limp, which only became more pronounced as the morning grew hot.

Long.

Agonizing.

Add to that a team that carried two years of loss and a defeated attitude into this season, and he just wanted to go home, soak his leg, and figure out why he'd ever thought he could do this job.

The fact was, after three days of practice, Caleb could admit he needed help. An assistant to help him run the plays, put action to words. He never thought he'd actually have to go it alone— the school board had specifically mentioned volunteers.

Days like today stirred the old urge to reach out

to God, to ask for help. But God had done enough, hadn't He? Caleb needed to stand on his own two feet. Well, figuratively. Still, gratitude didn't include whining.

God had given Caleb this job, and he intended to do it well.

"They're looking good," Caleb said to Dan, his voice tight. "I think we have the makings of a powerful team here. Of course, this is only half of them. The other half takes the field this afternoon with Coach Brewster."

"You coming back to watch?"

Actually, he'd planned on mowing his lawn. But that sounded feeble, didn't it? Mow his lawn rather than size up the competition? However, perhaps Isadora Presley *was* his competition. He hadn't thought about it until late in the night, but what if . . . what if she really didn't like him? Would she say something to her father? To the school board?

No, it was only his fears calling up lies, winding his brain into knots of worry.

"I'll wait until they're in position, then do a couple drive-bys," Caleb said as he glanced at Dan, dressed in a dark polo shirt, a pair of khaki pants. "How are you doing? How's Ellie?"

"Still wanting you to join the volunteer fire department." Dan sat next to him on the bench. "She sent me by to twist your arm."

Dan smiled, but Caleb turned his attention to

149

the field, where Ryan practiced a sweep play. "Okay, Ryan, I want you to just work on getting the snap from Merritt. McCormick, Walker, and Benson, line up, practice taking the handoff, left and right."

He should get up and run the drill so they could see it, but after three hours on his leg, he just might fall on his face.

Still, McCormick at running back was sloppy, dropping the ball too often to make him reliable. And the kid gave little effort with his fake. The defense would see right through it, take him down on his first step.

"You handled yourself well at the accident. Cool head, focused. Like you had training."

Caleb's eyes stayed on the field. "I have had training. I was a medic in the National Guard."

"Really?" This clearly got Dan's attention. "We could also use EMTs—"

"I'd like to, Pastor, but I'm here to coach football."

"We have three former football players and two school board members on our crew."

The man knew how to go for the jugular.

Unfortunately that could prove to be the perfect opportunity to reveal his weaknesses. "Let's see how the next two weeks go, okay?" By then, maybe he'd have the job.

By then, he could tell them the truth.

"Sounds fair." Dan clamped him on the shoulder.

"We're having a men's Bible study on Saturday morning. Would love to see you there." He got up.

"Hey, Dan, can I ask you a question?"

"Sure."

"What exactly happened to Coach Presley's daughter? Mitch said she has PTSD."

"Oh, that's a sad story. It was raining, about this time of year, actually. Coach and his wife were in the front seat, and a semi hit them as they slid through the light at the corner—"

"The one from last week."

"The very one. Spun the car around. Her mother was driving—she was trapped in the car. Coach flew through the windshield. And Issy was in the backseat, nearly without a scratch. For a long time I couldn't get the scene out of my brain. Coming up on the accident . . . the car had already caught on fire, and Issy wouldn't leave her mother. I think she might have stayed there until the flames engulfed the car. We finally got the fire out, freed them from the car, but Gabriella died there on the street. Horrible accident for everyone, but it was especially rough on Issy."

His pause, his tone, made Caleb glance at him.

Dan wore a grimace, as if witnessing some-thing fresh and raw. "She had a terrible panic attack the day of the funeral and locked herself in the bathroom. The police had to take the door off the hinges. And she was incoherent when we found her, had a sort of breakdown. She's . . .

she hasn't really left her house since then."

That was more than PTSD. Still, Caleb knew about that kind of fear, the kind that seeped inside you, took you apart piece by piece, made you believe that you'd never be whole again. "She lives next door to me."

"You saw her?"

"At the library, actually."

"Good. I'd heard she'd been making progress. Maybe you can reach out to her. I know Coach worries about her." He turned to the field. "By the way, your running back needs to sell his fake a little more. He's too easy to read."

Caleb stared at Dan as he started to walk away, the swell inside him making his mouth open nearly without his permission. "Hey, Dan, one more thing."

Dan glanced at him.

"Wanna . . . help me coach? I could use another set of hands."

A slow smile spread over the preacher's face. "I'll be here at 6 a.m."

The sun had crested in the sky when Caleb drove home. Roger met him as he lowered himself out of the truck's cab. He rubbed between the dog's ears. Then, circling around to the truck bed, he opened the tailgate, pulled out a ramp. He'd found the only self-propelled mower at Schuman's Sports, and it set him back about a fourth of his disability pay for the month. He grabbed the gas can from the back end and unscrewed the lid from the tank. As he gurgled the gas in, he let the wind off the lake cool his face. He'd start with the front yard, move to the back tomorrow.

Then, maybe, he'd replant her pansies.

A couple hard pulls and the mower roared to life. Not unlike a four-leg walker, really, it balanced him as he directed it down the row, moving slowly to mulch the grass, spitting moisture onto his jeans, his shoes.

He made another pass. Yes, it had grown into a jungle. His mowing job might not be pretty, but already the lawn shimmered, an emerald in the sunlight. The smell caught him, sent him back to his youth, to sprawling out on a fresh-cut lawn, running his toes between the prickly blades. In his mind, he gripped the football, stiff-arming his brother, going down, tussling in the front yard.

Someday he hoped to tussle with his own sons, watch them outrun each other. He didn't have big dreams—not after Iraq. He just wanted to build a normal, small-town life. The kind of life his parents had.

Roger bounded out from the driveway, toward the sidewalk, barking, and Caleb turned.

Wow.

Isadora Presley had amazing legs. So maybe he shouldn't have let that be his first thought, but nonetheless, Isadora came down the sidewalk in a pair of shorts, wearing a blue baseball cap, her curly dark hair pulled through the hole. It swung behind her like a tail as she ran with those tanned, long legs that belonged on a distance runner.

She stopped—or rather slowed. Looked at his yard.

At him.

He raised a hand. "Howdy, neighbor."

She stood there a moment longer before she smiled too, something quick and obligatory. Then she took off again.

She passed his house five times before he finished, not stopping, not slowing again. He locked the mower in the backyard, climbed up the back porch and into the house, then lay on the floor and tried not to weep at the pain.

Mow the lawn, check.

"It's the Seb-a-na-TOR!"

Just once, Seb would like to walk into a room without Big Mike, all-state center, announcing his presence.

Although for a second, something hot and sweet swelled inside him. He'd spent years being nobody. It felt good to be someone again.

A hero, even.

No one really needed to know the truth, right?

He raised a hand to Bam, seated on a high top

154

at the bar. With his bullish shoulders, not much of a neck and his head shaved to a nub, the defensive end could still strike fear into anyone opposite him, including, probably, the poor saps who came into the credit union searching for a loan.

"Six ball, left pocket. Hey, Seb." Pete Watson—P-Train, they called him—slid the ball into the corner pocket, smooth as silk, just like his running game.

Above P-Train, the neon lights in the window advertised the specials on tap, and beyond that, pictures of those members who'd served in the wars lined the walls. The VFW also served the best burgers in town, hosted a free pool table, and let JayJ and his band practice every Wednesday night.

JayJ stepped up to the mike. "You drink free tonight, Sebanator."

Seb acknowledged him, but he wasn't a drinking man—not anymore. He should have been warned off that night Lucy had caught him and Bree Sanders in a post–homecoming game clench. Sadly, there had still been a few dark years after the fiasco at Iowa State. He had to do something to forget his mistakes.

But about two years ago, he'd straightened up, found his way into a church, fallen hard at the foot of the cross, cried his eyes out over his sins, and promised to start over.

Even, someday, in Deep Haven. And he'd meant it, even if he'd had a couple rough starts after that. But not with alcohol. He only had to look at his father to let that lesson sink in.

He stepped up to the bar and ordered a Coke. Bam gave him a look, but he ignored it and found a stool at the high top where Big Mike considered his pool bets.

"P-Train knows how to sink 'em, but he still has a wild shot. Now, Deej, he's got the touch. He'll sneak right up and pretty soon he's grabbing the game out from under you."

DJ Teague looked up, smiled. Always had a smile—it wasn't easy being the only African American in a town pocketed so far north, but he knew how to pluck the ball from the air, and to the town he, like everyone else, appeared Husky blue.

Funny how Seb still saw each of these boys in their uniforms, their numbers emblazoned on their backs. Probably each of them could trace every play of that last game in their sleep, especially Coach's trick "Quarterback Chaos." Sometimes, he still saw himself taking off for the sideline. *Coach, Deej doesn't know the play! He doesn't know the play!* See, out of his periphery, the defenders loosen their stance, even stand up.

Enough for the offense to mow them over, for him to cut down the side and into the end zone. One of Presley's famous magic plays.

"How's practice going?" Mike picked up Seb's drink and sniffed it, made a face.

Seb took it back. "Good. I finally put them into positions today. First two days, I ran them until they couldn't see anymore."

P-Train sank another shot, then leaned on his cue. "I went by the field after my shift at the sawmill. Saw your guys running the bleachers. I hated those. You have any pukers?"

"No. I hated the feeling of being wrung out. But I still worked 'em hard. Had them run some drills, too. Then we played a little touch, just to have some fun."

Bam came off his stool. "Fun? Is football fun?"

"When you win!" Deej said and sank the eight ball.

P-Train chalked his cue. "So we got a state championship team, Seb?"

"Dunno. Depends on the other half—Coach Knight's team. He's got the senior QB, Jared Ryan, on his team. I'm still trying to figure out who can throw the ball on mine."

When Seb woke up this morning, he'd had the strongest urge to drive by World's Best Donuts. Instead, he'd driven to Coach Knight's practice, watched him run some drills, made a mental game plan of how he might do the same. Then he drove down to the beach and pitched rocks into the water for a good hour, the fear settling into his bones before deciding to put his players into positions, see what they could do.

Complain, was what. He didn't remember ever complaining when Coach Presley made them run.

Seb hadn't a clue how to turn these boys into a disciplined championship team. Sure, Knight might have sat on the bench sometimes, but most of the time Seb saw him standing out in the field with a clipboard. He'd gestured to his running back, drawn him in to speak close, then sent him back out. And sure enough, next time out, the kid sold his fake.

Seb saw improvement on Knight's team already and it was only day three.

He clearly needed help. So he'd come to the VFW to track it down.

"What if Coach Knight's team slaughters us? That can't happen, guys. I want to be the coach. I want to be the best, to see us get another trophy in the case by the gym. So . . . I need your help."

P-Train smiled. "I'm all over that. What time?"

"If I move practice to after dinner, you think you can come out? Mike and P-Train can teach some running plays. Bam, you could teach them how to tackle while Deej works the receivers. I'll focus on the QB."

"What's the plan?" Mike asked.

"Knight is teaching them fundamentals. We're going to outplay him. I have the secret weapon: all of Coach's trick plays, right here." Seb tapped his head. "And we're going to teach them to our boys."

Bam raised his glass.

Mike gave him a fist bump. "See, we just needed real Husky blood back at the helm. And who better than our all-state QB?" He picked up a cue. "What took you so long, bro?"

Seb kept his smile. "After college, I got into a few things." A few things? Sometimes his own words curdled his insides, but he'd already started the play—he had to finish it. "Started a couple businesses." If you could count selling coupons door-to-door as his own business. That had certainly been a dark time. Or perhaps, part of the darkness.

"Hey, really? You owned your own company?" Bam took Mike's place as P-Train racked the balls for a new game. "Ever made a business plan?"

"Sure, dozens of them. Business was my major." Okay, one of them. He'd done a lot of switching, declaring . . . failing. He took a drink and tasted his lies. "Actually—"

"We had someone come in today who needs a loan. But she hasn't a clue what she's doing, and she needs a business plan for me to approve the loan." Bam slapped ten dollars on the table. "That's on P-Train."

Mike glared at him.

"I . . . I guess so. I have some time before school starts," Seb said. Couldn't hurt, right? He

159

fished out a five, added it to the pile. "On Train."

"Great. I'll tell her you'll stop by. You two will have fun catching up, I'm sure." He glanced at Seb, gave him a wink.

A darkness slid through him even as he asked, "What's her name?"

Mike broke and pocketed two balls. He grinned shark teeth at Seb.

Bam finished off his beer. "Oh, sorry, man. I thought I said. It's Lucy. Lucy Maguire."

Seb closed his eyes. Of course it was.

It didn't matter that BoyNextDoor hadn't called again, right?

Really, it didn't matter.

Issy sat in the family room, feet propped on a wooden coffee table, painting her toenails deep pink. ABBA's "The Winner Takes It All" played on her iPod docking system. With the windows open, the fragrances of the lake, the pine, and the roses that twined up her front porch stewed a heady brew of summer, especially mixed with the aroma of freshly cut grass.

Her neighbor had mowed. And not just the front—as she might have expected—but this morning she'd awakened to the chewing of the mower as it devoured the savanna grasses of his backyard. She climbed to her office, peered down on him.

And probably peered for too long, really, but

Coach Knight had great shoulders, strong and bronzed, marred only by the burned skin that covered his right arm and a good portion of his neck. She was a little embarrassed to admit that she'd winced, again, at his scars. But she'd stopped seeing them by the time he finished the yard and mostly noticed that, when he took off his baseball cap to wipe his forehead, he had a nice head. A sort of distinguished, even solid look about him.

Still, sweat glistened off him, dripping into his now-scraggly beard, which seemed oddly incongruent with his clean-cut head.

She did appreciate a clean-cut man.

That's when she forced herself away from the window.

She'd visited the forum while he finished mowing and discovered that not only she had missed hearing from BoyNextDoor again. The forum lit up with scenarios about his absence.

Cupid87: I'll bet he didn't do anything Miss Foolish Heart said. He probably got off the phone, plopped onto the sofa, and fell asleep with the remote in his hand. He was too embarrassed to show his face.

Proverbs31: No way. He wouldn't have called in if he didn't want to get her attention. I'll bet he spent the day working on her list of complaints, probably fell into an exhausted lump.

DorothyP: I only wish my boyfriend would do one thing on my list.

Issy had logged in and pointed out that maybe the girl had noticed what he'd done to impress her and they were out for dinner all night long.

"Issy?" Lucy's voice came through the open screen door. She stepped inside without waiting for a reply.

"Over here." Issy applied the last of Berry Blast on her toes, then leaned back. Uh-oh, the way Lucy shuffled in, practically threw her donut bag on the table, and plopped into Coach Presley's favorite recliner . . . well, someone probably needed a donut more than Issy did.

"You okay?" Issy picked up the bag, opened it. A glazed raised.

"Mark Bammer turned me down for a loan." Lucy leaned her head back on the chair. "I can't believe it. He says that if I want a loan to build a drive-through, or even an outside serving counter, I need a business plan."

"So write a business plan."

"I stink at math, at numbers . . . at business in general. I make donuts. I sell them to people. I smile and ask about their grandchildren or their dogs. I don't write business plans. I've never had to." Lucy drew up her legs and rolled up her pant legs.

"You can learn. There's so much information on the Internet—"

"That's your world, not mine. I wouldn't even know where to start."

"What if you hired an accountant?"

"*Money.* It's a word I know you're unconcerned about, but I can't pay an accountant in donuts." She reached over and grabbed the nail polish.

"Ha." In fact, Issy tried very hard *not* to think about money. The settlement from the trucking company felt like blood money, and she hated the fact that it paid her father's bills, even if he needed it. She wanted to provide for him. "I don't know. You do make great donuts."

Lucy gave her a narrowed-eye look as she propped her foot on the table and began to paint her toenails. "I'll go to my grave with the words *She made great donuts* written on my tombstone."

Issy pulled the glazed raised out of the bag and bit into it. "What's so bad about that? Mine will read, *She helped others fall in love but never had a date.*"

For a second they stared at each other; then Lucy smiled. "The good news is, Bam left a message on my machine at work this afternoon. He says he has someone who can help me. Without the donut payment. I'm meeting him for coffee at the Blue Moose tonight."

"Hence the fresh coat of polish."

"He's probably a retiree from the Cities, looking to fill his time. But I'll take any help I can get. You can't imagine what it felt like to sit across Bam's desk and hear him say, 'No, I won't loan you the money.'"

"He always had a thing for you. Couldn't believe you shot him down sophomore year, then went out with Seb a year later."

"He does have a hard time with *no*." She didn't look at Issy as she finished her toenails. She finally capped the polish. "Anyway, I came to take you to the grocery store."

"I feel like I'm an old lady."

Lucy raised an eyebrow. Issy threw a pillow at her.

"Hey, who's grilling?" Lucy asked, waving her hands over her toes.

Indeed, the redolence of hamburgers smoking on a grill drew Issy from the sofa. She turned to look out the window. "Now he's grilling. He actually moved the grill off the porch, put it in the middle of the yard. He's sitting there in a lawn chair throwing a football to Duncan."

And she had to notice that he handled the ball well, balancing it with one hand, pitching it underhanded high into the air as the dog crouched, then bounded after it, crazy as it zagged around the yard. Duncan picked it up in his massive jowls, returned it to—

"He was at the library earlier this week. I found out his name."

"What did you do? Steal his library card?"

Issy made a face.

"You are pitiful."

"Knight. Can you believe that? Caleb Knight. And that's not all—he's the new football coach."

"You're kidding me. The new coach? See, the perfect romance might be right next door." Lucy winked.

"Are you here all week? Because you're downright hilarious." Issy turned back to the window.

Caleb held out the ball, faking the throw, the dog jerking with anticipation.

Lucy came over to join her at the window. Watched him for a long time. "Too bad about rule number three, huh?"

Issy glanced at her. "Maybe football players aren't all alike."

Lucy settled onto the arm of the sofa. "You come up with that yourself? Because you're simply profound."

Issy sighed. "I'm just saying, maybe I could modify rule number three. Maybe I don't date *some* football players. The stars-in-their-eyes kind. Maybe I date football players who didn't win state championships."

"*Losing* football players." Lucy raised an eyebrow. "I see where you're going with this.

Maybe only the ones who had to sit the bench for half the season."

"Most of the season. Four games, minimum." Issy smiled. "Okay, fine. Dumb rule. We'll scratch it. But seriously, for a coach, the guy is a mess. He needs a shave, and how about wearing a shirt that isn't ripped? And ditch the hat. Can you imagine how it smells?"

Lucy made the appropriate face.

Issy glanced at him again. He'd pushed himself out of the chair, now lifted the lid to the grill, flipping the burgers. "It's probably the only thing he knows how to cook. Charbroiled meat."

In a different world, a different life, she might have gone next door, asked him over for dinner. How many times did her father have the entire team over for burgers on a Thursday night before the Friday game?

Issy sat back on the sofa and grabbed a pillow. "Wouldn't it be nice if you could just . . . I don't know, order up the perfect man? Give your specifications to God and wait for Him to wrap him up and deposit him on your doorstep?"

"Or next door?" A smile played on Lucy's lips.

Funny. "Don't you have an old man to meet?"

"Number nine." As Lucy stood, she slipped her feet into her flip-flops. "He has to be able to cook."

"Something else besides burgers!"

"You are hopeless."

"Not hopeless . . . just . . . well, better safe than brokenhearted, right?"

Lucy's smile dimmed. "Right. Yes. C'mon. It's time to face your fears."

8

This was not the Lucy he remembered, the one who made him stand on a picnic table and recite Rochester's impassioned speech when he asked Jane to marry him.

Nor the Lucy who wouldn't even look at him in the hallways at school. Wouldn't let him chase her down to apologize.

Had he done that? Apologized?

No, this wasn't pretty, shy Lucy. Nor wounded Lucy. This Lucy wore a decade of determination in her eyes when she'd walked into the Blue Moose, spotted him sitting in the back booth, and come over to say, "Are you the one Bam sent to help me?"

For a long, panicked moment, all breath left him. Just sucked right out of him, along with his heart, and all he could do was nod. Like he still might be seventeen years old and assigned to work with her on their English project.

Then she sighed and offered what looked like a sincere smile.

The band of pain around his chest loosened. "Hey, Lucy. Uh, how are you?" He stood, extended his hand. She held hers out too, and it fit so perfectly in his, he held it too long.

Lucy slid into the booth. "Hi, Seb."

He might have been the one who betrayed *her,* but as he looked at her, at her sweet smile, everything he'd tried to deny burst open inside him. He wasn't in the least over her. Not at all. And the years of dodging and trying his charm on other girls came crashing on him as he sat back in his seat, his body still a little stiff from practice today. *Oh, God, I'm sorry for what I stole from her.*

"So," she said, slipping her bag off her shoulder, "are you here for a while?"

"Yeah, I'm . . . actually, I'm moving home. I'm going to be working at the school. And hopefully coaching the football team."

"You're really going to be coaching football?"

"Why not?"

She seemed to consider this. "How's it going?"

"Good, I think. We're having a scrimmage next Friday. A sort of tryout for the coaching position. I have some of the old team helping me with practice."

"I'll bet they're loving that." She studied him again for a moment, then, "How's your shoulder?"

This he hadn't expected. "Better. I did some throwing today, though, so I'll ice it."

"It was a brutal hit to watch. I'm sorry." She looked at the tabletop as she said it, so perhaps she didn't see his mouth open, just slightly.

Lucy had seen his career-ending game with Iowa State? He took a breath, fighting the joy that buzzed through him. "It was brutal to experience. And they never were able to fully repair the tear. Even had surgery."

"I know. It made the paper." She did find his eyes then, as if it might be more acceptable to read about his trials in the local paper than search for his games on the cable channels on a Saturday afternoon. Yes, that would take some amount of commitment.

That brought a smile, and suddenly he felt very much like the seventeen-year-old boy dating the prettiest girl in the school. "So Bam mentioned a business plan? Why? Aren't you running the donut shop?"

"Yes, but—" she leaned over the table as if including him in a secret—"the Java Cup has started serving donuts."

"Wow. That's . . ."

"I sold, on average, six hundred fewer donuts a day last weekend."

"Six hundred." He refrained from adding, *That many?*

Apparently six hundred less donuts put a hole in her business.

"Stop smirking."

169

She always could read his mind, and even now, she bore the hint of a smile. "This is a big deal, Seb. I'm already losing money this season, and I finally figured out why. It's not that I don't make great donuts—"

"You make awesome donuts." This he said with a straight face.

"I know, but that's the problem. I'm *too* popular. But I can't keep up. I . . . need to expand. Jerry says I need a drive-through window."

"A drive-through?"

"Or a walk-up. Something outside that can take the overflow."

"A hole in the donut shop." He really couldn't stop grinning.

"You're cute, but yes. Only problem is, that costs money. And I don't have it."

"So you need a business loan."

She nodded. "I think I can get Gary Starr and his crew to make me a . . . donut *window* before Labor Day, but not if I can't pay them." She drew in a breath, her face solemn. "Will you help me, Seb?"

It was how she said it, without a trace of their past in her voice, with so much hope, he wanted to leap to his feet, shout, *Yes!*

"I . . ."

But see, he'd never actually written a business plan or even owned a business. He'd been hoping—in the part of him that knew his own failures—that she wouldn't show, that he

170

wouldn't be forced to make a fool of himself, that he might slink away, his lie unrevealed.

But he'd returned for second chances, hadn't he? And most of all, he knew what it felt like to work your entire life for something only to have it slip out of your hands, your fault or not.

How hard could it be? "I'd love to help you."

She sat back, and the smile on her face could reach right down and light the dark places inside him. "Really?"

"Yeah. Of course. I . . ." He so didn't want to say, *I owe you* and suddenly rush their past at them, but he did owe her. He amended his words, softening the truth for both of them. "Well, you probably helped me pass my English class, so it's the least I can do."

"You would have passed without me, Rochester." Lucy slid out of the booth, grabbed her messenger bag. "I gotta get home. It's past my bedtime, you know. Someone has to get up and make the donuts. Thanks, Seb."

She held out her hand again. Somehow he took it. Somehow he smiled. Somehow he let her walk away without running after her.

Maybe he could be a hero again.

Seb Brewster had returned, and if Lucy guessed the expression on his face correctly, he was every bit as shaken to see her.

She crossed the street, headed up the hill toward

her house. The air held a soggy breath, the trees shivering. In the distance, thunder grumbled.

It seemed that Seb had grown up, no longer the shy boy who could barely read—only she knew about his dyslexia, how he struggled. How she'd helped him sound out nearly every word of their dramatic reading from their English assignment until he knew it by heart, could recite it with passion.

She smiled at the memory of him standing on the picnic table down by the harbor, thundering out his words over the roar of the waves.

"I sometimes have a queer feeling with regard to you—especially when you are near me, as now: it is as if I had a string somewhere under my left ribs, tightly and inextricably knotted to a similar string situated in the corresponding quarter of your little frame. . . ."

She might have dreamed herself into his arms a little then. Might have let herself be Jane, poor and obscure, plain and little, yet loved. Probably his drama had conspired to make her believe he loved her. Made her say yes that summer night with the stars sprinkled like dust overhead.

She never should have believed soft words like *forever* and *love* on his lips.

Lucy, I'm so crazy about you. . . .

Sure he was. So crazy that right after the homecoming game he'd gone out to celebrate and ended up fogging his car windows down by the beach. The same beach across from World's Best Donuts.

Too bad she'd spotted his car on the way to work in the wee hours of the morning. Too bad she'd been too curious.

It took her years to expunge the picture of Seb and Bree from her head. And worse, she had never really been able to scour away the one of herself in his arms. Which probably accounted for why, when Lucy walked into the café tonight and saw him sitting in the booth, wearing a white shirt and tie, his black curly hair cut short, it all rushed back to her—the feeling of being his girl, being in his arms, the hope of Happily Ever After.

Issy's light still glowed—her show would be about half-done. In her neighbor's house, the light also burned.

Wait . . . didn't Issy say her neighbor was the new football coach?

She didn't know much about football—just what she learned hanging around Coach Presley, which she'd tried to do whenever Seb happened to be around—but she knew this: Seb Brewster could lead any team to victory.

She'd never figured out, however, why he hadn't made it back onto the Cyclones after his injury. He'd dropped out of school, and out of the conversations around Deep Haven, and she'd lost him. He'd simply disappeared into the annals of Husky football.

But now . . . Coach Brewster. Yes, she liked that.

The neighborhood seemed more ominous now than in the early morning. Thunder rippled, closer. She picked up her pace.

Will you help me, Seb? She'd pulled everything out of her with those words. Pushed out every ounce of desperation and hope and saw herself, at that moment, small. And plain.

Broken. Until . . .

His eyes. They filled with a look she recognized—or thought she did. The look he'd given her the day the teacher assigned them to work together. And in that moment, she knew.

He hadn't forgotten her, not at all.

She reached her street, turned left. Overhead the stars blinked at her, perhaps as surprised as she was at the way she wanted to skip, even find a song.

Please, God, don't let him destroy my life again. She'd learned her lesson—she wouldn't betray her virtues again. But the way her heart had stirred to life since he returned to town, he had the potential to do great damage.

She simply couldn't give him her heart; that was all. She was smarter, not naive little Lucy anymore. She could handle working with Seb Brewster without losing herself, right?

Caleb had never been the kind of guy to find his fun online. Not with weights to lift and game

174

tapes to watch and weekend drills that turned him into an all-state running back. And growing up on a farm in southern Minnesota, he never lacked for something to do.

Never in his life would he have dreamed that he might spend his evening calling a talk show hotline. About love.

Good thing Dan didn't know. Who would have thought that his first friend in Deep Haven would be the town preacher? And a fairly decent football coach too, the way he drilled the guys and even helped the wide receivers lay out their routes.

He had a good team; Caleb could feel it in his bones. As long as they stuck to the basics, resisted the urge to be fancy, and simply kept their heads about them, they had a chance at winning.

If he could get through to Jared Ryan, of course. Although he'd figured out at least one source of the kid's lousy attitude today, when he'd nearly gotten into a fistfight with Bryant. The other team had drawn Ryan's buddy, wide receiver Chase Samson, and from what he'd heard, the two made magic on the field.

Caleb hoped his words, after Dan had gotten between the two players, sank into Ryan. *A great quarterback leads the team, finds their talents, and makes them better. Figure out how to help Bryant, and you'll turn him into the player you want him to be.*

Ryan barely looked at him, and when he did, Caleb saw distrust.

Apparently he'd have to prove himself to Ryan before the kid would listen to him. Oh, to take him down in a tackle or, better yet, throw a deep pass right into Bryant's skinny arms. Caleb had been a fairly decent quarterback before he'd settled into the running back position. But his leg had burned all the way through his body—he couldn't drop back into the pocket for a pass to save his life.

Sometimes his limitations could eat clear through him.

Navigating to the *My Foolish Heart* web page, he clicked on the radio player. He couldn't deny the urge to report in, to tell her that yes, he'd done his homework.

Perhaps it was the teacher inside.

The voice of Miss Foolish Heart came over the line. "Tonight we're discussing beauty. Can you love a man or woman you find unattractive? Consider Jane Eyre and Rochester. Neither of them could be called beautiful; in fact Rochester is actually called an ugly man. Yet Jane falls for him, even after he becomes blind and scarred. Why? Cupid, you're on the line."

"Rochester fell in love with Jane because of her intellect and because she connected with him. She understood him. That made her beautiful."

"Thanks, Cupid. How about you, NiceGirl?"

"It's not beauty on the outside that he wanted. Blanche was beautiful, after all. But she was not for him."

"Good comparison, NiceGirl, but let's not forget that Rochester was no catch, either. In fact, Jane even says, 'Had he been a handsome, heroic-looking young gentleman, I should not have dared to stand thus questioning him against his will, and offering my services unasked.' She doesn't see herself as beautiful, nor him, so that made him attainable. Go ahead, DorothyP."

"So are you saying it's impossible for an ugly girl to marry a handsome man?"

"No. But a girl doesn't want to walk into the room and feel like everyone is looking at her date."

Oh, brother. Caleb scrolled down to the show information. No picture of the hostess, Miss Foolish Heart. And by the tenor of the conversation . . . well, he didn't want to guess what she might look like. He clicked on the forum link and logged in, hoping to find something about her.

Oh . . . my . . . They'd created a discussion titled "BoyNextDoor." He hovered his mouse over the link, debating.

Clicked it.

Wow. Women had such fertile imaginations.

"I just think that Rochester saw her as his equal; that's why she became beautiful to him." This from someone who sounded about nineteen.

He couldn't stop himself. He dialed the line, then gave his name to the producer.

"BoyNextDoor, you're on the line." *Her* voice. Soft, with a hint of question. Talking to him. Oops, he hadn't thought Miss Foolish Heart would take his call immediately. Wasn't there some sort of queue?

"Uh. Hi." Was that him, on the air? He sounded like an idiot, deep voice, sort of confused. He cleared his throat.

"Would you like to add to the conversation?"

She didn't sound unattractive. In fact, he sort of pictured her young. Maybe with brown hair, kind gray-blue eyes.

"I . . . I just wanted to say I think you have it all wrong."

Silence. "Oh?" But not an angry *oh*. More curious, as if she might be playing with him.

"Yeah. Uh . . . look, men like pretty girls. They don't want their equal. Every guy out there would date a movie star if he could, but that's beyond his means."

"Wow . . . BoyNextDoor, that's fairly Neanderthal of you."

He shifted the phone to his other ear so he could scroll down, read the comments. Ouch, these women knew how to take a guy apart.

"It's the truth. The way we are. Sure, beauty's not the only thing that matters, but it's what gets your attention."

For a second, Isadora running down the side-walk stepped into his mind. Yes, she'd gotten his attention.

"Like my dad used to say, 'Beauty's only skin deep, but you don't want to have to skin a girl to love her.' "

Miss Foolish Heart gasped. "That's terrible."

"That's the truth, Miss Foolish Heart." But he smiled, wishing he could see her face. "But that's not the only truth. Beauty to a man is more than just curves and a smile, great hair. It's her laughter at your jokes, the way she makes you feel, the way she treats other people. It's the whole package. And that's why this Rochester guy loved Jane, because even if she wasn't the prettiest girl on the block, she was the one who made him feel like he was the most handsome man."

A beat of silence. Then, "Thank you. Yes. I believe Jane has this exact thought when she says, 'You are not beautiful either, and perhaps Mr. Rochester approves you: at any rate you have often felt as if he did.' "

He hadn't a clue what she might be talking about, but he could nod. Or, "Uh-huh."

"So, BoyNextDoor, I think all our listeners would like an update on your true love."

His true . . . "Listen, she's not my true love. Just . . . a girl I'd like to win over."

"But she *might* be, right?"

He glanced up at the lit window of the night

179

owl next door. "I don't know. I started her to-do list, and she barely noticed. In fact, I'm wondering why I did any of it."

Silence. "Oh. Hm. Well, let's see, BoyNextDoor. Your oh-so-sensitive quote goes both ways—beauty's only skin deep, but you don't want to have to skin a guy to love him. Have you given the girl something to look at? Make sure you look good; don't dress like a hobo. Women like a man who can clean up."

He couldn't help the quick glance in the mirror. Not that he'd noticed, but yeah, he'd gotten a little shaggy. Maybe a few weeks since he'd shaved.

He pulled at a string on his National Guard shirt where he'd ripped the arms off. Maybe she had a point. "Take a bath; got it."

She laughed. Something about it wheedled right through him, deep inside, warm and sweet.

"Thanks, coach," he said, his voice tough.

He heard the smallest intake of breath, then a tremulous laugh before she said, "Go get 'er, champ."

He hung up.

Smiled.

Maybe a guy could learn something from Miss Foolish Heart.

9

"I haven't had the courage to speak to my neighbor since Saturday. He was even mowing his lawn the other day and said hi to me, and it was all I could do not to run back inside my house, bar the door. The man must think . . . Well, who knows what he thinks."

Issy sat in her father's recliner, staring past Rachelle. Dressed in a pair of casual khakis, an oxford shirt, and sandals, the counselor always looked as if she might be going to a potluck down the street. She wore her black hair down, streaks of gray suggesting wisdom to go with her enigmatic smile, and Issy felt as if she were talking to her favorite aunt.

"Let's talk about when you went over there on Saturday. Did you feel a panic attack coming on?"

Issy closed her eyes, remembered the heat in her chest. "No, actually. I was just so angry."

"See, you didn't worry about panicking. You didn't even think about your actions; you just marched over to his house."

"Or I was blinded by rage. And I said such terrible things to him."

Rachelle held up her hand. "You apologized. Let it stand at that. He has obviously forgiven you. He mowed his lawn, didn't he?"

Issy looked out the window. He'd also parked his truck on the street—imagine that. So maybe he'd been listening to her tirade.

"Do you think I'll ever be the person I was before the accident?"

"Do you want to be?"

Did she want to be the confident, almost too-ambitious woman she'd been before that terrible weekend? The woman who'd vowed never to return to Deep Haven? "I always imagined myself showing up for my ten-year reunion with some sort of triumph. Maybe as a television host of my own show. Someone Deep Haven could be proud of."

"You don't think Deep Haven is proud of you?"

"Would you be? I was the class valedictorian. Now I'm the town victim."

"I think you might spend more time thinking about what the town thinks of you than they really do."

The words made her wince. "I thought you therapists were just supposed to ask how that made me feel."

"How does that make you feel?"

"Ha. Funny."

"Well? Do you think you put too much importance on what others think?" Rachelle said.

"I know I do. But I can't help it." Issy drew up

her legs, tightening herself into a ball on her father's chair. "I can't help thinking that everyone is so disappointed in me."

"Define *everyone*."

"Everyone. The people of Deep Haven."

Rachelle raised an eyebrow.

"My church?"

"Pastor Dan asked me to say hello. He'd like to come by and visit."

She hadn't seen him for nearly two weeks. He and Ellie had hovered over her after the accident like they were family.

"Lucy?" she offered. "Me?"

Rachelle nodded as if waiting for more.

"God?"

"Do you think God is disappointed?"

Yes. "I don't know. Maybe there is just something wrong with me. I look out and see everyone else living a normal life, a happy life. You know, there are times I actually believe that I could have that. I get up in the morning, hear the birds, stand at my window, and stare out at the lake and think, *Today. Today I'm going to change my life. Today I'm going to go visit my father.*"

"And then?"

"And then I do something horrid like I did to my poor neighbor, and I realize that I'm different. A disappointment to myself and others. I can't trust myself. That's a terrible feeling."

Issy's gaze shifted across the pictures of her

parents on the bookshelf: She and her father holding up a stringer of walleye. Her mother pressing a kiss to her cheek at graduation. "I dunno. Maybe you're right. I do spend a lot of time thinking about what others think about me. What they see."

"Tell me, when are you most comfortable with yourself?"

Issy rubbed the arms of the chair. "When I'm doing my show. When I'm imagining the people on the other end of the line and helping them."

Rachelle smiled. "And I bet you're not afraid to talk to them at all."

"They can't see me."

"But you could have a panic attack on the air, couldn't you."

"Thanks for pointing that out."

"But?"

"Yes. I suppose. But I never think about it."

"So you never do. Can I offer a suggestion why?"

"You're the therapist; knock yourself out."

"It's because you're spending time helping others. Your focus is off yourself. You don't even see yourself, so you can't imagine yourself panicking."

"Are you saying that if I spent less time imagining myself panicking and worrying about what the town might think, it *might* actually help me get better?"

"Your panic attacks stem from what you think might happen. You let your fears determine how you live. You do the math."

"It's not that easy."

"Maybe it's only one door, unlocked. But tell me this—why have you never revealed to the town that you're Miss Foolish Heart?"

Well, that was easy. "Because if they knew, they'd laugh at me." She gritted her teeth even as she said it.

"Why would they laugh?"

She narrowed her eyes at Rachelle.

The counselor smiled. "Then let's try this. Why have you never had a date?"

"I'm undatable?"

"Do you believe that?"

Issy lifted a shoulder. "Maybe. I mean, I had a couple offers in college, but no one that fit the list. . . ."

"Issy, why did you create your list?"

"So I didn't end up like Lucy." She said it softly. Met Rachelle's eyes. "I just want to make sure when I put my heart out there that far, it is for the right one."

"Because you don't want to get hurt."

She lifted a shoulder. "Is that wrong?"

Rachelle pressed her hands together, leaned forward. "You said earlier that more than anything, you wanted to be normal. What is normal, Issy?"

She knew what it wasn't, perhaps. "It's getting up every day, going to work, falling in love, having a family, children."

Unlike other therapists, Rachelle never made notes while they chatted. Instead, she had an insightful, brown-eyed gaze that could pin Issy to the chair. "Would getting hurt occasionally be on that list?"

"Preferably not."

Rachelle smiled. "So you've fixed the world to be safe. Controllable. But it's not, is it?"

Issy pressed her fingers below her eyes, fighting the sudden burn in them.

"Miss Foolish Heart. You can't preprogram your life."

Issy gave up, wiped her hands on her pants. "Then how do I make sure that it turns out all right?"

Rachelle said nothing, and Issy heard the answer in the pulse of her heartbeat. Outside, the garbage man drove by, and a dog barked.

"Tell me about BoyNextDoor."

Issy looked at her.

Rachelle shrugged. "I was on the forum. And I heard your voice. You like talking to him."

"I think I could help him. I want to help him."

"Because it will boost your ratings?"

"Maybe. I don't know." Issy glanced at the clock. "If I could help him get a date with Miss Right, I might feel like my life wasn't quite so small. I might even be able to be the person I left behind."

Rachelle shifted in her seat, caught Issy's eyes. "Maybe you shouldn't strive to be the woman you left behind, but the one who is out ahead."

Sometimes after therapy she just wanted to curl up in her mother's afghan and hide. But she found her voice. "What does that woman look like?"

"I'm not sure. But I'd bet if you stop trying so hard to hold her back, to keep her safe, she might just surprise you."

Outside, a door slammed. Caleb had stepped onto the porch. "What does that mean, anyway?"

Rachelle followed her gaze, and Issy watched her as she took in Caleb walking down the stairs, a stack of tapes under his arm. He crossed the street to the library.

"Maybe it simply means that next time, you say hello."

Agoraphobia is a condition in which sufferers experience anxiety in situations or locations where they sense they have no control, such as open spaces, crowds, or traveling. It is often exacerbated by a fear of experiencing a panic attack or appearing afraid in public. Often, a sufferer might be afraid of a particular location where he or she has experienced an attack in the past. The fear of panic attacks may lead sufferers to confine themselves inside a safer world. Agoraphobia can also be caused by post-traumatic stress disorder.

Caleb sat in the library, where the sun slid in over the wooden table, the Palladian windows surveying the neighborhood—specifically Issy's house across the street. Her hanging plants, dripping with some giant pink flowers, and the roses around the door suggested welcome, yet Dan's words from practice a couple days ago kept tugging at him.

She hasn't really left her house since then.

Caleb knew that kind of fear. When he'd woken in the hospital, still in Iraq, bewildered, so juiced on pain medication that he couldn't think straight, the fear had crawled up his throat and nearly choked him. It hung on all the way to Germany, then Walter Reed. He'd never forget the day he took a good, raw look at what remained of his leg and the scars on his body and let his loss settle into his bones.

"Hello, Coach."

He looked up. That young librarian, the one with the blonde braids, smiled at him, a stack of books propped on her hip. "I like the goatee."

He'd caught his reflection in the window this afternoon as he walked into the library, after his visit to the barber shop and the thrift store for a pair of khakis, a couple dress shirts, some unprinted T-shirts. He looked like an upstanding citizen of Deep Haven. And he didn't hate it.

How foolish was he that he hoped Isadora noticed?

"I don't want to look like a redneck, but I need *some* hair on my head." He winked at the girl, having long ago discovered that humor helped everyone breathe. "Thank you, uh . . ."

"Mindy. Are you finished with your book? Because I can re-shelve it."

He closed the encyclopedia. "Thank you. Can you tell me where the care center is in town?"

"Go up the highway, out of town, take a left at the municipal pool, then up Eighth Street."

"Thanks."

"Oh, and good luck on the game." She wore a blush. "Curt McCormick is my boyfriend."

"He's doing a great job. You can tell him the coach said that." He smiled at her, pushed away from the table.

The Deep Haven Care Center sat atop a hill, over-looking the beauty of Lake Superior. Geraniums spilled out of planters anchoring the doorway and a *Visitors, Please Register* card pasted on the glass door made him stop at the reception desk.

"I'm here to see Coach Presley."

The nurse at the counter pointed down the hall. "Last door on the right."

Caleb signed his name on the registration pad, received a visitor's badge, then eased his way down the hall.

The patients lingering in the common areas could reduce him to tears. Some of them lost inside themselves, others with enough faculties to lift their eyes, question his presence. Nursing homes always smelled aged, as if life had left the inhabitants long behind.

Someone had pasted a football helmet decal on Coach Presley's door, and he heard voices as he pushed the door open with his knock.

He nearly dropped with relief seeing Dan look up from the man's bedside. Caleb met Dan's eyes, found inside them a hint of compassion.

"Hey, Caleb," Dan said. "Glad you could stop by."

Behind Dan, through the picture window, the sun blazed over the lake, bright and glorious in the milky blue sky. A television hung above the bed, the sound muted—Caleb glanced at it and recognized old reruns from the NFL channel. Beside the bed perched a picture of Issy and a woman Caleb could only imagine had been Coach's beautiful wife, with her long dark hair, big smile, sitting on the steps of their home. Finally he looked at the coach. He swallowed before forming a smile.

Why had he thought this was a good idea? Meet the coach, introduce himself? He'd blame it on Dan, who had suggested the visit again after practice this morning.

Coach Presley looked a thousand years older

than he should, his body bony and limp in his bed, attached to a ventilator, the skin on his lifeless arms flappy, his hair thinned and white. Caleb stifled the urge to turn and run.

That could have been him. He could have been the one to go through the windshield of the Humvee, to lie broken and gasping for breath on the side of the road. It could have been him puffing and exhaling and blinking just to communicate.

He'd only lost a leg. And a partial one at that. And so what if he'd been burned? He'd kept most of his fingers, his mobility. And God had spared his face.

"Howdy, Coach. I'm Caleb Knight. I'm trying out for . . . well, your job." He wasn't sure—was he supposed to shake his hand? It lay limp beside Presley's body. He grabbed a chair. "Do you mind if I sit down?"

The man had Issy's eyes. Or rather, Issy had his eyes, gray-blue and deep and looking inside him even as he smiled. He could trace Issy's sculptured face, too, the edge of a tough jaw, despite the folds of skin around Presley's neck.

"Go ahead . . . son." Presley's voice emerged from a distance, as if trapped inside his body, and it died at the end. He hadn't considered the man's inability to talk. Caleb glanced at Dan.

"Because of his trach, he can only talk as the ventilator expels the air from his lungs. So it has to be short and sweet. And he can't modulate his voice, so you might have to lean close to hear him."

Caleb scooted up his chair. "I just wanted to come by and introduce myself. I, uh . . . I know I can never take your place, but I wanted to tell you that I'll do my best for the team. You left quite a legacy."

The ventilator drew the air from Coach's lungs. "Meet my daughter?"

Caleb glanced at Dan.

"I mentioned you two were neighbors," Dan said.

"Yes. I have. She's, uh, a very pretty girl." Oh, good grief; he sounded like he might be in high school.

The coach's gaze moved to Dan, and he smiled. For a second, Caleb saw a spark of the coach who had heralded his team to state championship glory—tough, smart, and savvy.

"I recapped this week of practice for him, filled him in on the little competition the town has going on," Dan said. "I hope it's okay—I told him about lunch on Sunday. I'm glad you made it by."

The respirator made a round as Caleb wiped his hands on his pant legs.

"Where are you from?"

"Southern Minnesota. Played running back for a small town. We won our state championship for our division."

"College scholarship?"

"No. I . . ." He glanced again at Dan. "I was fast, but I wasn't the big leagues. I would have barely gotten off the bench for Ohio State. So I found a college that let me play and taught me the fundamentals of coaching. I got my degree in teaching there—psychology. My dream has always been to coach high school football."

His leg had begun to ache and now he longed to put it up, straight, on a chair. "The National Guard helped foot the bill for college, so I went to Iraq straight after. I had planned to finish my commitment, then come back and find a school where I could coach."

Coach waited until his ventilator wheezed the breath out. "Get hurt there?"

Had he been rubbing his leg too much? Caleb eased back in his chair, folded his hands. Coach might be just the man to whom Caleb could tell his secrets. But what if the old coach rooted for Brewster?

Despite the concern in the man's eyes, and with Dan sitting here, Caleb ducked the truth of his injury. "I did. But it doesn't interfere with my coaching."

Coach considered him, and Caleb looked away. Dan too wore a strange expression.

Finally, "You want to help my team?"

It was the longest sentence yet, and it spilled out almost as a gasp, desperation in his tone.

"Yes, actually. Yes." Caleb sat up and leaned forward. "I really do. I've always wanted to coach a small-town team, like mine. I want to help mold boys into honorable and courageous young men, and football is a great way to do that. I hope to lead the Huskies to a state championship. Or three." Nothing fake about his smile this time.

Coach nodded, blinked, and from his eye, moisture dribbled down his cheek. Caleb's own therapist back at Walter Reed warned him that trauma injuries could weaken a man's emotional threshold. Caleb himself could tear up at a Hallmark movie. Still, the coach's emotions made him turn away.

Dan still wore that strange expression. Like he and Coach Presley shared an inside secret. "Coach here has been praying for someone like you for a long time, Caleb," he said. "A very long time."

10

A person shouldn't be allowed to grill while his neighbor worked in the yard. Especially when Issy still had a bed of pansies to deadhead before she could go in, grab a flimsy grilled cheese sandwich, and hang out in the forum for an hour or two before her show. That always gave the ratings a boost—Miss Foolish Heart's appearance on the message boards.

She needed her online friends after today's grilling from Rachelle. Say hello? Stop thinking about what the town thought of her, how to make her world safe? Rachelle made everything sound so easy. Try living with her memories and see how safe the world felt.

Her stomach growled. Issy tried to ignore the aroma, as well as the country twang lifting over the fence into her yard, followed by Duncan's excited barking.

Figures the dog preferred Coach Knight-in-Shining-Armor to her. She only fed him donuts. She'd seen the coach feed him a couple burgers. Cheater.

She'd bet BoyNextDoor wasn't a dog stealer. Okay, fine, so her neighbor hadn't actually stolen his own dog from her, but Duncan had spent the day in her shade, on her porch, eating her left-overs.

BoyNextDoor probably had his own dog. Something pedestrian and well behaved. A miniature schnauzer or a poodle. Even a collie. Named . . . maybe Frank. Or Harold. Something all-American.

She threw the dead flowers into her compost bin and gave it a stir. The odor made her turn away, toward the scent of dinner.

Maybe tonight BoyNextDoor was outside,

throwing a Frisbee to his collie named Frank, after making a flank steak. And a nice arugula salad with pine nuts and raspberry vinaigrette. Maybe he was sitting on his front steps, waving to the neighbor in his suburb of . . . Chicago? Maybe Grayslake? Or Schaumburg?

In some strange way, knowing that Coach Knight was grilling hamburgers on the other side of the fence and playing with his dog stirred an almost-sweet warmth in her stomach.

Sort of like how she felt when Lucy showed up after work to chat.

Or a picnic on the front porch.

Or when she logged online, found her favorite people in the forum, or on the phone line. What if BoyNextDoor came on the show tonight?

See, this was why she shouldn't date. If she looked forward to seeing online or hearing the voice of a man she'd never formally met—a man whose real name she didn't even know—how could she be trusted to remain calm and keep her head around a man she actually liked *and* met in person?

Not that she liked BoyNextDoor. No, she just wanted to watch her ratings spike again. Every time he called in, activity exploded on her forum boards. Better, online memberships had nearly doubled this week over last.

BoyNextDoor was simply good for *My Foolish Heart.*

Most of all, he wasn't a living, breathing soul who could watch her unravel right before his eyes.

Even if that soul did . . . clean up.

She'd snagged a look at Coach Knight climbing out of his pickup earlier and something inside her simply . . . stopped. He looked . . .

Well, what was the man doing in Deep Haven? With that tan, chiseled jaw, his beard clipped to a smart goatee, wearing khakis—he probably had a meeting with the school board or the bank.

Still, he was certainly no BoyNextDoor. BoyNextDoor would be trying to find ways to meet the girl of his dreams. Make her smile.

Ask her out on a date.

She reached in past the thick, spiny stalks of her rugosa to yank the last of the weeds from the soil. "Ow!"

Watch those wild roses, honey. They have a bite.

Her mother's voice sank into her mind, a bitter warning that could bring tears to her eyes. She dropped the weeds into the bucket.

The sun had risen, hot, unforgiving, the breeze barely tempering that Labor Day weekend.

"I know how to weed a garden, Mother. I just don't know why we have to get up at the crack of dawn on the last day of my vacation."

Her mother had leaned back, her face shaded by a garden hat, and wiped her tanned arm across her brow. "I just wanted to spend more time with you before you left. We never see you anymore. I miss you."

After all these years, her mother still spoke with an accent, one that suggested she'd lived life in some exotic location. Indeed, had her father not played football in Italy, he and Gabriella would have never met.

"I miss you too, Mama," Issy had replied. Only, well, the two years since college graduation had felt a little like flying. Issy had poured herself into her journalism degree and landed a job at a cable station in Duluth, writing scripts and working as a producer. But what she really wanted was to be in front of the camera, doing a talk show about current issues. Books. Movies. Even, if she had to, sports.

"You'll be back for homecoming?"

Issy moved away from the roses to pinch the dead buds of the pansies into the bucket. "I'll try."

She didn't have to turn to see her mother's lips press together in a tight, hold-her-tongue line.

"I just don't love Deep Haven like you do, Mama. It's so small. Everyone knows everyone."

"That's the charm, honey. But perhaps you'll come home for your father's game, not the town."

Her mother didn't play fair. Yes, she would do anything for her father, including driving home three hours for a Friday night football game. Especially now that his championship team had graduated.

Indeed, she loved football too. Loved to watch him stalk the sideline. Loved to listen to him coach his players. Even loved his Thursday night burger and ice cream parties in her mother's backyard, the game of touch football in the front yard.

"I'll try."

"Good. Come here and smell these Pilgrim roses." Her mother snipped off a bloom, held it out to Issy.

"You're not taking them all off, are you?"

"I'm pruning them down so they'll produce more blooms."

"Ouch."

"Yes, but I promise, it'll come back fuller." She had stood, kissed her daughter on her forehead, leaving Issy standing in the sunlight, a line of sweat dribbling down her back.

Her mother hadn't lived to see how the roses bloomed again, double in size.

"Roger! Come back here!"

Issy heard a thump next to her and turned to see a football stuck in her burning bush. "Hey!"

A second later, Duncan blasted into a loose board in her father's impenetrable fence. He wiggled his beefy body through the opening and plowed head-first into the burning bush, emerging with the football in his mouth.

"Duncan!" Issy stood. The dog trotted over. Peered up at her, then dropped the football at her feet. Spittle and slime slid off the brown hide. He backed away, his tail wagging.

"I'm not throwing that."

"Please?"

She looked over, at the escape hatch. Her now-groomed neighbor had stuck his head through the fence.

"At least I know how he got into my yard."

Coach Knight made a face. "I promise, I had nothing to do with this."

She picked up the football, ignoring the slime, glad she wore gardening gloves. "And this?"

"Sorry. My throw got off. It bounced on the fence and angled into your yard." He glanced at the dog. "C'mere, Roger."

Roger? The dog so did not look like a Roger. "Duncan. We call him Duncan over here."

"We? You and your hosta?"

"They've earned the right, I think."

He grinned, and for a second, she felt her heartbeat in her chest. She lined her fingers up against the laces.

"Uh . . . do you want a burger? It's my brother's secret recipe. Herb butter in the middle."

Her stomach roared. Traitor. "Oh . . . uh, no thanks. I have to get to work."

"On a Friday night?"

"Yeah, actually. I work from home. But . . . maybe . . ." She swallowed, pushing the words out fast. "I'll take a rain check?" She added a smile. No need to break his heart, right?

"Rain check it is."

She held out the ball.

He stuck his hand through the fence. "Pitch it to me."

Pitch it to me, Issy! For a second, her father stood there, his hand outstretched. *You take the hike from Mom, then pitch it to me. No law says a girl can't play quarterback.*

She had a great throw—always did.

She considered Caleb, then waved him off. "Go long, neighbor."

He gave her the oddest look before disappearing.

She fired it over the fence, wishing she knew whether he caught it.

"It's your lucky day, Rog. Or I guess it's Duncan?" Caleb crouched in front of the dog and slid him the plate of leftover burgers. He'd slapped two extra on the grill . . .

Just in case.

Apparently he couldn't tempt Isadora with the smell of ground beef cooking over an open flame. Or a game of catch.

Although, admittedly, she had a nice spiral. He'd nearly caught it, too, but avoiding the potholes in his yard slowed him down and he opted to let it bounce rather than dive for it, land on his face.

She didn't check on him, however, so he

might not fess up that he hadn't caught it.

At this rate, he'd be better off dating Miss Foolish Heart than trying to make friends with his neighbor. He even caught himself thinking about Miss Foolish Heart, her show, her voice in his ear . . .

Except her methods simply didn't work.

He patted the dog on the head, climbed the stairs, and sat on the back steps, his residual leg stretched out on the top step, the pressure easing as he ate. He could go for fries, maybe a chocolate shake.

And someone with whom to enjoy dinner.

Next door, he heard her gate latch. He should fix that broken fencing, but . . .

Coach here has been praying for someone like you for a long time. He put his hamburger on the plate, his appetite gone.

More than anything, seeing a man like Presley —a man so much like the person he wanted to be—taken out, sidelined . . . it could turn Caleb's bones to liquid.

God had spilled out more than his share of mercy on him that night in the ditch.

What if he'd been sent here not just to help the team, but Coach's daughter, too?

Caleb got up, wishing he could see her from his porch, but the fence blocked the view. He'd have to climb upstairs, but that felt too much like spying.

How did he coax a woman trapped inside her own fears out into the world? He threw his burger to Roger, who caught it in the air, before hobbling into the house, where he lowered himself onto the sofa, worked the suction seal away from his leg, and eased out of the prosthesis. When—okay, *if*—he got the coaching job, and once people knew about his injury, he'd switch to his athletic prosthesis, one that allowed him better flexibility to move and cut and even run, even if it did expose his disability with the metal compression foot.

Until then, he had to prove himself with two supposedly good feet.

He settled his leg on the sofa, the daily burn already lessening. Lying against the arm of the sofa, he just wanted to throw his arm over his eyes.

Nope. He still had plays to work out for Monday's practice. And his limb exercises to do, and his prosthesis to clean, and . . .

What he really wanted to do was talk to Miss Foolish Heart. See if she had any brilliant ideas for cracking his neighbor's thick shell.

Reaching over, he hauled his computer onto his lap. Maybe he could dig around that forum.

He logged on, ignored the welcome page full of crazy literary quotes, then clicked on the discussion tab.

Three hundred posts since his argument with

Miss Foolish Heart. Didn't these people have anything better to do?

Still, the speculation over his mystery girl had him smiling.

She's probably his boss and he is just trying to get a promotion.

He broke her heart years ago and now wants to win it back.

I think he's shy. I want his number.

Good thing these things remained anonymous.

On a few of the posts, Miss Foolish Heart herself had replied.

Would she show up if he started his own discussion?

He clicked on the Start a Discussion tab and named it "How to Get the Girl." Pressing Enter before he could change his mind, he immediately wanted to delete it. But there it appeared, on the front page of the forum.

It felt a little like standing out in the rain in his skivvies.

How did he delete? He clicked on Help. A list of options popped up and he chose FAQs. Discussions could only be deleted by the administrator.

Perfect.

But when he scrolled down, he discovered the

Privacy settings. He went back to the discussion page, and since he'd started it, it allowed him to set it to private.

Good.

Except how was he supposed to get any advice? A screen popped up. *MissFoolishHeart would like to add to your discussion. Will you allow?* Would he allow? He clicked Okay.

Her daisy avatar popped up on his discussion.

MissFoolishHeart: Hello, BoyNextDoor. Do you need help?

Caleb stared at the screen, the blinking cursor.

MissFoolishHeart: I'm sorry; am I intruding? I see you made the discussion private. I just wanted to see if you needed help.

Help, oh, did he need help, because suddenly all the moisture had sucked out of his mouth and his hands turned slick.

BoyNextDoor: Hi. Yes, I need help.

MissFoolishHeart: I'm not a technical wizard, but I am an administrator, so I can try.

BoyNextDoor: Well, I mostly need help with . . . how do you get a girl to go out on a date?

MissFoolishHeart: Ask her.

He made a face. Yeah, the idiot meter went into the red with him sometimes.

BoyNextDoor: No, I mean, so far your advice hasn't exactly worked.

He stared at the blinking cursor. Oops. He wasn't sure how this online communication worked, but he hadn't said it with his angry voice. Just a fact.

MissFoolishHeart: I'm sorry to hear that. Are you sure she's not involved with anyone else? She could be sending you the go-away signals.

Isadora . . . and a boyfriend? Surely her father would know. And he hadn't exactly seen a guy.

BoyNextDoor: I think she's single.

MissFoolishHeart: And you've followed all my advice?

Wow, that sounded like a woman.

BoyNextDoor: Yes. To the letter. I even shaved.

MissFoolishHeart: Oh, BoyNextDoor, don't go overboard now.

Funny, real funny.

BoyNextDoor: The thing is, she needs a friend, and I thought I might ask her on a date.

MissFoolishHeart: So she needs a date? That's fairly arrogant.

BoyNextDoor: I didn't mean it like that. But I met her father, and I think he'd like me to get to know her.

MissFoolishHeart: This is just getting worse. Her father? What, are you Amish? Is this an arranged marriage?

Oh, how he wanted to hear her voice, because in his head, she was laughing.

BoyNextDoor: No! Of course not. It's just that she hasn't had many dates recently.

MissFoolishHeart: Why?

BoyNextDoor: She's sorta disabled.

That word didn't seem to fit, but he couldn't figure out another. The cursor blinked.

MissFoolishHeart: I feel terrible. Please forgive me.

BoyNextDoor. I should have taken your concerns more seriously.

Her tone caught him, made him settle back into the pillow. As if she truly cared.

BoyNextDoor: It's no big deal. I just want to get to know her better. There's something special about her. And I want to figure out what that is.

MissFoolishHeart: I knew there was something I liked about you. What about this girl catches your interest?

What did he like about Issy?
He had to let the cursor blink a moment. He liked the way she had rubbed Duncan's head, as if she cared about the dog, despite his destruction to her hosta.

BoyNextDoor: She can forgive.

MissFoolishHeart: That's a good trait.

His gaze fell on the yearbook.

BoyNextDoor: She loves her town and her neighbors.

MissFoolishHeart: So she's friendly.

He had a feeling she liked football—after all, the way she threw that pass spoke of a girl who knew her way around a football, wasn't afraid to get her hands dirty. And she loved her garden, whereas he could kill plants with a look.

BoyNextDoor: Most of all, I think she could be someone I want to know. But currently, that's all I got.

MissFoolishHeart: That's not much to work with. Why is this so important to you?

Why?

BoyNextDoor: Because I was given a second chance to be the kind of man I should be, and I am not a quitter. I like to finish what I start.

Like learning to walk again. And turning the town football mess into a winning team.

And proving to God that He'd made the right decision in saving Caleb's life.

MissFoolishHeart: Be careful—she still sounds like a project.

209

A project. Sometimes *he* felt like a project. But, no. How about an . . . incentive?

BoyNextDoor: What if she's the prize?

The cursor blinked for a long moment.

MissFoolishHeart: BoyNextDoor, you're lucky; I just about banned you with the "she needs a date" comment. Okay, time to get creative. You could ask her to share a picnic—maybe a pizza. Or better, spaghetti. That's easy and nonthreatening.

BoyNextDoor: I'm not sure she eats spaghetti.

MissFoolishHeart: Everyone likes spaghetti. What's not to like? Also, most girls like it when the men in their lives show an interest in the things they like. Does she have any interests?

BoyNextDoor: She likes yard work. And exercising.

MissFoolishHeart: Perfect. Strap on your tennis shoes and go ask her to play a game of tennis. Or take a walk by the beach. Or even throw around a football.

Throw around a football?

He liked Miss Foolish Heart much more than he should. And the fact that she assumed he could do any of those activities . . .

For a moment, he tasted the days before his injury, the easy ones when someone called to him from the end of the hall, "Caleb! Let's play some catch!"

Miss Foolish Heart saw him as whole.

And in that delicious moment, he did too.

BoyNextDoor: Thanks, MissFoolishHeart. I'll try that.

MissFoolishHeart: Good luck, BoyNextDoor. She's lucky to have you.

Shoot, BoyNextDoor had signed off, and watching him go, Issy tried—oh, she tried—not to hate the Girl.

What kind of girl had *she* become that she got jealous over unknown—and taken—voices in her discussion forum?

The entire conversation had her confused even as she picked up her grilled cheese sandwich and walked downstairs.

She heard whining at the door, opened it to find Duncan sitting on the porch, his dark shaggy tail swishing on the boards. "I'm not sure why you even bother to whine. Why don't you just come through the cardboard?" But she let him in and fed him the last of her sandwich.

He gulped it down as if he hadn't eaten in a decade. Then he lay on the floor, rolling over for a rub.

"And by the way, we need to talk about the destruction of my fence." She let loose a smile at the image of her own boy next door, following his dog into her yard.

What if he'd caught her pass?

What if he hadn't?

She rubbed a bare foot over the dog's chest. "I have to go to work. If you promise to keep my feet warm, you can join me."

Duncan followed her upstairs.

BoyNextDoor hadn't returned to the forum. Probably out lacing up his running shoes. Except if the Girl was disabled, she might not be able to run, so she'd given him lousy advice . . . again.

What kind of man didn't even notice, or care, about a woman's disability?

The kind of man she'd like to know.

The sun had already sunk out of sight, dusk scuttling around the yard. She switched off her porch light and looked out the window, then checked the lock on the front door before climbing the stairs.

Her neighbor's light glowed into the yard.

She can forgive.

Those words lingered, nudged her. Forgive. Had

she forgiven her neighbor? For . . . what? Annoying her? Not cutting his grass?

Invading her world and making her stare at her vacancies? Her limitations?

She stopped on the stairs, her hand on the rail.

Ever since he'd moved to town, careened into her life, something had unhinged inside her. As if her world had slipped just a little out of her control.

He reminded her of her town, her people. Her father.

Her loss.

Caleb reminded her of all the ways she let them down. All the ways she was locked inside her fear, all the ways she'd failed.

She sat on the stairs, staring out the transom of her door. The narrow strip revealed the Millers' house across the street and the far edge of the library. Beyond that, the view captured the spire of the lighthouse at the point, the glow over the dark expanse of the lake. But her world seemed, suddenly, about that size—a peek out her door, the edges cut off, only glimpses remaining into the real world.

Oh, God, how did I get here? The coach's crazy daughter, afraid of the world?

She pressed the meat of her hands into her eyes and heard Rachelle's voice. *Maybe you shouldn't strive to be the woman you left behind, but the one who is out ahead. . . . I'd bet if you stop trying so hard to hold her back, to keep her safe, she might just surprise you.*

Oh, she had her doubts. Just imagine her, out on a date. She'd end up under the table in the fetal position. *Sorry, but can you take me home?*

Nope, nope, nope.

Caleb only made that wound ache, too.

He made her want to fall in love. Or at least make a friend.

She still sounds like she's a project.

Had she really written that? Could she be ruder? But it had bothered her, BoyNextDoor's fascination with his Girl. He seemed to know so little about her. She was *friendly?* Hardly an intriguing attribute on which to base an attraction.

She'd nearly written that, nearly flirted with him, nearly tried to get him to forget about this Girl and perhaps stay on the forum and talk to her . . . and then . . .

What if she's the prize?

Issy buried her face in her knees. See, that was what made the BoyNextDoor so . . . devastating.

He was the perfect catch.

But she'd never be the prize. Not for BoyNext-Door, not for Caleb, not for anyone.

11

All these years, Seb had believed that Lucy's family rolled in the dough.

He smirked at his own pun, but really, looking at her chart of accounts, he shouldn't be laughing.

Lucy hung on to World's Best Donuts by a thin . . . well, scrap. And with his very meager business skills, he couldn't figure a way to get her out of her financial mess.

It didn't help that she leaned over the Formica table, watching him scratch out numbers, her eyes on his work as if he might do magic. "Okay, Seb. Give it to me straight."

Outside, gulls dive-bombed the shore, searching for leftovers from the Saturday picnickers. A toddler in a saggy diaper stood at the edge of the water, letting the waves run over her sandals. She jumped back, then scampered up to her parents. A larger man with cropped curly hair swung her over his head.

"Just so I get this right, your parents didn't actually own the building."

"No, they rented it. Our family had a fifty-year lease, and it ran out four years ago. So I bought the building."

"Which is why you're having trouble making payments."

"Yeah. The building alone I could handle. The taxes on the shoreline property . . ." She shook her head. "That's why I need to move more donuts."

He hid another smile. Everything she said over the past three days had elicited a sort of crazy smile. Even at practice, he found himself grinning.

It made for ineffective drills. Good thing Bam and the gang showed up to whip his boys into shape.

Sort of. They certainly weren't the championship team. Michaels could hardly keep the ball out of the snap, let alone hand it off. And Samson never ended up in the right place, let alone grabbing his sophomore quarterback's end-over-ends.

Seb banked on Coach's magic plays to save the day. If they could get two, even three down . . .

"Seb?"

Oops. He did that too, with her. Drifted off to a happier time, when he could still hear the cheers. "I was thinking about football practice."

"How's it going?"

"Okay. Bam and DJ are out there every day after work. And the guys like hearing about Coach Presley."

"You should go up and see him sometime."

Seb blinked at her. "Go . . . Oh, I don't think so."

"Why not? He needs visitors. I try and visit a couple times a month. I'm sort of a physical link

216

for him and Issy. I know he'd love to see you."

"No, I don't think he would." He looked away from the confusion on her face. "I didn't live up to his hopes for me."

"Oh, Seb, c'mon. You blew out your shoulder. That was hardly your fault."

"I quit, Lucy." He let the words simply burst out, fast and hard.

She grew still across from him. "What?"

"I . . . walked away. After my injury, I sat the bench for half the year. Then at preseason practice, my coach told me that I wasn't going to start junior year, that the sophomore quarterback behind me had outplayed my position, jockeyed me out of starting. I lost my temper. I turned into my old man and just walked off the field."

"You gave up your scholarship."

"Yeah. Dumbest thing I ever did. And wouldn't you know it, Coach Presley got wind of it and called me."

"What did he say?"

"He said that I could get back in the game if I wanted to. That the man with heart could accomplish anything. But I didn't have heart. I had anger. And fear, I guess."

Lucy slid her hand over his, held it. He looked at her small hand and didn't know if he had the right to close his around it.

"What were you afraid of?" she said softly.

"I don't know. Maybe sitting the bench. Maybe

217

working harder than I ever had and not playing another second of football. Maybe letting myself down."

"So instead of failing, you quit."

"I sat there during the first home game, in my dorm room, and just kept reliving all those jobs my dad lost or quit, all those times I listened to my mother and father fighting, how many times she threatened to leave, until she finally did." He took a breath. "I kept remembering how many times he crawled home, so sloshed out of his head that he didn't even recognize me, and I knew that just like him, I had flushed my life. Knew that I had destroyed any hope of playing pro ball."

He sighed, waited for her to let go. But she didn't. In fact, she squeezed his hand. "But you're back. You're not a quitter. You got your degree, and you're here."

He was here. Yes.

She drew in a breath. "Seb . . . why did you come back?"

Why had he come back? He'd fought it for years, really, until he got his diploma. Until he'd heard about Coach's accident. Until he lost his job as a clerk in a sports store and read over the Internet about the math job opening. Then something clicked inside, something that tasted of redemption.

Something that he'd known he should have done all along.

"I thought that since it all started here, I might be able to go back to the beginning, to reset my life. Get it on the right track."

She met his gaze, and for a second, he saw her wide eyes as he woke to her staring at him, his arms around Bree in the backseat of his Pontiac. Words escaped him—then and now.

But she rescued him like she always did.

"That's why you want to coach."

She was smiling, and it felt like forgiveness.

"Yes. I guess a part of me thinks that if I can get the team back on track, maybe get them to a championship, then . . ."

"You'll be the town hero again." Her words emerged gentle, almost . . . kind.

"Is that terrible?"

"I think it's honest. And maybe you wouldn't be a man if you didn't want victory again."

Her kindness could truly stop his heart in his chest. He swallowed, tried to smile.

But he couldn't because the look she gave him had not a hint of pity or disgust. Not a twinge of regret or even pain. Just . . . a smile.

His mouth opened without his permission. "I thought of you all the time after I left Deep Haven."

Her smile vanished. Biting her lip, she looked away. "Oh."

He reached out to take her hand. "I . . . Did I ever say that I was sorry?"

She looked at his hand holding hers. "Probably. But thank you anyway." She drew in a long breath. "It's no big deal."

No big deal? It felt like a big deal. The hurt on her face had tunneled inside him, found him every time he took a girl back to his dorm room, reminded him that he was a jerk.

"I am sorry, Lucy, for hurting you. And I'm going to figure out a way to get your shop back in the black. I promise you, you're not going to lose it."

"And you're going to land the coaching job, Seb. I believe in you." She looked up then with that smile, and everything dropped away. There was just Lucy, the sunshine in her eyes, and he couldn't stop himself.

He leaned forward, now really holding her hand, and kissed her.

She didn't move at first, not at all, and he froze, stuck in that position, over the table.

Feeling like an idiot.

Then she wove her hand around his neck and kissed him back. Sweetly, with the taste of sugar and coffee on her lips. *Lucy.* How he remembered her touch, her taste. Nothing had ever been so right as when he'd been her guy.

Maybe this time he could do it right.

Caleb Knight stood in the yard, spraying his glorious white stallion with a garden hose.

The magnificent truck had endured an entire

three days without a wash, and Issy definitely saw a smudge around a rear wheel panel. Oh *no*.

Issy ran past Caleb, averting her eyes, but not quick enough to miss his long-sleeved black shirt outlining his football physique as he sprayed the truck's roof, then aimed the hose at Duncan. The dog veered away from tailing her on her run to lunge at and bite the water. She paused her iPod in time to hear Caleb laughing.

He had a solid, deep, and reverberating laugh, one that tremored her insides.

Next time around, she'd say hello. She started her music again, turned at the end of the sidewalk, and ran up the block. Seven times around; she had one more to go. Eight times around the block equaled two miles—her father had clocked it back in high school. Eight times around, nineteen minutes of freedom. And if she didn't say hello this time around, she might go two more.

He couldn't have waited until after her run to wash his car?

She rounded the corner, ran along the next block, parallel to her house, passing Lucy's.

She could always make a quick escape through their backyards.

Say hello; say hello.

Lucy's front yard could use some cleaning up, the bed weeded, the roses cut back, the lawn mowed. But Lucy barely saw it in the light of day, poor girl.

Issy turned at the next street, headed south. Funny that she hadn't seen Lucy for two days— although she'd left donuts on the front porch like some sort of May Day basket and a scribbled note that said, *I'll call.*

But she hadn't. And Saturdays were always her most chaotic. Poor woman was probably working overtime; otherwise she would have stopped by long before this.

Coach Knight had the chamois out, rubbing down his gallant steed, as she turned back onto their street. He glanced up as she passed him and stopped to take her pulse while running in place at her walk.

Out of the corner of her eye, she saw him move her direction.

Oh . . . no . . .

But she looked up at him, pulled out her earbuds.

"Hi, neighbor," he said, wiping his hands on the chamois cloth. "Isadora, right?"

Oh, she didn't want to know how . . . She swallowed, found a smile, too much teeth. "Hello."

"I met your father. Pastor Dan is helping me coach, and he introduced us."

She glanced at the house. Caleb's words bit at her, just a little. What had her father told him?

"I thought maybe I could come by and fix the fence? You know, where Rog—I mean, Duncan busted through?"

Maybe her father *hadn't* said anything, because nothing in his eyes communicated a curiosity, a *so this is the hermit* kind of perusal.

He waited for a response. She dug deep for her voice. "I guess that would be okay." Coach Knight, in her yard? She took a breath. Glanced again at her house. Duncan had sprawled in a spot of shadow on her porch.

"How about around dinnertime? I need to finish cleaning my car, and then . . . I could also fix your back door."

"My door?" Her words seemed to just burp out. How did he know about the door?

He seemed to read her thoughts because he lowered his voice to something soft and even conspiratorial and said, those dangerous eyes on hers, "Lucy over at the donut shop ratted out our pal Duncan this morning." Then he winked.

Maybe it was the combination of the voice, the wink, the way the wind blew his scent her direction—something rich and spicy—that nudged something familiar inside her. Something sweet and not at all terrifying.

Something she wanted to lean into.

She wanted to like him. Wanted to let him into her yard to fix the fence, fix the door. Wanted to be the kind of woman who might smile back, might invite him over for . . .

"And while I'm over, how about if I bring along a pizza? Or take-out Chinese?"

223

"We don't have take-out Chinese in Deep Haven." Her voice emerged so small, she couldn't be sure she'd even spoken. She drew in a quick breath. Swallowed.

"That's okay," he said quietly, his eyes still holding hers. "I love pizza; don't you?"

"Uh . . . well . . ." She swallowed again, found a boulder lodged in her throat. Took a step. "I'd rather have spaghetti," she said—or thought she said.

"Spaghetti. Okay." A smile curved up his face. "I'll see what I can cook up. How about five-ish?"

She tried a smile, but it felt like she might be catching flies, her lips drying. She took another step.

"Is that a yes?" Again that soft voice, and it sounded so . . . familiar. As if she might know it, as if he'd already spent time in her thoughts.

Was it a yes? She drew in a long breath and pressed her hand against her stomach. "Yes. Mmm-hmm." She nodded too, in case she wasn't communicating, because in her state, who really knew?

But apparently something had emerged from her knotted chest because his smile returned. "I'll see you at five then, Isadora."

"Issy. Call me Issy." That, she heard. He whistled to Duncan, who rose and trotted down the steps.

Then he glanced at her, still wearing that warm smile. "See you later, Issy."

She made it into the house before she realized . . .

She had a date. A real date.

Two giant steps forward in a single bound.

"Issy, you're not going to believe what happened!"

As Lucy closed the door behind her, she listened for Issy's reply in the quiet house. The radio chatted upstairs, a low hum of voices, but otherwise the house seemed still.

She headed down the hall, through the house to the back door, opened it. "Issy—!"

No one in the garden.

She turned, ran down the hall, checking in the parlor. No Issy.

"Where are you?"

She listened over the thunder of her heartbeat, then scrambled up the stairs.

Issy's office door stood ajar, but in the other room she heard a thump. She pushed open the door to Issy's parents' room.

What on earth . . . ? Issy stood in the center of the room wearing her prom dress, her earbuds in, playing the air guitar.

She caught sight of Lucy in the mirror and froze. Turned. Pulled out her buds. "Hi."

"What are you doing?"

"What happened?"

They stood a moment, then—

"I asked you first." Lucy pushed into the room. Issy had washed the bedspread—it bore no scars from Duncan's nesting. But what looked like Issy's entire wardrobe littered the bed. Jeans and sweaters, blouses, two dresses, and probably eight pairs of heeled sandals and pumps. She even saw a couple suits, one of which still dangled the tag.

Lucy picked it up, then sat on the bed on top of a pair of jeans. "Having a rummage sale?"

Issy grinned—a sort of grin Lucy might assign to a mental patient. It ran all over the place, dipping, rising. In fact, it might not be a grin but rather a new form of panic. "Are you okay?"

"I . . . I have a date." The words emerged more question than statement, but Issy turned away, smoothing the prom dress, staring at her reflection. "I. Have. A date."

"Really? With whom?"

"The neighbor."

"Coach Knight?"

"Yes." Issy's eyes widened and she nodded. "I have a date with Coach Knight."

"Okay, listen, are you having some sort of low blood sugar attack? I know I haven't been around for a couple days, but you're acting weird."

Issy smiled and Lucy saw her friend return. "I'm just getting used to it before I start panicking over what to wear."

"Please tell me you aren't wearing your prom dress?"

"Note that it still fits me."

"You're amazing. I'll send your name into *Woman's Day* magazine. However, I'm thinking Coach Knight might make a break for it if you show up in your prom dress."

Issy slipped the dress off, let it puddle on the floor, grabbed her bathrobe. "I wasn't going to wear it. I was looking for the right pair of shoes and found it in my mother's closet. And then, well, she has the full-length mirror . . ."

"Why did you turn your room into the studio instead of the guest room downstairs?"

"I like the view of Deep Haven. And my mother's garden."

"You should move in here, you know. Your dad is never coming home."

Issy took a breath, and Lucy instantly wanted to grab her words back. "I didn't mean that. I'm sorry."

"You did, and you're right." Issy picked up the suit, the one with the tag. But her hand shook. "I bought this for the interview at KQRD. I never wore it." She hung it in her mother's closet. "Tell me what your big news is."

So many wounds, little nicks that still bled as Issy walked through every day. But if Issy wanted to change the subject . . . "Seb kissed me."

"What? Seb *Brewster?*"

Oops. Lucy hadn't quite meant for the announcement to tumble out like that. She'd meant to go at it slowly, to prepare Issy. *Seb Brewster is helping me save the donut shop. Seb Brewster kissed me. . . .*

No, she should back up even more. "I've been meeting with Seb the past two nights. We've been sorting out the finances of the donut shop so I could get a loan."

"So it was Seb you met the other night?"

"Yeah, I couldn't believe it. He took business in college. He's teaching math at the school, and . . . oh!" She stared at Issy. "He and Caleb are vying for the same job. It's all over town. They're having a big scrimmage next Friday to see who's going to be the new coach."

"You met Caleb?"

"Today. He came into the shop and introduced himself."

"You told him about the door."

"Should I be sorry?"

Issy smiled. Then, "Wait—so Caleb and Seb are both going to be coaching?"

"I think it's a competition. Seb has all the old Huskies out coaching his team. They're running their old plays, the ones they can remember."

Issy sat on the bed, began folding the debris. "Poor Caleb. I hope he has help."

"Pastor Dan is helping him. And according to Seb, Caleb has a coaching degree. He's teaching psychology at the high school. I've already seen posters around town advertising the scrimmage."

"I remember it being a big deal even when my dad was coaching. All the boosters, the parents, most of the community came out to watch the guys play, gauge their potential."

"After the last two years, we need a little enthusiasm for Husky football."

Issy held up a black sweater before pulling it on. "I wonder if my dad knows."

"And which one he'd choose."

Issy grabbed a pair of jeans.

"Is that it, your outfit for your date?"

"Not so fast. We're still talking about you. And Seb. You *kissed* him?"

Lucy reached for a sweater, folding it on her lap. "I did. It sort of just happened. He was there, talking about his dad and why he quit football, and then suddenly, he kissed me." She smiled, remembering the look in his eyes as he drew away, as if he'd knocked over a glass of milk. "I don't think he meant to, but . . . it was like everything reset. As if we started over."

Issy hadn't moved. "Lucy, I don't know. You and Seb . . . there's a lot of pain there."

It's no big deal. Her own words rushed back to her. No big deal. Except she hadn't forgiven herself for betraying everything she believed in since then. And, well, there had been some dark times when she gave in to her wounds and went searching for comfort. No big deal.

I am sorry, Lucy, for hurting you. This time,

229

seeing the honesty in his eyes, she believed him. And if she hadn't forgiven him before, she did now.

Lucy reached for another sweater. "I think it can be different this time."

"You're stronger. Smarter."

"And he's different. Humbler. And sweet. He really wants to help me, too. I think I can save the donut shop."

"I thought you hated donuts." Issy smirked.

Lucy had a nice pile of clothing growing. "I can't lose the donut shop. It's been in my family for three generations. Besides, I'm changing the world, one donut at a time, right?"

"And I'm changing the world one foolish heart at a time."

"Hey, if God can use me one donut at a time, then He can use you, even trapped in your home. You would've never started the show if you hadn't been here. And think of the people you're helping."

"Oh, right. I haven't a clue what I'm doing. Poor BoyNextDoor keeps trying out all my ideas, and apparently the Girl won't even talk to him."

"She will. There's nothing more irresistible to a woman than a man who's in love with her."

"Thank you, *Sound of Music*. Sort of."

"My best line. So are you leaving the house for your big date?"

Issy turned away from the window. "No, we're

not going out. He's coming over to fix my fence. And my door."

"Uh . . . not to rain on your parade, but are you sure that's a date, Issy?"

"He's bringing spaghetti."

"Spaghetti. Oh yes, that qualifies."

Issy returned to the pile of clothing. "I can't wear this." She whipped off the sweater, grabbed a brown T-shirt.

"What are you doing?"

"If I wear the sweater, I'm trying too hard. It's too dressy, too full of expectation."

"Do you have expectations?"

"No!" Issy glared at Lucy. "Of course not. It's just . . . spaghetti."

"Mmm-hmm. Yeah, well, the T-shirt screams, 'Hey, dude, go out for a pass.' "

Issy stilled. "Oh . . . I told BoyNextDoor on our chat to play catch with the Girl."

"So?" Lucy riffled through the pile and found a seersucker blouse with short, ruffled sleeves.

"Don't you get it? The boy next door offered to bring me spaghetti."

"You are making no sense."

Issy sat down hard on the bed. "No, it couldn't be him. He said she was disabled. And besides, everybody likes spaghetti."

"*Who* is disabled?"

"The Girl."

"BoyNextDoor is dating a girl with a disability?"

231

Issy took the blouse, then stood and pulled the T-shirt off. "Yes, except he said it didn't matter." She pulled on the blouse, buttoned it. "Isn't that just the kind of guy you'd want to know? A guy who looks at a woman for who she is beyond her handicaps?" She smoothed the shirt.

Oh . . . no. "Issy, you like him."

Issy frowned. "Well, sure, we had a rough beginning, but . . . I said hello today. And he's going to fix my fence—"

"Not Coach Knight—BoyNextDoor. You *like* him."

"No, I don't. He's not . . . real. I mean, he's a voice on the end of the phone line. And yes, we chatted in the forum—"

"You chatted in the forum?"

"That's how I found out about her disability. And I told him to buy her spaghetti."

Huh. "Well, everybody likes spaghetti."

"Of course they do." She went to the bureau, picked up the pearls.

"Definitely not."

She put them down. "I just wish I could find someone who might see me the way BoyNextDoor sees this girl. Who would come into my world . . ."

"And get you."

Issy lifted a shoulder. "Maybe someone who isn't afraid of my world, dark as it is." She looked out the window again. Lucy followed her gaze.

The sun shone against the birch trees that parted their yards.

"Your world's not as dark as it used to be. How many times did you go around the block today?"

"Eight. But I could have done nine." She met Lucy's eyes. "I think."

"I *know*. And I know that there's light ahead. Just keep walking toward it."

12

Did a guy buy a gal who loved to garden . . . flowers? Caleb stood before the rack of potted flowers in the Red Rooster Grocery Store and tried to decide if Issy might like an iris or—he checked the tag on the other pot—chrysanthemums.

What if he brought her something cut? Like the bouquet of pink and white flowers? Or maybe nothing at all? He didn't want to spook her.

But Issy had fueled all sorts of happy, crazy thoughts with the look she gave him over her shoulder as she walked into the house. As if he'd done something right.

Finally.

A part of him couldn't wait to tell Miss Foolish Heart. Only, perhaps he'd wait until *after* the date.

He reached for the iris.

Down the aisle, he heard the tumble of cans. He glanced over, spied the stock boy in a white apron struggling with a box.

Caleb left the flowers and limped over to grab the edge of the falling box and hoist it onto the dolly. "Hate it when those things get away from me." He grinned at the stock boy.

Jared Ryan.

Ryan narrowed his eyes at him, then chased after the scattering cans.

Caleb held the box while the kid tossed them into the container. He predicted a special on dented cans of corn in the store's future. "Go easy there—"

"Don't coach me in my job." Ryan dumped the remaining cans into the box. Grabbing the box with one hand, he started to wheel away.

"You're welcome."

Ryan stopped. Turned, his eyes cold. "I don't even know why you're here, man. What good are you? All we're doing is learning the stuff we learned in fourth grade. We're never going to win with those plays. The draw, the sweep, a reverse —every defense in the state knows those. What we need is something magic, like the stuff the Huskies used to run. Like what Coach Brewster is teaching his team. We're going to lose and we're going to look stupid. We need to outplay those guys or they're going to run over us."

Caleb schooled his voice. "You win with fundamentals. I'd be happy if you boys could even manage the basics. You're so messed up from two years of bad coaching—"

"You're the bad coach. And I don't want to play for you. I'll go play for Brewster."

"Sorry, son, but you can't do that. Brewster's not going to let you play for him."

"He will if he wants to win."

Oh, boy. Caleb hated to think that he might have been this arrogant back in the day. "I thought the flashy plays were what'll make us win."

Ryan glared at him. "If I can't play for Brewster, then forget it. I'll save my energy for hoops. I was an all-conference forward last year. And I ran hurdles in state."

"Perfect. We'll miss you. But don't think that when I'm Huskies head coach, I'm letting you on my team."

"You won't get the job."

A can of corn escaped and clattered to the floor. Caleb bent over and picked it up. He didn't care about the pain that burned through him. He held it out to Ryan.

The kid swiped it from his hand.

"You get one more chance to show up at practice." Caleb turned, ignored the flowers, and walked out.

He got into his truck, staring at the storefront, watching Ryan trundle the corn down the aisle, listening to Ryan's words replay in his head. Fancy plays. No, they didn't need fancy plays— they needed fundamentals. Blocking. Tackling. Rushing.

He closed his eyes, leaned his forehead against the steering wheel.

I promise, I'm doing my best, Lord. But what if his best wasn't good enough?

This morning at the men's Bible study, he'd met a couple guys who he thought might be friends, someday. The local plumber. Joe, a firefighter whose wife ran a bookstore. He had a kid on Brewster's team, too.

Dan had reiterated Sunday's Philippians text about God's provision. God had provided Caleb an opportunity. Now he'd just have to work harder, be smarter, to be a good steward of it.

Caleb blew out a breath, then returned to the store. He avoided Ryan and picked up a box of spaghetti, Italian sausage, and the fixings for his mother's homemade sauce.

He could make a mean spaghetti.

Three hours later, he had his tool belt on and had nailed the loose board in Issy's fence into place.

"Make sure you put a lot of nails in—he's pretty big!"

Issy stood on the porch looking clean and pretty in a white short-sleeved blouse and a pair of jeans. She had a way of making the evening beautiful, with her long brown hair, those freckles over her nose, the way she wandered through her garden, picking flowers.

Good thing he hadn't attempted a bouquet—he might have insulted the spray she'd put on her deck table. Dahlias and roses. That, however, constituted the extent of his flower knowledge, thanks to the limited time he spent in his mother's garden. But it allowed him to sound a little like he knew his stuff when Issy toured him through her masterpiece.

"My mother planted these." She stopped next to a bush of yellow roses. "Pilgrim roses. She loved them." She moved to a V trellis. "But these are mine. Pink climbing tea roses." She smelled one, then held it out toward Caleb.

Yeah, it smelled good. Whatever. But he could stand here with her all night, probably. Because between this afternoon when he'd intercepted her running and tonight, he didn't exactly recognize the girl next door.

Not with the way she'd unlocked her world, invited him in. Whoever she'd become, he liked her. A lot. Liked her easy smile and the way she seemed to relax with him. Liked the way she watched him fix her fence. Liked the way she ran her hand over Roger's mug, tousled his ears.

More, if his radar hadn't completely fried out from lack of use, Issy liked him, too.

She'd finished clearing the table of the spaghetti plates, pouring the last of the lemonade from a glass pitcher. He'd already measured her door for a new pane of glass—he'd stop by the lumberyard tomorrow and see if he could order one. Until then, the cardboard was ingenious.

For the rest of the evening, he'd enjoy the whisper of the wind in the leaves of the birch and poplar, the lavender twilight on his back, the sweet taste of victory.

Miss Foolish Heart and BoyNextDoor had finally won the heart of the Girl—or at least a date with her.

He just had to play this evening correctly, not spook her with conversations of the past, keep it easy and friendly.

He finished driving the last nail into the wood, then slipped the hammer into his belt. Unhooking it, he set it on the porch, easing himself down on the steps.

"Want some more lemonade?"

He nodded.

She came down the steps, handed him the drink, sat beside him.

"That was amazing spaghetti."

"My mother's." He took a drink. He really needed to lay his leg straight. "She would be proud that I remembered how to make it."

She looked at him, a smile creeping up her face. "So you cook."

"My mother told me that all her boys should know how to cook and dance. Lessons in the kitchen every Sunday night."

"Cooking?"

"And dancing." He grinned, hoping she wouldn't ask him to do a waltz. Someday, maybe he'd dance again.

"I can't dance. Or cook, really. It sounds like you have brothers."

"Collin—he's the oldest. Lives in Minneapolis with his wife. And Levi. He's a basketball player, in his last year of college."

"What do your parents do?"

"My dad owns a hardware store in town, but we also worked a farm."

"Hence the tool belt."

"It helps to be handy. That's from my dad."

"Wise man." Issy clasped her hands between her knees.

"Are you cold? We can go inside."

She shot him a look, shook her head fast.

Okay, not inside. Maybe that was too personal, too invasive.

"It's just that, uh—"

"Really, Issy, it's okay. I shouldn't have suggested it."

Her eyes widened. "Why?"

Why? "Because it's more comfortable out here, right?"

She drew in a breath, seemed to accept that.

239

"Can I ask what you do for a living? You seem to be . . . always at home."

"I . . . I work at home. E-things."

"E-things?"

"I work online."

Oh.

"How's the team?"

"Good. They're getting their kinks worked out. I think they'll be ready for the game next week." The run-in with Ryan skidded through his head. "Most of them, at least."

"I remember my dad coming home after the first week of practice. He'd ice his legs, just like the guys. He liked to get in the dirt with them, loved to show them new plays as a sort of taste of the new season." She shook her head as if dismissing the memory. "Do you think you'll get the job?"

"I hope so. I've always wanted to live in a small town."

"Why?"

"Because I grew up in one. I remember the games, and I loved—"

"Being the football star?" She gave him a smirk, one he didn't know how to read.

"No. I loved knowing everyone in town. I loved going to the malt shop and having the waitress know my order. And yes, I liked winning football games. I liked the way the team worked together. I liked being a part of something bigger than me." Not unlike how he'd been a part of his unit in Iraq. Losing that life had been nearly as agonizing as losing his leg.

"Did you pull a muscle playing football?"

He removed his hand from his leg. Apparently he'd been rubbing it again. Oh, he didn't want to lie. Not when they were just getting started. But . . . "Something like that."

"So do you think we can win? Go to state?"

"I think the year is early. And frankly—" he made a conscious effort not to rub his leg, forming a fist on top of it instead—"I'm having an issue with one of my players. He's . . . not happy with the fact that we keep working on the basics. He wants to be a star, I think, and I'm not fancy enough for him."

"My dad spent the first week or two just on drills, on the basics, before he taught them any of his gadget plays."

"Gadget plays?"

"You know, the trick plays? The ones that win championships?"

He did know. In fact he had a few of his own formulating. But nothing he could try on the team . . . yet. "Not always."

"No, not if you can't execute them. Which why you need the basics."

"I think you'd make a great coach," Caleb said and was rewarded with the wrinkle of her nose.

"Nah. I'm just the coach's daughter."

"You have a great spiral."

She looked away, and he couldn't help it—he pushed her hair from where the wind twined it into her face.

She jerked away.

"Oh, sorry, I . . ."

She swallowed fast, however, and he recognized a fake smile when he saw one.

"Issy, I'm so sorry. You're safe with me."

Her lips closed. "Why would you say that?"

"Because . . . I . . . I guess I like you, and I want to get to know you better. I don't want to wreck anything."

Had he really said that?

She seemed to take in his words, roll them through her thoughts. "Why do you like me, Caleb? You don't even know me. Why would you make me spaghetti and come over here and fix my fence?"

"Because you're my neighbor? Do I have to have a reason?"

She bit her lip and looked away.

He resisted the urge to brush her hair back again. And this night had been going so well.

She palmed her hands together. For a gardener, she had immaculate fingernails. "Seb Brewster was my father's trick play man. He loved running all the funky stuff my dad cooked up. They'd sit at the dinner table long after everyone went home—even after I went to bed—and sometimes

I'd wake up and Seb would be crashed on our sofa."

She looked at him, her mouth darting into a smile. "Seb was a great player. You'll need something up your sleeve to beat him."

She had amazing eyes. Full of intriguing, silvery layers, they reached out to him and pulled his breath from his chest.

"One of my dad's tricks, too, was his Thursday night barbecue before the big game. He'd have the guys over after practice and feed them hamburgers. They'd sit around and talk plays and strategy. They trusted him."

That's what Caleb needed—the boys to trust him. "I should do that. Have them over. Grill hamburgers."

She pressed her hand to her mouth.

"What?"

"Have you taken a good look at your grill?"

"Yeah. I cook on it every night."

"I know. And one of these nights, it's going to explode. Preferably not with the entire team standing around with paper plates, waiting for a hot dog."

"What do you suggest, neighbor?"

"Uh . . . I guess you could have it . . . here."

"Really?" He searched her face. "Listen, you don't want a bunch of teenage boys—"

"Yes. Yes. I want to." The words came out fast as if she might be forcing them from her body.

"Issy—"

"Absolutely. Thursday night. We'll have the pregame barbecue here." She nodded, smiling into the night, but it seemed tinny, almost too bright.

"Issy, really. You don't have to do that."

"But I can. If you can bring the burgers and soda. And keep them from crushing my hosta."

He smiled. Oh, he could like a woman who pushed past her fears. "I'll threaten them with laps if they do."

She glanced at him, nodded. "I used to sit right here and listen to the guys talk, thinking, *Hey, there's more to life than football.*"

"No, there isn't. Please take those words back."

She giggled. The sound dipped into his bones, stirred something there.

"I'm serious. Life is football. It's pushing ahead, and maybe you make yardage or maybe you don't, but you get knocked down all the same. And right then, you have the choice to stay down or get back up. If you have enough people cheering for you, and enough heart, you push to your feet and get back in the huddle and go another round. Life *is* football."

"Sometimes, though, players get hit so hard they're slow to get up. And then they're afraid of getting hit again. Afraid of really throwing themselves into the game." She looked at him, her expression drained of humor. "What do you tell those players, Coach?"

He wanted to wrap his hand around hers. Hold

it. More than that, he wanted to say that he understood. For a long time, he'd been afraid to get up. To run full speed into life again.

"I tell them to shake it off. And then I tell them to get out there and give it back. Don't let them beat you. You'll never feel good if you don't play with all your heart."

She wiped her cheek, and he stilled. Oh no, he hadn't wanted to make her cry.

"Issy?"

"I was going to leave this town and never really come back. I wanted a bigger life. I didn't need fame or glory, but I did want to prove to my town that I could step out of my father's shadow and be someone. Never in my life did I think I'd be . . . well, working in my garden."

She looked at him with eyes that seemed so needy he knew he couldn't keep dodging the truth. "You have a beautiful garden, Isadora. But there's also a beautiful world out there, and if you'll let me, I'd like to help you see it."

There, he'd laid out his cards.

She covered her mouth with her hand, turned away. "You talked to my father about me, didn't you?"

"No, not really. But it was obvious . . . your father loves you."

"I miss him so much that it feels like I'm walking around with a hole the size of a fist through my body."

Oh, Issy. He knew there was a woman on the other side of the fence that had a heart he wanted to know. He drew in a long breath. "Maybe you could try visiting him."

She didn't even pause before she shook her head.

"I don't understand. I'd go with you—"

"I'm not getting into a car. Maybe ever."

"We can walk."

She closed her eyes. Her fists tightened. "Here's what you don't get. I . . . can't cross Highway 6."

She couldn't cross the highway?

"Every time I get near the intersection where the accident happened, I start to panic. And it's not just the intersection—it's the highway. I see the accident over and over and . . ."

He took her hand. Softly, winding his fingers in between hers.

She hesitated for a moment, then closed her hand around his.

"I'd like to help you get across the street, Issy," he said. "Off the bench and back into the game."

She didn't look at him, but he saw the edge of her smile, the way she ducked her head. Warmth layered her voice when she said, "Oh, brother, I'm back on the porch with the football players."

He didn't let go of her hand. "You betcha."

Issy had nearly missed her show. There she'd sat, holding Caleb's wide, warm hand, letting it bathe her with an unfamiliar heat, and she'd nearly lingered right there, through her radio show.

She'd had to figure out a way to disentangle and excuse herself, and . . . she hadn't wanted to.

For the first time since she'd started the radio show, something tugged her out into the real world.

But the lovelorn needed her.

Or she needed them.

Whatever.

So she'd done a not-so-sneak peek at her watch and Caleb had gotten the hint. He'd packed up faster than she thought necessary, gathered his tools, and bid her good night.

Without a kiss.

And she was fairly pitiful because she actually had hoped that . . .

No. She didn't need to lose her mind just because for a moment she'd felt not alone. Like she'd found a man who might look past her . . . her own disability, she supposed. In fact, more than looking past it, Caleb seemed to want to help her overcome it.

She didn't know how to interpret the crazy, sweet swirl in her chest.

She'd had a date.

And not one panic attack.

Issy introduced her show and went immediately to calls. Saturday night often saw a flurry of activity on the message boards and a full queue of callers, too many lonely hearts sitting at home.

Within a week's time, she'd seen a double bump in her ratings. One week.

She owed it all to BoyNextDoor.

And she really was pretty pitiful because, despite her amazing date with Caleb, she still hoped BoyNextDoor called.

You like him. Lucy's accusation swelled in her head even as she fielded calls. No. She merely had an academic interest in seeing if her advice had worked.

"Go ahead, HoneyBunny."

"Hello, Miss Foolish Heart. I want to tell you that I'm a huge fan, and I'm holding out for my perfect romance."

"That's great, Honey—"

"And I think you're absolutely right about making that list and sticking to it. I just dumped my boyfriend of three years. I only wish it hadn't taken me that long to see that he was only an eight."

An eight. Issy did a mental calculation. With *no football players* taken off the list, and *no Neanderthal, well-groomed,* and *responsible* checked off, not to mention *kind to animals* and *courteous,* that landed Caleb soundly at five out of nine. And if she counted *good listener,* Caleb was up to a six. The biggie—his faith—still remained. But an eight didn't sound so bad, perhaps.

"Maybe you should wait, HoneyBunny. See if he doesn't eventually—"

"Nope. It's ten or nothing. Thank you, Miss Foolish Heart, for helping me set my standards."

She hung up.

Issy listened to dead air.

"Okay. Uh, next caller . . . Romeo?"

"Hello." A man's voice, low, deep. "I want to know if all the stuff you're telling that other guy—about doing her list and cleaning up—is working."

"BoyNextDoor?"

"Yeah. I want to know if it works."

"It works, Romeo."

"Would it work on you?"

She paused. "Yes. It would."

It would. Because she'd advised BoyNextDoor to do exactly what she'd wanted Caleb to do for her. Take care of his house, clean up, do something kind for her. Make her spaghetti.

And it *had* worked.

Weird.

"I think BoyNextDoor should call in and tell us himself," Romeo said.

"Me too. BoyNextDoor, if you're out there, give us a call. We want to know if you landed a date with the girl of your dreams."

Even as she said it, though, a screw turned in her heart. What if he had? And enjoyed it? What if he was falling for the Girl?

Wasn't that what she'd hoped for?

"Thank you for calling, Romeo."

249

She let an advertisement play, then opened the message boards, checked the online users.

No BoyNextDoor.

He was probably out on his date.

She glanced next door. Caleb's light fanned out into the night.

What on earth was she doing up here, hoping a faceless, even nameless man might call in when she'd driven out of her yard a perfectly good . . . six.

The advertisement stopped, and she scrolled through her callers.

BoyNextDoor waited in the queue. Her heart gave the slightest unruly jump.

She shouldn't, but . . . she ignored the other calls and clicked on his name.

"Hello, BoyNextDoor. Great to see you tonight."

"I know a challenge when I hear one," he said, a smile in his voice.

Was it possible to fall for someone, just because of his voice?

She cleared her throat and hopefully her head. "Inquiring minds want to know—did you get your date?"

He paused, and in that moment, she hoped . . . No. It wasn't fair, she knew, but she wanted BoyNextDoor for herself. Okay, maybe not herself, but . . .

She closed her eyes. How could she have a crush on a name in a discussion forum? A voice over the air?

"Yes, actually, I did. Just like you told me to do, Miss Foolish Heart. I did something she liked. And we had dinner."

"That's great, BoyNextDoor." But even she heard the wavering in her voice. "Now, just keep it up."

He laughed again. "Miss Foolish Heart, how can I thank you?"

"Live happily ever after." She laughed too, and it sounded wretchedly fake. She prayed her listeners wouldn't see—er, *hear* through it.

"The fact is, I didn't think she'd like a guy like me," he said.

"Why?"

"I don't know. Baggage, I guess." He drew in a breath. "She's not the only one disabled. I lost part of my leg in Iraq."

Oh. *Oh* . . . "I'm so sorry."

"I'm okay now, but I remember, after the attack, realizing that my leg had been blown off, I just wanted to die. I only saw myself for what I wasn't. How I was less of a man. It took me about six months to realize that maybe I could be more of a man than I had been. My injury made me work harder and think about my life and how I wanted to live. It made me see that God had spared me. And it made me reach beyond myself. I did that today. Reached beyond myself and into her life. And I think . . . I think she likes me too."

251

She saw him then, a guy with a crew cut, maybe on some military base in Texas or Georgia, his leg propped up on a sofa, his upper body thick with muscle. Blue, solemn eyes, filled with determination.

"I am sure she does, BoyNextDoor. Now don't be afraid to give her your heart."

He took another breath. "Let's not rush things."

She laughed, and across the line, he did too.

"I'm not done with you yet, Miss Foolish Heart."

Something about the way he said it slicked the moisture from her throat. Oh, this was bad.

"Call anytime, BoyNextDoor." She disconnected and went immediately to commercial.

His avatar appeared on the forum, requesting a chat.

No, no, she had a show to run and . . . She hit Accept.

MissFoolishHeart: I'm fine. Just thinking about your story. I'm so sorry about your leg.

BoyNextDoor: Thanks. Although, if you knew me before the attack, you'd know that this probably saved my life.

MissFoolishHeart: Oh?

BoyNextDoor: I grew up in a small town, followed by a small college that seemed a bit too tame at the time. So I sort of decided to make my own rules. Then when I went full-time in the military, I ended up living a life I wasn't real proud of. Really embarrassed myself and God, frankly. He got my attention in that ditch. Now I live each day grateful for grace.

MissFoolishHeart: Still, it sounds terrifying. How did you live through it?

BoyNextDoor: 2 Timothy 1:7. "For God has not given us a spirit of fear and timidity, but of power, love, and self-discipline." I kept repeating that until a medical unit found me. I determined that if I lived, I wouldn't let fear take over my life but would instead let His power and self-discipline pour through me.

MissFoolishHeart: And love?

She gritted her teeth. Sometimes her fingers got away from her.

BoyNextDoor: That too. In fact, God's love is perfect, and He puts that into us, so we can love the way He loves. Most of all, because of His perfect love, I can trust Him, whatever happens.

MissFoolishHeart: Trust. I don't know. How do you trust a God who seems so unpredictable?

BoyNextDoor: He's only unpredictable to us. Even as night came and the pain invaded every cell in my body, I kept thinking, God is light and in Him there is no darkness at all. Which meant that even in this dark place, He knew what He was doing, and no matter what happened, it was good.

MissFoolishHeart: How can it be good for you to lose your leg?

BoyNextDoor: I don't think God is as interested in my leg as He is my heart. And I wasn't exactly the man I could be at that time. He woke me up in that ditch, made me realize that He'd saved me from destruction so many other ways. Sure, it took everything inside me to learn to walk again, but I'm not the man I was before I lost my leg. And that's a good thing.

MissFoolishHeart: So you can walk?

BoyNextDoor: Yes. And run. And even, when no one is looking, dance. But it's not pretty.

MissFoolishHeart: I'd like to see that.

Shoot, she should delete that.
But she waited, her cursor blinking.

BoyNextDoor: I wish you could.

The commercial ended, the intro to her show spooling back up.

MissFoolishHeart: Don't be a stranger.

BoyNextDoor: Not to you.

As she went off-line, Issy hated herself just a little for wishing he could truly be the boy next door.

13

"You put this all together? I'm impressed, Seb." Bam paged through the business plan, enclosed in a file folder and printed out with Lucy's ancient ink-jet printer last night. "But why didn't Lucy bring this in herself?"

"She's up to her neck all day at the donut shop. She said she already met with you and I told her I'd run it by. She'll make an appointment with you after you've reviewed it."

And he'd wanted to plead her case without her around. She had enough stress in her life already, not to mention fatigue. Seb had dropped her off from their date way past her bedtime at the late hour of 9 p.m. after they returned from dinner at the Trout House. His second first date with Lucy —the perfect way to spend a Sunday evening.

At the restaurant, they'd watched an otter gambol around the dock as they sat outside on the deck, cordoned off with thick white ropes. He missed Lucy's long hair, but the wind would have made a shambles of it, and the short hair only accentuated her face, made her eyes appear twice as beautifully large.

They'd pulled him in all during dinner and he barely twined together reasonable conversation.

He forced his focus back to Bam. "As you can see, World's Best Donuts could easily turn a substantial profit with the addition of another window. It would double the foot traffic and pull customers off the street. And she can probably do it for less than five grand."

Bam set the folder on his desk. "The problem is, she's three months behind in her loan payments, and she has a contract for deed on her place. I'm not sure the holder of the contract will go for more debt."

"If she can get the window in by Labor Day, she'll make enough to cover her back payments and meet this new loan payment. You know, with the autumn colors up here, she can make enough to pay the entire thing off before November, when the tourist season ends." Seb scooted forward in his leather chair, flipped the pages. "I made a payment schedule here. It's nearly risk-free."

"Nothing is risk-free, Seb." Bam sat back. "But you're right. It's a solid plan. I'll take it to my board and see what they say."

"The sooner the better, Bam. She needs that window, and now. Gary Starr and his crew could get on it this weekend."

"Gary does good work." Bam tossed the proposal onto his desk. "What's the plan for practice tonight?"

"I'm planning on drilling the team on the play we taught them at the last practice." It had scored at least twenty-one points during his last season as quarterback, and he'd even felt the old magic as he and P-Train ran the play for the boys. "I think they'll be ready for Friday."

"Listen, I didn't want to say anything, but I've been working with these guys, and I'm worried they can't make the tackles. They're hitting with their weak side—if Knight's team knows how to slough off the defenders, they're going to walk all over us. We need more practice on fundamentals."

"Of course we do. But we'll get it after Friday, after they name me coach. Right now, I just want to have fun and win." Seb sounded confident, smiled broadly, but . . .

He had noticed their sloppy tackling. Noticed the fumbles, the missed passes. And his team tired fast. He might have spent more time on conditioning—but he'd do that later too. After

Friday's scrimmage, they still had two weeks before the first conference game.

Plenty of time to whip the boys into shape. And think of all the amazing plays they'd have in their playbook.

"Your call, Coach. I can't make it to practice today—school board meeting. But I'll be there tomorrow. And of course, I expect the entire town will turn out for the game." Bam raised a dark eyebrow, added a smirk. "By the way, I saw you at the Trout House last night. With Lucy."

"Yeah. We had a date."

A date that ended with him kissing her on her porch, Lucy wrapped in his arms.

Bam shook his head. "Maybe it's none of my business, but Lucy Maguire is not the girl you left behind. She's not in your league, pal."

Seb blinked at him. "I'm trying hard not to hurt you right now."

"I'm just saying that Lucy hasn't exactly done anything with her life since high school."

"Running her own business doesn't count?"

"You can do better. I don't want to see you taken out at the knees again. Especially for a girl like Lucy."

Seb stared at him, a terrible roaring in his mind. "What do you mean, a girl like Lucy?"

Bam gave a harsh laugh. "Do you seriously think you're the only one who's slept with Lucy Maguire?"

Seb could barely form words. "Listen, Bam, we all did things years ago we want to hide."

"Lucy and I had a one-night stand a few summers ago."

The words punched Seb, then sank low, into his chest. He fought to find his voice. "You've been married to Joann for five years."

"We were separated at the time. I'm not proud of it."

Seb stared at him, a violent whooshing in his head. "I don't believe you. You always had a thing for her—you never could believe that she chose me. What is this, some sort of payback? I thought you were on her side—"

"She's broken, Seb. You need to see that before you get hurt."

Through the window behind Bam, a thunderhead hovered over the lake, turning black. *She's broken.* He met Bam's eyes. "Has it ever occurred to you that I might be the reason for that?"

His own words shook through him. Seb stood. "Just give her the loan, Bam."

He let the door bang as he walked out of the office.

Caleb was living a double life.

Was it cheating on Issy to call *My Foolish Heart*? It sort of felt like it, although he wasn't dating Miss Foolish Heart, just . . .

Thinking about her. Thinking about her laughter

259

through the phone line and her words of encouragement and the way she'd talked to him about his leg.

Just telling someone had released the vise around his chest. His deception had begun to choke him. And he liked how she didn't pander to him, didn't act like he might be some tragedy.

But then there was Issy. On Saturday night, she'd held on to his hand like it had the power to set her free.

He couldn't nudge that feeling out of his mind. Nor her smile, the way her eyes held him, untainted by pity or sorrow. At least for now.

Yes, in a way his life tasted of cheating, although he wasn't really dating Issy, and Miss Foolish Heart was only a voice on the radio.

Still, he'd never been the kind of man to dish out his heart to multiple girls.

One woman at a time, one for all time. Just like his father. And his brother Collin.

The thought had nagged him all through the day on Sunday, as he'd attended church, as he'd parked himself at the Laundromat, then checked in with Collin.

He might have also listened to the Sunday recap of *My Foolish Heart* as he did it. He heard his own voice, twice.

Probably he liked Miss Foolish Heart too much. So maybe he'd just focus on Issy. And winning Friday night's game.

Which meant calling the boys in from practice before they got too winded. He needed them to feel strong this week. He'd deliberately moved their practices to the afternoon so they would get used to playing with the sun low and in their eyes. Now he blew his whistle to round them up from where they were running around the track. Ominous cumulus clouds hung over the field and a soggy wind lifted the collar of his Windbreaker. But the cool drizzle had always been Caleb's favorite condition for practice.

Dan huffed in, having taken a final lap with the boys.

No wonder the team loved his assistant coach. He even got a couple back slaps as he gripped his knees. The man had lost a few pounds, it seemed, with all this practice.

Caleb walked onto the field, his shoes squeaking on the clipped grass. "Bring it in, boys, and take a knee."

He would stand. He found his balance, leaning heavily on his good leg as the team pulled in.

Ryan flopped down, lying flat on the field.

"Ryan, either sit up or take a walk."

Ryan muttered something under his breath as he pushed to a sitting position, bracing one arm on his helmet.

If he only had another quarterback. But the backup QB—Michaels—played for Seb's team.

"We have four days until the big game. Some of

you are giving it your all—and like I said, this game is about heart. If you've shown up at practice every day and shown me all you got, you can expect to get some playing time on Friday. Frankly I'm not as much interested in winning as I am in seeing what you give me out there."

From the back, Ryan shook his head, pulling at the grass. "We're not going to win."

Caleb glanced at Dan, who went and stood behind Ryan. Oh, to be able to haul this kid up, make him run until he showed some respect.

Yes, if Caleb landed the job, Ryan might be sitting the bench his senior year. They didn't have to win the first year. It took a while to build a football program from shambles.

"Whether I end up as coach or not, I'm going to be assessing every single one of you for playing time in the fall—"

"Teach us a play that we don't know, Coach!"

He hadn't expected the words from Bryant, nor the look Bryant exchanged with Ryan, a sort of smirk.

Perfect. Now Ryan had riled the team.

"We can win with what we have. We just have to play solid ball."

Bryant shook his head, leaned back on his hands. "Nope, we're not going to win."

Caleb tightened his jaw and drew in a breath. "Yep, you're right. You're not going to win."

A couple heads shot up.

"In fact, Bryant, you might not even play."

"Coach—"

"Because you've already lost. You believe it in your heart, then you believe it in your head. And that's where you lose the game."

He debated a moment, then got down on one knee, on their level, facing them. Fire burned down his leg, but he wanted this moment to feed truth into them.

For a second, he wished he could share his story. Tell them that when he woke up in Germany, he'd believed the voices that told him he would have to settle for less. That he couldn't see his hopes and dreams happen. That it was okay to have an out.

The words climbed up his throat, nearly made it to his lips. He could almost see their expressions, the shock and then the courage.

Or . . . disgust. With Ryan leading the pack, they just might turn on him. A handicapped coach. Not the glory coach they wanted to follow.

No, Caleb had to prove himself first. Had to show them that he could be their coach without their sympathy-induced loyalty. He had to win their hearts through pure coaching.

"Guys, listen to me. No one wins by quitting. And if you play with all your heart, fight with everything inside, even if you lose—" he swallowed as he spoke out of the dark, pained places—"you can stand proud."

263

He had their attention. Even Ryan stopped fiddling with the grass.

"I believe in you guys, and I believe you can win. If you give everything you have and leave it out there on the field, you'll never lose. I promise."

He couldn't get up. Not without them seeing him fall, because with the soggy ground eating his good leg, his prosthesis dug into his stump and turned it to liquid fire. Instead, he motioned to the boys. "Bring it in."

The team rose and huddled in.

And suddenly Caleb had the urge to pray. The words nearly came out on their own. "God, we ask for Your help to play our best. To give all our talents and our skills, our hearts, to playing this game. It's not about the game, but life. And how we live it. But it starts on the field, so . . . protect us, and bless our efforts."

"And help us win."

He wasn't sure who said it, but a murmur went through the huddle.

He wouldn't mind winning either. "And . . . help us win. Amen."

The team looked up, and something seemed to have changed because a few of them smiled at him. Genuine smiles that said perhaps, for the first time, they might have the makings of a team.

"Thursday night, we're having a barbecue at my

neighbor's house. After practice. I hope to see you all there."

They ran for the locker room as rain began to spit on the field.

Caleb still had to figure out how to get off the turf. Or maybe he wouldn't. He leaned back, caught himself on his hands, and straightened his legs. Oh yes. He breathed out fully for the first time in ten minutes.

Dan started picking up footballs, dropping them into a mesh bag. He shot a glance at Caleb. "Great speech. And it was good to pray for the team."

"But?"

Dan tightened the bag, then picked up the various water bottles littering the bench. "You might want to consider just one trick play. These guys have earned it. I was here for the run of the championship team. Coach Presley had some great plays. We could ask—"

"I'm not using Coach Presley's plays." Caleb lifted his face to the rain. Cool, soothing. "This is a new era, a new team, and we're going to have new plays."

"I don't think Coach would care. He might be honored."

"I care. I need to prove to the school board that I can do this job. That I don't need any crutches— like the legacy of Coach Presley helping me along. I can come up with my own plays."

"Really? Because I'm thinking you can't even get off the ground."

He stared at Dan, blinking. "What do you mean?"

"I mean you have a bum leg, and the entire team knows it. You've been limping around for a week. What happened—old football injury?"

"I can get off the ground." In fact, to prove it, he crossed his good leg over his residual leg, rolled over, and pushed up. Smooth.

Without even a hop.

He held out his hand, and Dan tossed him a ball.

"And just so you know, I *have* been thinking about a trick play. But I'm not sure they're ready."

"I am." Dan came over to the line. "Show me."

Great, he had another Ryan on his hands. But he could hardly back down now.

Especially with Coach Brewster in the bleachers.

Caleb had seen him as the team dispersed.

Now he debated: if he showed his hand, Seb might duplicate it. But didn't he have an entire Presley playbook of trick plays? He hardly needed Caleb's.

"Okay, I've been working on something. It's sort of a reverse flea-flicker or a double pass . . . I call it the Rough Rider. The QB takes the hike with the wide receiver in motion, who stops short of the line of scrimmage. The QB then laterals it to the wide receiver, drawing the defenders over. Meanwhile the QB runs a hook pattern and is hopefully wide open to get the pass from the wide receiver."

"Let's run it."

Let's run it.

Okay, it didn't have to be fast and hard. And he could catch just about anything, even if he'd been a running back.

"Fine. I'll take the snap; you go in motion." Caleb lined up, called it, and Dan set off behind him. He took two steps back, turned, and pitched the ball to Dan.

He didn't wait for Dan to catch it but followed the imaginary fullback blocking for him down the field.

For a second, he saw himself young and whole, heard the crowd, tasted the sweet adrenaline of a well-executed play.

Then, he turned on his prosthetic leg to hook inside.

He'd blame it on the rain transforming the freshly mowed lawn into a sheet of ice. Or perhaps that he had worn spikes to catch his footing. Whatever the reason, it all happened in a flash. He planted his leg, turned, but his prosthesis didn't.

His good leg slipped and he went down, tearing the suction away from his prosthesis and twisting it under his jeans.

If he'd had two good legs, the injury might render him a cripple, the way his leg seemed to twist ninety degrees at the knee socket. For Caleb,

267

it just meant he would have to lie there, his knee wrenched nearly out of joint, and explain why he wasn't screaming in pain.

Even though he wanted to. Because as the football sailed past him, as Dan ran over to him and Seb rose from the stands, Caleb knew . . .

His double life had come to an end.

Seb looked like a dog left out in the rain.

Lucy looked up as the door jangled, watched him walk in, past the counter, and slide into a curved Formica booth seat.

The rain drenched him to the bone, his curly dark hair in ringlets, his Windbreaker slicked to his body. Even his shoes left a trail along the black-and-white linoleum.

Folding his hands on the table, he hung his head as if he'd lost his best friend.

But she didn't have time to slide into the booth across from him, find his eyes, and ask the question. Not with a lineup of customers finishing off the last of her daily production. She'd been deliberately staying open later, hoping she might sell another hundred or two donuts, staying until she'd peddled the very last crumb.

"I'd like a powdered sugar cake donut, and two—"

"Chocolate glazed. Absolutely, Mrs. Howard." Lucy pulled out the wax paper and scooped up the donuts, dropping them into the bag.

Seb had peeled off his jacket, now hung it on the edge of the table to dry.

"Hello, Jerry, what can I get you?" She smiled at the mayor, although she still couldn't get over his rather callous response to her predicament. See if she voted for *him* in November. He might want to consider his campaign donuts before he started shutting her down.

"I want that last skizzle, please."

She dumped it into a bag, glad that it had sat under the glass for a while. A hot skizzle could make her mouth water from ten feet. A skizzle after an hour crunched in her mouth and shattered in her hand. She hoped Jerry found it in pieces on his pressed black jeans.

"Hey there, Lucy." Tall, thin Bree, with her finished nails and smoky eyes, that bleached hair. Where she put her donut-hole-a-day habit baffled Lucy because the woman probably painted on those jeans.

Lucy handed over the bag with the lone donut hole. Bree winked at her and dropped the eighty cents into her hand.

"Next?" A tourist—Lucy smiled as the woman cleaned her out of plain cake donuts.

Out of the corner of her eye, she watched Bree sit opposite Seb. He looked up but said nothing.

Lucy took the tourist's money.

See, Bree, he's not interested.

But Bree opened her bag, dumping her donut

hole onto the table, then leaned close to him to say something.

He smiled.

"Can I buy a donut?"

She glanced at the customer. Oh, the hotel owner from across the street. "Sure, Anthony, what would you like?"

"That last glazed knot."

She dumped it into the bag for him.

Bree was touching Seb's arm.

"And those last two bismarks?"

She glanced at Anthony. "What?"

He had kind blue eyes, and they even followed her gaze into the eatery. "I'd like the last two bismarks, too."

Right. She found another bag, dropped those in.

"Can you put it on my account?"

And if Lucy wasn't mistaken, the girl was leaning—

"Lucy?"

She still wore her smile—she always wore her smile. "Huh?"

"Can I put it on my account?"

"Yes. Of course." She tapped it into her computer. "Thanks, Anthony."

No one stood behind him.

Bree nodded now, listening intently to something Seb should be telling *her*.

That's it. They were closed. Lucy slid the remaining trays of donuts out of the case and began carrying them into the back. She hoped Issy was hungry.

"I got it from here, Bree, thanks." She stood over her with a wet cloth, then made a point of swiping at the table where Bree had spilled glaze.

Bree looked at Seb, back at Lucy. "Uh . . ."

"We're closed. See you tomorrow." Lucy still wore the smile, but Bree shouldn't be deceived.

She got up. Lucy didn't even watch her go. She slid into the booth. "You don't look so hot. What happened?"

"With Bree? Aw, I was just telling her that she looked great and that she should come to the game on Friday."

She looked great? Lucy stared after her. Bree had exited and stood outside on the porch, lifting her hand, her blonde hair glorious despite the gloomy day. "She looks like she did when she graduated." Cute. Every teenage boy's dream.

Seb Brewster's dream.

Seb gave her a smile. "But she's not you, Lucy. I never thought about her after . . . well, after that night you saw us together."

And just like that, the coil in her stomach vanished. See, Seb wanted *her,* not a fling. "Okay. So why do you look like you've lost the big game?"

Seb's smile dimmed. "I'm not going to get this coaching job. I know it."

"What are you talking about?"

"I'm talking about the new coach. He . . . well, he's disabled."

"What?" She'd seen Coach Knight. Sure, he had scars, but he looked capable enough. "What are you talking about?"

"I can't be sure, but from where I stood in the stands, it looks like he's got a prosthetic leg."

"You're kidding me."

Seb shook his head. "I saw him fall. Right there, on the field. He went out for a pass, landed on his backside."

"That could happen to anyone—you know that."

"His leg came off."

All the air blew out of her. "His leg came *off?*"

"Not all the way. But it twisted, and when the reverend helped him up, it sort of dangled, and he couldn't walk on it." Seb closed his eyes. "This is a nightmare."

"Do you think the school board knows?"

"I don't know—but I can't tell them. It would just sound . . . petty. Desperate."

"But can he even do the job? It's not like he's teaching computer science. He has to be out there running and showing them plays and—"

"Guys with prosthetics can do that. They have all sorts of advances today. And before he fell, he ran just fine. Maybe with a little limp—"

"I've seen his limp. I thought he must have pulled a muscle."

"Probably everyone does."

"Don't you think the school board should know?"

"I don't know. But I can't be the one to say anything. Besides, when they find out . . ." He sighed. "You should have seen him, Lucy. He was out there, working his way to his feet, and nearly wouldn't let Dan help him. Can you imagine what it takes to be a guy out on the field, missing a leg?"

"Wow." Did Issy know?

Seb pressed his hands through his wet hair. Leaned back. Stared at the waves now angry upon the shore. The downpour had stopped. Lucy wanted to take his hand—

"Am I a good man, Lucy?" He looked at her then. Frowned. "I want to be a good man."

"You . . . you are. You are a good man, Seb."

"What makes a good man?"

"I think it's who he is, right? His choices."

He pulled out a napkin and wiped the moisture from the table.

She took his hand. "I do know this: being a good man has nothing to do with how many touchdowns you score. But maybe, rather, how you play the game."

He looked up and made a face at her.

"That did sound a little cliché, didn't it? But let's remember I've been making donuts all day. My brain is a little doughy."

He laughed, shook his head. "Lucy, you always know how to make me smile."

She ran her thumb over his. "What was that thing Coach always used to say? About teamwork?"

"He told us that we needed to be men built for others. Not just for ourselves."

She lifted her shoulder.

"I can't fight a crippled guy. What does that make me?" He didn't meet her eyes.

"Seb, you didn't know he was handicapped—because he didn't tell anyone. He clearly doesn't want people to know. Which means, he wants you to fight him, fairly. Not with pity. Maybe it makes you a good man to honor him with a good game. You're just going to have to outplay him."

"Knight just got back up." Seb looked at her. "I don't get back up. I stay down like my old man. I stay down and crawl away."

"No, you *did* stay down. But now you're back, and you're getting your footing."

He sighed. "Yes." He reached out to her, the strangest look in his eyes.

She leaned into his cold hand on her cheek. "Are you the Sebanator or aren't you?"

"I don't know who I am, Lucy."

"Then maybe it's time you found out."

14

Issy simply didn't recognize herself.

Not only had she applied makeup—for the second time in less than a week—but she wore jeans rolled up at the ankles, a pair of Sketchers, and a white blouse, crisp and fresh like she might be waiting for someone to come home.

Which, of course, she was.

But she didn't want to look obvious, so over the top of her garb she threw on one of her father's blue dress shirts, now turned into a gardening shirt.

She'd decided to weed the front rose beds. Even though she'd weeded a week ago. Or less. But weeding was easier when the earth was softer, after a good rain.

Right.

The evening, filled with the early sounds of crickets, the low slant of the sun over the rooftops, the smells of a hickory grill or maybe a nearby fire, held the nostalgia of her youth. She half expected her father to drive up in his SUV and wave to her from his window as he pulled in after practice.

Your father loves you.

She wasn't sure why Caleb had said that, but

something about it could prick tears in her eyes, even two days later.

As she straightened up to consider her paltry pile of weeds, she blew through the tightening of her chest. She had made steps, hadn't she? Like having the football team over this week? That counted as a step toward freedom, toward her father, right?

I'm proud of you, honey. Her father's words today, when she'd told him about Caleb, about the barbecue. She hadn't mentioned Caleb's offer to bring her to visit him.

On the porch steps, Duncan rose and began to bark. She glanced over her shoulder, then turned back to her bed of flowers as Caleb drove up.

The car door slammed. "Hey! Isadora!"

She smiled a second before she looked over. She liked his using her full name.

He must have showered at school because he didn't look like a man fresh from a workout. No, he wore a white long-sleeved baseball shirt with black arms that did a devastating job of enhancing his physique. That and his requisite baseball hat, and he held white restaurant bags in both hands.

"There's a new Thai place in town." He gestured with his head. "Come over to my porch for dinner?"

She leaned back, pressed herself to a stand. Glanced past him. "Your porch?"

He nodded, a kind smile on his face. "Bring Roger with you."

Duncan had come off the porch to stand beside her. His porch. She could see it from her place, and twenty steps would bring her home. "Okay."

"I'll get silverware and meet you in ten."

Ten agonizing minutes to consider his porch. See, it was one thing to run a route around the block, cocooned inside her earbuds. But this involved her walking to his place.

Sitting on his steps.

But he knew about her . . . struggles.

What if BoyNextDoor had the same trouble with his girl? Not that she was Caleb's girl, but for argument's sake, did Boy have to coax Girl out of her world, into his?

Or had he gone in after her?

And really, she shouldn't be thinking of BoyNextDoor on her date with Caleb.

She wouldn't.

Going inside, she unbuttoned her father's garden shirt and hung it on the hook in the kitchen closet. She stopped by the sink and scrubbed her hands clean, then dried them.

Her hair . . . well, maybe she should get Bree in for a house call to trim her split ends. She couldn't do much else with the dark mop her mother bequeathed her.

Standing in the kitchen for another five minutes, she searched for the tightening of her chest. Nothing.

Huh. Maybe Rachelle was right. Maybe she should stop expecting herself to panic.

After ten minutes to the second, she opened the door, walked down the steps, across the lawn, over the driveway, and into Caleb's yard.

He'd spread out a picnic on his porch, seated against the column of his steps with one leg straight, the other pulled up. True man style, he'd grabbed a towel from the bathroom for a table-cloth and set out a couple of white paper plates.

"I didn't know if you wanted chopsticks or a fork." He held out both.

"Did you know that in most of Thailand, they use forks, not chopsticks?" She took the fork and sat on the step. "Did you really say Thai food?"

He nodded, opening a white container. "Pad Thai with chicken."

She fished out a noodly mix of chicken, egg, bean sprouts, and peanuts. "This looks delicious."

"And here's green chicken curry."

"Really?"

"Don't forget the sticky rice." He handed over another container.

"Where did you find this?"

Caleb had opted for chopsticks and was shovel-ing noodles into his mouth. "I think it's the old taco place. I saw sombreros painted on the window."

"That went out of business two years ago. Before that, it was an Italian place. And before that, a burger joint."

"Wow. You know your town."

She smiled. "I actually wrote an essay about it my senior year in high school."

"Really? I want to read it."

The way he said it, with a sweetness in his grin, she could probably stay here on the porch all night without a twinge of fear.

"Oh, I promise it's riveting. Absolutely compelling. Like the part about the logging truck taking out the fish shack at the end of the hill—high-action stuff. As was the flooding of Main Street in '87. My father actually got out our canoe and paddled to the donut shop. Had to get his donuts, you know."

Caleb laughed. "So I guess you could probably tell me why the T-shirt shop has a bar and stools in it?"

"Used to be a soda fountain."

"And the large, uninhabited monstrosity in the middle of Main Street?"

"The old theater. Last showing, *The Sound of Music*, late 1970s."

"And is Honeymoon Bluff really . . . you know, Honeymoon Bluff?"

She put down her fork and reached for a bottle of water. "I'll never tell."

"C'mon. You can tell me." He waggled his eyebrows at her, and the look nearly made water come out her nose.

"No, I mean—I am telling you. I never went

there." She wiped her mouth, reached for the chopsticks.

"Never?"

"Nope, I . . . well, I never dated in high school."

"What? Are you kidding me?" He put his plate down and the genuine surprise sent a curl of heat through her.

"No. I made a rule not to date football players."

He frowned.

"My dad was the coach—I couldn't date anyone on his team."

"Whatever. But what about the geeks? You know, the *soccer* players. Or the theater kids."

"Spoken like a true jock."

"Hey, my best friend in high school starred in all the plays, so you can take that back. I was kidding."

"We didn't have soccer, and there were three boys in our theater program, all taken."

"That's just not right. A pretty girl like you should have had boys lining up at the door."

The word *pretty* wrapped right around her. "Even if they did, I have . . . rules."

"Rules?"

"Yeah . . ." Except, she suddenly wished she didn't. Wished she could just trust that the right man might walk into her life without having to be so . . .

"Rules kept me from dating the wrong guys."

"I think rules kept you from dating, period."

"Hey—they're good rules. Like he has to be clean-cut."

"It does rule out the rednecks who might show up with a scraggly beard."

She smiled. "And there's the *no big trucks* rule."

"You know, that's not really mine. I'm just driving it for a friend."

"And he has to be well-read."

"Did I mention I read the sports section of the *Deep Haven Herald* cover to cover?"

"Clearly, you'd have no problem making the list."

As soon as the words escaped, she wanted to yank them back, wanted to bury them inside, where they belonged.

Because, yes, he *would* make the list. She hoped . . . "Are you a Christian? What do you believe about God?" Please, please. Because even though she hadn't set foot in her own church in years, and even though God might not want to see her after the way she'd embarrassed Him . . .

"Yes. I'm a man who loves God and is trying to be His man. And I'm in church every Sunday. Even during football season."

"Good." Her voice emerged high, and she chased it with a smile. A smile that stayed on her mouth too long, especially when he looked at her—or maybe *through* her—with those amazing blue eyes.

They could swipe the thoughts right out of her

head. Even the ones that might have said no when he leaned over, caught her eyes for a question.

She wasn't fast enough, wasn't used to—

He kissed her. Sweetly, his fingers brushing her cheek, a kiss that seemed more a whisper against her lips. A taste really, and it ended too fast.

He pulled back, met her eyes.

Then he kissed her again, his hand curling around her neck, moving into the kiss, gently but without question.

Although she hadn't the first time, she let herself kiss him back. He tasted of sweet peanut sauce and the slightest tang of curry, and his goatee brushed her chin even as she touched his face too.

Right then, the past two years slipped away, and she was simply a girl, sitting on the front porch, kissing the neighbor boy, lost in the charm of being wanted.

Of being normal.

When he pulled away, he wore a smile in his eyes. "I have a little thing for you, Girl Next Door."

The way he said it ran a jolt through her, but of course, he couldn't know about her show, right? The guy probably didn't even own a computer.

"Me too," she said, but it emerged fumbled and not how she'd hoped. Still, he seemed to take it in and eased back against the post.

"So . . . do you think you'd be willing to go to

the football game on Friday?"

And right then, the moment crashed upon her. The game. Which meant a crowd, which meant that if she started to panic—

"Issy, are you okay?"

The swirl began low, a hot circle inside her belly, and she caught her breath. "Uh . . . yeah . . ." Oh no, she was making little whimpering noises. *Get control. "Perfect love expels all fear." And what was that one BoyNextDoor said? "For God has not given us a spirit of—"*

"Issy, you're white. Listen, you don't have to go to the game." He took her arm, and she yelped, yanked it away, making it worse.

"I gotta . . . I gotta go." As she stood, she clutched the rail. "Thanks for dinner."

Beside her, Caleb had pulled himself to his feet. He grabbed her arm. "Stop. Issy, what did I say? I'm sorry."

She pressed her stomach, but the swirl found her chest, tightened. "I . . . can't. I . . . Thanks for dinner, Caleb."

And this was why she couldn't really be in a relationship. Why she never should have kissed Caleb. Why she was better off dreaming about a man online, through the computer. Because a real man could never love a woman who darted down the stairs and ran back to her home, opening the door and seeking shelter in the safe place behind her piano bench.

• • •

Why wasn't he faster? "Issy!" Caleb hobbled down the stairs, across the lawn, but she'd already slammed her door.

He never should have mentioned the game. Or maybe . . .

Could it have been the kiss?

He had pushed her too fast, and while it took everything inside him not to wrap his arms around her, she'd probably been just trying not to scream.

Nice, Caleb.

Only, it had felt like she'd kissed him back. Had felt like she wanted to be in his arms.

He climbed her steps. Knocked on the door. "Issy!"

Nothing.

He tried the handle. Locked.

Turning, he slumped down onto the porch. He leaned his head against her door. "Issy, I'm sorry."

He wanted to tell her he understood. Wanted to tell her that this afternoon, when he'd sprawled on the field, his body mangled, he just wanted to recede into that dark place inside. Wanted to give up and howl.

But God expected more from him. And after all God had done, Caleb owed it to Him to get up, to pull himself together, to keep moving forward.

Caleb had debated a long moment before he

284

let Dan hoist him up. And only because he really couldn't hop all the way across the field on one leg.

Even if he could, it occurred to him that any of his players might return to the field. And that would surely make for an interesting conversation. Not to mention the end of his coaching bid, because even if the school board did hire him, he'd never know if it was because of his skills or because they were fulfilling some sort of affirmative action clause.

Dan had lowered him onto the bench. Straddled it as he sat beside him. "Is there something I can do?"

"Just make sure none of the guys come out." Then Caleb had lifted his jeans as well as he could and adjusted the prosthesis. It hadn't come all the way off, just turned on his leg. He lowered his pant leg. "I'll wait until they've cleared out of the locker room, then fix it right."

Dan had that look, the one Caleb hadn't wanted to use to win the job. "I can't believe it. All this time—"

"Borrowed time. You knew something was off—I could only hide it for so long. But the thing is, I wanted to wait until after Friday's game. Until the town could see what I hoped to accomplish with this team. I wanted to earn it."

Dan nodded. "I get that. But I can't get past the fact that it's also deceitful."

"Why? Do you tell your congregation every wound you've had?"

"I never lost a limb."

"But you might have lost your faith. Or your hope. Or even your way. Those are wounds too, right? Does it mean God can't use you?"

Dan drew in a breath. "You should be a lawyer."

"I was a soldier. A medic in Iraq. And a good one. But I've always wanted to be a coach."

"And you're good at that, too."

"I want to be. Especially after God saved my life. I'm just trying to do my part." The rain had died to a drizzle. Caleb lifted his face to it. Closed his eyes. "He's done enough. The rest is up to me."

"You and Peter and Ben Franklin."

"What are you talking about?"

Dan picked up the bag of balls. " 'God helps those who help themselves.' C'mon. Let's sit in my car." This time he didn't offer his hand to Caleb.

As Caleb followed Dan to his car, he saw a couple parents waiting to pick up his players. He waved, trying to hide his limp, and surrendered to Dan's dry Suburban.

Dan started the car to add some heat. "Remember when Jesus washed the disciples' feet?"

"Sure. In the upper room, the night He was arrested. After dinner."

"Yes. Of course, having spent years with Jesus,

Peter knew He was the Son of God. He'd seen His miracles, seen Jesus walk on water. And Peter also knew himself. He knew the man he'd been —he was the one who cried out, 'Get away from me; I'm a sinful man.' "

"I understand that. For a long time, I couldn't bear the fact that God had reached out of heaven to save me."

"A lot of men have a difficult time accepting grace. We know ourselves too well." Dan gave him a wry smile. "Which is why, I think, Peter reacted like he did when Jesus got to him. He said, 'No, you will never ever wash my feet.' He couldn't bear to have the Son of God serve a sinner like him."

Caleb drew a breath as Ryan exited the school. He met Caleb's gaze with a stoic expression.

"But that was Peter's pride speaking. He didn't want God to have to help him. He wanted to be the one who didn't make Jesus wash his feet. But see, Jesus wasn't in a position of helplessness— He knew who He was and what He'd come to do, and washing Peter's feet was intended to show Peter the grace of God. Jesus told him, 'Unless I wash you, you won't belong me.' He wasn't talking about salvation—in a later verse He points out that they are already clean. He's talking about that continual communion with God, that humility to let God work in our lives. It takes the washing of our feet by Jesus to be His disciple.

We have to be willing to accept His love and grace. And only then are we able to turn around and do it for others. Daily grace, for you, for them."

"I have accepted grace—"

"But have you let Jesus wash your feet here? Or is your pride saying, 'God, You've done enough. Don't wash me'?"

Caleb drew in a breath. "It just seems weak. I can't go through life constantly needing God."

"Why not? That's the point, I think. God says, 'My grace is all you need. My power works best in weakness.' " Dan turned the heat down. "God is glorified not in your strengths and not in your gratefulness, but in your weaknesses and in your trust in His future grace. In your faith that God didn't let you down in the past . . . and He's not going to let you down in the future."

Dan clamped him on the shoulder. "Let God wash your feet, Caleb. Or foot, as the case may be."

Caleb smiled at him. "Funny."

"Just a little prosthetic humor." Dan's smile faded. "Think about telling the school board. It doesn't make you weak. But it does make you honest."

"Honest isn't going to get me the job I want, on my terms."

Dan considered him. "I understand why you don't want to tell the board before the game. But you can't keep this secret forever."

"I'll tell them right after the game. That was my plan all along. After they decide on the job."

"No more secrets?"

No more secrets.

He let Dan's words hum in his mind as he sat on Issy's porch.

No more secrets. What if Issy knew that he understood? That he knew the taste of fear crawling up his throat, choking him, and if he could have run and hidden, he would have?

What would Miss Foolish Heart say?

It didn't matter. She wasn't real. Issy was. Issy had the smile that could right his world. Issy had the laugh that could—

Issy's laugh. That was it. She sounded exactly like Miss Foolish Heart. And tonight, as he'd sat with her, listening to her voice as she told about her small town . . .

No . . .

I do e-things.

No.

I work online.

No. *My Foolish Heart* was a national show like *The Bean.* And Issy . . . Issy was the girl next door. Besides . . . she'd never even had a *date.* Miss Foolish Heart, on the other hand, knew all about love, the ins and outs, the techniques. She had to be a seasoned dater—probably even married.

Phew. Imagine if Issy knew he'd been asking a talk show host for help in wooing her. Talk about feeling exposed. Yes, that might set off the panic attack of all time.

And considering that he'd told Miss Foolish Heart his deepest secrets, well, that panic attack might apply to both of them.

The first time Seb met Coach Presley, a low fog had rolled in off the lake and settled like cotton over the flag football field. Soggy, muddy, and angry not only that his wide receiver had dropped the ball but that his team trailed by two touchdowns, Seb just wanted to tackle somebody. But being only a sixth grader, he had to wait a year to join the school team.

Seb had been crouched in the huddle, fuming, when out of the fog, like he might be a war hero, strode Coach Presley. And as Coach stopped on the sideline and folded his arms over his barrel chest, he fixed his eyes on Seb. Right then, Seb was speared with the knowledge that Coach had come to the flag football scrimmage to watch him.

Maybe it wasn't true, but he only had to believe it to his core, only had to believe that Coach waited for him to call a quarterback sneak and run the ball forty yards into the end zone. And two plays after that, pick off the pass while on defense and return the ball for a win.

He always became the quarterback—and the man—he wanted to be when Coach watched him.

Good thing Coach couldn't see him seven years ago when Seb answered the phone, his head in his hands as he listened to the Cyclones game on the radio.

I believe in you, Seb. Don't let this beat you.

But he had no ears to hear Coach then, his anger, his fears drowning the words.

Now, he heard the voice again as he stood outside Coach's room in the care center, staring at the blue and white football helmet pasted on the door.

What on earth had driven him to see Coach Presley? Maybe the grumbles he'd received from his team today during practice. Worse, when he'd benched Samson, the boy nearly walked off the field.

He'd watched them fight the drills and realized he had cultivated a team of superstars, a team driven by the fading glory of his coach's legacies.

More, Seb had no idea how to really coach these boys into men. Because, well, he wasn't sure what that might look like.

He'd spent so many years looking behind him for guidance, for significance, that he didn't know what to fix his eyes on in front of him.

He pushed the door open with two fingers. The familiar hospital smells seeped from the room—body odors, disinfectant—and right behind that, he heard the whish of the ventilator, the hum of the television set on low.

His breath seized inside his chest and he ground his molars together to keep from crying.

He'd heard about Coach's accident, of course, but he had no idea. No idea how the coach's injury might tear away his stature and reduce him to a shell. No idea how his face might lose its features, settle into a wide mass above the ventilator tube.

Nor how his eyes might have the power, still, to fix upon Seb and send heat through him.

Coach smiled.

"Hey, Coach," Seb said, pulling up a chair in the room. A picture of Coach and his family angled toward him on a side table, but the room seemed strangely void of personal elements, as if Coach might not be here long.

"Heard you were back." Coach's voice emerged raspy and thin. He kept his eyes pinned to Seb.

Seb waited for more—maybe a question about his past, where he'd been over the past few years—but nothing came. Until he figured out that Coach couldn't talk more, not with the trach vent in his neck.

The back of his throat burned. He swallowed fast, forced a smile. "Yeah. I'm teaching math at the school. And, you know . . . coaching. But . . ." He drew in a breath, wishing he wasn't looking down at Coach but was twelve years old again, seeing him stride out of the fog. "I'm not sure I know what I'm doing. I thought maybe I needed to focus on some flashy plays, get the team excited about the game. My team, however, is . . . well, they're more interested in listening to the glory days and running the fun plays than digging in with drills, conditioning."

He scrubbed his hands together, unable to look any longer at his coach, hearing Bam's words in his head. *Do you seriously think you're the only one who's slept with Lucy Maguire?*

They tunneled through him like acid. Sure, Lucy had made her choices, but he'd been her first.

The first to win her heart, the first man she'd loved, the first to betray her.

The first to tell her that men were after one thing.

She's broken.

"Coach, I'm so sorry. I messed up." He drew in a breath and realized he was crying. As he wiped his cheeks, he stared out the window past Coach's bed. "I just wanted to be the kind of coach that you were. The kind of man you were."

"Get my playbook," Coach's voice wheezed out.

"Your playbook? But I know the plays, Coach. I remember them—"

"My playbook, Seb." He recognized the tone, the don't-argue-with-me gaze.

"Where—?" But he knew where. Or at least where it had been when he'd been a senior, staying over at Coach's house all those nights when his father had stumbled home drunk—or not at all. Seb would return to Coach's house, usually find him up late, reading.

Coach always invited him in and listened. Or sometimes just handed him a blanket.

The playbook always sat on the floor, next to his recliner, under his Bible.

"I'm still proud of you."

Seb took Coach's hand and wept.

15

Issy didn't need Caleb Knight, his dog, or his Thai food.

Not when she had the *My Foolish Heart* forum.

Not when she had BoyNextDoor. Except she hadn't heard from him in two days. Maybe he had run off with the girl of his dreams.

While she'd run out of the arms of a perfectly good man and back into her online world.

"Hello, Lovelorn, welcome back to the second hour of *My Foolish Heart*. We're going to wrap up the first hour's discussion about love letters with a note from Elizabeth Barrett Browning to Robert Browning:

"And now listen to me in turn. You have touched me more profoundly than I thought even you could have touched me—my heart was full when you came here today. Henceforward I am yours for everything. . . ."

Issy refrained from glancing at Caleb's window, her voice almost hitching on the last line. She didn't love Caleb. But he had filled her heart with hope. With him, she'd felt almost normal, not a hint of panic when he'd run his hand into her hair, kissed her so sweetly. She'd wanted to run her fingers through his goatee and—
No.
"Have you ever received a romantic letter? Could you love someone without ever meeting him? Let's take one last caller. The lines are open."
Of course she wasn't in love with BoyNextDoor, either. But something about his friendship felt easy and fun. Even comforting, like she could share with him something of her heart.
She could fall in love with someone like BoyNextDoor. Someday.
"MissElizabeth, you're on the air."
"I think letters are romantic. And like you pointed out last week, what if the person you fall for isn't attractive? You can love them if you know their heart—but how will you know it if you don't give them a chance?"
"Good point, MissE. But it brings up my next topic—when do you call it quits? How much do you invest in a relationship before you know that it won't work? Miss Foolish Heart normally

recommends three dates. But if you see it's not going to work, how do you break up? Should you use a letter?"

In the background, Elliot had cued up "Breaking Up Is Hard to Do" by Neil Sedaka. Nice touch, Elliot.

"UnluckyInLove, you're on the air."

The voice that came on the line sounded husky and dark and anything but lucky, as if she'd nursed her own broken heart. "Breaking up over e-mail is a cheap trick. It's easy and quick, but the best breakups help each other grow."

"So you're saying that breaking up isn't about blaming, but about helping each other become better people?"

"I'm saying people need closure, and it isn't fair to shut someone down over e-mail, is all." Her voice ended with a crack. "They deserve a reason." She hung up.

"Um, thank you for the call, Unlucky. Miss Foolish Heart agrees with you. A mature relationship talks through why it isn't working and respects the other party." She hoped her voice didn't betray her on that last line. Caleb had knocked on the door twice today. She hated herself for staying upstairs, locked in her office, but she couldn't embarrass herself any further. He deserved an explanation, although a smart man without a foolish heart would have already figured it out.

"What about timing? Is there ever a time to break up because you're not ready? Or do you hold on until you are?"

In the caller queue, PrideAndPassion appeared. Hopefully not with more pleading for Issy to attend her wedding.

"GotMyHeart, nice to see you back. How are you doing today?"

"I'm good. I wanted to respond to your letter conversation. I met my boyfriend online in a chat room. We're going to meet in a couple weeks, and . . . well, I'm not sure if it's the right timing. But I don't want to break up with him. It's just that I'm in school and I want to finish before I start anything serious. What should I do?"

"Miss Foolish Heart always recommends sticking to the plan. Tell him you're not ready to meet and that if he wants you, he'll wait for you. Good luck, Heart.

"It's true that in our new age, many relationships start online. And without having to look the person in the eye, it's easier to share intimate thoughts, so it's something to beware of. Miss Foolish Heart suggests keeping your conversations casual and light and saving the intimate sharing until you are face-to-face."

Except, of course, when you're unable to meet face-to-face. Oh, Elliot should just pull the plug on her right now.

They had thirty seconds to commercial and only

PrideAndPassion left in the queue. Well, she could cut her off if she started making a scene. "Thanks for the call." Issy took a breath and found her cheerful voice. "PrideAndPassion, you're on the air."

Sobbing, and a hiccup of breath.

"Pride?"

"Miss Foolish Heart, I think I made a terrible mistake."

Issy kept her voice calm. "What's the problem?"

"I think I should call off the wedding. I don't know if he's the right one."

See, this was why she made her callers remain anonymous, so when they announced they were getting married, then backed out, they didn't all end up in the tabloids.

"Pride, what happened?"

"Nothing. I mean—everything is great. Except . . . what if it's not?"

"You're not making sense."

"What if, one day, he decides that he doesn't love me? Or that I'm too neurotic? Or he meets someone else? How do I know that this is going to be my Happily Ever After?"

Issy's own words filled her mind. *Is he a ten? Does he have the big three? Are you caught in the love fog?* But for the first time, the platitudes she offered seemed more like military rules than wisdom. "The truth is, I don't know, Pride. It could be perfect one second, and the next, some-

298

thing could happen. You could have an illness, or yes, he could decide he doesn't love you." *Or a truck could run a red light and destroy your life.* "There are no guarantees."

Silence. Then, "That's what I thought. I . . . I can't live like that, being afraid it's all going to crumble."

Issy heard something in her voice, something she couldn't place. "Pride, is that why you broke up with your last five boyfriends? Because you were afraid?"

"They weren't tens, Miss Foolish Heart. And you always said, if he's not a ten when you're dating, he's going to be even less when you bring him home."

She had said that, but it was based more on a guess than reality. And frankly, were there ever any tens? Issy knew better than anyone that you had to look beyond the facade to the person behind the mask. Even then, there were no guarantees that the person you loved wouldn't jump up and go running out of your arms. Still, a gal had to protect her heart. "I did say that, Pride. If you aren't ready, then . . ."

"The wedding is off. I have no choice. I'm going to have to wait until I find the perfect ten. Thank you, Miss Foolish Heart. You saved me again."

Pride hung up.

Issy went to commercial, still hearing Pride's

words. *I can't live like that, being afraid it's all going to crumble.* She stared at the forum, at the activity. Not all of them agreed with her, and indeed she didn't entirely love her response to Pride.

In the phone queue, BoyNextDoor appeared, and warmth coursed through her. She didn't care what Miss Foolish Heart advised—she liked her online friendship with BoyNextDoor and planned to hold on to it.

If she couldn't have Caleb, then BoyNextDoor might be enough.

Her studio phone rang and she picked it up.

"What are you doing?"

Elliot, and she could picture him pacing.

"What are you talking about?"

"Did you just tell Lauren O'Grady to break up with her fiancé? Are you nuts? Maybe I should give out your home number to the governor when he calls."

"Elliot, you heard her. She wasn't sure."

"*Life* isn't sure! It doesn't mean you stop living it!"

She drew in a breath. Opened her mouth. Nothing emerged.

Elliot's tone softened. "Sorry. It's just . . . we can't have people saying that Miss Foolish Heart sabotages relationships."

But she did, didn't she?

She fought the quiver in her voice as she went

back on the air. "BoyNextDoor, so glad you could show up. Give us an update on the Girl."

"She's not talking to me." He sounded . . . annoyed? Angry? "And there's nothing I can do about it."

"Are you breaking up?" She didn't know what to make of the swirl of heat in her chest. Happiness? Panic?

"I don't know. She won't tell me what I did wrong. Or let me fix it."

"What happened?"

"I did everything you told me to—I asked her out, we had a couple nice dinners, and then . . . it isn't fair. I did everything you told me to and she still shut me down."

She recognized this tone—had heard her father use it too many times after a loss.

"Maybe she needs time to figure out what she lost, Boy. Women are like that—we get lost in the emotions and need time to see clearly."

She glanced at Caleb's window.

"I don't know. Maybe she's not into me. I might be trying too hard."

She wanted to reach through the line and take his hand. *I won't hurt you, BoyNextDoor. I won't shut you down.* But that could be because he was long-distance. Safe.

"It's possible that she is just afraid." She didn't know where that came from, but it felt right—the first right thing she'd said all night. She took a breath, wanted to give him more. "I had a date last night. It was nearly perfect—simple, you know? Take-out Thai food that we ate on his porch. We talked and even shared a kiss. But sometimes what seems perfect has hidden flaws. Even dangerous ones. She might be trying to protect you from something."

His voice had changed, taken on a kind of tremor. "Uh . . . protect me from what?"

"Herself?"

Silence on his end, and she realized that she'd probably revealed too much. Never had she told the audience about herself, and now she knew why. But like Rachelle said, they couldn't see her. BoyNextDoor wouldn't possibly dream that Miss Foolish Heart was Isadora Presley, trapped in her north woods home.

Isadora Presley was Miss Foolish Heart.

Caleb froze, unable to move, to speak. *I had a date last night. It was nearly perfect. . . . Take-out Thai food that we ate on his porch.*

He ran through her tidbits of advice, his body turning to ice. What was this, some sort of game to her? How long had she known he was her caller? She was making a fool out of him with all those things she told him to do—and he did them. Like some sort of . . . puppet.

Or one of her father's plays.

Why? Was he an experiment? Or maybe an

302

advertisement for her show? He'd heard the replay show on Sunday, the few ads about how Miss Foolish Heart could even help the boy next door find his true love.

She'd used him.

No. She'd *lied* to him.

And he'd told her his secrets. She knew about his leg. No wonder Seb Brewster had watched his practices—probably waiting for him to fail. In fact, the whole town probably knew.

They'd been playing him the whole time—all of them. Pitying him. No wonder Ryan didn't want to play for him, why the kid showed him no respect.

He wouldn't respect a coach who could fall on his face any second either. Or a coach who lied.

Worse, after practice, Caleb had actually purchased flowers, appeared at her door, knocked. And knocked. Then, desperate, he'd called the *My Foolish Heart* hotline asking for help on how to win her back.

Funny that he didn't hear crazy laughter filtering out of her office upstairs.

"BoyNextDoor, are you still there?"

Two could play at this game.

"Tell me, Miss Foolish Heart, what do you think is the definition of a foolish heart? Is it someone who gives their heart away too easily?"

"Uh . . . I suppose—"

"Or is it someone who believes in the actions,

303

the smile of another, only to find out she's been mocking him behind his back?"

He'd opened the forum and watched the discussion light up. It was almost like running a quarterback sneak—it confused the defense.

Ellery09: He sounds angry.

HeartLikeHis: Maybe she broke up with him.

He wanted to type in *Miss Foolish Heart is a fraud,* but he couldn't bring himself to eviscerate her because of his own hurt. He wouldn't out her on the air.

"Did your Girl mock—?"

"Or how about someone who just flat-out lies to you? Makes you believe she's someone, but in reality, she's another person altogether?"

Her voice cut low, added in compassion, and he would have believed her if he didn't know the truth. "What happened?"

He fought to keep the anger from his voice. "I just found out that the Girl—you know, the one you've been trying to get me to date—"

"Of course."

"Yeah, well, I guess you would." Whoops.

"I don't understand, Boy."

"Let me clear it up for you, then. I just found out the Girl is using me. She wasn't really interested in knowing me, but only in what I could do for her." He winced even as he said it.

He expected an indrawn breath, expected her to catch on, but . . . "That's terrible. I'm so sorry."

"You're . . . sorry?"

"Of course. Anyone who uses someone else is . . . Well, it's not your fault, that's for sure. Let's get back to your original question. The definition of a foolish heart. I think that's a great question. What do you think a foolish heart is, listeners?"

Oh, she was good, and he'd played right into her hand. He hung up.

But she hadn't finished with him yet. Her avatar popped up and asked him for a chat.

He accepted on impulse and regretted it instantly.

MissFoolishHeart: BoyNextDoor, is there something I've done to hurt you?

He stared at the cursor. Something to hurt him? Seriously?

MissFoolishHeart: Are you sure the Girl is using you? Why would she do that?

What if . . . what if she *didn't* know it was him? He considered his question for a few beats before he typed.

BoyNextDoor: MissFoolishHeart, how many dates have you been on?

He watched the chat box, waiting to see her type. If she knew it was him, she wouldn't lie, would she? But if she didn't . . .

MissFoolishHeart: I've had enough dates to know a good one.

Interesting.

BoyNextDoor: What made last night's date nearly perfect?

He wasn't sure exactly why he asked that, but it *had* been a nearly perfect evening, including the kiss. Until she ran away.

MissFoolishHeart: My father is a football coach, and sometimes when he came home from practice, he'd bring a bucket of chicken with him. He and my mother and I would eat it on our front porch. There was something about those simple picnics out in the open air, waving to our neighbors, enjoying the fall colors, that felt easy. Safe. Last night, I had a picnic date, and for a while, it felt the same way.

He hadn't expected that. Nor the growing surety that she didn't know the avatar on the screen was really her boy next door.

BoyNextDoor: When did it stop feeling safe?

Please don't answer when I kissed you.

MissFoolishHeart: He asked me to go to a football game Friday night.

Right. He had.

BoyNextDoor: You don't like football?

MissFoolishHeart: I love football.

He watched the cursor blink.
Oh, Issy.
On the air, they returned from the commercial break and her voice came over the Internet player. "We're back with five more minutes. Thank you for the definitions of a foolish heart. Miss Foolish Heart has her own—a foolish heart is one that loves recklessly. Any last callers?"
Loves recklessly. Perhaps that was the only kind of love. It made him pick up the phone again. He couldn't help it. He had to hear her voice.
"BoyNextDoor, uh, thank you for calling back."
"Thanks for taking my call, Miss Foolish Heart. I'm sorry for the abrupt hang up earlier. I want to ask you a question about the Girl."
"Go ahead. You know I'm here to help."
Yes, he actually believed that. And that she

didn't have a clue as to his real identity. Why else would she have hesitated telling him the truth about her fears? He already knew them.

He couldn't just let her go. *She might be trying to protect you from something . . . herself.*

He didn't need protecting from Issy, thank you.

"I take it back. I don't think the Girl is using me. I think she is afraid of me. Afraid of getting too close."

Issy drew in her breath. "Yes. I agree."

"So what if she already agreed to another date? Do you think I should ask her to keep it?"

"A lady keeps her commitments. But then again, a gentleman lets her beg out of them."

"What if it would be good for her?" Having a slew of football players in her backyard, reminding her of all she once had?

"Are you ready to risk losing her for good if you push?"

No, he didn't want to lose her. But he had the sense that she might already be slipping away. Maybe BoyNextDoor was his last hope to hang on to her.

"What if it's my last chance?" He said it softly and let his emotions show. "What if I don't take it and I lose her anyway?"

Please, Issy, hear my words.

"Then go for it, BoyNextDoor. You gotta play with all your heart, right?"

Her words caught in his chest, and he had no

response before she rolled over to her closing lines. "Thanks for the calls, Lovelorn. Remember to visit the forum and post your comments. This is Miss Foolish Heart saying, your perfect love might be right next door."

A love song closed out the show.

He waited for her to appear online, but her avatar showed that she'd signed off.

Above him, in her office, everything went dark.

16

"Where do you think my mother would've hidden the recipe for her potato salad?"

Lucy looked over to where Issy sat on the floor in front of her mother's bookshelf, surrounded by a stack of cookbooks, recipe boxes, and three-by-five index cards. "The Thursday night football salad? You don't remember it?"

Issy stacked the books, shoved them into the bookcase, and came over to sit on a stool at the island. She wore her hair pulled back today in a long French braid and the slightest hint of makeup. She appeared, in a way, as if she'd woken from a deep sleep, a vibrancy about her face that Lucy barely recognized. "I can't remember what she called it. My mom was in the process of putting all the recipes on the computer, so who knows where she filed it. But do any of these look familiar?" She dealt them out like playing cards. "I have to find that salad recipe."

Lucy read them over. "I thought you said you weren't going to see him anymore."

"Oh, it's Miss Foolish Heart. She said something a couple nights ago that I can't get over."

Lucy stared at her. "Are you having a split personality moment? *You're* Miss Foolish Heart."

"You're right. Foolish." She shook her head.

"Okay, what is up with you?"

Issy sighed. "BoyNextDoor called in on Tuesday night."

"Uh-oh, here we go again."

"His Girl dumped him. He asked if he should try again, and I told him yes. But it wasn't his call that bothered me so much. PrideAndPassion called too."

"Isn't she the one who invited you to her wedding?"

"Yes, only now the wedding is off. She got cold feet. And I foolishly told her to wait for a ten."

"That's foolish? It's how you live your life."

"And look where it's landed me. Maybe having such high standards isn't a great idea."

"I think high standards are a very good idea."

"What if I reject a guy because I think he's not the one, but he is? What if Caleb is my last chance?" Issy got up and went to the counter, where a spray of fresh-cut red roses fanned out in a vase. "This is the second bouquet he left on my porch in two days. This one came with a card."

"I thought those were from your garden."

Issy handed her the card.

Please let me in. Barbecue Thursday night? I promise to be on my best behavior.

Lucy returned the card. "That's very sweet."

Issy slid back onto the stool. "Elliot called during the show and yelled at me. Told me that just because life is scary, you don't stop living it."

Lucy folded her hands on the table. "Profound. Wonder where you've heard that before."

"Stop. I just think I'm finally ready to start believing it." She studied the card, rubbing her thumb over the writing. "I left a note on his door this morning and told him that we'd have the barbecue anyway. I wish I could have apologized, too. And I wish I hadn't run away from him the other night. I was so lured by this guy who understood my situation that I totally forgot he was a normal guy, a guy who would want to do normal things. Like go to football games. Be out in public. I just can't believe he wants to be with a woman he has to talk off the ledge every time he suggests a social event."

"Oh, Issy. I wish you could see what I see— what Caleb sees. A strong woman who is trying to put her life back together. You're better than you

311

were a month ago, even two weeks ago. You went to the store today—on your own! And now you're actually inviting Caleb and a crowd of rowdy boys to your house."

Issy smiled.

"The fact is, we see our own limits much more than others do."

"Like BoyNextDoor not even caring about the Girl's disability."

"Yeah, uh, I'm starting to wonder at your attachment to him, Issy. I think you have a real crush on him. But you know he's as close to a figment of your imagination as you are going to get. He's not really real—he has his own life, probably in Houston or Milwaukee. You're never going to meet him—and never mind that he called you because he's interested in someone *else*."

"I know. I *know*. He just seems like the perfect guy. But you're right. He's only a name on a forum. For all I know, he's sixty-two and married."

"Okay, now you're creeping me out. He's not real, and Caleb is. And more than that, he's everything BoyNextDoor seems to be and more. He's sweet and encouraging and a good listener, and . . . Caleb is a good guy. A guy worth making two gallons of potato salad for." Lucy leaned over to sort through the recipes. "Which, I might add, is a pretty big step for you. Are you sure this is a good idea?"

"It doesn't freak me out at all. They're in my house. I grew up with football players in my house. Shall we start with how many times Seb ate Saturday breakfast with us? No, this isn't hard. It's the idea of attending the game that makes my chest tighten. I can't control the game. I *can* control dinner. If I can find that salad recipe."

Lucy picked up a recipe. "Try this one. It says, *Salad for the Hungry*. If that's not a football player, then I don't know what is."

Issy took the card, read it over, and looked at Lucy with a triumphant smile. She pulled a pot from under the stove and set it in the sink, followed by a ten-pound bag of potatoes.

"Hey, your dad's playbook." Lucy reached out and snagged a bound, thick book with *Presley Plays* scrawled on the cover.

Issy opened the bag of potatoes, dumping them into the empty side of the sink, then fished out her potato peeler. "I was thinking I'd show it to Caleb. He might like to see some of the plays Seb might cook up."

"The magic Presley plays. Yes, I'd bet Caleb would give his right arm for these. Especially since . . ." She glanced at Issy, who had begun to wash the potatoes.

Issy paused. "Especially since?"

Uh-oh. Issy would have mentioned Caleb's disability if she knew, wouldn't she? "Since . . . he's never run them." Caleb should be allowed to tell her, right? "Has . . . has Caleb talked about his scars at all?"

Issy turned off the water, grabbed a towel. "No. But I think he will, when he's ready. I haven't even told him about my parents' accident yet." She came back to peer over Lucy's shoulder. "Oh, I remember this one. The Quarterback Chaos play."

Lucy read it through. "Are you serious? Is this legal?"

"Yeah—he did it in the state championship game. Don't you remember—the last play? Seb ran to the sideline shouting that Deej didn't know the play? Totally baffled the defense. It's funny and completely legal. Dad thought it up himself—didn't have the guts to call it until Seb came along. But I don't think he's used it since because everybody in the league has heard about it."

"That's hilarious. Your dad was so funny."

Issy looked at her, her face pale. "*Is* so funny. Is. He's not dead."

Oh. Yes. "I'm sorry, Issy. Of course he's alive." Lucy closed the playbook, cleared her throat. "I think Seb is worried about my business plan. He spent last night drawing up plans for my walk-up window."

"Have you heard anything from the bank?"

"No. But Seb said the meeting with Bam on Monday went well, so I have high hopes. He's already talked to Gary about starting work on Saturday. He thinks if the crew works hard, they could finish it over the weekend, in time for Labor Day. I'll probably have to hire more help, but according to his plan, we'll make enough to pay for my current back debts as well as go into the black."

"The Sebanator," Issy said. "Always the champion."

"I think he does want to be my champion, a little." Lucy let herself linger on the memory of his hand in hers, the taste of his lips. And this time around, it didn't feel quite as dangerous, as if he'd keep his promises. "I think he wants to be the town hero, too. He's really worried about tomorrow's game."

Lucy fished a stack of letters out of her bag. "I probably need to stop by my PO box more than twice a week, although all I get is junk mail. Oh, the bank sent me something."

She sawed her thumb through the lip of the envelope, then pulled out the letter and read it. "Are you kidding me?"

"What?" Issy dumped a clean potato in the pot.

"They're foreclosing on my loan."

"What?" Issy grabbed the towel again.

"It's from Bam. He says that due to loan default, he's calling in the loan on World's Best."

"Can he do that?"

Lucy laid the letter on the counter. Drew a

breath. "Yes. Because the loan is technically a contract for deed. And the previous owner of our property can take it back if we default."

"Why would they do that?"

Lucy shook her head, but she had a pretty good idea. And it all started in Bammer's office, probably when Seb handed over her stellar—*his* stellar—predictions of her earnings with her new addition to Bam the banker. Bam the all-state blitzer.

Bam, the holder of her contract for deed.

Bam, the married womanizer who'd made a nonfootball pass at her during the Fish Pic street dance a few years ago, one that ended with her climbing out of his truck in the wee hours of the morning, a moment she wanted to erase. Unfortunately Bam wasn't used to having a girl slam the door in his face. Add that to his high school crush and he had a pride to soothe.

And Seb had helped his pal betray her.

"Stay in your lanes! Hustle all the way to the ball!"

Seb gritted his teeth as he watched the ball slip as if greasy through the hands of his receiver. It squirreled around the field while one player after another on the receiving team pursued it.

The defense and offense tangled up in the middle of the field.

"Grab the ball!" He couldn't watch.

"They're not wrapping up. They're not staying in the hip pocket to tackle. They're getting stuck on their man, not getting by." Bam listed off his complaints under his breath even as, next to him, DJ nodded.

"You can't make yards if you can't hold on to the ball."

Seb had taught these boys nothing in the space of two weeks. Not even spending the last three days in drills had made a difference, not when all they wanted to do was run the handful of plays perfected by the old state champs.

"Maybe you should run a few tackling drills." He glanced at Bam, who had shown up for every practice since Monday without a word of apology. It didn't matter—they were here to play football.

Bam shook his head. "It would take another week of hard practice, and we got a game tomorrow. Call 'em in; let 'em rest. We've already overworked them."

Seb blew the whistle, his gut burning. The boys pulled off their helmets, ran in as he walked to the fifty. "Take a knee, guys."

Most of them simply flopped on the grass. So much for discipline. He'd watched Knight's team huddle up for another prayer today.

Not even praying would help, probably, although he hadn't exactly sought God's help—hadn't really thought he needed it.

He threw his clipboard to the ground, his hands

on his hips. Bam and DJ edged over, their eyes on him. The old quarterback, rallying his team.

Only he'd never had to rally his old team. Not with Coach Presley at the helm. Coach always knew what to say, how to encourage, how to push. And if this had been Presley's team, they'd be barbecuing tonight in the coach's backyard.

The sun hung low, the evening stretching dark fingers into the field. Gnats hovered in swarms over the boys' heads, although fatigue kept them from shooing them away. Crickets sawed into the night, and a languid summer breeze swept through the air.

They were going to get slaughtered.

And they had no one to blame but Coach Brewster and his glory days.

He swept off his baseball hat, ran his hands through his hair. Blew out. "Boys, I owe you an apology."

Bam narrowed his eyes. DJ looked at the ground.

"I failed you. I haven't taught you what you needed to know these past two weeks."

Eyes considered him, wary, angry.

"I taught you some fun plays, yes, but without knowing how to tackle, hold the ball, or even block, a great play doesn't matter. Substance matters. Not flash."

Bam shook his head and turned away from him. DJ folded his arms over his chest.

"The reason our team won state wasn't Coach Presley's fancy plays; it was because he drilled us until we knew how to play good football. How to be men who wouldn't quit. Men built for others, for their team."

He stared at the boys, the way a couple of them bore down on him with a hard look. Others looked at the turf or away, as if embarrassed.

He should have picked up that playbook like Coach said, stopped by Issy's to ask for it. But what could be in it that he didn't already know?

"Are you saying we're going to lose?" Michaels asked. His sophomore quarterback, lean, blond, slippery as an eel with a throw that could make it all the way to the end zone with the right blocking, wore a stripped look.

Yes. But watching the boys . . . they deserved a coach who believed in them.

They deserved a coach they could believe in. A coach like Caleb Knight, who knew how to be a man of honor, who didn't let his past cripple him.

He'd given Lucy a chance to tell him about her past last night, and she'd said nothing. Why were Bam's words eating him? So she'd dated— okay, slept with—other guys. He hadn't exactly been a choir boy since leaving Deep Haven.

Bam watched him, one eyebrow up.

He had to find something to give them. "I'm not saying we're going to lose. But maybe . . . maybe it doesn't matter. Maybe we get out there and have fun and see what we can do. We worked hard and we owe ourselves—and them—a good fight. And we're going to give it to 'em. We're going to play hard, hit hard, and most of all, remember that you're playing for your position for whoever the coach may be, so go out there and give all you got."

He got a few nods, but nothing that would set the world on fire. He wasn't particularly enthused either.

A good part of him wanted to run off the field and never look back.

"Go home and get rested. Be here at three tomorrow for warm-ups."

The boys pried themselves off the field.

Bam walked over. "What kind of pep talk was that? Have fun? We're not playing flag football here, Seb. We're in it to win. Do you want Knight to get your job?"

Yes, maybe. "Knight is a good coach. The team would be lucky to have him."

"He doesn't belong here. *You* belong here. You're the coach we need."

Seb picked up his clipboard. "Hey, did you hear back from the board on Lucy's loan? We got Gary's crew lined up for Saturday—"

"Board turned her down."

Seb looked at him. "What? Why?"

Bam drew in a breath. "Lucy's defaulted on her loan for three months, Seb. I can't fix that."

320

"You saw it in the business plan—she'll make the money back, and more."

"She's got a contract for deed. Which means the owner can call in the loan or foreclose at will if she misses her payments."

"Let me go talk to him. Who is it? Let me explain—"

"It's me, Seb." Bam met his gaze when he said it.

Seb blinked, not sure how to process his words. "It's . . . What do you mean it's *you?*"

"My family owned the property where World's Best sits. They want it back."

"Only because you saw the moneymaking potential. You can't open a donut shop. You don't know the first thing about making donuts."

"But Java Cup does. And I'll hire them to come in and make donuts. People don't care about the secret recipe. They care about having a donut with their cup of coffee. And yes, your business plan helped us see the potential of the place. It's not our fault Lucy dropped her loan payments."

"You never intended to give Lucy that loan, did you?"

Bam picked up a football. "Get over her, Seb. Everyone else has."

Seb didn't realize he'd dropped the clipboard until it banged on his foot, but by then, he didn't care. By then he'd launched himself at Bam. Tackled him into the turf, snuffing him so hard it rattled his own bones. Then he cocked his fist and committed the first of a string of personal fouls.

Practice ended with the team watching the quarterback of the Deep Haven Huskies get bloody with his star defensive end.

So much for team spirit.

Issy had traveled back in time to the days of the Thursday night Presley barbecue. Hickory-smoked hamburgers, hot dogs, teenage boys talking swagger and smack on the deck, some of them pitching a football around the garden.

"Watch out for the hydrangeas!"

"No problem, Miss P.!"

On the grilling deck, wearing a white apron and a pink oven mitt, Caleb served up burgers.

He looked way too much like her father after the Thursday night practice. Smiling, confident, trustworthy.

Safe.

"Is that number three for you, Jackson?" She remembered the names as Caleb had introduced them, mostly by their position. "Being a tackle doesn't mean you have to be built like a brick."

The blond, pimply kid had the girth of a moose. "Saving room for cookies, Miss P.!"

Caleb grinned at her as she came up to the deck after making the rounds with Kool-Aid. "That potato salad is a thing of joy and beauty." His paper plate, scraped clean, lay on the railing.

"It was my mother's secret recipe. She always served it at the barbecue."

"No wonder the Huskies always won." He winked at her.

Yes, she very much could get used to this.

It nearly felt like attending a game. She let that thought sink into her, waited for the swirl of panic. Nothing.

"I'll get the cookies."

"We *do* want these boys to be able to run tomorrow."

"They're my mother's secret recipe too."

"Bring them on."

She had propped open the back door, still waiting on the glass from the lumberyard, and now nearly tripped over Duncan, sprawled in the middle of the kitchen floor. The team's quarterback sat beside the dog, rubbing his head, reading—

"That's my dad's playbook."

Ryan, she thought his name was, looked up. "Really? It's got some cool plays."

"He won three state championships with them."

Ryan nodded. Went back to the book.

Lucy stood at the sink, stirring a new batch of punch. Stirring, staring out the window, stirring.

"I think it's ready," Issy said, slipping her arm around Lucy. She still appeared as if someone had just set fire to her house. Drawn. Hollowed out. "Are you going to be okay?"

"I lost my parents' business. The business that has been in our family for three generations. How could I do that?"

"I don't think it's entirely your fault—"

"You're right, Issy." Lucy turned to her, something wild, unrecognizable in her eyes. "No football players. Number three. I should have listened to you and your list. Miss Foolish Heart knows best."

"Shh—"

Lucy opened her mouth, then clamped her hand over it. "Sorry."

"Ix-nay on the ow-shay. There are extra ears in the room." Her gaze darted to Ryan, still paging through the playbook. Maybe someday she'd have the strength to part with it, bequeath it to the school. After her father okayed it, of course. Until then, she could almost hear his voice in her ears when she read his plays, could see him on the sideline. No, she was far from ready to part with it.

"Sorry. I just . . . I was so stupid. Here I thought . . ." Lucy's mouth opened again, some sort of conspiracy playing behind her eyes. "What if Bam set me up? What if he sent Seb to spy on me? What if they deliberately got my hopes up in order to watch me fail? Bam has reasons not to like me. And I'm sure he told Seb."

"What kind of reasons?"

Lucy shook her head.

"What are you talking about, Lucy?"

"What if this entire thing was just payback?" Her voice sounded strained. Lucy closed her eyes, something that looked like real pain on her face. "Payback from Bam. And Seb helped him. I knew he never really cared for me. This was probably some joke to them."

Issy took her hands. "Payback for what?"

"Everything okay in here?" Caleb stepped inside, too cute in his pink oven mitt. "I have some big boys outside who are willing to separate you two."

"We're not angry at each other," Issy said over her shoulder. "Not ever."

He came over to lift the cooler from the sink as Lucy moved back. "You sure?"

"Hello, the house. Are there pancakes here?" The voice came from the hallway, and Lucy froze.

Issy turned, not sure if she should smile or not. She glanced at Lucy, who turned away. Oh, boy. "Seb Brewster. It's about time."

The years dropped away as he walked into the room. He'd filled out, his shoulders bigger, although he still had the look and build of a quarterback, along with the Saturday morning bruises. Apparently he'd been working hard with his team, too, although he'd taken a tackle on his chin.

Seb always had a sheepish smile for her—

325

usually when he showed up on a Saturday morning, eating pancakes at their breakfast table. He produced that smile now. "Hey, Issy."

She walked into his arms and let him hold her.

When she broke away, she turned to the duo eyeing them. Caleb holding the punch, Lucy looking like she wanted to deliver one.

"This is Caleb Knight, the new coach . . . or, uh . . ."

"No, you're probably right." Seb held out his hand. "Caleb."

Caleb set the cooler on the counter and met Seb's hand. "Nice to meet you, Seb. You have a good team out there."

"You too."

"They'll be amazing when we get them on the field together."

"Tomorrow's game will be good—"

"Actually, I meant when we get past tomorrow and see how they combine. I know Ryan here is looking forward to playing with his pal Samson. Right, Ryan?"

Ryan glanced at Caleb, no smile. But he'd scrambled off the floor when Seb walked in and now turned to him, held out this hand. "I'm Jared Ryan, quarterback. Great to meet you, Coach."

Seb shot a glance at Caleb but took Ryan's hand. "You too. I saw you out there. You look good. Can't wait to see you play this year."

"Hope to play for you, sir. I've seen every tape

326

from the championship season—even listened to it on the radio."

"Thanks. But it doesn't matter who you play for—just how you play. You do your best out there tomorrow."

Ryan's lips pursed.

"Hey, is that Coach's playbook?" Seb reached for the book in Ryan's grip. "Wow, does this bring back memories."

"I remember you sitting at the table and going over some of these," Issy said.

"Look at this one—the Doctor. Such a great play. It's made to look like a run, even though it's a deep pass."

"I know that one—Doc Dorman, who was the head coach at Upper Iowa University, was the first to use it in a game." Caleb moved toward Seb, so much verve in his voice, Issy could nearly see him running it on the field.

"We ran it once. Beautiful play." Seb caught Caleb's eyes, and Issy saw the old Seb. Not only that, but for a moment, she could see Caleb in the kitchen, surrounded by a slew of teenagers, or even middle schoolers, listening to him prep them for the game. He'd be leaning over, like now, his voice intimate, rich with excitement . . .

She could be with this man. The thought caught her, swept her breath from her chest. She could be with this man because he brought her to a place she'd been before—and a place she wanted to go.

A place of safety.

"So I guess if you run that play tomorrow, I'll know it," Caleb said to Seb.

"I might have a few others up my sleeve," Seb said, but his voice lacked the cocky smack talk of his youth. He glanced at Lucy, who had her arms crossed, and closed the playbook. "Can I talk to you?"

Lucy lifted the cooler of punch, splashing some onto her shirt. "Sure, talk all you want. It's all lies anyway. I don't know why I ever believed you."

"Lucy—"

"Don't. Don't even start. I should have never let you back into my life. You'll tell me how much you missed me, how you only thought about me the last eight years. Yeah, I'll bet you thought about me."

"I did." A muscle pulled in Seb's jaw as he held the playbook in both hands. "Just like you thought about me."

She stared at him, and even Issy frowned at his tone.

"You want to tell me *how much* you thought about me, Lucy?"

Lucy's mouth opened. "I knew it. I'm such an idiot. I should have seen you setting me up."

"Wait one second—"

"That's some ego you have on you; but of course you are the *Sebanator*. You're used to lugging around that massive ego, the kind that doesn't care how they trample on someone, destroy them." Lucy slammed the cooler back on the counter, grabbed a washcloth, scrubbed at her stained shirt. "What, you think I couldn't get over you? That you were so wonderful I couldn't go on without you?"

Seb flinched as if her words actually bruised. He curled the playbook in his hands. "I think you got along without me just fine."

She rounded on him. "That's right I did. I stayed here, ran my donut shop . . . dated other guys. I'm sure you know all about it. It's exactly the sort of thing you jocks love to talk about—you probably told the entire locker room about us. I'll bet Bam couldn't wait to return the favor."

Seb drew in a breath and shook his head. "I never told anyone what happened with us. And I couldn't care less what Bam said. I told you, I want a fresh start for us."

Lucy and Seb stared at each other, so much in their eyes Issy had the strange urge to run from the room. What were they talking about?

"I'm sorry, Lucy. I'm sorry for hurting you, and for . . . for everything."

Lucy looked away from him, her voice strange. "Like I said, it's no big deal."

Seb unrolled the playbook. It curled at the edges, warped by the strength of his hands.

Lucy wiped up the bloody puddle of Kool-Aid where it had spilled onto the counter. "I thought I was over you. I thought I could put it behind me. But the fact is, I gave you who I was, Seb. I gave you everything I had—and you threw it away. Threw *me* away."

Seb flinched. "Lucy, I didn't know Bam was going to take the donut shop from you, or I would have never shown him the proposal. But you *knew* I was going to show him. That was the point—to show him the donut shop could turn a profit."

"No, your point was to prove that you were still the superstar, that we couldn't live without you. Well, guess what?" She turned away from him, wringing out the towel. Red liquid dripped from it as she said, her voice shaking, "Get out, Seb." She faced him again. "Get out of this house; get out of my life. Thank you for coming back and destroying me yet again. I am an idiot for ever trusting you."

Issy actually hurt at the blitzed expression on Seb's face.

"Do you really want that?"

"Yes," Lucy answered. Quick, sharp. Like the fine edge of a blade. She turned on the water, let it run into the washcloth, flushing out the dye until the water ran clear.

Seb's shoulders rose and fell as he looked at her. Finally he tossed the playbook onto the counter. "Yes, you certainly can live without me. I'm sorry I ever came back to Deep Haven."

Seb glanced at Issy, then at Caleb. "Good luck tomorrow, Caleb."

Caleb nodded. Issy noticed how he'd taken a step in front of Lucy.

Issy turned to Lucy. "What's going on?"

"I'm going home."

Issy reached for her, but Lucy scooped up her mail and dumped it into her bag. "Please, just let me go home."

Caleb stepped outside, hollered at the boys to start cleaning up.

"This isn't about the donut shop, is it, Lucy?"

She held up her hand. "I don't want you to miss your show." But she looked at Issy with big eyes, and something in her expression seemed so painfully familiar.

"I won't. Elliot put together a 'best of' intro for me tonight." Issy reached out to Lucy, but she backed away. "Lucy, I'm here if you need me."

Lucy kept retreating, through the open door. Issy watched her cut through the yard, her bag banging against her leg.

She should go after her.

Maybe it was time for Miss Foolish Heart to make house calls.

17

"Don't follow her."

Caleb had watched Lucy nearly flee through Issy's garden, and he ached for her. He knew a little about having someone break your heart. But the look on Seb's face as Lucy took him apart told Caleb that perhaps Lucy didn't have the entire story.

Whatever the case, she and Seb needed to work it out. Without the assistance of Miss Foolish Heart. Not that Issy didn't have good advice, but with Lucy's luck, Issy would list all Seb's faults and he'd end up at a negative three.

Caleb hated to think where he might end up. Now, as Issy frowned at him, he added, "She needs to be alone."

"She's my best friend. And she's hurting. You don't know their history. She and Seb dated in high school and he broke her heart when she found him making out with Bree Sanders."

"It looked to me like she broke his right back."

"Hardly. He went on to win a state championship, remember?" She pushed past him onto the porch, but he caught up, stepped in front of her. "Really? You're going to block me?"

"Just . . . hear me on this. Let Lucy and Seb

work this out. They don't need your advice. This is real, Issy, not . . . not entertainment."

She stared at him, blinking, and he grimaced. He hadn't wanted to tell her like this. Around him, the guys had started to collect the trash from the yard. He'd rather pick a different time and place to reveal that he was BoyNextDoor and had swindled her into this dinner.

"What do you mean, it's not entertainment?" She backed away from him a step, and he lowered his voice.

"Issy, please, don't. Let's talk about this later."

"Talk about what later?" She had reached the door, had a whitened grip around the handle.

"I have to drive some of the guys home, but I'll come back, help you clean up."

"What did you mean, Caleb?" Her voice had a sharp edge, and he remembered Seb's wince.

He drew in a breath. "I'm just saying that you don't always have to fix other people's problems."

"I don't . . . I . . . Listen, you don't know anything about Seb or Lucy or what they need. What do you mean, I don't have to solve other people's problems? You don't even know me."

He stepped toward her. "I know you better than you think I do. And you know me."

"I don't know you at all."

"As a matter of fact, we know each other very well."

She had backed fully into her house now, and

333

he closed his eyes as she shut the door in his face.

He packed up the boys as quickly as he could and left to drive them home.

He dropped McCormick off last. The running back lived in a box house, with overgrown juniper like a carpet around his front steps. A wan light flickered by the front door.

The kid hesitated just a fraction before he opened the door.

"Everything okay, McCormick?"

He stared at the light, then finally nodded.

"You'd tell me if . . . if something wasn't okay at home, wouldn't you?"

He glanced at Caleb, tried a smile. Caleb too well remembered guys on his team who had played simply for the escape. "You know if you ever need to talk, I'm always around."

"Thanks, Coach." McCormick reached for the door. "Great barbecue."

"Get some rest."

He stayed, his headlights shining on the house, until McCormick let himself in.

Caleb drove by Pastor Dan's house, grateful for the man and his willingness to carry Caleb's secret, at least until after the game.

"My power works best in weakness."

He tightened his grip on the steering wheel.

How he hated his weakness. And nobody won by admitting their limitations, did they?

He drove past the school, around the unlit field,

and parked his car, then scanned the dark field and imagined tomorrow's game. Ryan at the helm, working out the plays, Bryant downfield, pocketing the ball. McCormick rushing through the center of the pack. The boys knew their basics—at least as well as they could after two weeks of practice.

Now it was time to fight a good fight, turn the lights on the Huskies.

"It's all about tomorrow, God. Please help me not to let You down. Please—"

It takes the washing of our feet by Jesus to be His disciple. We have to be willing to accept His love and grace. And only then are we able to turn around and do it for others.

Dan's voice seemed to be haunting him tonight.

He wanted to be a disciple; he did. But did that mean he had to do it on his face? Couldn't he stand up?

Still, maybe he didn't get to call the plays. He closed his eyes. "God, I want to be Your man here, for these boys, for this town. Help me to accept Your grace in my life." He swallowed, drew in a breath. "However You choose."

The moonlight ducked behind the clouds as he drove back to the house. The forecast for tomorrow's game suggested a chance of rain.

Caleb loved cool game days. And he wanted Issy there. He could see her in the stands, wearing a Huskies jacket, her long hair in a ponytail, her dark eyes shining as she cheered.

In fact, he could see her in his life. He'd watched the way she shone when he talked about her father's playbook. She loved football. She loved this town.

And he could love her.

Maybe that's all she needed to hear. He'd simply explain it to her—he hadn't set out to deceive her. After all, who would guess that he had a talk show host living next door?

He pulled up, parked on the street, and walked to her dark house. He pressed the doorbell. Waited. Pressed it again. "C'mon, Issy!"

Nothing. No footsteps. Nothing but the light streaming out of her studio. Figures she'd run back to *My Foolish Heart.*

Fine. He knew exactly where to find her.

Lucy stared into her mirror, at her cropped hair, her unremarkable hazel eyes, her less-than-womanly body.

She certainly looked innocent.

But the look in Seb's eyes tonight brought it all back. The shame. The sense that she would never be clean again.

Hence the hot shower. It had always been the safest place to cry.

She toweled off her hair—it stuck straight up as if it had been gelled—then tightened the cinch on her bathrobe and switched off the bathroom light.

I think you got along without me just fine.

That's right I did. I stayed here, ran my donut shop . . . dated other guys.

Yes, she'd dated. Two guys, to be precise. And Bam, which she wouldn't even count as a date, simply a horrible event during which she ended up weeping in his arms. Over, of course, Seb. No wonder he wanted payback.

Seb Brewster simply couldn't help turning her into a fool. She closed her eyes. See, there was a reason she hung on to the donut shop. Through the eyes of her customers, she saw the woman she wanted to be. Sweet Lucy.

But thanks to Seb and Bam, she didn't even have that anymore.

She walked down the hall, catching the blinking red light on the answering machine in the den.

She paused by the door. Then, going in, she pressed the button.

"Lucy, it's me, Seb. I'm on my way to Issy's house—I was just hoping to catch you. Bam told me he denied your loan, and I wanted to say how sorry I am. We'll figure something out. Call me back."

She deleted his message. Stood there, seeing the pain in his eyes, as another came behind it.

"It's me. I . . . wanted to say that I don't care what happened in the past, Lucy. I know that I'm to blame for so much of it and—"

She deleted that one also.

Shoot, she would have liked a third. Maybe to not delete. Maybe to try and believe.

She returned to the living room and picked up her bag to read the foreclosure letter again.

Bam couldn't foreclose. Not on a Deep Haven institution. She sat on her parents' sofa—one of these days, she'd hoped to earn enough to buy her own place. But with her family in Florida most of the time, free rent had helped pay the bills.

At least, what she could pay of them.

What was she supposed to do if she didn't have the donut shop?

Leaning over, she brushed her fingers against the touch lamps. Light splashed over her, onto the brown plaid sofa.

She opened her messenger bag, pulled out the stack of bills, and . . .

Oh no. Coach's playbook. She must have simply scooped everything into her bag. Issy would be furious. Or maybe she wouldn't even notice, not with her attention on Caleb.

Finally, finally, Issy Presley had found a man who just might break her free. Who saw more of her than she saw of herself.

Lucy fought the burn in her eyes. Flipped open the front cover of Coach's book. He'd written an inscription on the front page in his tight handwriting.

"Receive and experience the amazing grace of the Master, Jesus Christ, deep, deep within yourselves." Philippians 4:23

Lucy leaned her head against the sofa. Had she ever received that grace? Or allowed herself to receive it?

She closed her eyes, hearing her conversation with Issy—was it already almost two weeks ago? *Donuts have a hole in them. Which says that something is* missing. *Probably a good metaphor for my life.*

Missing. Losing Seb had felt like having a piece of herself ripped away. And when he walked back into her life, he'd made her feel whole again—or at least nearly. But perhaps it had only patched the wounds on her heart. He couldn't heal the wounds on her soul. The wounds of her self-betrayal.

The wounds only grace could heal.

"Receive and experience the amazing grace of the Master . . ."

The voice whispered inside her. Resonant. Strong. Heat filled her eyes.

"Receive and experience . . ."

Had she done either, really? Had she let grace change her, make her whole? Was it even possible to feel whole after she'd given away so much of herself? She'd asked God's forgiveness long ago. But she'd never believed it. Never let it inside, to heal her, change her. Cleanse her.

No, she'd been trying to do that herself.

Lucy covered her face with her hands. "God, I'm so sorry. I don't know who I am. I don't know who I was supposed to be. I'm lost."

She drew up her legs, buried her head in her knees.

"Lucy?"

She looked up. Seb stood over her, his hands out as if in offering.

Seb was here?

Lucy wiped her eyes with the heels of her hands. "You let yourself in?"

"I'm sorry. I knocked, but maybe you didn't hear me." He swallowed hard, then got down on his knees. "I know I shouldn't have let myself in, but I . . . I had to see you. I keep thinking about what you said. No big deal? Of course it's a big deal. I slept with you. And I know it went against what you believed in. I know you did it for me, and I feel sick that I took that gift and I trampled on it. I manipulated you, and then I betrayed you. And I can't get past it. I keep thinking of you and how you told me you wanted to wait, and I pressured you anyway. If I could take that back and honor you . . ."

He looked so broken, his breath hiccuping.

"I'm just sick about what happened with Bam. I don't blame you, even if the thought of you with him eats me alive. I guess I deserve it." He closed his eyes, looked away, a muscle pulling in his jaw. "Probably how you felt when you caught me with Bree. I'm so sorry."

Oh, Seb. She wanted to touch his face, gentle the wounds of their past. "The worst part about seeing you with Bree was realizing that I had given myself away to a man who didn't cherish me. And then, suddenly, I was just like Bree. Thirsty for someone to love me. But that wasn't me, and I couldn't figure out how I got there."

"We're all thirsty for someone to love us, Lucy."

Lucy rubbed her hands together. "Yes, but—" she drew in a breath—"I did sleep with Bam. It was a bad moment during Fish Pic a few years ago. I was lonely and . . ." She closed her eyes, feeling again the dark shame that seeped through her. "I can't believe I did that. With him."

"It's okay. I wasn't the guy I wanted to be either. After that night with Bree, I knew I'd destroyed everything between us, and I hated myself. I don't know why I did it—I didn't think. I let her make me feel like I owned the world. Until, of course, I didn't. Until I saw your face. I thought if I won the state championship, I could be a hero, but seeing everyone cheering me, knowing the kind of man I was . . . it only made it worse. So I left Deep Haven in hopes of becoming someone. And then got hurt and quit football. Then I thought if I got my degree, became successful . . . but I couldn't do that, either. So I thought I'd come back and try to coach football, but I realized

I just wanted to feel good about myself again. I don't want to be a man who betrays the people I love. And I do—I do love you, Lucy. I always have. I was just so stupid about it."

She pressed a hand over her mouth. Nodded. Tears shook out of her. "After what happened with Bam, I kept trying to believe that if I was just . . . just a good person, then maybe God would fix the broken place inside. And then, after the Presleys' accident, I thought, *Hey, I'll help Issy. I'll be her world.* And that worked until . . . until you came back."

"Until I betrayed you again. Or you thought I did."

"I know you didn't betray me, Seb. Bam did. I did. I was just so thirsty for someone to love me even though . . . I was no longer sweet Lucy."

His voice roughened, his eyes red. "You'll always be sweet Lucy to me."

"But will I be sweet Lucy to God?"

Seb wasn't exactly sure how he got into Lucy's family room. He'd sat in his car, his chest burning, until he drove to Lucy's house. There he'd let his car idle in her driveway for nearly an hour, dredging up the courage, listening to her voice in his head.

Get out of this house; get out of my life. Thank you for coming back and destroying me yet again. I am an idiot for ever trusting you.

Staring at her in Issy's kitchen, he'd known her hurt had nothing to do with the donut shop. The fear of losing it only brought the truth to the surface.

Instead of helping, he'd somehow stirred up the past.

It nearly took him out whole to find Lucy curled into a tight ball on her sofa. Now her question dug through him: *But will I be sweet Lucy to God?*

"I . . . don't know, Lucy. I know I can't give back to you what I took. But I would like to prove that I can honor you."

Lucy swallowed. But she nodded.

He closed his eyes.

"What is it?"

He opened his eyes, shook his head. "I don't know. What if I turn into my father? What if I hurt you again? What if I don't know how to be that man?"

She sat back, reached behind her, and handed him a book.

"Coach's playbook." He took it.

"I accidentally took it from Issy's house. Look inside."

He drew in a breath, then opened it in the middle.

Plays, and there, in Coach's handwriting, verses in the margins.

Philippians 3:13-14. "I focus on this one thing: Forgetting the past and looking forward to what lies ahead, I press on to reach the end of the race and receive the heavenly prize for which God, through Christ Jesus, is calling us."

Lucy read it with him, then looked up and met his eyes.

He turned to another play. The Bronco. He remembered running it but didn't know it came with Ezekiel 36:25-26. *"Then I will sprinkle clean water on you, and you will be clean. Your filth will be washed away, and you will no longer worship idols. And I will give you a new heart, and I will put a new spirit in you. I will take out your stony, stubborn heart and give you a tender, responsive heart."*

He turned the page and found another play— a standard option play, alongside Ephesians 2:8. *"God saved you by his grace when you believed. And you can't take credit for this; it is a gift from God. Salvation is not a reward for the good things we have done, so none of us can boast about it. For we are God's masterpiece. He has created us anew in Christ Jesus, so we can do the good things he planned for us long ago."*

Whatever God had planned for him, Seb had messed it up but good.

Lucy took the book, flipped to the front cover. "This one, Seb. Read this one."

"Receive and experience the amazing grace of the Master, Jesus Christ, deep, deep within yourselves."

She wore a soft smile. "Maybe that's what we thirst for. What made me say yes to you, what made you say yes to Bree, what made us search for it in others. That need for grace. For unconditional love, despite our wounds and mistakes."

She took his hand. "I think God did bring you back here, Seb. You thought it was for you, and I thought it was for me. But I think it was for us. I think He meant for us to have a second chance. To receive His grace. I think He did plan a good thing for us, long ago. And we derailed that. But maybe He's giving us another chance."

He looked at her hand, then at her sweet eyes. "So we can do those good things?"

"Like be a coach?"

"Or a donut girl?"

Lucy smiled. "How about just your girl?"

Lucy. His throat thickened. "Yes. Please be my girl."

And when he kissed her, it indeed felt like the first time.

18

As a matter of fact, we know each other very well.

Issy wanted to expel Caleb's words from her brain, but they lodged there, despite trying to focus on her calls.

"NorthernHeart, you're on the line."

"Thank you for taking my call, Miss Foolish Heart. I've been dating a . . . well, he's definitely an eight, but he could be a ten . . . for about a month. Is it too soon to know if I love him?"

"Miss Foolish Heart's standard answer has always been the three-month rule—but sometimes, yes, you might be able to know if you can love someone . . . much earlier."

"How?"

How? Was it the way he made you feel? The way you saw the woman you could be in his eyes? The way you saw him in your future, serving up hamburgers, maybe someday attending a football game?

Until Caleb's cryptic words, she had felt real courage building inside her. With Caleb on the sidelines believing in her, she could tuck herself into the crowd and be a part of the world again.

On the forum, replies already scattered in.

Is he a ten?

You haven't dated three months!

Does he share your values?

All her rules, her litmus tests. But none of it included the most important thing, the words coming from a place inside her that felt natural. Whole. "He sets you free of the things that trap you and helps you be the person you want to be."

Silence over the phone line. Oops. "I mean, of course, he . . . We all have our own fears, right? Perhaps when you love someone, he shows you that you don't have to be so afraid. Maybe he holds your hand. Maybe he makes you believe in yourself. Does your man make you believe that you can be the person you want to be?"

"I think he does." NorthernHeart sighed, and Issy understood it. "I know he does. Thank you, Miss Foolish Heart. You really helped me."

No, NorthernHeart, you helped me.

She went to a commercial, looked down at Caleb's window. It remained dark. Perhaps he hadn't returned home from dropping off the boys yet.

As a matter of fact, we know each other very well.

Maybe he meant his conversation with her father. What exactly had her father told him?

If his light glowed after her show, she'd venture next door and . . .

BoyNextDoor popped into the phone queue.

She smiled. "Welcome back, Lovelorn; let's take another call. Hello, BoyNextDoor. How are you tonight?"

"I'm . . . confused. And frustrated."

"Oh. Well, what can I help you with tonight?"

"I want to know if you have feelings for me. If you're ever going to let me in."

"I'm not sure I understand. Let you in?" She opened a chat box, requested a chat, but he seemed to ignore it.

"How about I make it clearer for you." His sigh niggled something inside her. " 'Everyone likes spaghetti'?"

"Everyone *does* like spaghetti."

" 'Help her with yard work'?"

"Uh . . ."

"Like maybe fix her fence?"

She froze. She hadn't said anything about a fence, that she could recall. "That's a nice thing to do."

"How about 'Give her something to look at'— like shaving my beard?"

She swallowed, suddenly remembering Caleb's transformation.

She pressed a hand against her mouth.

"Did I make the list, Miss Foolish Heart? Did I meet your standards for the perfect romance? Because it's starting to feel like I didn't."

He hung up and she listened to the silence, let the show go to dead air.

And in Caleb's house, the light flickered on.

No . . .

BoyNextDoor couldn't be Caleb Knight.

Wait a doggone minute. She'd hardly planned this. He'd called in to her show. He'd asked for her advice. He . . . was the soldier with the missing leg? Their online conversation tunneled back to her. How he'd lain wounded in the ditch, the night closing in around him. How his understanding of her fear had calmed her.

But Caleb didn't look like he was missing a leg, did he? She'd seen him walking around—sure he had a limp and his scars, although she'd stopped seeing them long ago. . . .

No. A guy with a missing leg wouldn't apply to be a football coach, would he?

But why would Caleb lie to her?

The coaching position. The playbook.

She threw off her headphones, scrambled downstairs. Ran down the hall.

Where—? She flicked on the light, tore the books from the bookshelf, then searched the kitchen.

Gone. Of course, gone.

Caleb had invaded her world and stolen the only thing she had left of her father.

She yanked open the front door, her bare feet

chilled in the tall grass, ran across his driveway, up his stairs, and pounded on the door.

No answer. She tried the handle. It gave and she pushed her way inside. "Caleb, how dare you!" Her words caught on a sob as he looked up from the sofa.

His computer lay open on his lap, his face solemn, on defense.

"You took my father's playbook?"

"What?"

"Don't lie to me. I figured it out. Why, oh why didn't I stick to my list? I'm an idiot. I made it to keep jerks like you out of my life."

"What? No, Issy, you've got this all wrong."

"That wasn't you on the call-in line?" She heard her voice on his computer, a replay of an earlier show, and realized Elliot had caught on to the fact that she'd gone AWOL.

"Yes, but—"

"So you didn't just set me up to look like a fool in front of the entire world?"

"No!"

"You didn't play me, try to get me to fall for you?"

"You started this. And I quote: 'I'll help you woo this girl.' "

"I'm not the one who called in! You must have been laughing behind your hand every time you did something, knowing I'd be stunned at your Casanova abilities to win my heart."

"You've got to be kidding me. Listen, until a couple days ago, I had no idea it was you."

"Give me a break. You had to know I was Miss Foolish Heart."

"Why's that?"

"Because why else would you be interested in a—" her breath caught—"a girl who is *disabled*."

"Issy, I didn't mean it like you took it."

"Nope, you're right. I'm a mess. My world is two blocks wide. And I can't leave my house without feeling like I'm undressed in front of the entire town. I have so much baggage, you'd have to hire a cargo plane every time we went out on a date."

"Then what are you doing here?"

"You stole from me. You stole the most important thing I still have of my dad."

"I didn't steal anything. I don't have your father's playbook. I don't need it—I have my own plays."

"I'm sure you do. Your own specialized sneaky plays."

His face hardened. "You want to talk about baggage? How about meeting a pretty girl for the first time only to have her scream and run away?"

She stilled. "You know I regret that."

"But it's still true, isn't it. I know how I look. And I know that after a while, you'd notice it too. Pity is a terrible foundation for love."

"I don't see your scars, Caleb. But I guess you do."

A muscle pulled in his jaw.

"I can't believe you asked me, on the air, if I had feelings for you. What did you want me to say—yes? Yes, I have feelings for you?"

He stared at her as if that was exactly what he wanted her to say.

She shook her head. "I wouldn't date you if you were the last man in Deep Haven."

"Then you really are Miss Foolish Heart," he whispered. "And by the way, your dad isn't dead."

Her breath hiccuped in her chest. Then she turned and walked out of his house.

Caleb hated how his disability had the power to beat him. How it kept him from running after Issy. He'd had to practically launch his computer off his lap, untangle himself from the sofa, then grapple for his crutches and force himself upright before he could take off after her.

By then, of course, she'd slammed her front door. He rang the doorbell, pounded. "Issy!"

Then you really are Miss Foolish Heart. Oh, he was a jerk. He'd just been so . . . frustrated. And yes, angry.

Perhaps he *had* only been seeing his scars. Because he couldn't get past the dark fear inside that he didn't measure up to Issy's top ten. That he simply was too . . . damaged.

Okay, a guy could be at least as resourceful as his dog. Caleb moved around the back and through the gate. He climbed the porch stairs and, finding the kitchen door locked, called out, "Issy, I'm coming through the door."

Nothing but the sound of crashing, thumping. "Are you okay in there?"

He debated a long moment, then pushed the cardboard from the frame enough to reach inside and unlock the door. Good thing he hadn't received that pane of glass yet.

Issy sat on the kitchen floor, surrounded by books, most of them upturned and open. She looked at him. "I can't find it."

Then, before he could sit down next to her, she got up and backed away, her face crumbling. "I can't find it."

"Issy, listen, we'll find your dad's playbook. I'm sure it's around here."

But she just kept shaking her head. "I . . ." She turned and disappeared around the stairs before he could navigate the minefield of litter on the kitchen floor.

"It's going to be okay."

He heard thumping in the other room, and by the time he got there, she'd dumped out the contents of the bookshelf.

"Where is it?" Her voice had a wild edge to it.

"Issy, breathe. Just . . . stop. It's going to be okay."

"It's gone, Caleb. It's gone." Her voice turned whisper thin. "He's gone."

"He's not gone. I'm sorry for what I said."

When she reached out for the piano, she missed and collapsed onto the floor. Moving back between the bench and the wall, she drew her feet close. Clasped her arms around her legs. Put her face against her knees.

He dropped the crutches on the floor and hopped over to her.

She looked up at him, and her mouth opened as if seeing him for the first time. Her gaze went to his leg, to his crutches.

He tried not to let the horror in her face take him apart, tried to steel himself for the blade that went through him, but it still made him wince. "Yes, I lost my leg. Just like I told you."

"BoyNextDoor told me."

"*I* told you, Miss Foolish Heart. I didn't know it was you at the time. But I was going to tell you. I wanted you to know."

She pressed her hands again to her mouth, closed her eyes. Her shoulders shook.

"It's just a leg." He used the bench to brace himself as he lowered himself to the floor. Then he reached out and touched her cheek, running his thumb across it. "I'm still alive. That's the part that took me a while to get my brain around. I'm still alive. And living life as wholly as I can."

She opened her eyes, an ache in them. "You're

more *whole* than anyone I've ever met. You were so kind to me, even when I ran from you. You have no business with someone like me. I was horrible to you . . . and I'm so sorry, Caleb."

"Of course I forgive you, Issy. But you have to know I wasn't trying to deceive you. It's just that . . . you're so hard to get to know, and I loved being the guy you shared your thoughts with at the end of the day. And I'm not going to lie and tell you that it didn't feel good to have you pay attention to me, to see me beyond my scars. I thought that maybe if you got to know me on the radio, it might be easier to—" he took a breath— "to love me in person."

He swallowed, letting that word hang there.

She looked at him then, her expression stripped, and all he could think to do was pull her into his embrace, right there under the piano. "I'm not going to let you go, Issy. Not when I just found you. I might have needed a little help getting started, but everything after the spaghetti was all me. I meant everything I told Miss Foolish Heart about you. Everything I told *you*."

He pressed his lips against her hair, loving the smell of her, the lingering scent of her garden, the perfume she used. And she fit perfectly, right there in his arms.

Filling in all the blank places of his life.

She let out a trembling breath, and something inside him gave way when she grabbed his shirt, fisted it. "Don't go anywhere, Caleb. Please, hold on to me."

Attagirl.

She looked at his leg. "Does it . . . does it hurt?"

"Sometimes. When I'm standing for a long time or often at the end of practice. And I can easily wrench my knee if I'm not careful."

"I'm so sorry."

He drew in his breath. "Issy—you swear you didn't know it was me? BoyNextDoor? I mean, I didn't think so, but how could you not know? I did everything you told me to."

"I . . ." Her voice caught. "I didn't know. A couple times, I thought your voice sounded familiar, but . . . no." Her eyes softened. "But I wanted it to be."

He ran his hand down her face. "When I found out it was you, I didn't want to mess it up. I'd given away some big pieces of myself to Miss Foolish Heart, and I felt foolish too. But it was worth it if you would let me into your world." He couldn't look at her then, but she found his eyes.

"I know. I loved those parts you gave to me, loved seeing inside your heart. And that's probably why I had such a horrible crush on BoyNextDoor. Here I'd been on the air for two years and never once developed feelings for a caller. Then suddenly, I was thinking about your voice, checking the forum to see if you appeared.

And then, when you—Caleb—started . . . invading my life—"

"Hey, you were the one who came over and barged into my life—"

"Your dog invaded mine first!"

"He's not my dog, by the way."

She stared at him. "Really?"

"Really."

"But that first day, when I—"

"Nearly bit my head off, blaming me for my terrible beast? Yeah, well, you scared me a little. I didn't want you mad at me."

"Sorry."

"I just have to know—how did you start this radio show if you'd never had a date?"

"Oh, it happened a couple months after my parents' accident. I called in to a radio station to make a comment about a community discussion and I quoted *Jane Eyre*. The station's manager happened to be a friend of my father's, so he asked me to host a book club from my home. It started as a book club for romantics, and he posted it online as a podcast. My producer, Elliot, heard it and turned it into *My Foolish Heart*. I took it online not long after and . . . well, apparently it's a hit."

"You were invited to a wedding in Napa for Lauren O'Grady."

Her face fell. "Which, of course, I did a great job of destroying. But even if she hadn't called it off, I couldn't really go."

He ran his thumb down her cheek. "Someday, maybe."

She let her breath shudder out like the last shiver of a tree after a rain. "It's funny—ever since that attack in the grocery store, I hardly had a moment's hesitation about going over to your house or letting you into mine. Meeting you was a sort of breakthrough for me."

"I'm so glad I can infuriate you into healing. I have a feeling I'll be rather good at that."

She wore a small grin. "By the way, yes, I have feelings for you."

"You have feelings for me?"

"I'm sitting here under my piano with you."

"That's significant?"

"It's . . . my safe place. My mother used to play the piano, and I'd climb under here while she played and listen. I can imagine her alive, here. Being here . . . it keeps my world together."

"I heard she died in your arms."

She nodded. "We'd just had tense words, too, about my leaving. I was in town for homecoming, but I wanted to leave on Sunday morning. She'd wanted me to wait until after church. We fought and finally decided to go out for dinner Saturday night. It was raining, and the semi skidded through the light." She sighed. "I still can't figure out why I was in such a hurry to leave."

"I'm so sorry, Issy."

She leaned her head against his chest.

"Thank you for letting me under your piano."

"Thank you for breaking in to my house."

"Sorry about your door."

"I think maybe I shouldn't bother with glass."

She looked at him, and he caught her face in the cradle of his hand.

"Issy, you are so beautiful." He leaned forward, stopping himself a breath from her lips. "Can I . . . ?"

She kissed him. Just leaned up and pressed her lips to his, sweet and full on the mouth. Issy Presley, Miss Foolish Heart, kissing him. She made a little sound in the back of her throat, and he wrapped his arm around her neck and moved into the kiss.

Issy. I have feelings for you, too.

She broke away, took a breath. "Wow, I break my rules fast with you, BoyNextDoor."

"What rules?"

"No kissing on the first date."

"Well, we already kissed. Besides, this isn't actually a date. It's more of a rescue mission."

She held a finger against his lips. "Then there's 'No dreaming up a future on the second date.' "

"Are you dreaming up a future with me, Miss Foolish Heart?"

"Then there's most definitely 'No saying the *love* word until you're absolutely, positively sure—' "

"Are you in love with me, Isadora?"

359

"Well, you are pretty easy to love, Caleb. Online . . . and off."

His eyes filled. He looked away, and she kissed him on his neck. His devastated skin.

They sat there in quiet, listening to the thunder begin to rumble outside, the faintest tapping on the house.

"Are you ready to leave the piano yet?"

"Why, don't you like it under the piano?"

"Actually, I think I've found exactly where I belong."

19

The seagulls called from the shore as Seb chased his shadow into town after running out to Kadunce River. The cool breath off the lake dried the sweat from his brow, his back, and the sweet scent of pine called him home.

Oh, God, let me win.

He didn't know how else to say it. Could he live in Deep Haven if he wasn't coaching?

He climbed the deck and opened the door to the mobile home. It squealed, and at the noise, his father turned away from the stove.

Seb stood on the small patch of linoleum that served as an entryway and stared at him. "What are you doing?"

The man wore a pair of jeans so saggy on him he might not have bones beneath them, and a blue T-shirt with *Deep Haven Fire Department* embroidered by the pocket. He had shaved, his eyes clearer than Seb remembered. He'd even . . . showered?

"Making eggs."

"Making eggs?"

His father turned again, this time with the pan in hand. "I always make you eggs before your games."

Did he? But even as his father walked over to the tiny Formica table, the memory rose, vivid and sharp and burning his eyes. Yes, he had. Even when they went uneaten.

His father slid a couple eggs, over easy, onto a plate. "You still like yours with the runny yolk?"

Seb nodded.

"Well, sit down, kid. You need your energy." He plated two more eggs for himself, then set the pan back on the stove.

"Dad, I—"

"Sit down, please."

He didn't really need a shower, not yet. "Okay." Seb pulled out a chair. His father poured him a glass of—milk? "Did you go shopping?"

"Got paid."

"You have a job?"

His father didn't look at him as he cut his eggs. "Cleaning the fire station."

Seb looked away, blinking.

"I'm coming to the game, if that's okay."

He picked up his fork. "You're coming?"

"Of course. I love watching my boy play ball." His father gave a sort of half smile. "Out there you were bigger than what I gave you. Not a quitter like your old man."

"Dad . . ."

"No. Listen to me." He put his fork down. "You got something special in you, Son. A magic that can make people listen to you, make them want to play for you. The Sebanator."

"You knew about that?"

"I chanted it with the crowd." His smile fell. "I went to every game, Seb. You probably didn't know that. And that last couple years when everything fell apart, you probably didn't want to know it. I know I hurt you and especially your mother. Even when I couldn't tell you, I was so proud of you."

Seb stared at the runny eggs, the yolk now bleeding into the plate. "I did quit, though, Dad. I quit the Cyclones."

His father shoveled a bit of egg into his mouth. "But you got back up. And you kept going. And you came back to Deep Haven."

"What if . . . ?" Seb's throat tightened. "What if I'm not cut out to coach?"

His father considered him a moment. "Then you find something you're good at, kid. You just keep trying. It doesn't matter what you do, just that you do it with heart—isn't that what Coach Presley always said?" He looked down, away from Seb. "At least, that's what he kept saying to me all those years ago. I just wish I'd believed it sooner."

Coach had talked to his father? He shouldn't be surprised, perhaps.

His father drew in a breath, looked up, smiled. "Be a better man than I was."

Seb had no words. Instead, he reached for his milk. Smelled it. Yes, his old man had gone shopping. "You promise to keep making me eggs?"

A chuckle, something deep and fresh. "Deal."

The conversation clung to Seb all day, even as he went to the school, stood in the field, played the game in his head. Overhead the clouds hung low, bleaching color from the sky, and over the piney hills, thunderheads gathered. The wind carried the smell of rain.

Seb finally climbed into the bleachers, sat on the fifty-yard line.

He heard the verse from last night again. *I will give you a new heart, and I will put a new spirit in you. I will take out your stony, stubborn heart and give you a tender, responsive heart.*

He contemplated that stony heart, the miracle of a new one in his chest. Once upon a time, on this field, he'd lived for the cheers of others instead of the cheers of God.

Seb drew in a breath. Not anymore. He didn't

want to worship at the altar of the Sebanator any longer. He wanted a new heart, a heart free of the filth—the mistakes, the failures, the selfishness of his past. A heart that understood and drank in grace.

"God, this game is Yours, whatever You have planned. Make me a man built for others. A man built . . . for You."

He lifted his face skyward, closing his eyes as the first drops of rain began to fall, splashing like tears over his face.

It felt like a game day. Issy woke with a soft hum under her skin, and when she turned on her radio, Ernie had already started taking callers at the local station, waging war on the airwaves over who would walk away with the win.

The Brewsters against the Knights, and the town picked Brewster on top by two touch-downs. But they didn't know Caleb like she did.

Didn't know that they had a coach who'd forgotten how to quit.

"Can I touch your leg?" she'd asked when they finally climbed out of the shadow of the piano and he let her see his wounds.

Amazing how the skin on his stump so neatly folded over itself, the reconstructive surgeons bending his flesh over, almost like an envelope. Four inches remained of his tibia, enough to create a solid residual for his prosthesis. The extra length gave him more motor control and balance, "and when I wear my athletic prosthesis, I'm still fast. I probably could beat you around the block."

And yes, he'd let her touch his leg and met her eyes when she looked at him. Clear and solid, they reached inside and told her the truth.

She could beat this fear. She could beat it because he was right—God did not give her a spirit of fear, but of power and love. And He'd reminded her of it by having the last person she thought she could ever love move in next door and invade her life.

Her perfect world . . . with the perfect romance.

"I'd love for you to go to the game," Caleb had said as he left last night, a new moon hidden behind storm clouds, a turbid breath in the air.

Her father would have loved it. Something about playing in the rain stirred his competitive edge, although Issy never understood it. Rain made her want to shut herself in her room.

But maybe that was starting to change. "I would love to go," she'd said last night. "But . . ."

Caleb had cupped his hand to her cheek and run his thumb across her lips. "I know." Then he'd kissed her again, and with everything inside her, she'd longed to see him on the field.

Even now, as she turned up the radio for the kickoff, she could see him, wearing the blue Huskies jacket he'd purchased at the Ben Franklin, his red cap. For the occasion, she'd dug out her mother's foam finger, the Huskies stadium blanket, the bleacher cushion, and even her father's old megaphone. She'd set up camp in the family room, with Duncan wearing a Huskies bandanna.

She could see the game in her mind. The three sections of bleachers crammed with familiar faces—Jerry and the staff of the paper, of course, with Brian down on the field, taking shots. And Nancy from the diner, Anthony from the hotel, probably having dragged along a few guests for the hometown showdown. Nothing like small-town football to attract tourists. Nelda and the booster club on the top rows, their own foam fingers affixed, wrapped in blankets.

The blue and white scrimmage had always rounded up the town for the start of the season. Issy guessed, from the buzz she'd heard on the local radio station and from Lucy, that the stands might even be full.

In the announcers' box, Ernie and Wade would be waving to the crowd, cracking jokes, reading off advertisements from the hardware store, Pierre's Pizza, the bait shop.

If it were a real game, not a scrimmage, the pep band would be warming up with something cheerful—"Go Big Blue!"—the band wannabes with their horns and cowbells manning the rail.

If the pom-pom girls had shown up, they would be rousing the crowd with a few rallies, warming up for the game with some antics on the field.

And the players—they'd be in the locker room, listening to her father—no, listening to Caleb.

She closed her eyes, imagining them as they ran onto the field, even as Ernie announced the starting lineup, then asked everyone to stand for the national anthem.

Issy rose, put her hand on her heart. Sang along.

Kickoff, with the Brewsters receiving. They fielded the ball, brought it back twenty yards, and as the crowd cheered, a swipe of pain went through her.

She should be with her father. Listening to the game with him. Wouldn't that be a triumph?

But the thought still took her breath, still clamped a fist over her throat, her chest.

I'm sorry, Daddy. I'll visit. Soon. Tomorrow, perhaps.

The Brewsters inched the ball forward with a couple running plays, then fumbled on a handoff, and Knight's nose guard jumped on the ball.

"C'mon, Knights!"

They executed a sweep, moved the ball a few yards.

Next time at the line, Ryan kept the ball, moved it forward again. If they could keep this up, they would inch it all the way to the goal line.

A screen pass out, and Bryant dropped it. She could almost see the kid, hard on himself as he lined up on defense after the punt.

The Brewsters gained a few yards up the middle on a quarterback keeper but nearly fumbled on an option play. On the next play, the defense caught the quarterback in the backfield and the Brewsters had to punt.

Back and forth, the Knights would inch the ball forward on solid but predictable running plays, then try a pass without reception. The Brewsters would gain a yard on something basic but lose it on a play straight from the Presley playbook.

The first quarter ended scoreless, the crowd restless.

Issy dialed the care center. "Hey, Jacqueline. Can I talk to my dad?"

"Hi, Issy. Sure. He's listening to the game right now."

"Me too." Her attention caught as Caleb's team pushed the ball to a first down.

"Hello." His voice came across the line wheezy and soft. She turned down the volume.

"Hey, Daddy. What do you think of the game?"

"He needs to change it up."

"You're talking about Caleb?" He had to be, because Seb had been running flashy but limp plays all night.

She waited for his words.

"Quarterback Chaos."

"The trick play from the state championship? But I can't tell him how to call his game."

"It'll work."

"Really? Are you sure?"

"Quarterback Chaos."

"Okay. I'll tell him. I miss you, Daddy."

She hung up, picked up her cell. The Quarterback Chaos. Caleb had his own plays, of course, but he might take this one, a sort of gift from her father. And she remembered it well enough to pass it along.

Her phone call flipped to voice mail. "Caleb—call me. My dad had an idea."

At eight minutes left in the half, she left another message.

When the Brewsters fumbled and the Knights picked up the ball, ran it back to the forty, only to miss the field goal, she called again.

She listened with the phone in hand as the Knights drove it all the way to the red zone only to be held at the five-yard line. She dialed again when the kicker for the Knights set up for his field goal. The ball squirreled through the slippery grasp of the holder, and a Brewster picked it up and ran down the field untouched for a six-point lead.

Issy pounced to her feet, yelling at the phone. "Pick up!"

But he probably hadn't even brought his phone to the field.

The rain teared down the window, the sky pellet gray. She stared outside, her hand on Duncan's head, rubbing.

If she wanted Caleb to win, she'd have to go to the school.

The basics. Just teach them the basics. Caleb heard his own strategy echoing back to him and wanted to put his fist into the wall. With the basics, they'd moved the ball forward every time.

But not enough for first down yardage. Not enough to score.

And now the Brewsters, despite their sloppy ball handling, had points on the board.

Dan had followed him into the gym, where they'd been relegated for their halftime pep talk and now stood against the door, arms folded, the rain shiny on his blue slicker.

Caleb's gaze slid off Dan, onto his team, their stained jerseys, their soaked breeches, the way they didn't meet his eyes, and he realized . . .

They'd already quit.

Bryant straddled a bleacher, his head down, probably reliving all those dropped passes, feeling them slip through his hands. And McCormick, sitting on the floor, his hands over his updrawn grass-stained knees, grimy and sodden, wore a snarl on his face.

But Ryan. Ryan stood with his back to the team, his hands braced against the wall as if pushing back frustration or perhaps anger.

They needed a game changer. Something . . .

"They're killing us out there. Just like I said

they would." Ryan turned, his voice low, but it bore a ragged edge of fury. "We look like fools."

"We don't look like fools. We've got good ball-handling. You haven't fumbled once—"

"Bryant can't catch anything I throw at him." He spun to face his teammate. "What, you got bricks for hands? Grab the ball!"

Bryant raised his head, something sick in his eyes.

Caleb kept his voice tight, schooled. "Ryan, the ball's slick. And it's our first game out. Ideally, we'd have another week, even two, before we'd have a game."

"It wouldn't matter. We're running the same five plays and guess what—they know them all. We're a bunch of—"

"That's enough." Caleb watched the shift of energy in the team, the way Ryan's words stirred them.

An angry, united team could put points on the board. But an angry, divided team would end up in a locker room rumble.

They needed inspiration.

"You're beating yourselves out there, guys. You can win this. We'll change up the game, run it more—"

"It won't matter! They know our plays, and we don't know any of theirs."

"Which they can't complete," McCormick said, glancing at Caleb.

"That's right. They've lost every drive on a turnover. Good, solid playing will—"

"No. I quit." Ryan gripped his helmet in his hand. "I'm joining Brewster's team."

"If you leave, you'll never play for me again." Caleb kept his voice calm. "And you'll regret it for the rest of your life."

"You're not going to be my coach."

"Are you willing to stake your future on that?"

Ryan stopped. Drew in a breath. Stared at him.

Caleb looked at his team, needing their coach to win this round. "Ryan, I can't figure it out. I've taught you good football, given you a thousand second chances. We're *not* beaten out there. Six points is nothing. Yet you want to throw it in. Why? What did I ever do to you?"

Ryan glanced at the ground. "You're weak."

Caleb frowned.

"Or maybe you're just afraid, but you never get onto the field with us. You make Coach Dan show us all the plays, how to hit, how to handle the ball. You're a clipboard coach, not a real coach. I've seen Brewster out there. He's running with them; he's playing with them. He's one of them—he *plays football*. You . . . you talk about football, but I've never seen you play it. Maybe you don't even know anything beyond these five plays. And most of all, you don't know what it's like to get kicked around there on the field."

Dan had shifted on the other side of the room

and now lifted his eyes to Caleb's. He saw their conversation in the pastor's gaze. *We have to be willing to accept His love and grace. And only then are we able to turn around and do it for others. Daily grace, for you, for them.*

Daily grace. The courage to get back up. The courage to stay in the fight.

Maybe it was time to reach out, knowing who he was and what he'd come to do, and wash his team's feet. "Actually, Ryan, I do know."

He drew in a breath, then sat on the bench and raised his pant leg.

"It's a transtibial prosthesis with a flexible keel foot. Just above my 'ankle' it narrows into a solid piece of stainless steel. A sock covers the suction cup that covers the end of my limb." He rolled the sock down for his players to take a look.

Then he sat back and met their eyes. A few blinked, looked away. A few more stared at it as if they were the spectators of a train wreck. McCormick looked like he might burst into tears.

Ryan wore a stoic expression as if he'd been socked in the solar plexus and, instead of crying out, held his breath.

"I lost it in Iraq. I was transporting injured soldiers to a field hospital when a bomb hit our vehicle. We lost the soldiers inside the medevac unit and the driver. I alone lived. I spent the night in a ditch, in the cold. I had to tourniquet my own leg, and I passed out long before help came. I woke up in the base hospital where they were transporting me to Germany. It wasn't until I was there that I found out I'd lost my leg, although I'd suspected it as the hours drew out."

He rolled his pant leg down again. "I was an all-state running back in high school and helped my team win a state championship. But I never knew what it really meant to pick myself up off the turf until I had to get out of that bed on one leg and learn to walk again." He got up. Picked up his clipboard. "So yeah, I know a little about being kicked around on the field . . . and off."

Ryan looked away, but his jaw trembled.

"I didn't show you that because I want your pity. Actually, I kept it from you because I *was* afraid of being weak. But . . . I was wrong. Ryan, I was wrong. I should have shown you. No one is rooting for you more than I am. No one believes in you more than I do. And no one knows what it'll take to win more than I do."

Ryan met his eyes.

"But maybe it is time for a little trick of our own. A play they've never seen before. A pass to the quarterback. Ryan . . ."

"Yes, Coach?"

"Can you catch the ball?"

Seb stood in the dank locker room and hated the way he saw himself—the old self, the *Sebanator*—in his players. The cocky way they marched into the school, banging their fists on the lockers, followed by an equally arrogant Bam, who glared at Seb as he and DJ passed by. Even the fact that the school board had granted Brewster's team the use of the locker room instead of the gym for halftime seemed arrogant.

Seb stood in the center of the room, thick with the hot breath of his players, sweat stenching the air while his boys high-fived each other, and searched for words. He wanted something solid to bequeath them. A legacy of truth. The kind of legacy Coach Presley left him. So he folded his arms and spoke in a voice he'd heard Coach Presley use. "Calm down, everyone. Six points on the board doesn't clinch this ball game. If you get cocky, we're going to lose."

"We can beat them, Coach!" Michaels said.

"Maybe we can; maybe we can't. But we can be proud of what we do if we leave everything we have out there on the field."

DJ nodded. Bam's lips tightened in a knot of disapproval.

But the truth welled up inside him, and Seb added emotion to it. "You can't be proud of what I saw out there—a fumble, a touchdown that you got lucky on? They practically put it in the end zone for you. All you had to do was fall on it. That was a freebie. You didn't earn it. Get out there, remember your basics, and play good ball. Be the players that make the Huskies proud."

Bam then stepped up with a note to the defense before the team broke and headed out to the field.

Seb watched as each player slapped the giant *H* by the door on the way out. Bam smacked the letter, then DJ, who looked back at Seb.

DJ's glance stirred the past, revived the echo of the crowd, the earthy smell of the turf, the clip-clop of cleats on the cement hallway. The Huskies, charging onto the field to clean up the other team.

Seb reached up to the *H*, pressed his hand on it. Good-bye, number 10; good-bye, cheers and days of triumph.

Good-bye, Sebanator.

He'd decided during the first quarter that he wouldn't fight to be the Huskies' coach. Regardless of the win. Something about the entire competition, the way he—and the board—had handled it, didn't seem right.

"Coach?" The school board president propped the door open with a foot, coffee in one hand, a donut clasped in wax paper in the other.

"Hey, Mitch."

Mitch glanced out into the hall and drew a breath. "I gotta talk to you."

"What's up?"

"Did you know that Caleb Knight has an artificial leg?"

Seb nodded. "I've known for a couple days. Why?"

Mitch stared into his coffee. "I saw him show

his team his bum leg. Just sat down, right there in the gym and pulled up his pants leg. I nearly had a heart attack."

The donut in his grip might have had more to do with that. Seb's gaze fell on the green coupon clasped between his fingers. Buy one, get one half off at World's Best Donuts. *Way to go, Lucy. You're still in this game.*

"Thing is, it puts the board in a bad position," Mitch was saying. "Knight's kept it to himself— didn't tell the board. We had a right to know."

Seb had feared that. But given the same position, the same choice, he might have done the same thing.

Nothing like being judged for your weaknesses.

"I've seen him out there with his boys, Mitch. He can't exactly get into a three-point stance, but he can show them the plays, and he certainly knows what he's doing."

"I don't know. His team's not exactly moving the ball."

Seb had no words for that. Sure, his team could read the five basic plays the Knights ran, but if Caleb decided to pull a trick play out of his game book, they'd run Seb's team into a snarl.

"So I need you to do me a favor out there, Seb."

"What's that?"

"Win your game. If you win, it'll seal the coaching job."

"I don't want it."

"What?"

"I don't want it." Seb looked at the *H* and tapped it one more time, pressing his hand into the smooth, cold paint.

He took a breath, then moved toward the door. "I will always love Husky football. But I'm not a coach, Mitch. I don't love the job. I love the game, sure, but I don't have the patience to work with these kids."

"Please don't tell me any more. We need a coach, Seb, and you have a history here. The boys worship you—"

"That's the problem. I don't know what I'm doing, really. I know Presley's plays, but there is a theory to coaching, and it's not enough to run plays. The truth is, I came back here wanting to stir up the old glory." Something about just saying it out loud freed the knot in his chest. "I am not the coach for the Deep Haven Huskies."

They walked outside. The fading sun had parted the clouds, turned the wet field to fire under the twilight.

Mitch stopped him. "What a shame, because I'm not sure we have enough in the budget to pay a coach *and* a math aide."

Seb stared at him, deciphering his words. "So you're saying that if I don't win this game, I'm out of a job?"

Mitch lifted a shoulder.

"Nice, Mitch. The fact is, you can take your

job—" He bit off the rest of his words. "Did you know I don't even have my teaching certificate? So technically, I'm a bigger liar than Knight."

"Hey—"

"No, you hey. Knight is a good coach. And he can heal this team. I know it."

"You just going to leave? Quit?" Mitch shook his head.

Seb's gaze tracked to Lucy at the concession stand. She wore a blue Huskies cap on her head, smiling over the counter, handing out green coupons to the scraggly line at the window. "No, actually. I think I'll get into the donut business."

Then he marched to the concession stand. "Hey, donut girl." He smiled at her, and she looked up, her eyes bright. Yes, perhaps he didn't need football at all to feel like a hero. He scooped up the majority of the coupons.

"What are you—?"

"Just keep selling donuts!"

He trotted out to his team, now watching as Caleb's team huddled on the sideline.

"Bring it in, guys." He handed the coupons to DJ. "New halftime warm-up. I want you to split up, run the bleachers, and make sure every person here has one of these coupons. Don't come back until you've given your coupons away." He nodded at DJ, who handed them out by the fistful to the team. "And make sure you run to the opposite bench!"

"Is this another trick play, Coach? Are we trying to intimidate them?" Michaels grabbed his handful.

"Yep," Seb said, pounding him on his pads. "This is one game I intend to win."

Issy sat in her two-year-old Chevy Aveo hatchback, running her hand over the blue polyester seat, smelling the new-car fragrance.

She'd vowed to never drive this car.

She closed her eyes, gripping the steering wheel with both hands. *"I can do everything through Christ, who gives me strength."*

Issy had managed as far as opening the garage door, sliding into the car with the keys. They dangled in the ignition.

Turn on the car. Turn it on.

She could do this. Sure, her chest tightened; her breaths fell, one over another. But she could do this, right? She just had to reach out, turn the key.

Back out of the driveway.

Go one mile down the hill, to the game.

Park.

And from there . . .

What if . . . what if she had a panic attack, right there in front of the entire crowd? What if she fell apart on the sideline, crying, curling into the fetal position?

The entire town could relive her grief with her, all the wounds reopening in a giant, ragged gash.

See, she stayed home, inside her house, to protect them all.

Issy reached for the key and ran her fingers over it.

"Perfect love expels all fear."

"Perfect love expels all fear."

And remember, your perfect love could be right next door. Her own voice came back to her, along with images of Caleb washing the truck, then spraying Duncan with the hose. Caleb sticking his head through the fence, Caleb arriving with spaghetti, Caleb holding her under the piano.

Her perfect romance. Right next door. Driving away her fears. Then why did they still churn in her chest? Why—?

She saw Caleb then, lying in the ditch in Iraq, and heard his voice, soft, solid in her head. *In fact, God's love is perfect, and He puts that into us, so we can love the way He loves. Most of all, because of His perfect love, I can trust Him, whatever happens.*

Yes, "perfect love expels all fear." Yet the perfect romance wasn't with Caleb . . . but with God. The God who loved her perfectly, even when she was a mess. The God who hadn't forgotten her.

The God who had brought the one man who could help free her from the darkness and placed him right next door. The God who had a perfect future for her.

The God she could trust.

She pressed her fingers to her lips. "Oh, God, I'm so sorry for my fear, how it's held me hostage, how I've let it determine my life. I want to break free; I do. Help me to stop fearing what is out there and trust in You."

"For God has not given us a spirit of fear . . . but of love."

And she loved Caleb.

She turned on her car engine. Time for a game-changing play.

Easing out of the garage, she tightened her hold on the wheel as she backed into the driveway. The clouds had parted, a glorious, red-streaked sky pressing into the darkness. She drank in the smells of the summer evening as she rolled down her window for fresh air.

She passed Caleb's house, turned onto the street, and crept to the intersection at the highway. Pressed her brakes long before she reached the dangling stoplight.

Not a car on the stretch of highway that parted the town, the asphalt shiny as it unrolled around the corner, then down the hill to the school.

She put on her blinker.

Deep inside, she heard the echo of her screams, felt her mother's hot blood over her hands.

"I love you, Mama." She said it as she turned the corner and pushed herself down the road.

Sure enough, a Thai restaurant had taken over

the taco shop, a couple of Buddhas peering from the window. The fitness place had had a face-lift, a new studio space beside the treadmills and ellipticals. And next door, Bree's Hair Salon. So that was her new place.

Issy passed the Java Cup, where the road opened up to run along the harbor. The lake, as if spent, lay still, the sunset seeping into it, resigned to the twilight, the tide barely tickling the rocky shore.

It seemed the entire town had vacated their posts for the big game.

She drove past the fish shack, the Realtor's office, even the Footstep of Heaven coffee shop and bookstore. How she missed Mona's coffee, the smell of new books. Someday.

Someday soon.

She turned right at the entrance to the combined elementary, middle, and high schools. Cars jammed the parking lot, but perhaps she could squeeze her compact into something close to the gate.

The roar of the crowd tharrumphed into her breast, igniting her adrenaline. She swallowed, hard, to still the roil of her heart. She'd gotten this far. And she couldn't decide if the pressure inside might be panic or . . . joy.

She squeezed her car into a space between the ambulance and an SUV near the gate. Hopped out.

At once, the smell of the field, the cheers, the camaraderie that embodied a small-town football game engulfed her. She drank it in, opting to find strength in it.

The booster club member at the gate didn't even ask for her ticket as she wandered in, gritting her teeth.

Fans lined up at the concession stand, the redolence of a game captured in the smells of pizza, popcorn—and Lucy serving up donuts.

Issy turned away before she caught Lucy's eye. That would be a moment she didn't have time for.

She found Caleb instead. He stood on the far sideline, his team huddled up for last-minute strategy before the second half kickoff.

Quarterback Chaos. She just had to get the play to him, then shrink back into the crowd. How many times had she run out to her father during practice, cutting through the end zone?

She took a breath, put her head down, set off in a jog.

"Hey! Get off the field!"

When she turned, she saw a man gesturing to her.

"Yeah, you. What are you doing? Get off the field."

What are you doing?

She drew in a breath, froze. What was she doing? She looked at the stands, at the mass of people, all probably staring at her, watching, waiting. Issy, the hermit, out of her house. Issy, the coach's daughter, the one who never left Deep Haven. Issy, the town embarrassment.

Her chest tightened. Her breath left her.

No. Not here. Please—

She reached out, found the damp ground even as it came up to meet her.

And inside her head, the roaring began.

Caleb should have told his team about his challenges two weeks earlier. Two weeks of struggle, two weeks of misunderstanding, two weeks of hiding from them what it took to push past the pain and fight.

Adrenaline tremored through him as he watched his receiving team take the field. Especially as Ryan, beside him, shot him a look, something steely in his eyes.

Caleb had inspired them. And no matter what the second half held, he could leave them with something solid, something of value.

Now he just had to confess the truth to the school board. As soon as he'd seen the hardened respect on Ryan's face, he'd known: he should have listened to Dan. Deceiving the school board had nothing to do with wanting an even playing field, but with his own lousy pride. He had been like Peter, refusing to let Jesus have His way in his life. Insisting on getting the job on his own terms, not trusting in . . . well, God's perfect love for him. Why did he have to keep learning these lessons?

The referee placed the ball in the kicking tee, then moved away and held up his arm.

Ryan danced next to him, ready to take the field.

Ready to trick the Brewsters with Caleb's Rough Rider play, the one he'd tried to run with Dan. He'd earned their respect a little with that, too.

Maybe enough to win the game.

The whistle blew, but as the ref lowered his hand for the kickoff run, Caleb heard the crowd, the shouts, the dark voices. "Get her off the field!"

Who—?

"Oh no, it's Miss P.," Ryan said. "What's wrong with her?"

Issy. She'd shrunk into the grass, looking pale even from here, her hand clamped over her mouth, as if she might be trying to control her breathing.

No . . . *no* . . . Caleb glanced at his team, but the Brewsters had their backs to Issy and had already started running toward the ball for the kickoff.

"What's she doing?" Ryan said.

It appeared she was attempting to scoot back, behind the end zone, where she stopped, drew up her legs, wrapped her arms around herself, began to rock.

"Call the play, Ryan." Caleb started to walk down the sideline, eyes on Issy. What was she doing here?

She seemed to be searching for him, or perhaps he just hoped she searched for him. But she gave up as he cleared the end of his scattering of players, then broke out into a jog. He had to compensate for the slick grass, and a spectator would have to be blind not to see his limp. "Issy!"

The whistle blew, but Caleb didn't turn to watch the play, just kept his eyes on Issy. He heard cheers and prayed that Ryan had made the handoff, cut around the line for the pass.

Then Caleb turned, cutting through the back of the end zone.

Just like that, his world shifted. His leg slid out beneath him and hooked on an end zone cone, tearing the suction away between his prosthesis and his limb. He fought to right himself as his good leg slipped away from him, pitching him onto the turf.

He hit hard and rolled. For a second, his breath huffed out with the blow.

He lay there, staring at the darkening sky, the crowd wild behind him.

Wild, because even as Issy reached out her hand to clasp his, even as he realized that she had shaken herself free of her panic to run to him, to kneel at his side, even as he realized that his prosthetic leg lay separated from his body five feet away for the entire town to gasp at . . . Jared Ryan ran in for a touchdown.

Tie game.

20

Issy knelt beside Caleb, her jeans mopping up the wet grass. Why had she believed that rushing to the football game like some sort of running back with a late game play might be a good idea? That walking out of the house into the world would help Caleb win his game, win his job?

He didn't need her help. And because of her, he'd fallen right in front of the town, in front of his team, and his leg had—

She couldn't even think it as she leaned over him. "Are you okay?"

He nodded as he pushed himself off the ground, but his face said it all when Ryan picked up his prosthesis and brought it to him.

Oh, she had humiliated him in front of the entire town. She pressed her hand against her chest. "I'm so sorry, Caleb. I'm so—"

"Shh, Issy, I'm fine. Thank you, Ryan." He put the leg down beside him, almost an afterthought as he turned to her. "Are you okay? What are you doing here?"

"I—oh, why did you run out here, Caleb?"

He gave her a look as if her question might have been posed in a different language. "I think you know why." He reached up to touch her face.

"Your darkness can't keep me away. I told you—I'm not letting you go. No matter what the cost."

No matter what the cost. She glanced at his leg.

"Kiss her, Coach!" This from Ryan, and Issy came back to herself and found a frown.

Caleb shook his head. "Only if we win."

Win. Right. She cut her voice low. "My dad sent you a play."

"What?"

"Yes, he—well, he's rooting for you, Caleb."

"I think he's rooting for the Huskies." He looked at Ryan, then held out his hand. "Help your coach to the bench?"

Ryan handed Issy the ball, then reached out and pulled Caleb off the turf. He wrapped Caleb's arm around his shoulder, and another player lifted the other arm, hoisting him off the ground.

McCormick picked up the prosthesis and Issy jogged behind as they ran to the bench.

The crowd had died to murmuring. Now, they began to cheer—although Issy guessed they had no idea what was going on.

They sat Caleb on the bench and Dan came over. "You okay?"

"I have to get this prosthesis back on. So . . ."

The team turned around, their backs to Caleb, and formed a pocket. Issy wanted to weep at their faces, stoic—or perhaps proud? Something pulsed in their expressions she couldn't place, but she felt it too as she turned. This was their coach.

They gave Caleb a moment to pull himself together.

The ref ran in. "You ready, Coach?"

Caleb stood. Grabbed Ryan and pulled him into a huddle. "Get the ball back. We have a game to win."

"Right, Coach."

The lights shone now upon the field, pockets of gold puddling on the turf, a freshness in the air, the night crisp and bright. The town cheered as Caleb's team charged back onto the field to an even score.

Issy shoved her hands into her pockets, a warmth in her stomach, thick and rich . . .

Freedom.

She tasted it, pushed it through her teeth, let it seep into her pores. Freedom. He had come in after her, drawn her out to freedom.

As the team took the field, she sidled up next to Caleb.

He looked at her. "So, Miss Foolish Heart, what next?"

She grinned. "How about a little Quarterback Chaos?"

The moment Ryan hooked around the offense to receive the pass from McCormick, the moment Caleb Knight slid into the end zone, tearing his leg in two, the moment Issy unraveled herself from the fetal position to launch toward him, Lucy wanted to close her donut shop.

After all, one could hardly watch the game *and* count out change.

If only she didn't have a rush on donuts. Over the space of ten minutes, a line formed outside the stand that snaked around the end of the field, everyone handing in their coupons.

The coupons Seb had stolen.

"Where did you get this?" she asked Mindy from the library.

"One of the Brewsters gave it to me during halftime."

Seb's football players. She had no words. Especially when Bree entered the small hut, followed by Monica Rice and Abby Fieldstone.

"What are you doing here?"

"Seb told us to help you." Bree reached for an apron. "He said you needed more hands on deck, and that if we didn't help, the donut shop just might go under."

Seb said that?

Monica picked out two cellophane gloves. "This town wouldn't be the same without World's Best Donuts. Put me to work."

"Really?"

"Where would we meet, exchange the latest gossip? Get our sugar fix? World's Best is an institution, and we'd be lost without it." Abby turned to the first person in line. "What'll ya have?"

He pointed to the last two glazed raised on the

tray, and Abby scooped them up while Bree took his money.

"We need another tray of glazed, and you'll find another tray of chocolate cake donuts in the fridge," Lucy said to Monica. Then she considered the crowd. "First come, first served, and if we run out, they can use their coupons through the Labor Day weekend."

"You don't need to be here, Lucy," Bree said, taking another person's money. "I think Seb would like you to watch his game."

"Really?"

"We can handle selling donuts. It's inspiring Seb Brewster that takes work." Bree dropped the change into the customer's hand. "But then again, he only ever got his inspiration from the donut girl."

The words settled inside Lucy, filling her. Untying her apron, she wadded it into a ball and escaped the concession stand. She pushed through the crowd on the sideline in time to see the Knights haul Caleb to his feet—er, foot—and carry him off the field, back to the bench.

"Was that his leg that came off?"

She wanted to slug the guy behind her, but she could hardly deck everyone who murmured the questions as they watched one of Caleb's players carry his leg to the sideline.

"What a shame, too, because he would have made a great coach." This from, of all people,

392

Jerry. Traitor. "Good thing Seb's still around."

"Nope, he doesn't want it either."

She tracked the voice to Mitch. "What are you talking about?"

He searched, found her frown. "He turned it down."

"Why on earth would he do that?" She didn't exactly mean for her question to emerge with such force, such passion, but the man had been born to play football. He lived and breathed and dreamed football.

Mitch gave her an enigmatic look. "You tell me. He said he was getting into the donut business."

She glanced at Seb, standing on the sideline, hands in his pockets like he might be a father to the kids, watching, yes, but not armed with a strategy or a game plan.

This was not the posture of Coach Presley.

"Excuse me," she said, pushing through the crowd.

She picked up her pace as she cleared the last of the gawkers, ran down the field toward Seb, catching a few frowns from players huddled near Bam.

She narrowed her eyes as she stalked by him, not bothering to answer when he called her name.

But at the sound of it, Seb turned. The surprise—even delight—on his face did a little something to her heart. Oh, but he knew how to make a girl turn to batter.

"Lucy, what are you doing here?"

"What do you mean, you're not taking the job?"

His mouth opened a moment. "I'm not cut out to be the coach. I . . ." Then he grabbed her arm as if he'd said the wrong thing and kissed her.

Right as his quarterback fumbled.

The crowd on the opposite bench went crazy, but it couldn't match her heart, the way it exploded inside her as his lips moved over hers and he pulled her into his embrace. She let herself mold into his.

He let her go. And smiled. "I always wanted to do that. Had dreams of doing it after I threw a touchdown pass—run to the sidelines, find you, and kiss you in front of the town."

She stared at him. "Did you get hit in the head?"

He grinned. "Something like that." He glanced at Bam, who was pushing the defensive line onto the field. "I don't want to be a coach. Not really. I longed to come back and take the reins of this team because I thought it would make my life mean something again. But . . ." He pressed his hand, his huge hand that nearly eclipsed her face, against her cheek. "All I really want to do is . . . be with you. Make donuts."

"You want to make donuts?"

"Okay, maybe not make donuts. But help you make donuts. Be—" he rolled his eyes—"the donut guy. If you'll let me."

"Are you ill?"

" 'I sometimes have a queer feeling with regard to you—especially when you are near me, as now: it is as if I had a string somewhere under my left ribs—' "

"Seb!"

" '—tightly and inextricably knotted to a similar string situated in the corresponding quarter of your little frame.' "

Oh, Seb. She put her hands over his mouth. "Your team is watching."

"*Caleb's* team is watching. My team is sitting in the stands." He pulled her hands away, hooked his fingers into hers. "I have this great idea, Lucy. See, I think we can still save your shop, if you'll let me and my team help."

"Who are you? What happened to the Sebanator?"

"He retired."

And when she searched his eyes, nothing in them disagreed.

"Seb, I don't want you to do this for me. I—I'm not going to be responsible for you giving up your dreams—"

"It's not my dream."

"You aren't a quitter."

He flinched, but she didn't take her eyes from his.

Finally he said, "No. No, I'm not. But it's not my dream anymore." He ran his thumb down her cheek. "You are. And you always have been. I didn't come back to Deep Haven to coach. I came for you."

"For me?"

"Yes. You brought me home."

She pressed her cheek into his hand. She'd brought the golden boy home. "Then do me a favor."

"Anything."

"I want you to win me one last game."

He looked at her, then glanced at the field. Raised his hand to the ref. "Time-out!"

Caleb just wanted to walk—or in his case, limp—off the field and head for home. Or perhaps the state border. He pasted a smile on his face whenever he glanced at Issy, of course, but . . .

The entire town had seen him fall. And now they'd watch Brewster's team walk all over him.

He could only imagine what the school board might be saying.

"It's a fake! They're taking it around the end—watch your containment!" He refrained from slamming his clipboard to the ground, but Seb's team had advanced up the field like they might be the marching band. The Knights held them at the twenty-eight-yard line on the second down, but with less than two minutes left on the clock, Seb could score a field goal and wrap up the game.

And then Caleb could pack his bags.

He could just about grind his molars into dust

thinking about landing on that turf, seeing it in slow motion as the world rose up to slam into him, as the cool air separated the suction from his leg.

He should have worn his athletic prosthesis, but of course his pride had throttled his common sense. Why had he ever thought that keeping secrets . . . ?

Although he had to give himself credit for standing on the sideline for two entire quarters when all he wanted to do was dematerialize into the dark night that had descended on the field.

Except for Issy, he might have. Issy, standing beside him like some sort of cheerleader, cheering, screaming, believing in him, in his team.

And Ryan, running every play he threw at him with everything he had in him. Oh, give him two more weeks with these boys and they wouldn't miss tackles, wouldn't drop the ball. A month, and they'd be able to read each other's thoughts. By next season, he might even have them winning division titles. Okay, that might be ambitious, but—

"Reverse! Reverse!"

Thank you, Merritt. The defense shoveled the ball handler down on the line of scrimmage.

And Seb was sending out his field goal team.

"Wow, that Riley kid can kick. He's going to be great on special teams." Issy looked at Caleb as the ball sailed through the uprights for three points.

And the way she looked at him . . . Truly, he'd imagined this moment, her standing on the sideline—although, frankly, he'd prefer her in the stands because she made him nervous, the way the wind reaped her scent, driving him a little crazy. And he had to stick his free hand in his pocket to keep from pushing her hair from her face, maybe curling one of those dark locks around his finger.

Caleb nodded at her assessment of the kicker and glanced across the field at the Brewsters. Seb stood in the middle, the other coaches on the side. Lucy stood on a bench behind them.

Six-nine, Brewsters, with 1:49 left on the clock.

The Knights returned the kickoff to their own forty-eight.

"What should we do, Coach?" Ryan snapped the chin strap on his helmet.

"Twenty-two dive, up the gut." A standard run play through the middle of the line. McCormick might get two yards.

"Why are you doing that?" Issy looked at him. "You have less than two minutes on the clock. Do a flea-flicker or a reverse. We need to trick them. It's getting desperate."

Desperate, yes. And he was fresh out of game-changing plays.

"How about a draw?"

"They don't know those yet."

"What do they know?"

"Basic power plays, a few running routes."

"How about a sweep play?"

"How about you let me call the game?"

She gave him an I'm-sorry face as the Knights gained two yards.

He called a sweep play because she was right. McCormick put up five more yards.

Less than a minute, with the Knights stuck on the Brewsters' forty-five, still out of range of the field goal.

He had nothing. They needed a deep pass or some sort of flashy play that might spin Seb's team in a circle, but he had nothing he could show his team during a one-minute time-out and have them successfully execute.

"We're going to lose this game, Issy." He kept his voice quiet. "I'm sorry."

She stared at him, and the expression on her face, her soft words, drove the roar of the crowd from his thoughts. "Use my dad's play."

No. The minute her father's crazy play had left her mouth, he knew. He couldn't use it. Not and be taken seriously. The Quarterback Chaos? Only one coach could pull that off and not be laughed out of the high school football league. That was Presley's play, not his.

"No, Issy. I can't use that."

"Why not?"

"For one, it's your dad's play—"

"He gave it to you to use."

"And two, it's crazy. It barely feels legal."

"Oh, it's legal. I promise it's legal because when he won with it, the state high school football league analyzed it from every angle. It's legal. And you'll win."

He looked out at Ryan, who watched him for the signal.

"Don't you want to win?"

He drew a breath. "Not like this."

"Why not?"

He shook his head. "It feels—"

"Like you need help. This is my father's signature play, and you feel like you're weak, like you're asking for my dad's help, and the entire town will see it."

He looked away from her.

"Listen, my dad gave you this play because he believes in you and wants you to win, Caleb. Receive his gift. Let him help you."

Receive. Unless I wash you, you won't belong to me.

He looked up again at Ryan, now nearly desperate as he glanced at the game clock, and signaled a time-out.

Seb had to admit that he'd never had so much fun at a football game. Back when he played, he had a sort of coiled steel in his gut, the kind that wound tighter as the quarters ticked by. Even when he won, the coil only slowly worked its way free until he could breathe sometime around Sunday.

Not tonight. Tonight he watched football like a fan, feeling the thrill of the game in his bones. Yes, he could enjoy the sideline, especially with his boys fighting for their win. They'd actually earned those three points.

This just might be his favorite game ever. Especially with Lucy standing on the bench behind him, screaming for his team in a wildest-dreams-come-true kind of moment.

Knight called a time-out and Seb reeled his boys in.

They grabbed water bottles from Lucy, and Seb crouched in front of them. "We're going to take Johnson off the line and move him into a defensive back position. They only need three yards for the first down, but they're running out of time, so they'll probably go for a passing play. With five defenders in the backfield, that should stop them."

Lucy stuck her head into the middle. "Free donuts for the whole team if you stop them, boys."

See, this was why he couldn't be Coach. This kind of incentive and his players would roll down the field. "Stop 'em, boys," he echoed and sent them back out to the field.

"Since when did you become such a football fanatic?"

"I was always a football fanatic." She grinned at him. "Go Brewsters!"

Yes, he might have enjoyed coaching, with

Lucy in the stands cheering. But even better would be sitting beside her, her tiny hand tucked in his. That was enough glory for him.

The Knights came out and lined up with three wide receivers on one side. His defensive backs adjusted. Ryan lined up, called the first hut.

Then Ryan stood and yelled toward Caleb, "Coach! McCormick doesn't know this play! Coach!"

Seb saw it happening before his eyes, and the familiarity registered, niggled something inside, but he couldn't find the words fast enough.

Ryan, in motion, began to jog toward the outside of the line, as if running to talk to the coach.

Bewildered, his defense eased their stance.

No—no—wait!

Seb opened his mouth just as the running back called the hike and the center passed the ball to him, putting it into play. Ryan jerked into motion, cutting downfield toward the end zone, arms pumping.

Seb found the words then, nearly ran out onto the field as he—and Bam and DJ, who also recognized the play—screamed, "It's a trick play! Pass! Pass!"

And pass McCormick did—a deep, end-over-end albatross that found a home in the unprotected arms of Jared Ryan. He clutched the pigskin to his body as he ran it the easy ten yards into the end zone.

Quarterback Chaos. Coach Presley's champion-ship play.

And just like ten years ago, the crowd went crazy. A wild frenzy as they—like Bam and Deej and even Seb—realized that Coach Presley had bequeathed his winning play to Caleb Knight.

The rightful new coach of the Huskies.

The game clock hit zero and Knight's team descended on their coach. For the second time that day, they carried him across the field.

Seb reached for Lucy's hand, and they sat together on the bench, watching his team trot in to meet Caleb, watching the stands empty, watching the lights flicker on the chewed-up field.

"Great game, Seb," Lucy said, raising her sweet smile, those eyes he could find himself inside.

Yes, yes it was.

21

It made perfect sense, of course. Caleb in no way blamed Mitch for showing up on his doorstep, his hands shoved all the way into his pockets as he said, "Sorry, Caleb. It's just not going to work out—the coaching position or the teaching gig."

He didn't offer any more than that, but Caleb did the math himself.

The school board had added up the limitations

of a disabled football coach, the extra staff he might require to get the job done; then they'd simply subtracted from his job application the word *character*.

He could fight them, probably even win on grounds of discrimination. But this wasn't about his leg. He shouldn't have lied to them. No, he hadn't exactly denied his situation, but he hadn't revealed it either.

Still, no one could steal the victory of watching Ryan run the ball into the end zone, knocking those last six points on the board. And he'd never forget the image of Seb going berserk across the field as he recognized Presley's play.

Seb would land the coaching job, but Caleb would take with him the admiration he saw in his players' eyes.

Next time—if he ever got a next time—he'd lay his cards on the table and still prove himself. He rubbed Roger's ears, letting the dog slurp his chin. "You take care of her for me, okay, dude? Until I can figure this out."

He bit back the grimy ball lodged in his throat at the memory of Issy's hand laced in his, her smile for him as he'd called the last play.

In that moment, when he'd stood in the moist grass, listened to the roar of the crowd, watched the team victory-tackle Ryan, he'd . . . belonged. The team charged at him, scooping him up. As he slapped their helmets and drank in their joy, he knew he could belong to this town. These people. This life.

And to Issy.

By the time he exited the school, she'd left. He returned home to the light in her window. He caught only the last five minutes of her show and just about called in. *"Hey, Miss Foolish Heart, can I come over, watch the stars with you?"*

Instead he'd watched the game tape, conjuring up drills and feedback for the next practice. Foolishly believing that the school board would choose him.

Caleb rubbed the dog around his jowls one last time. He'd rented the house through Labor Day weekend, and then maybe he'd take his brother up on the extra couch where he could crash. He'd find a tide-over job until next spring, when he could start searching for another coaching job.

The lump in his throat had the power to choke him.

With a job, he might have stayed, just been the local psychology teacher. Maybe.

Roger got up and whined at the door for freedom, so Caleb pushed himself off the sofa, his knee so swollen from yesterday's wrenching that today he'd opted for crutches.

He hopped over to the door and opened it to let Roger out. "Say hi to her for me."

"Say hi to whom?"

Seb stood at the door, looking whole and

undefeated in a black T-shirt, a pair of cargo shorts, and running shoes. He moved out of the way as Roger barreled through. "Hey, I had a pal who had a dog that big. He used to come and sleep on my porch when he was a pup."

"It's not my dog. He just showed up."

"Funny. Looks a lot like Weatherby. But he was killed my senior year in high school. Tore up the entire town. Everybody knew Weatherby. He'd turn up on your doorstep, lick you until you cried mercy. We used to say he was the Deep Haven welcoming committee."

"I don't know who Roger belongs to. He just shows up and I feed him. Then he goes to Issy's house." Indeed, the dog disappeared around the end of Issy's fence, probably having made his own private entrance again.

"Great game last night." Caleb held back the rest, the part that bit at him, the voice that wanted to ask, *"Did you come here to gloat?"*

But he understood, really. Who wouldn't want a coach who'd been a part of the glory days, a coach who could inspire—even help heal this town?

Seb was the perfect choice. Caleb nearly held out his hand to offer his congratulations when Seb propped his foot in the screen door, folded his arms over his chest. "We barely hung on by our teeth. You did a good job whipping your boys into shape."

"They're hard workers, but you have some real

talent on your team. The hands on that Samson kid? Wow."

Seb nodded. "He'll do a good job for you." He delivered the words so easily, so believably that Caleb could only stare at him.

"What? I didn't get the job. Didn't they give it to you?"

"I didn't want it. I . . . well, I'm not a coach. I love the game, and I'd love to help with drills, maybe eventually work up to an offensive coordinator." He shrugged. "But I'm not the coach of the Huskies."

So if they hadn't given it to Seb . . .

They simply didn't want him.

Caleb exhaled, a long breath that razored through him. They didn't want him.

Oh, he'd like to blame it on his scars, his disability, but clearly . . .

They didn't want *him*.

A muscle pulled in Seb's jaw. "They didn't give it to you?" He shook his head, his eyes hard. "You're a great coach, Knight. I'm really sorry to hear that. I don't know why—"

"I do." He lifted his shoulder. "I shouldn't have tried to dodge the truth. I should have told them." He glanced at his missing leg, the fabric dangling below his amputation.

"Why? I don't see anything wrong with wanting to prove yourself. I should have tried harder to prove myself rather than ride in on number 10.

You gave it everything you had, and frankly, we could all use a little Caleb Knight in us."

He would have enjoyed playing for the Sebanator.

"So what's next?"

"I have a brother in the Cities. He's got an empty sofa."

Seb's eyes narrowed for a moment. "I don't think so."

It took a beat for Caleb to respond. "I don't have a job, Seb."

"Yeah, me neither. But I got a girl." He grinned. "And unless I'm wrong, you do too. Or wasn't that Issy standing with you on the sidelines yesterday?"

He noted that Seb tactfully omitted the wipeout in the end zone.

"You know, she had a rule not to date football players." Seb winked at him. "Don't quit at fourth and goal."

I'm not going to let you go, Issy.

Oh, he wanted to stay, but not in a town that didn't want him, a town that didn't need him.

Seb glanced past him. "Where's your leg?"

"Why?"

"You're going to need it. I need help on a project."

Seb's tone had changed, and for a moment, Caleb imagined himself back in the huddle, receiving a play.

"What kind of project?"

"My team and I are putting a hole in the donut shop. A little something for Lucy."

"Your team?"

"Some of the guys from town. We were wondering if you'd help."

"I don't know how helpful I'll be, since, well, I've got this bum leg."

Seb rolled his eyes. "Excuses, excuses."

Caleb backed up, gesturing Seb inside. "Are there donuts involved?"

"Could be."

Caleb looked out past him, to the glorious blue sky, his white truck in the driveway, Issy's house, quiet and dark.

"I guess I could do what I can."

"That'll be just fine, Coach. Welcome to the team."

Issy could smell victory in the Saturday morning air, in the bright sunshine heating the front porch, in the scent of fresh-cut grass across the street. It all screamed football.

And today, she'd see her father. Yesterday's game had stirred to life something inside her she'd thought dead. The image of herself, confident, strong, the woman she'd started out as.

The woman she would still be.

She had debated asking Caleb to join her, but perhaps this trip she needed to make alone.

Besides, if she could make it to the school for

Caleb, she could make it to the care center to see her father, right?

Perhaps they'd all have new victories after last night's game.

Including Lucy. "I didn't mean to take the playbook," Lucy had said as she stopped by after the show, way past her bedtime, bearing an apology. "Or to lie to you."

"You could have told me that you and Seb slept together. I would have understood."

"I was ashamed. Especially after Bree. I couldn't tell anyone."

Lucy sat on the porch swing, and Issy listened as Lucy told her about how she and Seb had started sleeping together that summer, the first time on the beach after Fisherman's Picnic. No wonder Lucy hated the celebration. No wonder she'd seemed like a grieving woman after she and Seb broke up.

"I tried to act like it was nothing," Lucy said, her knees drawn to herself, "but I couldn't. I felt dirty. And stupid. And like I'd given myself to someone who didn't care."

Issy sat beside her, one arm around her. "We all could be trapped by our past if it weren't for the perfect love of God."

They sat there, counting the stars until Lucy left for work.

Issy had gone to bed then and tossed the night away.

Lucy. Seb.

Caleb.

She liked Seb. She did. And if Lucy could forgive him, she could. But how could the school board give the job to Seb?

Especially since Seb didn't want it. Which meant the board simply couldn't get past the fact that Caleb had made them look foolish. They'd trusted him, and he'd lied to them.

But he'd won the game.

He'd won the game and the hearts of his players.

The heart of the girl next door.

But if she truly believed in God's perfect love, then she'd have to trust Him for Caleb's job. His future. Just like she trusted God for hers.

She drew in a breath as she stood in the garage, keys in hand. She'd found a new verse for today. Isaiah 41:13. *"For I hold you by your right hand—I, the Lord your God. And I say to you, 'Don't be afraid. I am here to help you.'"*

She sat in her car, prayed, turned the key, and drove all the way to the care center without one moment of real panic.

Issy hadn't imagined that the building would be so cheery, with overflowing planters of geraniums flanking the door, a flag waving as if in welcome.

She took a breath. A full one, without the webbing in her chest. She walked in and stopped at the front desk.

Jacqueline looked at her. Smiled. "Room 212."

Then she went back to her work as if Issy had been here yesterday.

She turned down the hall and could have found the room without direction. Laughter, voices, and behind that, cheers and whistles, the sounds of a taped football game.

She took a breath.

"I'll see you tomorrow, Coach." Pastor Dan emerged from the room and nearly ran right into her. He jerked back. "Issy. Hey."

Behind him, Bam exited. He glanced at her, gave her a small smile, then continued down the hallway.

"What's going on?"

A couple more men filed out, along with Diann, from the school library. She patted Issy on the arm as she might have done a few years ago, when Issy was a student.

"Impromptu school board meeting."

"Really? Why?"

Dan smiled. "Your dad called a time-out, pulled us in for some coaching."

Mitch exited the room. "Hey, Issy. Good game yesterday. I don't suppose we could rope you in to help with the cheerleaders? As long as you're going to be on the field anyway." He winked at her as he walked by.

"What's going on?"

"Your dad asked us to reconsider Coach Knight. Told us he was the one."

The one. Yes.

"Hope to see you at church on Sunday." Dan squeezed her shoulder as he walked away.

One public event at a time, thank you.

One private event at a time too. She blew out a long breath, then knocked on the doorframe. "Daddy?"

Oh . . . oh . . . The sight of her father hit her like a fist. He lay in the bed, the man he'd once been flushed away, leaving only the bones of a memory. Those big hands that could palm a football and scoop her up after a game lay at his sides. That barrel chest that bellowed out plays, fought the refs for bad calls, now shrank into itself. He'd lost most of his hair, and a breathing tube was affixed to his neck, tunneling air in and out of his chest.

She knew of his condition, of course, but she hadn't expected time and his injury to strip so much of him from her.

Oh, she should have been here years ago. The absence grabbed her, forced the breath from her lungs, started the dark swirl inside.

"Don't be afraid. I am here to help you."

His eyes darted over to her. "Isadora." Her name wheezed out of him, sounding almost like relief or perhaps simply longing. It caught her up. Drew her back.

"For I hold you by your right hand."

"Daddy." She rushed at him, pressed her face into his chest. Despite the hospital smells, she recognized him, the natural scent of his skin, strength, calm. "Oh, Daddy."

"Issy." He breathed her name again, and she looked up. She cradled his face in her hands and found his eyes.

There he was. And inside those gray-blue eyes, she recognized herself—strong and beautiful and resilient.

So that's where she'd gone.

"You made it," he said, his voice hoarse.

A tear leaked out of his eye, and she scrubbed it off with her thumb.

"I made it." She sank into his smile, and it pulled her away from the dark edges of fear. Of grief. "I'm sorry it took me so long to get here."

"I knew you'd make it . . . someday."

She ran her hand down his face, the familiarity of it sinking into all her broken places. "Daddy, I've missed you so much."

"I know. Me too."

She looked up at the television. "Just in time for the two-minute warning. Wait until you see the winning play."

He winked at her.

She nestled her head into his shoulder, slid her fingers into his lifeless hand. Listened to his heartbeat. Strong. Constant.

Daddy.

Behind her, she heard the cheers—probably herself—as Ryan ran toward the sideline yelling,

"Coach! McCormick doesn't know this play! Coach!"

"I love that play," her father said softly, his words thick with memory. "Takes guts to call it."

She met his eyes. "Thank you for giving it to him. I know he came here, that you met him. He has such courage. And he's a good man."

"God . . . sent him."

She nodded at that too. "I think he's supposed to be here, for this town. He can pick up where you left off—"

"No."

His word scraped the wind from her, despite its soft delivery. But didn't he just give Caleb . . . ?

"Start over. New coach. New team. Knight's team."

Oh. She laid her hand against his damp cheek. "I dunno, Daddy. This town needs you, too."

He drew in a breath and leaned his head against her hand. "I'm not dead, Issy."

She pressed her forehead to his, then kissed it. "I'm not either." Not anymore. She wanted to live, to walk into the light, to live there with God, with Caleb.

In perfect love.

In fact, she might even rename her show. *No More Foolish Heart.* Except, it still felt foolish for Caleb to love her, with all her wounds, her fears, her unpredictabilities. But perhaps that's what love was—foolish. After all, God loved most foolishly. He came into the dark world to rescue people who might never love Him back.

Maybe, in fact, the foolish heart *was* the perfect heart.

"Let's watch the game." Her father glanced at the television. She watched his eyes shine as Caleb's team carried him off the field.

Victory.

Epilogue

"This is the greatest town ever. Moose burgers. I think I'm in heaven."

Issy laughed as Caleb balanced the burger in one hand and held her hand with the other, his fingers laced through hers. How could she not love a man who wouldn't even let go of her hand to eat a hamburger? Er, moose burger, the official sandwich for Deep Haven's annual Moose Madness weekend.

"Thanks, DJ," Caleb managed between bites.

"Good practice on Friday." DJ wore a paper hat and an apron, the word *Elks* across the front.

"Thanks for your help." Caleb stepped away as ketchup dropped onto the pavement to join a mixture of soda, kettle corn, and ice cream. "We're going to look good against Elroy this Friday. See you at practice."

He finished his burger, grabbed a napkin, still one-handed.

"This is foolish, Caleb," Issy said, trying to disentangle her hand from his. Just because he'd started attending counseling with Rachelle occasionally, learned some techniques to help her push past her panic attacks, didn't mean he had to hold her hand constantly.

"Hey, you want me to trip and fall right here in the middle of the street? Have some mercy." He grinned at her as she shook her head. Like he needed her help. He'd been digging out his athletic prosthesis even before Mitch and the other board members restated their job offer and named him the head football coach of the Huskies. On his state-of-the-art limb, no, Caleb didn't need her to hold his hand.

But she wouldn't argue. Walk around town hand in hand with the most handsome man in Deep Haven? No problem.

And she might admit that she needed *him* after spending thirty minutes winding herself up for the crowds of Moose Madness. But here she was. Stepping out farther into the world every day. And tonight, she'd host *My Foolish Heart*'s first ever on-location broadcast, on World's Best Donuts's new outdoor patio.

Issy feared, just a little, what Seb might think of adding next. A gift shop, maybe? She'd already seen T-shirts and coffee mugs for sale.

She let Caleb lead her down Main Street amid the tourists buying cotton candy and artisans plying their wares in blue canvas booths. Lucy sold donuts hand over fist down at World's Best's new "donut hole" window. Built, of course, by the Deep Haven Huskies, Seb quarterbacking the entire thing, his brilliant idea to beat Bam at his own game. And smack in the middle of the hammering was Caleb, reading the blueprints, directing traffic, and embedding himself into the fabric of the town.

Now, children dappled the iridescent lake with stones, ducks waddled the shores, and dogs chased seagulls, brazen in their attempts to steal picnickers' sandwiches.

"I miss Duncan. I checked the animal shelter, but they haven't seen him."

"He'll turn up. Maybe he's found some other hermit to harass." Caleb winked at her before stopping at a pottery booth.

Liza greeted her, proving again that Issy hadn't been quite as forgotten as she'd thought. "Nice to see you, Issy."

Issy smiled at her, picking up a milk pitcher glazed brown with streaks of green.

Liza turned to Caleb. "Are you here to stay?"

He nodded.

"Good." She indicated the pitcher Issy held. "Remember the broken clay I was working with?"

Caleb touched the pitcher, and Issy let him take it. "You can't even see the scars."

"It's yours. A welcome-to-Deep-Haven gift." She packaged it up for Caleb and tucked her card inside. "Stop by sometime."

"You know her?" Issy took the bag.

"I met her at Fish Pic—"

"Hey, Coach, look out!"

She flinched as a ball whizzed by his ear. Caleb reached out, pulled it to his chest.

Jared Ryan ran up, followed by a face she didn't recognize. "Sorry, Coach. I was aiming for Samson."

Caleb passed him the ball as Issy's phone vibrated in her pocket. She tucked the bag under her arm, then pulled out the phone. "It's a text from Elliot. He said last night's ratings were our highest yet."

Tonight's broadcast just might be a warm-up to the one she'd do in Napa, at Lauren's wedding, if PrideAndPassion actually listened to the words Issy had spoken last night on *My Foolish Heart*.

"It's probably the first time Miss Foolish Heart has ever admitted to being wrong."

"Ha. You mean on the radio. I've been wrong plenty of times."

Caleb grinned at her.

It's not every day that Miss Foolish Heart admits to her mistakes, so listen up. Throw out your lists. That's right. There are perfect tens out there. And perfect eights and perfect threes. See, I've learned that you don't plan for the perfect romance; you work at it. And you trust God to bring the right one into your life.

Or next door. She'd loved how Caleb had leaned into the microphone, adding his voice, his opinion to the show.

Although he wouldn't allow anyone to call him Mr. Foolish Heart. "Coach will do," he said on their first broadcast, a few weeks ago.

Coach seemed to be very popular with her female audience. She didn't blame them. She'd fallen in love with his voice just as much as the man in the flesh.

She closed the phone. "The continuing adventures of Miss Foolish Heart and BoyNextDoor."

"I'm still not sure I'm cut out to share the airwaves with Miss Foolish Heart. I haven't any clue what I'm doing."

"And I do?"

"Oh, I think you know exactly what you're doing." The way he looked at her, the sweetness in his eyes . . . Why had she ever thought that he might not be a perfect ten—or eleven or eighty-seven? So far off the charts, she'd stopped counting. Stupid list.

They made it past Pierre's, then down to World's Best Donuts, where Lucy waved to them from her new window. "I'm just closing shop."

Sitting on the bench of the picnic table, Issy finally let go of Caleb's hand. He climbed up, sat on the table, and tucked her between his legs, settling his hand on her shoulders.

As if she might make a break for it. Not in this lifetime.

"I'll bet Napa doesn't have this view." The waves of the lake caressed the shore, the deep blue meshing with the far-off horizon, limitless.

She looked up at him and found him grinning at her. He bent down, brushed his lips across hers, a little fire there to heat her through. Who needed Napa, anyway? She could stay right here, forever, in Caleb's embrace.

"Stop necking and check out my newest creation." As Lucy straddled the bench, she handed her a bag.

"This is not a donut. It's not even a pastry."

"It's a cupcake. They're all the rage." Lucy grinned at them.

"World's Best . . . Cupcakes?" Caleb pulled out a chocolate cupcake, bit into it. "Not that I'm complaining. Yum."

"I'm just expanding my vision. Why not?"

"Lucy, I love your going into the cupcake business. You're a genius." Issy removed another cupcake. This one had pink sprinkles on the white frosting. "My father would love this. I'll tell him about it when I see him later today."

"How is he?"

"Good. I've outfitted him with new Huskies gear. We have a standing Saturday morning game tape viewing. And he's looking better—no more infections. We might even get him to the house for a visit for Thanksgiving."

Lucy met her gaze. Smiled. "By the way, I think I've tripled last year's donut sales just this weekend. I'll be all caught up on my payments, and Bam won't be able to foreclose."

"Where's Seb?" Caleb said, plowing through his cupcake.

"He's bringing a chocolate raised to his dad, over at the firehouse. Six weeks of sobriety today."

"He mentioned running for mayor during practice on Friday." Caleb finished his cupcake and wiped his fingers.

"He's going to run for school board first—take Mitch's spot."

Issy searched Caleb's face for any lingering hurt.

"Mitch thought he was protecting the town." His hand kneaded her neck. "He and I have made our peace."

"Hey, guys." Seb came down the sidewalk, a walking billboard in his red *Anybody want a donut?* T-shirt. "Wanna grab some dinner before the fireworks start?"

Issy glanced at Caleb.

"How about spaghetti? Everyone likes spaghetti," he said softly.

"Miss Foolish Heart says so."

"And don't you know," he said, his eyes in hers, "she's always right. After all, the perfect love might be right next door."

A Note from the Author

Life is scary. Why do unexplainable things happen —tragic accidents, disease, terrorist attacks? When watching the news, I find myself searching for a loophole—some guarantee that something like that won't happen to me, my husband, or my children. Like when I hear about the girl in a tragic three-car accident because she was texting. Well, I never text and drive, therefore I won't get into a tragic three-car accident. Loopholes!

If I could, I'd make some sort of bargain with God for the earthly safety of my loved ones. But life doesn't work that way. So what to do with the fear that could paralyze us, cause us to panic, and finally barricade us in our homes?

The answer: God's perfect love expels all fear.

While writing this story, I was struggling with my children leaving the nest—going off to college and out of the safety of my arms. I wanted, with everything inside me, to pull them back, to keep them safe. So wanting to set Issy (and myself!) free, I took apart that verse, let it seep into my life.

Perfect, in the Greek form of this adjective, means "complete." As in, all-encompassing. As in, nothing is lacking, and it touches every corner of our lives. Add the word *perfect* to the word *love,* and we might have some answers about how to handle fear. *Love,* meaning "affection," "benevolence," "feast of charity." (I love that—a *feast* of charity. Tasty, delectable, never-ending charity!) See, in God there is no evil. Not one smidgen. We sometimes act as if God doesn't care about the bad things that happen to us. Or even worse, that He is somehow laughing behind His hand at our hurts.

Never.

This is the problem with putting human attributes on God. He is always, 100 percent about invading our lives with His love.

Invading? Yes. *Complete* means that He loves us into our dark corners. It makes me think of a wave crashing into a cave, washing every part.

In short, we can't escape His love, His benevolence. Even in our darkest moments, His love is there.

Hard to imagine, isn't it? If anyone knows my testimony, they know about the violent years my family lived through as we served as missionaries in Russia. But if I allow God into my memories, I see Him there, pouring His perfect love into every corner. His grace, His love, is always greater than the wounds the enemy can inflict.

Life without God's love is terrifying. But God's perfect—complete, overwhelming—love drives out fear.

Try this: next time fear overwhelms you, praise

it away. Start singing the truth. Then step forward in the knowledge that God loves you (and your loved ones!) perfectly.

That perfect love even includes deep wounds. Like the loss of loved ones, and for Caleb, the loss of his leg and his future. I recently listened to Captain Scott Smiley, a soldier who lost his sight in a car bomb attack in Iraq. His courage and continued faith struck me, especially when he told the audience that he was *better off* now. That God was using him in a way he never could have imagined. That is trust in God's perfect love. I want that kind of faith; I believe that kind of faith changes lives, and that is the faith I gave to Caleb. He reminds me that we are not responsible for the things that happen to us, but only for our response to these things, and that God can use our surrender for the good of others.

Sometimes our wounds are not physical but emotional. Like Lucy's. In today's world, it seems that losing your virginity to your high school sweetheart is almost expected. But it shouldn't be. And neither should we, as a society, overlook the damage that giving oneself away before marriage might do, what lies one might hear as a result. I wanted to show how both Lucy and Seb were wounded by their choice, but also how God could give them a fresh start in His perfect love for them.

In every book I look for that profound moment

from the Lord to show me how He wants to change *me* through the writing of it. That moment came when I wrote, *God loved most foolishly. He came into the dark world to rescue people who might never love Him back.* I stared at that line for so long I almost deleted it. It felt blasphemous. God is not foolish. But He *is* love. Big, overwhelming, incongruous love that looks foolish. A love that, even now, doesn't seem wise. I mean, really, has He taken a look at the people He loves recently? What a mess they are! (And I'm not looking at anyone but myself when I say that!)

But see, that's the amazing part. His love is perfect. Not messy. Not uneven. Consistent. Overwhelming. Freeing.

Life-changing.

And He offers it to us, no strings attached.

May you have a foolish heart for Christ, just as He has for you.

Thank you for spending time in Deep Haven, reading Issy, Caleb, Lucy, and Seb's story. If you are interested in more Deep Haven stories, check out *Happily Ever After*, *Tying the Knot*, and *The Perfect Match*.

In His love,
Susan May Warren

About the Author

Susan May Warren is the RITA Award–winning author of more than thirty novels whose compelling plots and unforgettable characters have won acclaim with readers and reviewers alike. She served with her husband and four children as a missionary in Russia for eight years before she and her family returned home to the States. She now writes full-time as her husband runs a lodge on Lake Superior in northern Minnesota, where many of her books are set. She and her family enjoy hiking, canoeing, and being involved in their local church.

Susan holds a BA in mass communications from the University of Minnesota. Several of her critically acclaimed novels have been chosen as Top Picks by *Romantic Times* and won the RWA's Inspirational Reader's Choice contest and the American Christian Fiction Writers Book of the Year award. Four of her books have been Christy Award finalists. In addition to her writing, Susan loves to teach and speak at women's events about God's amazing grace in our lives.

For exciting updates on her new releases, previous books, and more, visit her website at www.susanmaywarren.com.

Discussion Questions

1. At the beginning of the story, Issy is showing symptoms of what disorder? Have you ever had something so consume your life that you felt trapped? What helped you or would help you overcome that fear?

2. Issy has a rather unusual "work from home" job. Have you ever called in to a radio or television show? What do you think about online communities like the one Issy has formed? What are their benefits and dangers?

3. Issy has a top-ten list for her ideal man. Do you think that's a good idea? Why or why not? What characteristics might be on your top-ten list?

4. Lucy can't believe it when Seb, her high school sweetheart, shows up in town. Have you ever been surprised by someone from your past? When and where? How did it affect you, if at all?

5. Caleb wants to prove himself despite his disability. Have you ever felt as if the cards

were stacked against you and you had to prove yourself? How did you handle that situation?

6. Seb returns home, hoping to relive his glory years. But some things aren't as glamorous as he remembered. What parts of your past would you like to relive? What would you gladly never repeat?

7. Issy runs from Caleb when she first sees him. Have you ever been ashamed by your reaction to something or someone? What did you do about it?

8. Caleb gets desperate and asks for the advice of a radio host. Where have you gone for relationship help? Looking back, do you think you were given good advice?

9. In chapter 14, Pastor Dan points out that Caleb has been unwilling to continually accept grace, as Peter refused to let Jesus wash his feet. Have you ever been like Caleb and found God's grace difficult to accept? Why?

10. Lucy and Issy are best friends, but Lucy hid the full truth of her past with Seb from Issy. Why? Would you have hidden such a secret from your best friend? Why or why not?

11. Near the end of the story, Seb and Lucy are able to come to terms with their past and are set free to start over. Is there any relationship you would like to start over with? What is keeping you from doing so?

12. Why is Caleb upset when he discovers that Issy is Miss Foolish Heart (as Issy is when she discovers BoyNextDoor's identity)? Have you ever felt exposed or betrayed? How did you respond?

13. Caleb's worst fear comes true when his secret is revealed in the middle of the pivotal football game. How would you have reacted in that situation?

14. Issy has let her fears create unnecessary distance between her and her father. Have you ever been estranged from a family member? Have you mended those bridges? If not, what holds you back?

15. What truth does Issy come to realize that helps her break free from her fears? Do you agree with what she learned? How could you apply the same truth to your life?

Center Point Large Print
600 Brooks Road / PO Box 1
Thorndike ME 04986-0001 USA

(207) 568-3717

US & Canada:
1 800 929-9108
www.centerpointlargeprint.com

Mount Pleasant Public Library

3 1024 15273 229 6

JUL   2012

LARGE PRINT

DISCARD

MT. PLEASANT

2/5/14